IN THE
WAKE

IN THE WAKE

"*In the Wake* is a subtle, heartfelt meditation on intimacy and the many ways we can lose those we love. Behind the seemingly tranquil backdrop of quotidian, seaside lives, a storm is building. As the novel moves towards its dramatic conclusion, Davison sensitively explores how grief and mental illness reverberate through families and across generations."
—SARAH FABER, AWARD-WINNING AUTHOR OF *ALL IS BEAUTY NOW*

"Memory's siren pull is as comforting and treacherous as the ocean in Nicola Davison's gorgeous debut novel. With striking acuity, *In the Wake* reveals how people's deepest desires are charged with danger, the bonds between those who love the most often fraught with self-deception. Nothing is ever quite as it appears to Davison's mothers of sons, who cling to their own visions of the past and present in this beautiful rendering of nouveau Nova Scotia."
—CAROL BRUNEAU, AWARD-WINNING AUTHOR OF *GLASS VOICES* AND *A BIRD ON EVERY TREE*

"*In the Wake* gathers like a storm wave, throwing the characters forward. Nicola's writing is a lighthouse catching moments of sorrow and joy. Here, mental health is not a hashtag, but broken glass under wounded feet. This novel can deepen you."
—JON TATTRIE, AWARD-WINNING AUTHOR OF SEVEN BOOKS, INCLUDING THE NOVELS *BLACK SNOW* AND *LIMERENCE*

IN THE
WAKE

NICOLA DAVISON

[signature] 2019

Vagrant
PRESS

Vagrant Press is an imprint of
Nimbus Publishing Limited
3660 Strawberry Hill Street, Halifax, NS, B3K 5A9
(902) 455-4286 nimbus.ca

Printed and bound in Canada

NB1328

This story is a work of fiction. Names, characters, incidents, and places, including organizations and institutions, either are the product of the author's imagination or are used fictitiously.

Library and Archives Canada Cataloguing in Publication
    Davison, Nicola, 1970-, author
    In the wake / Nicola Davison.
    Issued in print and electronic formats.
    ISBN 978-1-77108-664-6 (softcover).—ISBN 978-1-77108-665-3
    (HTML)
    I. Title.

PS8607.A9575I5 2018   C813'.6   C2018-902972-2
                                              C2018-902973-0

Canadä   Canada Council Conseil des arts   NOVA SCOTIA
           for the Arts   du Canada

Nimbus Publishing acknowledges the financial support for its publishing activities from the Government of Canada, the Canada Council for the Arts, and from the Province of Nova Scotia. We are pleased to work in partnership with the Province of Nova Scotia to develop and promote our creative industries for the benefit of all Nova Scotians.

For Chris, who always says, *yes, you can.*

"Memory plays tricks. Memory is another word for story, and nothing is more unreliable."

–ANN-MARIE MACDONALD, FALL ON YOUR KNEES

PROLOGUE

2000

The second-last thing he sees are fingers curled over stone. It's the shower of dirt that makes him look up. He's halfway there, gripping the side of the cliff for balance, almost up to that hollow box of a house.

The last thing he sees is the rock bouncing down the cliff. Straight at him. Half his life wearing a hard hat, just waiting for something to fall, and now that he's decided to really live it's to be bashed out of him. It was a foolish idea, climbing down here to drown his words in the sea. Should have just told her. Serves him right. He even hears the crunch as it connects. But before the lights go out for good, there's the highlight reel: laughter, his name a whispered groan in his ear, his son's newborn cry, the colour orange glimmering on water. Then warmth pulls him away.

CHAPTER 1

2003

For years, she missed this grey, almost colourless landscape, the air nearly as sodden as the ocean. On days like this, you can squint out at the water and not be sure what you're seeing, the dark triangle of a sail or only the shifting thickness of fog. It's probably because her strongest link to him, Da, is out there in the mist, away from the solidity of land.

Daniel drives the rented moving truck. It sways on the road ahead while she brings up the rear with the delicate cargo. It's a single-lane highway with a narrow gravel shoulder. She slows for the next bend and avoids a maze of potholes. A *highway* is what it's called on maps. Stunted evergreens line the road, the thickest of their trunks still smaller than one of her thighs. When she pointed this out to Daniel, he automatically disagreed, admiring the curve of her hip, savvy husband.

A faded sign is propped at the end of a driveway. *Whirligigs*, it reads, and next to it a yellow-clad fisherman in a red dory spins the oars of his boat to an ever-receding shore. Next it's the local convenience store with large black letters announcing "izza" by the slice. Signs don't fare well in the stiff onshore winds.

The steam of her panting dog warms her left shoulder, while her son sits in miraculous silence, gaping at intermittent views of the sea out his window. They're coming up on the beach. "See any surfers out there, Ryan?"

He puts his forehead to the window and reports that there are seagulls. A wave licks over the edge of the road, leaving a trail of small rocks. A line of cars is parked in the narrow lot at the edge of the beach, the occupants glorying in the power of nature from the comfort of their vehicles. Braking, she feels the wind push the car sideways and grips the wheel a little tighter. Six days ago they left Calgary on a bright day with no snow in the forecast. Though not a confident driver, Emily is fine if the roads are familiar and the weather reasonable. Driving across Canada in the winter didn't fall within these parameters. Ryan and the dog had a love-hate relationship that played out in her rear-view mirror. They had to get good stretches of driving in whenever it wasn't storming. A serious dump of snow could stall them for days. So, she kept going in moderately frightening conditions, like black ice, thick fog, and her personal favourite, freezing rain with the thermometer ping-ponging between minus two and plus two.

"Almost home!" she sings out, trying to whip up some excitement as they pass the parking lot for the larger beach.

Daniel, on the other hand, less bothered by winter driving, has spent hours in solitude, sometimes listening to an entire audiobook in a day. If she could manage a large truck she'd have switched seats with him in a heartbeat, but the idea made her percolate with anxiety. And so, they ploughed on, their daily journey punctuated by unhealthy meals and unplanned bathroom stops.

She flicks on her signal light and they wind their way up the hill. Their hill. "You see it?" It's just coming into view. "The one with the flat roof? That's our new home."

Sheltering in her porch, Linda enjoys her one smoke of the day—*really, this would be it*—steeling herself to meet the new owners and hand over her key, finally. She's arranged to be around most of the day, having run all her errands the day before and cancelled an appointment.

There's a squeal of brakes; she stands to get a better view. A large white truck makes the turn onto her road. With only the three houses up here, it's likely to be the new people. Or is it just movers? It lumbers past and she lifts her hand. You always wave—there's a good chance you know the person, but if not it's better than just staring. The truck backs neatly into the driveway. *Not bad.* Linda only puts her car in reverse when absolutely necessary, avoiding the debacle of parallel parking at all costs. A man hops down from the driver's side and nips around the side of the house, out of sight. *So much for gawking.* She sinks back onto her chair and turns her head to keep an eye out for the rest of the parade.

She'd watched the skeleton of the house appear from her kitchen window years ago, an anomaly amidst the traditional homes nearby. The people, she was told, were come-from-aways, their architect too, sketching out a house better suited for a warmer place. They must be from down south somewhere, live in one of those cities where life hums along predictably, where you don't have to prepare for the possibility of long stretches without power every winter. They must've walked the site on an August afternoon, a precious fog-free day, been wooed by the vision of children playing in the waves below, gulls surfing the air currents, bright umbrellas along the beach. Heck, they probably assumed there was a beach all year too, unaware that the sea gathered up all the sand in the winter storms, only returning it for the summer months.

She still has the magazine article that featured the house. It was staged with sparse furniture, a pair of wine glasses resting on a patio table with a stunning sunset beyond, a blanket draped just so over the arm of a chair, a book face-down on the table as if the reader had just stepped away to answer the phone. But there were no people in the shots, even with the fire blazing away in the wood stove. The first owners were too private for that. So private that Linda had never met them. Two years later the sign went up and it sat there waiting for its next people while the new landscaping wilted in the salt air.

The couple that moved in next had hosted a housewarming party and invited the locals as well as their urban friends. They loved to cook and talked of doing yoga side by side every morning to the distant sound of the surf. They planned to put in a kitchen garden and have friends come out for fancy dinners. *Foodies,* they called themselves. But the guests petered out as the ice settled on the roads. They made it through Christmas. Then he took an apartment in the city, *just to be closer to work.* She had emphasized this, placing a hand on Linda's arm like it was she who needed reassuring. Sure enough, the house was dark again the following spring.

Reluctantly, she'd agreed to take the key and walk through the empty house, to satisfy their insurance company. The last time around, when the first owners decided to sell, her husband was still alive and he'd done the honours. He'd only met them the one time and agreed to monitor the place without telling her. Martin would sometimes be over there for hours, doing what she never knew but he never turned any lights on. Her own visits were brief. She'd pad through each room in her socks, the chill of the floor spreading through her, and peer out the windows. From her house, just down the hill, she had glimpses of the sea but nothing like this. Martin must have liked it here, but it made her feel small, exposed.

One day it dawned on her that there was only one door on the inside of the house, mercifully it was for the bathroom on the main floor. Everywhere else, it was just a wall that would discreetly hide views where necessary. It felt more like a place to display art. How would her family have stood up to this environment? She needed to have a sense of privacy, even if it was just a cheap door in a small house.

Now this must be them, soft things squashed against the car's back windows. There's no room in the driveway with the moving truck there. She watches them turn around at the end of the road and halt in front of the house with two tires planted on the front lawn.

Finishing her cigarette, Linda listens to it hiss as she touches it to the snow, drowning its little fire. Might as well go up and say hello, give them the key in case they don't have one yet. God knows that realtor might keep them waiting half the day.

He'd seemed a touch flighty when he pulled up in front of her house. His eyes darted around her yard like he was tallying up the details for her listing—split entry in a quiet area, walking distance to the beach, a handyman's dream. It was a family moving in, he said. He'd walked them through a few places before they decided on this one—*moving back home*—he didn't say from where.

She sighs and quickens her pace as she sees the car door fling open. Her voice isn't strong enough to be heard at this distance, calling out to warn her new neighbour about the ice.

⌒

Emily hasn't seen it since the late fall when they flew out to find a place. It is unlike their old bungalow with its steep-pitched roof to shrug off the snow. This one is airy, in and out, windows framing the horizon. The landscaping is a blank canvas, except for the haggard tree at the side. Daniel, an architect, went on about clean lines. He told the realtor how as a kid he always drew houses with flat roofs. Emily stayed near the wall of windows, squinting at boats on the horizon.

She barely remembers signing the documents to put in the offer. But offer they did, and it was accepted within the day. The sellers didn't ask for any changes to the contract. Emily and Daniel had stretched their credit a bit to have the ocean view. It was, after all, a bargain compared to house prices in Calgary.

The moving truck is in the driveway, but there's no sign of Daniel. Sliding out, she lets her foot touch their lawn for the first time. She doesn't notice the ice until she slides, heavily, underneath her car door and is looking up at the sky. Her winter hat cushions the blow. She takes a second, suppressing the curses that would once—pre-mother-hood—have issued casually, satisfyingly, from her mouth.

"You all right?" A woman's face appears above, upside down. She's slight; grey eyes in a thin face, the wind ruffles her pale hair into whimsical shapes.

"Yes, I'm fine. Thanks."

"I'm Linda, I live next door, I have a key." She holds it up. "To your house. You'll probably change the locks but…let me help you."

"No really, I'm okay." She manages to roll onto an elbow. "Been sitting in a car for a week. I'm Emily." She offers a hand, and as Linda reaches to shake it she, too, loses her footing and lands beside Emily with a cry of alarm.

"Shit, I'm sorry."

"Fine," Linda croaks and erupts into a coughing fit.

"Right," says Emily. "Me first." Using the car, she pulls herself up, then helps Linda to her feet. It's less than graceful and they're laughing, brushing the snow from their coats, when Daniel appears.

"Ah, here he is." Emily slips her arm around his waist. "This is Daniel. Linda brought us a key."

"You all right?" he says, shaking her hand.

"Fine."

"And in there," Emily continues, "is Ryan. The one licking the window is Hoover."

The dog gazes at them through the smeared glass, his head swaying with happiness.

"Pleasure to meet you all. I live just over there." She waves her hand. "Just me now, my husband passed a few years ago. Oh, and there's the cat, Bert. He thinks he lives at your house." She turns away from them to cough into the crook of her arm. "Sorry, this just won't go away."

Daniel releases Ryan's seatbelt and the dog barks, demanding equal treatment.

"Daddy, you have to get *Bumpy* too."

Emily shares a look with Linda and mouths *imaginary friend*.

Another car pulls up. The bright letters on the side doors boast of how quickly the driver can sell a house.

Nodding, Linda says, "You have plenty to do, no doubt. Come over if you need anything. You too, Ryan. You like cats?"

Ryan nods then buries his face in his dad's pant leg.

"Lord love him." Linda smiles.

CHAPTER 2

She's the first to wake the next morning. Crawling out of her sleeping bag, she sits, yawning silently on the edge of the bed. Neither one of them could find the box labelled *bedding* last night, but the camping supplies were easy to locate in the battered backpack. A large unopened wardrobe box is in the corner of the room. Daniel has neatly folded his clothes on top. Her own things are heaped on the floor nearby, so she only need reach out a hand for her sweater. She tugs on yesterday's slightly stiff socks and tiptoes out of their room, craving her first private moments with the house.

When they'd first seen it, they had overlooked the lack of doors, dazzled by the views instead. The omission was a clever design feature. The rooms still had privacy, visually. But it would prove challenging with a little boy. Standing at the top of the stairs, she surveys the cardboard boxes below, clumped into the middle of the great room. They'd managed to drag it all inside by the end of the day, call for a pizza, then set up Ryan's bedroom as best they could.

Hoover opens one eye and, seeing her, thumps his tail against the floor. This brings to mind another matter: not a single carpet in the place. They'll have to remedy that with a few rugs to deaden the sound. She jogs down the stairs, intent on getting the dog outside before he can begin his morning routine, which—for reasons she can't fathom—always includes a round of explosive sneezing. As her foot hits the last step Hoover heaves himself up on his forelegs, wrinkles his snout, and begins to snort. Too late. She leans down and pushes him by the rear end toward the door while his sneezes ricochet off the high ceilings.

As she stands in the doorway, watching the dog snuffling the ground outside, Ryan begins mumbling in his bedroom. This is followed by Daniel, yawning loudly. So much for a few minutes alone.

Ushering the dog back in, she heads to the kitchen and begins restacking boxes in search of the coffee machine, no longer attempting to keep quiet. She has just about unearthed the familiar box—on which Daniel and Ryan doodled a pre-coffee portrait of her with hair standing on end—when she feels arms reaching around her.

"Welcome home."

It's Daniel, happy to wake up in his own bed and happy not to be driving a truck. Turning around, she moves into the warmth of him. They'll need to fire up the wood stove.

"Welcome home. I need coffee, a rug for the living room, and a way to keep our son in his bedroom."

"I'll do a coffee run."

Not an entirely selfless offer: it would get him out of the morning routine, something she'd been doing for the past week.

"That's okay, I have all the bits needed to get some coffee on. We'll head out later, get our first grocery run in. How about you see to Ryan?" She smiles and watches his face fall.

"Right. I'll do that," he says, pushing his glasses up on his nose, standing taller. Then, over his shoulder he adds, "Don't forget to add the windows to your list. You going to sew curtains this time?"

A parting shot. Few things make her feel quite as incompetent as being unable to sew a square. In the last house, after weeks of ripping seams, she ended up leaving the fabric in a heap in one of the closets, a sad offering to the new owners. Plus, there is the sheer height of these windows; they must be fourteen feet and god knows how wide.

Custom coverings would cost a fortune. The windows face the beach below, it's not like it's a busy street. They'll just have to remember not to wander nude through the house.

While she fills the coffee carafe with water she gazes out the windows. They should probably work on making things safe first. At the rear of the house, a cliff leads down to the beach. There's a ragged picket fence in the back. At best, it might slow down a small child and a dog. The gate's latch has rusted so that it moves back and forth like a pendulum in the wind. In the meantime, she'll make sure to be outside with them.

Hitting the *start* button on the machine, she wanders over to look at the yard. Why did the previous owners never build stairs down to the beach? Maybe it's not permitted. When they'd viewed the house the first time, walking around in the yard she'd thought she could see a worn spot where people had made their way down. The thought of it made her queasy. It must be more than sixty feet, although Daniel is always teasing her about her judgment of distance.

She pulls out a pad of paper and begins a list. *House Things*, she scribbles. *Rug. Wood.* They'd need more firewood than the dwindling pile behind the house. *Price Fences.* This she underlines.

"Ryan!" He streaks into the living room, diving onto the sofa with Daniel striding in behind, tiny pants and shirt in hand. "You have to get dressed. It's too cold to be naked."

The coffee machine is entering its grand, gurgling finale behind her and she's loath to delay her first sip, knowing Dan will soon give up the chase and expect her to step in. She holds her fingers up to Daniel. *Two choices*, she mouths at him.

"Ryan, you can walk back to your room or I can carry you…."

Ryan leaps from the couch and runs for his new bedroom. Muffled sounds of father and son continue upstairs while she scans the labels on the boxes.

She's done a fair amount of moving, from when she was single and had only a carload of things to the recent years with Daniel, every move requiring a larger vehicle. She locates the one labelled *pottery* and digs into the paper for their mugs, chosen for how they snug into the palm of the hand. She gives them a cursory rinse and pours the hot coffee just in time for Daniel to reappear, straightening his glasses.

"He's a worthy opponent, yes?" she says.

"You'd think I was torturing him." He reaches into the fridge for the cream that isn't there. "Ugh. Whitener?" Seeing her shrug, he says, "I'm still doing a Tim's run." They shuffle into the living room and plop down on the couch. Ryan wanders in and out of boxes, pretending they are tall buildings in a city. He'll be disappointed when the room takes on its regular appearance.

She allows Daniel a few sips before inclining her head toward the cold wood stove. "Fire?" His reply is a loud slurp. "I'd do it myself," she continues, "but there's no kindling and you do remember the last time I wielded an axe?"

"Axe. Any idea where that is?"

"With the tool things? I can picture where it was in the other house...."

Ryan tires of Box City and attempts to insert himself between them.

"We have to feed you, buddy. You hungry?"

He nods and grabs her arm, nearly spilling her coffee.

"I got up last night for the washroom, were you awake then?" she says to Daniel, watching Ryan sort himself into a horizontal position, feet on Dad, head on Mum.

"No."

"You didn't get up at all?"

"Nope."

"That's weird." She scratches at something stuck to Ryan's shirt, chocolate, hopefully.

"What's weird?"

"I thought I heard you coming upstairs but when I turned over you were in bed asleep. You weren't downstairs at all last night?"

"Did you get up last night, Ryan?" Daniel says.

His head moves back and forth. "Mm mm."

"No. These were heavy footsteps." She frowns. "It sounded like you had boots on."

"Probably just new house sounds."

"Mm," she says picking her cup back up from the coffee table. "I probably dreamed it."

IN JANUARY, THE snow comes every few days. Daniel scrapes the windshield in the blackness of morning, inching his way to the office in the city and returning in the dark.

On his third Monday of work, the power goes out. It must have happened in the night. Daniel tweaks to it when he realizes it's daylight and the clock's face is blank.

"Em, what's the time?" He shakes her shoulder.

"Morning," she mumbles into her pillow.

"I should be at work." The bed jiggles as he sits up and feels around for his slippers. "Where's your cell? It's got to be past seven." She doesn't answer, hoping it's part of a dream. He has to rush off without a shower.

After he leaves, she finds herself in the kitchen staring at the useless coffee machine. There will be no toast either. Then she remembers something and opens the fridge, frowning at the blood pooling on the bottom shelf. Dammit, she'd meant to cook the chicken the night before, but things had been too rushed. *Salmonella*, she thinks and reaches for the kitchen cloth. For some reason, she thought the plastic bag would contain it. She tries the hot water, then the cold, but nothing comes from the tap. *Right, no power, no pump for the well.* Her next thought is to go to the radio, find out how long the power company will take. *Of course, no radio either.*

The kitchen counter is icy to the touch so she retreats to the warmth of the wood stove and abandons the problem of the bloody bird. Oddly, Ryan is still in bed. She checks her phone for the time. Although loath to wake him when she could use the extra minutes, instinct makes her creep into his room. The sour smell hits her before she sees the mess. He must have been bone-tired to have stayed put, not even calling out for his parents. He is burrowed deep under the filthy blankets. She stands over him, silently cursing, before running downstairs to find the scribbled note stuck to the fridge and dialling Linda. It's a stroke of luck that she answers, Linda doesn't strike her as a cellphone person.

"Poor thing. You can come down. Plenty of room."

"You think it'll be back on soon?"

"No telling. Might be any minute...or it could be a few days."

Days, Emily mouths the word. Ryan's bedding is splashed a horrible shade of peach. He rolls away from the sound of her voice, fighting to stay asleep.

Emily cleans him up, using a full package of wet wipes, then carries him down the hill with his cheek on her shoulder. He watches her with glassy eyes as she tiptoes around the icy patches, calling over her shoulder to keep Hoover moving. The door opens as they arrive. Linda has boiled water with a propane burner. Tea is brewing in the pot and steam rises from a small wash basin set on the end table. She opens a can of ginger ale and stirs the bubbles from it before putting a plastic cup near Ryan.

"Thank you so much," Emily mumbles, still thinking of the crumpled pile of sheets in his bedroom.

"It's what we do," Linda says, pulling a blanket over Ryan. His eyes are closed again.

"And I have a whole chicken rotting in my fridge," says Emily.

"Oh, that's easy." Linda won't hear of food being wasted. So, Emily fetches it and watches as Linda prepares the bird for the grill. "You can do almost everything on a barbecue."

"Another thing for the list," says Emily. "We didn't bring ours from Calgary."

"Get one with the side burners." Linda closes the lid of the barbecue and they head into the house. "And an extra fuel tank. You'll want a week of fuel. Lucky you've got the wood stove."

Leaving Ryan on the couch, they head for the kitchen, where Linda pours them each a mug of tea.

"You said you're from here?" says Linda, plunking the sugar bowl on the table.

"Mahone Bay, originally, then Halifax." They sit on either side of the table, stirring their tea.

"Is your family still here?"

Family. They said they were moving here for family, but what they really meant was Daniel's parents.

"My mother and stepfather have a condo in the city, but they're in Florida until the spring."

She thinks of her mother's gleaming kitchen and the white furniture in the living room. And her stepfather, ever the deal-maker. *I never haggle, the price is the price for me, but not for Richard.* Emily could picture it, the seller merely keen to see the last of him.

"Ah, snowbirds." Linda wraps her hands around her mug and huddles close to the steam. They're both wearing winter coats. "We used to love a drive to Mahone Bay in the fall. Do the whole South Shore down to Lunenburg. That must have been a change for you, the city, after being in a little town like that."

"It was. Actually, we were a few minutes outside town, right on the water. Our boat was right there on the dock." In the house, it was faded rugs, bookshelves lining the walls (and everywhere), her father's abandoned mugs of tea. After, when they moved in with Richard and she was instructed to call him Dad, the house was spotless. The carpet showed twin rows where the vacuum made its daily passage, plastic covered the rigid sofa cushions. Every time Mary polished the kitchen floor and bleached the bathroom, she ensured that not a particle of their old life would resettle onto the new things.

"And now you're back. Right on the water again," says Linda, watching her face.

"Well, I can see it but I can't get to it. You don't know if they ever thought of putting stairs down to the beach, do you?"

Linda chokes on her tea. "Sorry." She leaves the kitchen and returns with a tissue box. "Not to my knowledge. That slope is a little steep for that."

"Yes, just a thought I had."

"There's a spot just down the hill." Linda points behind her, as if they can see right through the wall. "Just take a left at the bottom of our road and there's a dead end right next to the beach."

"Maybe you can come for a walk with us? Show us the local secrets," says Emily.

"Well, sure. If you think you can keep up with my brisk pace," Linda says, smirking.

The house powers up late in the afternoon, announced by a long beep as the answering machine resets itself. Linda helps them up the hill, carrying the cooked bird in a roast pan while Emily cradles Ryan in throw blankets from the couch.

"I won't stay." She puts the pan on the kitchen counter and turns for the door. "You'll want to get to that laundry. Try the vinegar. Works like a charm." She lets herself out before Emily can insist that she stay.

Emily expands her list of House Things to include batteries, candles, spare blankets, and the barbecue. Then she adds Linda's number to her speed dial.

IN THE MORNINGS, Emily likes to drive Ryan the short distance down to the beach, the two of them layered for winter on top, rubber boots on the bottom. It's a look she calls *Maritime chic*. Today, the sun has come out after another night of snow that turned to rain. Winters weren't so erratic here before, surely. At least she doesn't recall shovelling in the rain before. Maybe she didn't notice as much in the city. Then, living in tiny places with roommates, no one even cleared the steps. It was hard enough to negotiate the ownership of items in the fridge. They'd pack the snow down with their comings and goings rather than divvy up domestic chores between them.

Ryan dips the toe of his boot in the water. She watches him while listening to the crash of the waves, the bass of it vibrating her bones and the salt working its way into the back of her throat. She thirsted for it, in the years they'd spent inland, the smell, the sound, the constant movement of the water. The closest thing was the fields of grass swaying with wind under the big sky, but it didn't have this pull.

Da used to play a game when they were on the boat, inviting her to point her finger in any direction and he'd tell her where they'd end up. Curiously, it was always a place with warmer water, *a blue you just don't see here, Duck*. He said he'd take her out of school for a year. They'd make their way south before winter set in, spend a few months in the Bahamas. *We'll fish for our supper. Sail to the next spot when the weather is fine. No schedule.* She still wonders what life she'd have had, if they'd only made it to shore faster that day.

When they get back to the house, she widens the walkway. Her arms are getting that hollow feeling now and her mind turns to lunch. Ryan cheerfully shovels it back onto the pathway, leaving random clumps of slush where she's just heaved it away, something she's dubbed *unshovelling*. It is simpler to clean it up a second time and make him feel that he's helping, despite the ache in her back.

Leaning on her shovel, listening to Ryan's chatter, she watches a small green truck pull up. Winding down the window the driver calls out, "Hey, new neighbour!"

Taking Ryan's hand, she approaches the truck, smiling.

"I'm Jim, live just down there in the yellow house." He is pointing a finger at the bottom of the hill and she can just make out the faded yellow bungalow. "Thought I'd swing by and say hello. How're you liking the place?"

"Great. We're *still* unpacking." She makes the introductions while trying to keep the dog from jumping on his truck. "Sorry, he figures you're here for him."

"Smells mine." Leaning out the window, he offers his hand to Hoover. "Heard you're from out west?"

"Oh, no, we're from here. But we've been away for almost ten years. We missed the ocean."

"Do you sail?" The glint in his eye makes her smile.

"We do. Daniel can't wait to get on the water."

"Wooden boats or plastic?" He says it as if it's a crucial test.

"Wooden, even though they're more work. That's what we had when I was a kid."

"Yup." He inhales the word. "Mine keeps me busy. Got her hauled out. Getting ready for spring, if it ever comes. Course, a day like today and you can see it coming, but we'll pay for this, sure enough." He squints up at the sun, accusing. Then he looks past Emily at the house. "You *like* the house?"

She follows his gaze. "Yeah. We've got a great view. Bit different than what we're used to, bigger." Why she feels this need to tell him that is beyond her. "I can't believe the surfers, out there in the middle of winter."

"Mm," he says, still looking hard at the house. "You've met Linda, I take it?"

"Um yes, the first day."

"A good egg, Linda. Took care of this place, just like Martin did… before he passed."

She waits too long to pose the obvious question.

Jim takes a deep breath and looks pointedly at the clock on his dash. "Well, good meeting you." He puts a hand out to Ryan, who takes two fingers and shakes them stoically. "I'd best be going. Let us know if you need anything."

Backing away from the truck, she shoos Hoover toward the house, feeling as if she's missed something.

SHE BRINGS IT up with Daniel. The two of them in bed, side by side, addressing the ceiling.

"Do you think it's that the house is different?" Has he pegged them as pretentious?

"No, we're *from away.*"

She snorts. "We're from here."

"Right, we're come-*back*-from-aways."

"Mm, well we did choose to come back though."

"Still," he says, closing his eyes, as if that finishes things. His breathing slows right away. With the added commute, his days at the office are longer than they were out west. Often, he gets in too late to even say goodnight to Ryan. He spends most of his time hunched over drawings or squinting at a computer or explaining to the Calgary office that things work differently here.

He grew up in Halifax, spent his summers sailing the Northwest Arm with his younger brother, and attended Dalhousie University. "But my work experience isn't from here," he said earlier, frowning. It's not the homecoming he'd imagined. Maybe it will get better when his parents return home from down south or maybe when the days lengthen—coming and going with the sun on the horizon.

She rolls out from under the covers and walks around the foot of the bed, clicking off the lamp before going to the window. It takes a moment for her eyes to adjust to the dark but then she is able to see the moving water below. She watches, trying to let her mind go blank. Her attention is drawn to a dark figure below; she squints at it but her eyes are too weak. There's someone sitting on the edge by the gate. She retrieves her glasses and looks again. Nothing. She keeps scanning the yard. Nothing. Just to be sure she takes off her glasses, tries to see the scene in the same way. Maybe she'd mistaken the fence post for a person. It's happened before, much to Daniel's amusement. How many times had she clapped him on the shoulder, saying she could see a bear? It would turn out to be a tree stump or an errant bag of garbage. She stands this way for several minutes, her hand to the glass feeling the chill, unable to summon the figure again.

⌒

"Bert?"

Linda puts a hand on her hip and listens, still holding the package of kibble. Shaking the box usually draws him to the kitchen. She'll have a poke around while she's outside. Even though she makes a habit of leaving the shed door open for him, the wind and the snow contrive to push it shut from time to time.

It's a windless day. Not many of those around here. She reaches into her pocket and finds just three cigarettes left in the pack. Simple enough, just don't buy another carton, that's what a non-smoker might say. Pulling one out, she lights it and squints as the smoke curls past her eyes. She loops around the house and finds the shed door propped open. No cat to be found. There are paw prints though, heading uphill.

"Darn cat."

Bert probably thinks that's his name. That's what Martin called him most, pulling him onto his lap, one side of his mouth lifting up, *darncat*, ginger fur coating the sleeves of every one of his sweaters.

Maybe she'll mosey over to Emily's, see if she can call him without traipsing through their backyard. But it doesn't seem right to go up there, cigarette in hand. She takes a long drag and bends to put it out, soaking it through before putting it in the bin near the shed. Nothing uglier than a yard full of filters in the spring.

The white two-door is in the driveway. Most likely it's Emily who's home then, Daniel must be off to the office with their car. The white one is a lend from the in-laws. Fat lot of use it does them, without snow tires. Emily only takes it out on dry days. How they think they can manage here with just one car is beyond her. Sure, she might be able to walk to the convenience store—they have milk, junk food, a few dust-covered cans of things people resort to eating in emergencies—but even that would be a good half hour on foot, or more, trying to push a stroller along the gravel shoulder with cars whizzing past.

If only she still had Martin's truck. She just sold it last fall. It hadn't moved since he died. Jim was up for a chat and pointed out that the tires didn't look so good, going flat on the bottom. He had a friend with a used car lot down the way. So, the truck was towed off and made ready for the road once again. Too bad she hadn't held off. It was one of those heavy things that had no trouble getting through the deep snow. It cost an arm and a leg to fill the tank.

"Vehicles need to run." Jim patted her shoulder as they watched the truck being pulled away on its leash. "Just like wooden boats need to be in the water. Not good for them to dry out."

Jim always finds a way to inject nautical wisdom into things. It's probably his way of trying to start a conversation about his boat. If so, it never works with her. Not all Maritimers want to bob about in a boat. Linda is happy to watch from shore, thanks. And she resents the sea's pull on people, like a drug.

Since Martin passed, Jim comes up now and then, sometimes just a polite wave as he lopes past with his dog, sometimes with a shovel to help her dig out. He keeps the conversation light, complaining about local politicians and the weather. Maritime chit-chat. "Just give us a shout if you need anything," instead of a goodbye.

Some might say he is being a good neighbour. Sure enough, he is, but Linda can feel something under his words, underneath the long pauses, the way his eyes flit to the house up the hill. It haunts him. She was spared that part at least, finding Martin on the beach. They'd made him a little more decent for her at the morgue. She only looked at his face, keeping her eyes trained on his mouth, his eyelashes, avoiding the sticky mass at the side of his head. It was hard enough to look at his face—so still—but she made herself do it, even said his name, just in case. Just in case they had it wrong. But his eyes didn't open.

For Jim, it seemed necessary to check on her; that must be how he dealt with it, or didn't deal with it. Make sure she's still on her feet, moving about the world. This much he could do. Keep her from falling. Maybe he felt bad, the way they'd withdrawn, he and his wife. The two families spent some time together in the early years, when the kids were still young. That fell away after, though. After they found out about Tom. Nothing was said, really. Everyone was busy, that was the official line, accepted gratefully by all.

Peering around the side of the house, she can only see lumpy snow. No sign of orange fur.

"Bert?" and then "Darn cat?" Just in case.

They're home, there's woodsmoke in the air. But no, she won't knock. Bert will be back as soon as she gives up on him. It's like he's wired into her that way, like it's his game to lure her out and about. The moment she gives up, picks up the phone to report him missing, poof, he's there on the step. Probably, he's already there.

She hears a knock on the window and catches a movement by the door. Ryan's nose is flattened to the glass, steaming it up, his hand stretched above in a frozen salute. She waves back and blows him a kiss then turns for home, before she's discovered and coaxed in for a pot of tea.

Valentine's Day flyers litter the coffee table. Ryan managed to reach the mailbox on his tiptoes. One piece of mail suffered for it. Luckily, it's just a bill, torn in half, along with the envelope. Emily flattens it out on the table and wishes it meant she could pay half the amount. Shouldn't it cost less for power with the wood stove going all the time?

Emily leaves Ryan at the table, poring over the bright pictures, and runs up to the bedroom to tuck away the brass shackle before he can see it. For years, she kept it on her, in a pocket, or clipped to a loop on her jeans, despite the way her mother avoided looking at it.

Pop this in your pocket for me, Duck? We need to pick up another one at the boat store next week. She'd snugged it into her sweatshirt pocket and forgot it until the day of Da's funeral. She found it while rifling through her closet for a black sweater. The weight of it made her check the pocket. She held it in her hand until the brass was warm, until her mother came looking for her.

Just a few weeks after his death, her mother tried to open her fingers and remove it while she slept. *For your own good,* she'd pleaded. Emily had strong hands from sailing. There was no contest. But the attempt fractured something delicate between them.

Now it stays hidden away from a small person in search of shiny things. How had he managed to get it?

Standing at the dresser, wondering about her habits, she notices the message light blinking on the phone. It's Lola calling from work.

She dials the number, creeping to the top of the stairs to check on Ryan.

"Hey. Everything okay?"

"Hello to you too," says Lola. "Did you get my message?"

"I didn't listen to it, but I figured you're calling me from work so…."

"Just a slow morning." (Big yawn.) "I'm taking breaks at my desk to avoid Tanya."

"Right, she still trying to get you to do that Tupperware party thing?"

"It's not Tupperware, it's like extra stretchy clothing for women. I don't know. Just. Not. Me."

"I could use something like that." Emily yanks at the waistband of her pants.

"I'm sending out resumés," Lola says in a whisper. "If I'm not out of here by spring you can shoot me."

"Deal." Lola always has resumés out but won't leave the benefit package of the insurance company where she's been for the past eight years.

"You guys doing anything for Valentine's?" There's an edge to her voice because the last time they talked, Emily promised that they would not become shut-ins.

"No babysitter."

"Grandmother's?"

"Still down south."

"So take the little guy with you."

"Dinner out with Ryan, colouring on a paper tablecloth, if we are lucky. Back home by six after spending a hundred bucks on a mediocre meal."

"You're such a Scrooge."

"Wrong holiday but yes, it's just a money-grab from florists and card companies. Most people just feel guilty. And you?"

There's a long pause and she can guess why.

"So, I'm back online." Meaning she's dating after declaring her hatred for it three weeks ago. "And there's this guy, but I haven't met him yet. Still, we've had some good…phone time."

"Saucy woman."

Downstairs Ryan is tearing paper to shreds.

"Anyway, you ought to get out. I imagine you holed away in your grey house, with grey fog all around, talking to a three-year-old and a comatose dog, slowly going nuts."

"It's not always like that."

"You must have some old friends from school days?"

"Nope. The good ones moved away."

"You said, and I'll see if I can quote the words, *we won't be those people who talk about nothing but their own kid.*"

Emily snorts. "Speaking of Ryan, I have to go. He's gone silent down there."

"Me too. Boss is coming. Give him a big smooch for me? Ryan, that is."

Emily descends the stairs to find Ryan attempting to feed a twisted piece of paper to Hoover. She sneaks up on him and plants a loud kiss on his cheek, provoking a shriek.

"From Auntie Lola."

"Who?"

"Mummy's friend, Lola? Hair?" Emily holds her hair out to the sides.

"Oh! Is she here?"

"No, she's in Calgary."

"Can we go see her?"

"No, sweetie, it's too far. Remember the big trip?" It's been a couple of months, another lifetime at his age. But he's moved on.

"Look." He holds up a crumple of paper. "I made it."

"Ah. For me?"

"No, for the man."

"Daddy?"

"Nope, the man." He gestures at the backyard.

"That's very sweet of you." Another offering for the imaginary friend.

Linda pulls into her driveway. It's dark. It's always dark in February, or so it seems. She's pleased to see Emily's lights on. She likes that she's not the only one at the top of the hill now. When the house was empty, the previous owners had a motion-sensor light that would come on if people came near, but it was evident, even from a distance, that the house was bare. Now it glows, a lantern in the darkness.

She opens her front door and Bert dashes out. The cat must have been a coiled spring for hours. It's pointless to go after him now. Maybe he'll come back before she goes to bed, silly creature. She needs a dog, someone more content to lie at her feet on these cold nights, maybe let out the occasional woof if someone comes near.

Martin hadn't been one for pets. She'd gotten Bert anyway. Inherited him, really. A friend passed away and Linda felt the need to do something more than make a donation to cancer. So, Bert's litter tray moved in and Martin said surprisingly little in protest.

Bert took a shine to Martin, curling about his legs, arching his back, even meowing in a deferential way. Martin gave in, picking him up and stroking the top of his head, roughly. Bert seemed to like that sort of attention better than Linda's gentler ministrations. Soon, he was a fixture on Martin's lap and he'd follow Martin like a dog whenever he left the house. More than once she'd gone up to the empty house at the top of the hill and found Martin sitting near the cliff watching the sea, Bert beside him sharing the view. She supposes that's where Bert goes, keeping the vigil alone now.

A dog. Maybe one like Hoover, his drooling lips slung over her slippers as she watches television in the evenings. A small dog might be more manageable though, curled in her lap on the sofa, her hand kept warm on the fur of its back. It would be good to have a reason to go for a walk and feed someone other than herself at mealtimes. Bert only requires that she fill his bowl with kibble from time to time. He must prefer the outdoor cuisine to the domestic. Cats still have so much wildness in them.

She stalls in front of the hall closet, seeking the hanger on which to stow her coat. The closet should not be so overstuffed with one woman living here. The trouble is that despite advice from everyone, she hasn't gotten rid of Martin's clothes. Some things are in boxes in the attic, but the task left her weak. It did not feel right, nor cleansing, as advertised. It felt like she was deciding to let him go.

She knows he's dead. It's not like she's pretending he is still here. It's just that they built this house together. They were not wealthy, every little thing in here was earned. It was their house, to take away his things seemed wrong. Not yet, she tells them when they ask. Not yet. Three years is still too soon.

She puts the kettle on and locates her cigarettes. She's down to three—well, four—a day. An improvement. The government will soon make the cost entirely out of reach anyway.

She gazes out the kitchen window, waiting for the water to boil, her reflection a composite image over the distant glow of Emily's house. Is her face thinner? She's not one to look in the mirror for long. If she wears makeup she forgets and rubs her eyes, which is only a good look at Halloween. Aging doesn't bother her. It's the loneliness. Her grandmother, gone many years now, had a face filled with lines, but you could tell they were from smiling. That's the face Linda would prefer. The steam from the kettle fogs the glass, erasing her features, leaving only the soft smudge of her outline.

She pops a tea bag into a mug and goes back to the closet for her smoking jacket, reserved for winter nights on the porch. It's more a wearable sleeping bag than a coat; two sizes too big, it reaches well past her knees and is filled with feathers. A second-hand find and one that her son scoffed at for its incompatibility with lit cigarettes. Tom isn't keen on her smoking. He doesn't say it but his hugs are brief when he can smell it.

She hasn't seen much of Tom this past week. Sometimes this is a good thing, his life's in the city now. He has a roommate and a job, but sometimes these hiccups in their regular communication signal something else.

Emily's front door opens and Daniel appears with the dog on a leash. He comes out but doesn't see her there on the porch. He always puts Hoover on a leash, whereas Emily seems to take her chances. It's become a familiar sight, Emily in pursuit of her dog, clad in slippers and a bathrobe, Hoover oblivious to her pleas, nose glued to the ground. Linda smiles, she likes optimists.

She hasn't told Tom. She meant to at Christmas, but it wasn't the right time. He volunteered to do all the cleanup after the turkey. She finally went to check on him after she tweaked to the sound of water running for too long. The sink was starting to overflow. He was looking at it but he must have been seeing something else. She turned off the tap and teased him for daydreaming even though they both knew his visions are not so lightly named. He muttered an apology and went for the mop. Sometimes he'll tell her what he sees, but Linda could not bring herself to ask. So she waited, thinking she'd tell him about the new neighbours next time.

CHAPTER 3

Ryan fidgets in the cart, trying to reach the bright things on the shelf nearest him while Emily edges forward in the line, further frustrated that she only has three items but they are crucial things. If she goes home without them, tomorrow's breakfast will be a wasteland. It's five thirty, her stomach growls, supper has yet to be conceived of let alone prepared. She forces a smile at her son. Leaning into his ear she sings "Itsy Bitsy Spider," tracing her fingers up his arm, stopping at his shoulder then tickling through his hair. He stops reaching for the candy and waits for his favourite part, "down came the rain." He smiles, not waiting for her to finish before demanding an encore. They repeat this several times to the amusement of a grandmother in a neighbouring line.

The cashier wears a nametag that reads *Martha*, pinned to her blue polyester smock at a diagonal. She pushes her glasses up her nose and smiles as Emily takes her turn in front of the conveyor belt.

"Find everything you need, love?"

"I did, thanks."

"And you're helping your mum?" Ryan stares at Martha without understanding. "Do you like stickers?"

At last, a nod, mouth hanging open. She produces a sheet of stickers from under the cash register and hands it to Ryan.

"That will be twenty forty-seven, love, cash or card?"

"Oh, debit." Emily tries to assist Ryan in peeling a tiny fish from the page of stickers.

"Just enter your code when you're ready."

Emily dials in the numbers. The machine bleats. Martha lifts her glasses from her nose and peers at her display.

"Sorry about that. Let's try that again."

Emily reads *declined* and frowns.

"No, sorry. Something must have gone through on the account. Here, let's try this one." She produces a credit card from her wallet, and sees Martha flush and glance at her growing lineup. "Oh dear, we don't take that one. Do you have another?"

"Let me see what I have for cash."

Her cheeks redden as she tries to count the change in her purse. Ryan drops the sticker and grasps at the floor two and half feet below, a siren rising in his chest.

"Ryan, just a moment. I…I have ten-fifty here. I'll just have to leave the…" She looks at her three items and has a flashback to *The Price is Right* from her lunch hour as a child. "The coffee."

Minutes ago this was unthinkable, but now she wants to escape the store with her milk, eggs, and wailing child. Martha smiles and tucks the full sheet of stickers into the bag for Ryan.

Pulling out of the parking lot, she realizes that the mortgage payment would have come out. There had been a little left over from the sale of the house, but they bought a load of wood with cash, the new rug for the living room, and replaced all the usual condiments and so on that you can't pack for a long-distance move. The credit card still needs to be paid off or they'll be paying a hunk of interest on that too.

She pulls out onto the main road without doing a shoulder check—a horn blares behind her. "What's that?" Ryan's voice is tiny, he leans forward trying to see.

"Mummy made a mistake. It's okay." Her heart hammers away in her chest, hunger forgotten.

Linda is getting out of the shower when she hears the pounding on the door. She freezes, towel midway across her back. First thing in the morning? Closing her eyes, she wills it to be something else, a woodpecker, the washer off balance, maybe just a sliver of the past coming up to torment her, but it gets louder, faster. Please, not Tom. Wrapping the towel around her, she pads over to the window and tries to see who it could be.

Emily, in pyjamas, hunching, blowing into her hands and revving up for another round of door pounding. Hoover is behind her, his tail slung low.

"Lord Jesus," she mutters. Abandoning her task of drying off, she rushes down the hallway. A blast of cold air hits her as she wrenches the door open.

"Thank God! I thought you weren't home." Tears stream down her face and she's shaking. Linda waves them in. "I'm locked out. Just ran out after the dog and the door swung shut behind me."

"You must be freezing. Daniel's at work?"

Emily nods, her teeth still chattering. "You don't have another key, do you? Or some secret way of getting in?" she pleads with arms wrapped around her.

"No, love. You can't get Ryan to open the door?"

"I've been trying to tell him how, but it's the one on the doorknob. I hate those things. He's freaking out." Her eyes are wide. "Hoover was getting sick and I went out. It's so stupid, I was going to keep his ears out of it."

The dog looks miserable.

Linda flips through the phone book, propelled forward on Emily's tide of panic, trying to keep her towel from sliding off.

"Grab the phone from the kitchen. I'll dial, you talk."

Emily puts the phone to her ear and addresses a particle of dust seven feet away as it rings. "Daniel's going to kill me, this is probably going to cost hundreds of dollars. Fuckfuckfuck, hello? Yes, I'm locked out…."

Linda escapes to her bedroom, hears the muffled directions behind her. Knotting her bathrobe, she hears Emily hang up.

"Thirty minutes, he says. I'm going to head back to the house, talk to Ryan through the window."

"You can't go back out like that. I'll get you something."

"Your coats won't fit me."

"Oh, go on. I have plenty of things." She pulls Tom's lime green down coat from the closet. Emily slides into it, without asking why Linda would have such a thing.

"Now go, see if you can coach him to open the door." She pats her on the back. "If not, come back. I'll put on the coffee."

By the time she's dressed and the coffee is ready, a white van is parked in front of Emily's house. It takes the man a matter of seconds to get the door open. He steps aside and the dog disappears though the door. But Emily bends at the waist and straightens up with Ryan clinging to her, his head buried in her neck. They stand like that, her arms wound around him, swaying back and forth in a private waltz before going in. Linda opens the cupboard and puts the second mug away, swallowing a lump in her throat.

LATER, SHE HANGS over the sink, peeling potatoes, the phone rammed between shoulder and chin, listening.

"Still, you have to take them for now," she says. "At least until the appointment. Try eating some yogurt, I read that it helps with nausea." She pauses, listening to his rapid breathing.

"I'll see if Brad has some in the fridge."

"Thank you. I'll come by tomorrow afternoon. I'm bringing you a casserole."

"Mum, you don't have to do that."

"I know, but you still need to eat."

"At three, right?"

"Right. I'll call before heading out. Love you."

She drops the potato in the sink, puts down the phone, and rubs her neck. Then she picks it up and dials another number.

"Brad, it's Tom's mum."

"Hey, Mum."

"Is work busy? Think maybe you could swing by the apartment?"

"Did you talk to him?" It sounds like she's caught him walking somewhere.

"Just now. He said he'd take them but—"

"Yeah. No, I'll take a break and pop in. I'm in between meetings."

"Thanks. I'll be there tomorrow."

"Right. Call you back in a bit."

Without Brad, she'd be in the car right now, driving to the city. It feels like spying sometimes, but what else can she do?

⌒

"Wow, look at how tall." Daniel's voice comes from the living room. "Nice work, bud. Now we need to make a roof."

"Roof roof." Ryan laughs.

"Yes, rrrrroof. Should we make it flat like our house?"

Emily watches them while she tucks her hair into a winter hat, getting ready to head for the front door. Should she ruin the mood and mention the missing shackle? Chances are good that Ryan has made off with it again.

"Oh wait. Mum needs to say something. You going out?"

"Yes, our roof needs to go for a walk."

"Want us to come?" He's not looking at her, instead reaching out to tickle his son.

The wood stove is stuffed, it's almost too warm in here. She'd love to lie on her back, read a book for a few hours in silence. Last night, there was an awkward amount of wine left in the bottle so she'd finished it off. Just half a glass too much. Her tongue feels swollen this morning.

Just then Daniel finds the tender spot, just under the chin, and Ryan releases a peal of piercing squeals, each one bouncing off the hard surfaces of the living room and finding the fine bones of Emily's ears. She winces and raises her voice.

"No, it's fine. Just a short walk."

She rams on her boots and whistles for Hoover.

Outside, the cheerful screeching is muted. The sun is turning last night's snowfall to a dirty stew, the kind that sticks to the shovel. The plough has left a ridge of it at the end of the driveway. Emily turns from that chore and heads down the hill with the dog, his tail curved over his back. Clomping through the slush behind him, she sees Linda waving from her porch.

"I'm sorry about yesterday." She must have scared the bejesus out of Linda in the shower, pounding on the door like that. It was only after she got home that she thought about it.

Linda waves the apology away. "These things happen."

Emily gropes for a bag in her pocket. Naturally, Hoover has chosen to go in the middle of Linda's front path instead of a spot where people don't walk.

"Hoover seems happy today," Linda says, crouching down to stroke one of his ears.

"Last night he had me up at three." It would be nice if, just once, he would go to Dan's side of the bed and lick his face. "I was keeping an eye from the door, half asleep, when I started thinking he was taking too long. So, I get my boots on—making sure the door does *not* lock behind me—and there he is, eating it."

"Eating wha—oh. Christ, why do they do that?" Linda straightens.

Hoover moves on to a spot of yellow snow, his nose pulling in the scent in great, appreciative gulps.

"Man's best friend," says Linda.

"Oh, and when Dan got home from work Ryan tells him how *I left him in the house, all alone.*" They'd had one of their *talks* last night. Money. Never the best way to fall asleep. She sighs, looking at the house. They still need curtains. Last time she took Ryan to the library she noticed a posting for a job. It might be time to polish up the resumé.

"It's always fascinating to hear kids tell their version of things," says Linda. "Anyway, he was fine, if a little shaken up."

"True. Hey, you said we could take a little walk tomorrow?"

"Oh." The smile drops from Linda's face. "Tomorrow. I have something." It seems like she's about to go on but then she crosses her arms as if she's cold. "Another time?"

"It's okay," says Emily. "I'll use the excuse to stay in, eat a stick of butter." But Linda doesn't laugh.

"Next week?" says Linda. "Closer to spring anyway."

CHAPTER 4

Daniel finds her in the bathroom, clad in only a T-shirt, the digital scale's numbers whirling, the verdict unknown.

"Hah!" she says, raising her arm. "What's Ryan up to?"

"He's got the playdough out on the table, making us *cookies.*"

"Ah, glad I didn't vacuum."

"I wanted to talk to you about something."

She shimmies into sweatpants. "Mm hm."

He sits on the end of the bed and pats the spot next to him. It's an annoying gesture, something her stepfather used to do when she was a teenager.

"Everything okay?"

"What do you mean?'

"You're sleeping?"

She snorts. He revises his question.

"Getting *enough* sleep then?"

She yawns in response. Daniel is a textbook good-sleeper, nodding off in under seven minutes, getting his full eight hours most nights. He only knows about her wanderings throughout the house in the middle of the night if she tells him. But there's no point in complaining; he has to be rested and out the door for the office every day.

"You know why I'm asking."

"There's not much I can do."

"Sure, there is. The doctor said regular exercise, fresh air, avoid alcohol, no TV before bed…." He taps each one off on his fingers.

"I hardly ever watch TV," she says.

"And less worrying."

"Hard to control that."

"Alcohol."

"I'm not giving up my glass of wine." It is one glass, she just refills it sometimes.

He reaches an arm around her and kisses the top of her head.

"Maybe if I got a job."

"Why?" He leans back, surprised.

"Less worry? If we had just a bit extra, stuff like getting locked out wouldn't make such a dent."

"But then we'd be paying someone for childcare—"

"Not if it was evenings and weekends." It's not what they'd talked about, being there for Ryan in shifts. "I actually…applied to the library a couple of days ago." From downstairs, they hear Ryan narrating his playdough creations. "Plenty of parents have to do it this way. And it's temporary, right?"

"Right, I'm just a little concerned."

She puts her hand to her eyes and massages her temples. It feels so good. "I'll go to a walk-in clinic, get my sleeping pills refilled."

"It might be better to find a new doctor."

"I already put a call in to get us a new GP, but there's a wait-list of over a year."

"I don't mean a GP."

She studies his face.

"Is this coming from you or your mother?"

He looks away. Just as she'd thought. It was Maggie that Daniel called after Ryan was born, when he realized that she wasn't coping. The word *unfit* was used, something he'd never be able to take back.

"It's just that I read something the other day—okay, Mum emailed it to me—but the article said that sometimes it pops up again when the child turns three."

She closes her eyes and breathes. He won't even name it. Christ. Of course, she shouldn't be annoyed. He'd had to take time off of work to care for his infant son—unplanned—and watch her turn into a different person. When she found out she was pregnant, she'd warned him that she was at a higher risk for postpartum depression. Maybe he thought she'd exaggerated, expecting a sort of melancholy, cured by a hug, but he was shaken by her transformation. Regardless of his good intentions, it feels belittling, this checking in, like they're no longer on an even plane; him the responsible parent even though she's been fine for two years, slogging through the day-to-day.

"Yes, I'm tired. But it's not like before."

"You're not having the dreams?"

"God no. I'm just…restless at night."

He takes off his glasses to clean them on his T-shirt.

"As long as you're sure."

⌒

The car is frosting up inside by the time Linda spots the tow truck pulling up. He takes his sweet time climbing out too, and he's still chewing something when he raps his knuckles on her window.

"You the one who called?"

Linda averts her eyes from the smudge of ketchup at the corner of his mouth. "I am. It just started sputtering so I pulled over and that was it."

"They tell you that you only have a week left on your membership?" He raises his eyebrows at her, his tongue probing at a piece of food between his front teeth.

"Yes."

"Damn lucky that, eh?"

She nods, wishing he'd get on with it. It's been a long day already, and she'd only dressed for a warm car and the doctor's appointment, the one she won't make now.

"You have a place I'm supposed to take it or just the closest one?"

"Closest one."

He ambles off, wiping a hand on his plaid shirt.

They'd always had a membership to the automobile association. It's the first time she's had to use it though. In the past, her first call would have been Martin. She must have missed a renewal notice, maybe it looked like junk.

There seems to be no end to the reminders of Martin's vacated role in her life. The worst was the autumn after he died. There was a knock on the door, she'd opened it to a man with a clipboard, his truck already blocking her driveway.

"Your husband called about getting the roof done."

He said it as if it had been that very day, not months before, just after the snow had melted, revealing missing shingles. You could have knocked her over with a feather. The man swung his clipboard around to show her the familiar signature. Maybe Martin had told her about it. Maybe he hadn't.

The reason she is here is probably the result of some other dangling thing. It's hard not to feel anxious, uncertain of all these little things she should be doing to maintain the hum of life.

Dammit. This appointment was made three weeks ago. Now she'd be at the back of the line again. Not that she's keen for the icy stethoscope on her back and her doctor saying *still smoking?* The whole medical community makes her feel as if she's an inch tall. She'd spent enough time in stuffy waiting rooms in the last ten years, trying to make sense of things for Tom.

The knock on the windshield makes her scream.

"Jesus, Mary, and Joseph," she mutters, cracking her door open.

"Sorry." He looks a bit embarrassed for her. "I been trying to wave at ya. All squared away here."

⌒

"You shouldn't have…."

"It's a late Valentine's Day gift," says Daniel.

"But I only got you something small. I thought we agreed not to spend much." This is certainly not small.

"Just open it. You'll understand. Ryan, help Mum."

Daniel guides his son's finger under a gap in the tape. Together, they get all the paper off.

And there it is.

"I had it made. Someone at work put me in touch with a woman at the museum and she gave me a little guidance. I hope you like it."

Da's shackle.

"I kept finding it around the house, and I thought this way you'd know exactly where it is."

His words fade as she runs her fingers along the glass. It's a box of dark wood. The background is a nautical chart.

"Mahone Bay?" she says looking at him.

He nods, his eyes smiling. "And the photo, that's a copy I had made."

Emily glances at the shelf and locates the original in the frame. He must have taken it with him one day, and she hadn't even noticed.

"Mum took that picture just after he got the boat."

It's a black and white shot of Charlie in the cockpit, grinning up at the mast, squinting from the glare of the sun. Beside the photo, the shackle loops into a short piece of rope, tied into a bowline and stitched neatly to the chart behind. Da used to have her practise that knot over and over.

Forcing a smile, she means to say something kind, but says instead, "I've been looking everywhere."

"Sorry. I wanted to surprise you."

"You did. You did." She lowers her head to the box, sniffing. "It's teak?"

"Mm hm. I thought it would be good if it smelled a bit *boaty* too."

He has gone still, watching her.

She feels one hot tear break free.

"It's okay, Mummy."

"Mum's just happy," Daniel says, leaning in to pat her knee.

"Yes," she lies, removing her glasses and wiping her cheek with the back of her hand. If only it weren't so exquisite. It's a piece fit for a museum.

"Ryan, careful, it's glass. Don't bang it." He removes his son's hand from the front of the box. "Right. How about I make us some pancakes?"

One of Daniel's specialties. He leaves her sitting in the living room, hunched over his gift. God knows how much it cost. Beyond that, though, beyond the sentiment, beyond that non-glare glass, immune from dust and sticky fingers, is the shackle, never to be cradled in her palm again.

"THANK YOU FOR coming." Emily glances at Linda before putting the car in reverse. "It helps to have two sets of eyes on Ryan when I'm shopping."

It's a miserable afternoon but the parking lot is busy.

"Well, it beats sitting at the mechanic's for two hours. I'm glad I caught you before you left. And…"—she turns and gives Ryan a wink—"I love thrift stores. It's like treasure hunting."

Emily switches off the engine and they sit watching the snow fall on the windshield.

"I know. We had them in Calgary, but nothing like Frenchy's. It's crazy to buy new clothes for kids this age."

Inside, Emily takes off Ryan's wet coat and shows him the play area tucked in the corner where a few other kids watch *Sesame Street*. He lets go of her hand, edging his way into the corner, and scoops up a threadbare stuffed dog from the toy box.

Emily joins Linda at the pants table, putting a basket at her feet. They sort through the items, placing them against their bodies, one leg out.

"So, do you have a method?"

"Hm?" Linda looks at her over the waistband of a pair of white Levis.

"I've been here before and gotten in trouble for heaping in the wrong direction. I believe that the correct etiquette is to pick up things on your left and pile them to your right. I'm more of a colour hunter, I tend to just scan for the shades I want and snatch them. People can be remarkably protective of clothes that they don't even own yet."

Linda has abandoned the Levis and watches Emily, smiling.

"I've never thought about it. But I go through pretty much everything on the table."

"What about these? They're a size, let me see…zero. Christ. Anyway, looks like they'll fit you. Never been worn by the looks of it." She tosses the pants across the table.

"Can't hurt to try them on." Linda pops them in her basket.

"Mummy." Ryan is beside her holding a plastic fire truck, faded nearly to pink. "Look."

"Oh? You have one at home. You can play with this one while you're here." She takes his hand and guides him back to the play area. "Have you met the other kids?"

A little girl stares at Ryan. Her pigtails are high on her head and she's wearing a tutu over a pair of jeans.

"Why don't you see if you can share the blocks?"

Returning to the table she says, "I'm not sure how long he'll last."

"Relax, I can watch him. He reminds me so much of Tom at that age."

Of course, Linda mentioned him way back. "Your son!"

"Oh, he's all grown up, nearly your age. But I used to take him shopping, and he'd hide in the clothes racks. Used to scare the hell out of me."

The little girl points at Ryan, giving him directions, then goes over and restacks the blocks.

"Is Tom married?" says Emily but the question doesn't seem to register with Linda. "Tom, right?"

"Yes, Tom. Um no, he's single."

Has she put her foot in it? Maybe he's gay. Should she have said partner? Then again, not all families are close.

"You must have some old friends here still?" Linda says.

"In Nova Scotia? No, they're scattered around the country."

"What about your mother? Does she shop with you?"

Emily shakes her head. "Oh, she shops. But not second-hand." Her stepfather has a superstition about used things bringing bad luck from their past owners. It has always struck her as a thin excuse for snobbery. She lurches toward women's blouses, shoving the basket along with one foot. "I really need to get something to wear to a job interview."

Two hours later they pile into the car, bags of clothes crammed in next to Ryan's car seat. Emily offers a squirt of hand sanitizer to Linda.

"Thanks. So, how are you liking the house?"

"Pretty good. I just want to sit there watching the water." She checks the rear-view mirror to make sure Ryan is not making a mess with his snack then pulls onto the road. Finally, she glances at Linda and realizes that she's looking back at her. "Sorry, what was I saying?"

"The house."

"Oh, yeah. It's different, I've never lived in a young house. Most of our places have been older than me. I could be this one's mother."

Linda laughs.

"It's the noises. I keep thinking I hear Daniel in the day when he's not there. He says it's probably the windows heating up and cooling off. But I find cupboard doors open when I'm sure I shut them."

Linda tilts her head, indicating Ryan.

"No, it's not him. It's probably the house settling. Did you spend much time there when you were looking after it?"

"Oh, I'd take a quick walk through to check for leaks, but no."

They're interrupted by Ryan coughing in the back seat.

"You okay, buddy?" He's fine by the time she's pulled over, granola dotting his chin, his eyes watering.

Linda stays in her seat while Emily wipes his face.

"Enjoy this," Linda says when Emily is buckled up. "This stage goes so fast. You can't know it now, but things can get much more... complicated."

"Great," says Emily, pulling back onto the road. Every mother seems eager to tell her this. It starts when you're pregnant and, apparently, never stops.

"WHY HERE?" DANIEL says, wiping the foam from his upper lip.

"It's where we met."

They're seated at one of three long wooden tables that face the empty stage, each one stamped with the circles of beer steins from people thumping their demand for one more tune. It's still early. People order plates of food and talk quietly. Emily and Daniel will be out of here long before the night crowd rolls in.

"I know, but it wasn't exactly the most romantic way to meet. Plus we were here in November after we put the offer in on the house. Remember?"

"Right there." She points at the bar. "That's where I *first* saw you. You were trying to wink at me."

"No I wasn't."

"You were."

"Fucking Peter tricked me into buying rounds of rum. You know I can't wink."

"I said *trying* to wink."

Daniel still cringes at the story of how he accidentally threw up on her, so she won't rub it in. His friends did enough of that at their wedding reception. But to her, this pub is a special place.

Late at night on weekends it feels like you're below deck on an old ship, the whole room swaying with the music, people shouting out the lyrics along with the band. She worked here for a stint, not downstairs but at the restaurant above. That's how she knew where to take Daniel to get them both cleaned off when the rum came back up. He'd tried to contain his mess. Even in his state, he was mortified. She grabbed his hand, they bumped their way through the crowd and climbed the stairs. Afterwards, they walked the waterfront to clear his head. In the morning, they were still talking when Daniel's appetite kicked in. That's when they'd really got to know each other, over coffee and eggs Benedict.

"What time did you tell the sitter?" Daniel checks his watch.

"Nine, at the latest."

"Okay, good."

He leans back in his chair and rubs his neck.

"Everything all right?"

"Tomorrow is coming too fast."

"Sorry, next time we'll come on a weekend. It's just that she was available, and I wanted Ryan to meet her before my interview." The cellphone is on the table next to her drink, but she picks it up and checks it anyway. "She must have got him to bed."

"He was probably easier on her than us."

"Probably." Emily had never left him with anyone but Maggie or Lola. Both of them claimed he went to sleep right away for them. "How's work?"

"I shouldn't complain."

"But." *You're going to.*

"Do you know that they still work in imperial here? The *building code* is in metric." He's got that look he gets when he's about to launch into techinal jargon, so she jumps in.

"What about the people?" She used to get together for after-work drinks with Daniel and his co-workers when they were in Calgary.

"They've been working together for years, then they're bought out and I come along and start telling them to do things differently—and faster. But, at least I'm not away in Fort MacMurray for weeks at a time."

"Or months."

"Yeah." He stretches his arms behind his chair and cracks his back. "This is good."

"Yeah?"

"Talking without filtering everything. Ryan's always right there, you know?"

"Mm."

She could point out that it was he who loved the house's open concept and she who has to live with it most of the time. Trying to get Ryan to stay in his room and nap when there's no door to shut is a losing battle. But that's not what this evening is about. Instead, she eyes his empty drink. "Want another? I'll drive."

EMILY IS IN the bathroom, her face two inches from the mirror, glaring at a red lump at the tip of her nose. Aren't pimples the bane of teens? Of all days. She dabs some makeup on it and leans back. There, no one will notice. She ought to become a makeup artist.

In the kitchen, she's busy making breakfast when Daniel swings by and offers a kiss. He hums to himself as he turns away.

"Christmas music?" she accuses his back. She's the one guilty of this offence at warmer times of the year, simply because she remembers the lyrics. He chuckles, then she recognizes it: "'Rudolph the Red-Nosed Reindeer.' Nice! Like you should be teasing *me* on this subject."

From the living room, a wail rises to a screech. A toy has refused to bend in the right direction, or maybe the dog has casually wandered by, disturbing the careful order of things. She closes her eyes and hopes it will resolve itself. It does not. Maybe Dan will feel bad about the teasing and intervene, allow her to finish making coffee. No, instead the phone rings.

Calls at breakfast time are rarely simple. Even before motherhood, she resented the phone. Too many jobs required her to cheerfully respond to cranky callers. She longs to pick up a telephone, say something thoroughly honest, and hang up.

It's the sitter. She can't come today. It's her mother, the hospital, she is worried, she is sorry. There is no railing against this kind of excuse. True or not, Emily would be the bitch in this situation. Murmuring polite concern, she hangs up. She has been trying to squash her left ear shut with her hand while listening, unaware that the wailing has stopped.

Ryan appears, eyes hopeful. "Chocolate chips?"

Right. If he is quiet when Mum and Dad are on the phone, he gets three. Of course, that deal wasn't meant for pre-breakfast. Her shoulders droop. The phone rarely rings in the morning, after all.

"You were so good! But not before breakfast. Remind me later and you can have them then. After lunch, okay?"

Surprisingly, this seems to satisfy him and he retreats to the other room to continue bossing his toys around. Turning back to the counter, she tries to remember what she was doing. Looking blankly at the coffee machine, she drums her fingers on the counter.

"Who was that?" Daniel says.

"The sitter. She cancelled. It's her mother."

Neither one of them know her enough to comment on this. She's only been here the once. It's possible that she doesn't even have a living mother. Emily pictures her rolling over in bed, smiling sleepily at a man, reaching for a cigarette, smirking at her own cleverness.

"Shit," Daniel says.

"Yes. Exactly."

And right on cue, from the other room, an echo but in a small voice: "Shit," and again—gleeful this time—"shit, shit, shit."

Holding a hand up to Daniel, she says, "Ignore it. If we pay attention, it'll make it worse. He doesn't know what it means."

"Anyway, what are you going to do? What time is the interview?"

Emily looks at the clock. "Ten. Too soon."

"Have a coffee and think about it for a few minutes. I have to run. Early meeting. Will they reschedule?" He is shrugging on his coat, one foot hovering above an open shoe.

"I don't know. I'll call and see. First, I'll wrack my brains for a different solution. Surely the dog is old enough to babysit."

But he's switched off his Dad persona, his head is at the office, rehearsing his part in the meeting.

"Yes, sure. What about Linda?" He doesn't wait for an answer, he just picks up his bag, calls out a goodbye to Ryan, and marches off.

"Lucky bastard," she mutters, remembering when she envied the notion of a stay-at-home mother.

Back to the coffee, she fills the water tank and adds beans. Not one person comes to mind. Grandparents are still away. Even if her mother was here, she's not sure she'd want her to do it. Linda's car isn't there.

So that leaves two options. Postpone, though they might insist that this is the only day of interviews. Or take him along? What the heck. If they say they can't reschedule, there is little left to lose. Libraries are filled with small children. She imagines sitting in a comfortable office, Ryan in a miniature chair in the corner, quietly flipping through the pages of a picture book while she talks to the interviewer. It could work.

Hitting the *start* button, she wonders if it's too early to call. The outgoing message reports that they don't answer their phones until ten, when the library opens.

"Ryan, let's get you dressed."

SHE PULLS INTO the parking lot at five past ten. It would be easier to pull off a robbery at the Louvre than to get Ryan anywhere early. Her carefully applied makeup is now shining with sweat despite the winter wind. The end of her nose is itchy but she forces herself to leave it.

There is no time to search for picture books to amuse Ryan—maybe a magazine from the shelves nearest the door? She comforts herself with this as she unbuckles him. All the while he points at the sky, asking about airplanes.

"Okay, we have to be fast. Can you get down quick? Pretend it's an emergency. No time to waste." If she tries to help him he will melt to the ground, yelling, then climb right back into the car to show how he can do it himself. "Go, go, go!" she yells, smiling tightly at people getting into the car next to them.

He pitches toward the door, catching his toe on the frame and falls sideways, bashing his head on his car seat. *Always the head.* Now he's hurt, angry, and crying.

They push into the library, his cheeks wet with tears. Before going to the front desk, she grabs a magazine from the rack. There is a smiling child on the cover.

"I'm here for ten. Emily. I have an interview…."

She trails off, realizing she has forgotten with whom the interview is, along with the title of the job. She stares at the woman at the desk, who looks freshly washed, unfettered, coffee mug in hand, eyes searching Emily's hip, taking in the small sniffling boy.

"My babysitter couldn't come at the last minute. I'd have postponed, if I could. He loves books so I was thinking he could sit in…."

Deliberately, she leaves an opening for the librarian to jump in with reassurances. She only furrows her brow and looks at her computer. Maybe the screen contains information on a scenario such as this. Finally, she says, "Oh. I'm sure it will be fine. I'll just go and check with Barb."

Barb! Yes, that's it.

She's dreamed of this sort of work: hidden away in the stacks, surrounded by books, called away infrequently to assist in the search for a novel. It would be time with grown-ups, time to complete a thought.

She is left to stand at the desk while Barb is consulted. Ryan buries his snotty face in her coat. Her hand rests on his soft hair. She crouches, automatically wiping his cheeks with her fingers.

"Remember what I told you? I'm going to talk to this person for a little while. You can look at this book." She waves the magazine at him like a parade flag. "But while we're talking, I really need you to be quiet. Can you do that for Mummy? You can have a treat after. *After.* Okay?"

He nods, his mouth down-turned. "Is it about airplanes?"

"Oh." Her heart plunges, if only she had five minutes. "There might be some planes, you'll have to look and tell me. *After.*"

The librarian has returned, clearing her throat. "This is Barb, she says it's okay."

Barb takes over. "It's too bad it's not Wednesday. We have storytime then." She offers her hand briefly, eyes skirting the top of Ryan's head, then turns and heads for a corridor filled with grey doors.

Emily grips Ryan's hand and tugs him along.

"I'm so sorry, my sitter gave me two hours' notice."

Barb doesn't respond, ushering them into the little office. It's easy to tell that she is not the person who runs the storytime for the children. Books line every wall, leaning in precarious towers on the floor, sticky notes adorning their covers. There are three chairs. Ryan heads for the swivel chair right away, brushing past Barb.

"No, Ryan, that's not your chair. You're here." Emily's voice is too loud in the small room. She pauses and tries to sound friendly. "You sit next to Mummy."

Barb waits patiently until everyone is settled, then quietly closes the door and seats herself, smoothing her cardigan. Emily opens the magazine in Ryan's lap, noting that it's a medical journal, featuring mostly text with a few small·images that seem to detail skin afflictions. *Shit*, she thinks.

"Shit," a smaller voice says aloud.

"SO HOW WAS the interview?" Daniel asks, coming through the door, kicking off his shoes.

"Once Ryan broke the ice we were off to a rollicking start."

Her back is to him as she cuts cheese to go with supper.

"You took him with you?"

"Mm hm, you should try it. It changes the tone completely."

Turning, she puts a hand on her hip; he reads her face, realizes she's not joking.

"So, no job offer?"

"Oh, I don't know. When Ryan started swearing it really lightened the mood."

"No."

"Yes, I was thinking I'd have to just leave when she started to laugh. I'm guessing she'd had enough of the standard interview questions over the past couple of days. At the end, she said that my 'honesty was refreshing.'"

"Shit?" he whispers at her.

"That's the one," she says, pointing the knife at him.

"Jesus," he says, reaching in the fridge for a beer.

"Yeah, all those years of nervousness over interviews. Next time, I'll bring the dog too." She plucks his beer bottle from his hand and takes a swig.

"Get your own." He grabs the bottle back from her. "So, did you get it?"

"They're deciding next week." She turns back to the cupboard and pulls plates out. "Ryan! Supper!"

⌒

Strange how your subconscious can niggle at you. Something...some chore neglected? It finally dawns on Linda when she sees Daniel pull into the driveway. She doesn't have to check on that house anymore. Weird, how that had come back this morning, that burden, after they'd been living there more than two months. A dream? Yes, Martin was still alive, she'd only forgotten that he was up the hill. All this time, he'd only been checking on things.

Back when he was responsible for the place, he often did it right after work, before he even came in to say hello. One night, she spotted his truck parked in the driveway. She waited for over a half-hour and when he still didn't come in, she put on her coat and headed out, curiosity getting the better of her. He stepped out the front door just as she reached the house, locking it behind him.

"Hey, Lin." He was casual, like this was their routine.

"We checked out that apartment today."

"Tom like it?"

"Seemed to."

He shoved his hands in his pockets and joined her. They ambled back down the hill.

"You're still not sure," he said.

"I just don't know who is going to sign up to be his roommate."

"It'll work out." He looked up at the sky, watched the stars winking in and out as clouds scudded past.

"You're just…" Linda started.

"I'm just what?"

"Nothing."

There was no point in hashing it out again.

"Someone will go for it."

"But the right someone."

"Has to happen one day, Lin. You know that. And it's not like we're buying the place."

Inside, they wouldn't discuss it like this. Tom's hearing was better than theirs.

"I guess."

"Good for him. You'll see."

She reached out, looped her arm through his elbow, and gave it a playful little tug to try and uproot his hand from the pocket. But he didn't put his arm around her waist and reel her in. She settled for walking up their driveway arm in arm, until the path was too narrow and he let go.

Emily pauses in the shower with one leg up, razor in hand, a hunting dog on point. She feels something, a change in the air, or maybe she heard it. Relaxing in the shower is not possible with a small child in the house. Even with the help of cartoons, she is always listening for telling noises or dubious silences. The running water deadens the sound from the next room. She cocks her head in the direction of the door and hears a commercial on TV along with the small sound of Ryan's voice. She lets out a breath and then catches a deeper voice speaking. It's probably the TV. She puts down the razor and strains to make out the sounds. Too many horror movies as a teenager. It's easy to imagine terrible things happening while naked, wet, and blinded with soap. Or, more likely, this would be the time Ryan would fling open the front door and run into the street, suddenly filled with speeding cars, or turn on all of the burners on the stovetop piled with stuffed animals. No, it's just the TV.

But something feels wrong. Call it paranoia or call it mother's intuition. She rinses the soap from her half-shaved leg and switches off the water.

"Ryan?" she calls out.

She dries her face, then holds her breath, listening. There it is again, the deeper voice. A fresh fear blooms in her. The front door is locked. She must have locked it after letting the dog back in. The dog. Hoover would bark at a stranger. Surely he was good for that. That is, once he woke from his drooling sleep.

Grabbing her robe, she pulls it around her damp body and is about to open the door when she hears him.

"Hi, Mummy!" he mumbles around a lollipop, leaning through the door to see her; the sound of the television comes with him.

"Hi, sweetie. What have you got in your mouth?" She peers around the edge of the door at him, sliding into her slippers and knotting her robe. Her shoulders relax, he was just sneaking a treat.

"Lollipop! The rocket man gave it to me!"

Emily stares at the stick protruding from his mouth, his smiling eyes.

"You're not supposed to have candy in the morning, Ryan. Too much sugar, it's bad for your teeth," she says, picking her towel back up to finish drying off.

"But the rocket man thought it was okay," he reasons, crunching the candy. "I brush my teeth."

"Rocket man? Do you mean on the TV?" She really must stop using the TV as a babysitter.

"No, the man gave it to me. He says he likes the stars and the moon."

An old soul, that's what people say. He lives inside his head like a lot of three-year-olds, makes up imaginary friends. She keeps this in mind, watching him reaching for his toothbrush.

"A man gave it to you?"

She can't remember having any lollipops in the house. There's a small box of sugary treats tucked away, from whenever people have offered Ryan candy. This happens randomly, even at the doctor's office. Instead of letting him have it right away, they put it in the little box and let him have it after a meal. Still, she can't remember any lollipops like this one being in there.

"Yup, but he left," he says, popping the brush into his mouth.

She pulls her robe more tightly around her, peers around the door into the living room, sees the dog deep in sleep, and then she catches the change of light playing across his nose as the front door moves with the breeze.

CHAPTER 5

Ryan acts it out for her, the man's *pointy* hair, one arm shaking, "and tall, like Daddy."

"You're sure he said your name?"

"Mm hm, Ry-an."

"It wasn't Jim or someone we know? He wasn't like Bumpy?"

"No, Mummy, a real man, sat down here." Ryan runs to the couch and shows her the spot on the cushion.

"But what else did he say? Did he look…mad?"

"Not mad. Rocket man."

"Did he…touch you?"

"Uh uh."

He does a pirouette, still on a sugar high. She switches off the TV and puts on the classical music station. Ryan spins in circles, arms flapping.

She rifles through the lower drawers in the kitchen, hoping to see other pieces of candy, something put away in the wrong spot. Nothing. And what of the wrapper? It's not in the garbage or abandoned on the floor somewhere. If he had helped himself, there would be something.

Daniel is in meetings today. Even if she called him, what would he do?

She goes to the front door again and tests the lock. It's firmly shut this time. Hoover drifts along behind her. She turns to him and squats to his level, running her hands along his ears, staring into his drooping eyes.

"What happened?"

He wags and tries to lick her chin. He had a sniff of the floor once he finally woke up. His head popped up like he'd forgotten he needed to be somewhere, one cheek squashed flat from his power nap. He woofed once then his nose pulled him out of bed, drawn to the front door and back to the couch like a magnet. Then back he went to the front door and waited for it to open and reveal the source of the smell. This didn't ease her mind at all.

No one's out there, she checked all sides of the house through the windows; no monstrous footprints in the snow. If someone came in, it was via the shovelled walkway. The front and back gardens are still a design of paw prints and patches of yellow snow.

"So, what do you think, Hoover?"

Her gut tells her that someone did come in, while her mind provides the counterpoints. Even with the sleeping pill last night, she's groggy, as if there is cotton wool in her head. Things aren't always where she leaves them. Maybe Daniel had the candy in a coat pocket.

Hoover sits in front of her while she strokes his ears, gazing into her eyes as if he can read her thoughts and sympathize.

"It doesn't make sense, does it?"

Lick.

"Nothing's missing."

Emily looks around the room, sees that her keys are there. Daniel's laptop is on the desk. Her purse hangs from a hook by the door, containing the five-dollar bill and change from yesterday.

"So why, Hoover? Why would a person walk in and walk out again? If he was going to take Ryan…."

The dog cocks his head sideways.

"Casing the place?"

She knows nothing of how to be a good burglar, but she figures that being unobtrusive is key. Hoover has left her side and stands below his dangling leash by the front door.

"No walk. No, you'll have to wait."

She shakes her head at him. What if the man is out there? Jesus, what about Linda? She straightens up and goes to the window. Linda's car isn't there, that's right, she'd checked that earlier. These things happen all the time, everywhere in the world, especially the quiet places where the neighbour will inevitably testify to the news cameras that *nothing like that happens around here, people don't even lock their doors.*

Pull yourself together.

Maybe a walk is a good plan, a good look around the house to set the mind at ease. First, she goes down to the laundry room and digs around in a basket. The pepper spray is a few years old but it's better than nothing. If it can disable a grizzly bear, it should do the trick.

Outside, she feels better; it seems less real without the walls and ceiling closing in. She makes Ryan stay inside while she does a circuit of the house, ready to blast someone with a cloud of orange mist. Meanwhile, Hoover—on his leash but not held back by her—snuffles his way towards Linda's house.

"All right, we'll go." She opens the door for Ryan and locks it before jogging to catch up with the dog.

Ryan finds a stick and dawdles behind them, poking holes in the snowbanks.

"Look, Mummy. Windows for the snow people."

"Ah, an excellent idea. They'll like that." This keeps him busy for several minutes, allowing her mind to wander. They'll carry on down the hill and make a left until they get to the little lane that gives the locals access to the beach.

Ryan lets out a scream, jangling her nerves once again. His stick has broken in half of its own accord, nothing to do with his actions, of course. She swivels around and picks him up, her heart hammering.

"We'll find another one when we get to the beach. Okay?"

They continue their journey down the hill with Ryan on her hip. Despite the added weight, she's glad for the closeness. He goes into a trance watching the seagulls drifting above them, while Hoover noses the shoulder of the road for treasure.

When they reach the beach, Emily puts Ryan back on his feet. A long smooth rock serves as a couch for her as Ryan crouches to play in the sand.

It's early March, a bright grey day. She pulls in the salt air and exhales deeply. Her old therapist recommended four or five of these. In, slowly, then out, feeling her ribs rise and fall. On her third inhale, she feels a prickling on the back of her neck. Turning, she expects to see someone, but there is no one. On a hill in the distance, modest houses face the distant views of the ocean. You can't see their house from this angle but you can make out snippets of Linda's place. Emily puts her hand to her forehead, trying to block the bright sky. It's hard to keep her eyes open in this light but she locates Linda's shed amongst the trees and shrubs. That's when she catches a movement, a figure. But her eyes are closing, a reflex against the bright sky. It might be a person, but then the sneeze forces her away. When she looks back at the spot there are only long grasses, swaying slightly, as if shaken by a gust of wind.

Linda spent the afternoon with an old friend. Her face aches from wearing a smile. Doris likes to listen to the CBC and never hesitates to call in with her opinions. She has gotten louder with age, surer of herself, and does not save her soliloquies for the airwaves. This has been the basis of their friendship from high school onward. Doris broadcasts while Linda listens.

In the car home, Linda moves her mouth into a silent scream, a little trick of hers to help loosen the tightness in her cheeks. The drive to Doris's house is too far in these cold months. It's nearly an hour on a winding road. The black ice, the short days. The excuse will do for now. In the summer, she'll have to think of something else. Volunteer work, real or fictional. She is beginning to question, belatedly, the necessity of this friendship. In fact, she is not feeling the need for human companionship at all at the moment. A puff on the porch will be even sweeter.

She's halfway up her front walk when she sees that the kitchen curtains are closed. Linda always has them open, they're creased from being drawn back to the very edge of the window and don't shut properly in the middle. But they have been pulled in tightly so that the outer edges are bent inward.

She halts, staring at the blank window. How long has he been here? Someone must have dropped him, maybe a cab? That's one small consolation, he didn't drive this time. She tries the front door but it's locked so she has to choose whether to knock on her own front door and give him warning or to just come in with her key. She decides on the latter but does it audibly, not trying to sneak in.

"Tom?" Nothing.

"Tom? It's Mum."

The curtains in the living room are shut too; he's pacing back and forth, still unaware of her. The TV is unplugged and turned to face the wall. Linda sees this and knows that she'll have to make a phone call if she can't calm him herself. How many days since she spoke to him on the phone?

Sometimes it's best to wait for him to speak. He has to find a pause in the noise within his head. He is deafened by it when things are at their worst. His pacing ceases and he looks at her. It takes him a moment to piece her features together—nose, eyes, cheeks, hair—but finally she sees it, there's recognition. He's described it to her, the brilliance of colours and light, the jumbled information arriving at the switchboard within his mind, out of sequence.

"It's poison. They're trying to poison me."

Linda has learned not to argue these statements. It's taken years of practise.

"Show me. Where is the poison?"

"They're in the toilet."

"What's in the toilet?"

He resumes his pacing so she goes to the powder room down the hall and stares at the pills floating in the bowl. Plan A obliterated. The doctor thought this one was working but the dosage was too high, they've been trying to reduce it.

"Tom. I am so tired, I'm going to sit down for a few minutes. Will you sit with me?" She keeps her voice even. "I was just visiting Doris and I'm always exhausted after our visits and then the drive home."

She keeps chatting as she sinks deep into the couch, makes a show of putting up her feet. He paces the room two more times then perches at the edge of an armchair, his right hand shaking slightly.

"Has Bradley gone away?"

"Mm? Yes. Yes, Brad went away for work."

She curses his roommate. They had an agreement; he was to leave her a message when he wouldn't be around. That is why he pays less rent. He's not a caregiver per se, just someone to take a read on things and sound the alarm if things are going downhill.

"When did he leave?" She tries to sound conversational. Tom has begun to chew his nails.

"Yesterday…I think."

"You don't work today?"

"No. Yesterday."

Maybe he's only missing one day of meds.

She gets up and makes her way to the kitchen, chatting to him over her shoulder. "I saw a kite surfer out on my way back today." He doesn't reply.

The phone number is on the fridge. She'll take the handset into the washroom upstairs with her and turn on the fan. She stopped resenting the need for this delicacy years ago. No point in mourning a different life. But seeing Ryan has brought back the simplicity of Tom's early years, when things were easily solved with a hug or a warm bath. Touch is a minefield now.

The phone call is brief. They'll be expecting him within the hour, whether she can persuade him into the car or has to call for assistance.

She returns to the living room to find him with his head in his hands. He hears her footfalls on the carpet and speaks through his fingers.

"I saw Dad."

She waits for him to go on but he doesn't.

"Did he…talk to you?"

He drops his hands and lets her see his face.

"Tom. He loved you…. " But it's best to stick to the truth. "You know he's dead. Part of you knows that."

"It's so real."

"I know it's real to you. I know." Of all the hallucinations, this one is the hardest for her. "What did he say?"

"No." He is up again, wearing out the carpet. Linda stands too.

"I could use a cup of tea. I'll make a pot. After that, I think we need to head out." She doesn't say where and she takes his lack of response as encouraging. He has come to her for help, one of the few people he trusts when he feels himself sinking.

She stands in the kitchen, feigning relaxation, readying a Thermos and two cups to go. She can hear him, back and forth across the living room, quiet mumbling. Is he answering the voices or simply talking to himself?

Just today, Doris lectured Linda on selling the house.

"Not good for either one of you to live with his ghost."

Despite Doris's shortcomings, she is the only one of her friends who has weathered the storm of Linda's past decade. While others dwindled to occasional greeting cards at the holidays, Doris is always willing to speak the truth, as she sees it. Sometimes it is bang on. Linda argued that Tom might still go to the old house looking for her, forgetting.

"Rubbish, he's looking for you. Draw him to a new place, a new future. It doesn't have to be that far away either. Just…away."

Linda tries another silent scream as she pops the tea bags into the Thermos.

"Mum?"

Tom's voice sounds alarmed in the doorway. He's watching her with her mouth open wide, eyes slammed shut.

"Oh. It's okay. I'm just loosening my jaw. You haven't seen me do that?" She laughs. How many years ago did she hear that? And where from? An actor on TV maybe. "It's a facial relaxation technique. Tiny face. Big eyes. Silent scream. Try it."

He looks at her carefully. If he weren't sifting through the voices in his head, he'd be laughing, teasing her. The books advise to behave normally, opt for a distraction. It seems to get through to him, watching her go through it a few more times before trying it himself.

"Okay. Tea's ready. I'll get my coat. Did you wear one?"

He shakes his head. Just as she thought, he must have left the house and flagged down a cab before he knew his own plan.

She fills his hands up with the Thermos and cups and marches out the door.

"We'll stop at the beach for a bit."

Another distraction.

Even inside the car, she is not certain they'll get there. He could try to get out halfway there. It's never happened but she's heard stories; support groups are a mixed blessing. Tom seems calmer.

She doesn't bother to tell him to put the cups in the holder, holding them seems to help steady his hands. They park the car at the spot favoured by surfers, but no one is there. Linda fills the cups and looks him in the eye.

"We have to go into the city. We should talk to Dr. Miller. Just… talk. I'm going to stay with you. Okay?"

Tom drops his gaze, follows the steam escaping from his cup, while Linda holds her breath.

"Okay."

⁓

They trek back up the hill, heavier with the damp sand on their boots. Hoover's face sags, tongue lolling from his mouth. He stops at regular intervals to lick the snow. Dogs know nothing of conserving energy for the journey home.

"Your face looks mad, Mummy."

She leans down and scoops him up, nuzzling into his cheek. "Not mad, just thinking."

It brings to mind her mother, the yellow rubber gloves and the rough clatter of dishes as she rammed them into the dishwasher. Da liked to cook his roasts and use every available pot and pan. He'd take over the kitchen on Sundays while her mother stuck to her salads. They sat at opposite ends of the table with Emily in between them. *More for us, eh, Duck? Pass the gravy.*

"Can we go see Linna?" Ryan looks toward her house, they're almost there.

"I don't think so. Her car's gone."

Emily thought she caught sight of Linda's tail lights disappearing around the bend when they turned onto the main road. Funny, that she'd be out all day and come home so briefly. Maybe she opened her fridge to discover the milk was gone and headed back out. Or maybe that wasn't Linda's car. Maybe she needs new glasses.

It's nearly time for supper when they get back to the house, locking the door behind them.

"Pizza?" Ryan says with a big smile. He would eat pizza every night if he could.

"Let's see what we have in the fridge…." She pulls out several packages and puts them on the counter. "Pizza, it is." Before she starts cooking, she pours a glass of wine and takes a few long sips.

She doesn't hear Daniel pull into the driveway, so she is startled by the knocking on the front door. Hoover doesn't even lift his head, spent from his beach walk, proving himself to be a part-time watchdog at best.

"Why is the door locked?" When she yanks the door open, Daniel is trying to fish his keys back out of his pocket, juggling drawings and his briefcase.

"Sorry. I'll explain later." Going back to the kitchen, she tucks her wineglass out of sight.

"Explain what?" He's trying to find a piece of floor to rest the drawings, free of boot slush and the small stream created by Hoover's massive drink.

"The door. I'll explain the door."

"Okay," he says, the corners of his mouth turning up, deciding on whether to make a joke of it.

"You're home early. It's still light outside. Congratulations."

He responds by stretching his arms above his head, speaking through a yawn. "This morning I decided I was going to come home in the daylight, see my boy before he's ready for bed." He steals a slice of pepperoni from the cutting board.

"Daaaaddddy!" Ryan has left his imaginary world at the sound of his father's voice. He holds a mangled cardboard box in one hand, decorated with streaks of crayon.

"Hi, bud. What do you have there?"

"Moon lander."

"Very cool. Did you just make it?"

Emily goes still, listening. If he's had help from the imaginary friend, that might settle it.

"Mm hmm. It can suck up candy on the moon."

"Candy? Wow. What did you do today?"

"I got a lollipop."

"Lucky you." Daniel is looking at her to elaborate.

"Ryan, tell Dad what happened when I was in the shower. You were watching TV and…."

"Rocket Man came in and gave me a red lollipop." He grins.

"While Mummy was in the shower?" Daniel looks at her.

"Tell him what he said to you." Maybe it will be a different version this time.

"His hair was like this." He puts his fingers on top of his head to demonstrate. "Um, he said, you like candy and he likes rockets too then he went away."

"And you said he knew your name."

"Mm hmm."

"Who was it?" Daniel asks, turning to Emily.

"I have no idea."

"How did he get in?"

"The door."

"It wasn't locked?" Daniel's voice rises in pitch.

"Apparently not."

"Did you call the police?"

"I thought about it, but here"—she gestures at their son, who has pulled open the drawer of Tupperware and started to search for rocket accessories—"is my only witness. I'm not entirely sure how...real it was."

"You should have called me."

"But maybe I left the door unlatched when I let the dog in. Maybe that was it."

"You mean the door was open while you were in the shower?"

"It was...ajar when I came out to check."

"Sh...oot, Emily."

"Don't look at me like that."

"I didn't say anything." He turns away. "What about Hoover? He didn't bark?"

"He was as you see him now. Has he greeted you in the last few minutes?" The dog's head hangs at an impossible angle from his bed, one ear covering his eyes.

"No."

"In his defense, he just got home from a walk with us. Oh, can you get Ryan some dry pants? He's wet from the knee down."

He hesitates, his eyes on the front door. "Sure," he says slowly. "Ryan, come on, let's go up to your room."

Ryan stands up with several trophies from the drawer and skips off. Daniel pauses, looking thoughtful. "We didn't change the locks when we moved in?"

"No. But Linda's the only one with a key."

"We don't know that. All those realtors. It's only the two doors. I'll call around, okay?"

"It's expensive."

"It's worth it."

⟞

Linda stays the night in the city. Tom's apartment is comfortable enough, considering the inhabitants. The fridge has a few items in it, enough for a quick breakfast in the morning.

She spends the first hour cleaning the washroom even though it's two hours past her usual bedtime. It's a good way to clear the mind and avoid chain smoking on the balcony. It's something that she can visually improve in a short amount of time and that brings some measure of satisfaction, scrubbing at the gaps between the tiles.

Her cleaning supplies are just where she left them on her last visit. Tom had watched her come in his door with the little plastic bin containing her chosen chemicals and sponges.

"You know me, I can't help it. Last time I was here I could see mould developing in your bathtub grout. You guys are tidy but you're not doing the deep cleaning."

She marched straight down the hall and nearly collided with Brad, emerging from the room of discussion.

"Morning, Mum. You might want to wait to go in there."

Brad started to call her this once he realized she'd be dropping in on them regularly, usually carrying pre-made meals for their freezer. She didn't object. In a different marriage, she would have had more than one child.

And so, she hadn't cleaned it on that visit but left her supplies in their cupboard. In the meantime, the mould had grown from a gentle pink to a dark line extending along the back wall. She does not understand how people can call themselves clean after bathing in this environment. But she's seen far worse in her days.

She had her own little business and a few employees while Tom was in school. Top Deck Cleaners, with her own business cards and an ad in the Yellow Pages. The hours were flexible and the wealthier residents in their oceanfront properties tipped well. She employed students in the summers to help with the houses that were only open in the warmer months. It did fairly well, the little business. She sold it the year before Martin died. They talked of becoming snowbirds, wintering in a place where they never had to shovel snow. Looking back, she should have known that they couldn't have done such a thing. Tom needed her.

Tom will be in for observation for seventy-two hours. By the time she left, his symptoms were fading, his gaze was clearing, and she could see the exhaustion taking hold instead.

"I'll be back first thing. I'll bring your tea."

She couldn't tell if he heard her. The nurse gave her a sad smile as she passed the station.

She showers and puts the same clothes back on. It would be a good idea to keep a simple change of underthings in her car, but she hasn't done it.

She counts back; it's been about nine years. Things have improved. The relapses are farther between, and he has been living somewhat independently for four years now. As much as she curses Brad, he has taken on more with his roommate than most guys his age. Tom's doctor had hinted that living at home wasn't allowing him to grow. It's better for him to be less isolated, be able to walk places within the city and hold down a part-time job.

She makes Tom's bed and climbs under the sheets. Lying on her back, she can watch the lights from cars move across the ceiling through the thin curtains. She wanted to be open about it in the early years. It was Martin who felt differently, insisted that it was better to be private about it. That was how he liked to put it.

"It's our business. Why should the neighbours know?"

But they did know. How could they have missed the change in him? He was a chatty child, offering to help out with mowing lawns and shovelling snow before the paranoia set in. People would have assumed something worse than the truth if she didn't tell them. So, she'd quietly done so and asked them not to mention it to Martin. They were good people, they probably stayed away to avoid lying to Martin.

It was the beginning of their isolation as a family. Fewer people came by the house and when they did, there was tension between father and son. Tom would refuse to take his meds, telling his father that he didn't need them if there was *nothing wrong with him.* He sensed his father's shame even if he never came out and said it. Martin drank more, staying out after work, while she kept the house very clean.

⌒

After the phone call with the library's HR person, Emily tries to work out how many weeks have passed since the interview. She had given up on the job and begun applying for positions waiting tables. Too much time has gone by for her to have been their first choice. She's holding the page of the calendar in her hand, thinking, when Daniel walks in.

"Hey, you look tired."

"So I've been told." He removes his shoes and heads for the fridge. "Any beer?"

"No beer. New locks though."

"Ah yes. Did he take Visa?" He continues to survey the inside of the fridge, not one to give up so easily.

"Yes, thank God."

"Where's Ryan?"

She gestures toward the living room where Ryan is slumped on the couch. "Don't worry, it's educational." She clears her throat. "So, I have some good news."

He straightens up and closes the fridge.

"I got the job at the library."

"No way. Congratulations."

"Yeah. They want me there Monday. I'm hoping your parents are back tomorrow." The job itself is easily slotted around Daniel's schedule but the training isn't, take it or leave it. "It will be a rush but… what?" She stops, reading his face.

"Mum called the office. They won't be back for two more weeks. I'll tell you about that later."

"Shit."

"What about *your* mother?"

"No way. I mean she might but…."

"Come on, it's for…how long?"

"The two of them here?" Meaning, her stepfather too. "And it's a favour we'd have to return. You know him."

Richard had warmed easily to Daniel. He'd turned on the charm for Dan's parents at the wedding and that had turned Daniel right off. She remembered watching her new husband's face tighten in response and feeling a profound sense of relief.

"Okay. Who else?" says Daniel.

"Maybe Linda."

"Hm. What about that babysitter from before?"

"The one who cancelled on me?"

"Right."

"Or"—and she grins—"you could work from home?"

He doesn't answer. She enjoys the idea of him attempting to talk on the phone while his son hangs from his leg declaring his imminent need for a bowel movement. Even the TV can only hold his attention for half an hour, at best. Then Daniel would have a taste of what it is to live with distraction.

He leaves her standing there thinking and returns a moment later with a mop. He sops up the puddle around the dog's bowl.

"I thought you said you asked your mother to stop calling you at the office."

"I did." He shrugs.

"So, what is it?"

Maggie could just as easily call here, talk to Emily, maybe get a chance to listen to her grandson babble on the phone for a few minutes.

"That they're staying on in BC for a bit, to look at real estate."

"Seriously?"

They stare at one another, no need to say anything. Daniel was baffled by his parents' lukewarm reaction to their announcement that they were moving home to Nova Scotia. His father had encouraged them not to buy a house but to rent for a year instead.

"How long have they been planning this?"

"No idea."

"Have they listed their place?"

"I doubt it. They've been in that house for—it's got to be forty years."

"They're probably just tempted by the weather. They don't know anyone out there."

"Dave and Celia and their other grandchild?"

"I mean, besides them, all their friends are here. And us."

"I know, I know." He shakes his head and goes to put the mop away.

"And here I was thinking Ryan would be spending all this time with his grandparents."

"Me too." Daniel comes back and leans a shoulder against the wall. "Anyway, they're probably just looking. Have you thought any more about calling the police?"

"About yesterday?" She glances into the living room at Ryan. "We talked about this. There was no crime, nothing taken, what would I even tell them?" All questions she'd asked herself while holding the phone in her hand before hanging up again.

"Still."

"Oh wait. You told her?"

"I regretted it the minute it was out of my mouth."

"Why did you...." They'd agreed, hadn't they?

"I think I just wanted to bring her down, she was sounding giddy about moving. It was stupid."

Emily doesn't answer, just lets his words hang there.

⌒

It's late in the day when they discharge Tom. The only thing they need to do is stop by the apartment for some of his clothes.

Bradley is there when they get in, the TV on and an empty plate beside him on the couch. He switches channels when he hears her voice behind Tom. She catches a glimpse of skin on the screen and makes a point of looking down at her purse when he turns to greet her.

"Hi, Mum." Brad has begun to say this with an English accent for reasons he doesn't explain.

Tom nods and makes his way to his bedroom to get his things.

"He's okay. Pretty flat right now. He's going stay with me for a week."

"You called work?"

"Yes, I called them right away. The manager was a little short with me."

"Yeah? Must be the new guy, Tom mentioned him. You don't think they'll lay him off, do you?"

She shrugs, tired of worrying. It's a job stocking shelves. There are plenty of grocery stores in the city with similar work, but this one was more understanding, until now, about his unique situation.

"I'm really sorry I didn't call before I left. Work gave me no notice on this trip and he seemed fine."

Linda gives his shoulder a little punch. "It's all right."

She would've seen it coming, knowing Tom's speech and mannerisms better than her own. But a distracted roommate could easily have missed it.

"They, ah, they want me to travel more now. My boss said they're tightening things up. Doing more with less. They let some of the staff go, so I have to take over another region until they've worked out another arrangement."

"I'm sorry."

"Yeah. The thing is, I'll probably be away for part of the week every week for the next little bit." He's looking at the door of Tom's room. "I don't want to move out or anything, but it kind of puts a dent in things around here."

"I don't have anyone else right now. Even having you around part of the week so he can work, that helps. You think this will be temporary?"

"I don't know."

"Okay. Well, let's assume that it is for now. Just keep me posted and I'll fill in the gaps."

They sit in the living room with the news silently playing, an apologetic anchor consults papers on a desk; car crashes, war, and hospital beds flash onscreen. Linda finally gets up and goes in search of Tom, knocking on his door lightly.

"Just about ready?"

No response. She cracks the door. He sits on the bed holding a small bag.

"Sorry?" He looks up as if waking from a dream.

"You ready?"

"Yeah, I just was trying to remember. There's another thing I wanted."

"Sketch pad?" Tom often finds art to be a good way to cope.

"Maybe."

Linda goes to his shelves and runs her fingers along the spines of the books. "Here." She pulls out the spiral-bound pad of thick paper.

This one is nearly half full. One day she'll frame some of his work, if he'll let her. Some of it deals with his inner world, the hallucinations and distorted portraits of people in his life, but others are quite serene, landscapes and abstracts.

It's dark by the time they get home. They pile out of the car and bring their empty brown bag from the drive-thru into the house for disposal. Bert is on the doorstep, tail coiled tightly around him.

Tom gets in the door and stands looking at the closet jammed with coats.

"You should put some of these away."

She's wedging her jacket in amongst the others, scanning for a spare hanger for Tom.

"I know. I was thinking that the other day."

He leaves his coat on and heads upstairs. "I'm going to take a shower."

"Okay." She goes to the thermostat to turn up the heat. When it's just her she keeps it low, but Tom tends to like it a little warmer. She feels a gentle bump against her calf.

"Silly cat."

Leaning down, she strokes his back. Bert usually sleeps at the foot of Tom's bed when he's home, spending less time outside. Maybe he should get a cat at the apartment. It's supposed to be helpful. But then she'd have another creature to worry about.

She hears the water start running upstairs so she slips on her smoking jacket and steps outside. She doesn't bother with the outside light, it allows her to look at the sky. Orion's Belt is the first thing she can pick out. Martin was a great one for pointing out the constellations. It took her a few years to realize that he was making them up. One night they were out walking, still early in their marriage, when he traced the line of one above her head.

"That one, right there."

"Really?"

"Mm hm. Striking resemblance, don't you think?"

"You're telling me that someone named a constellation Rectum."

"Yup. Rectum. Damn near killed him."

He couldn't hold his laughter in, a more frequent sound then. Afterwards, he said the real name of the constellation was Reticulum, but he'd lost credibility. If only Tom had known that version of his father, but he only shakes his head when she tells these stories, as if she's telling a tall tale.

The nicotine settles her mind. It makes no sense, she thinks, addiction to things that will kill us. Every time she is frustrated with Tom's mind working against him she thinks of the lure to the cigarette for her. But hasn't she passed a point in life where it's useful to quit? Isn't the damage done? And yet she assures everyone, including herself, that she'll give it up. But there's no substitute for the break it provides, just stepping out onto the porch for a few minutes. At a party, you could find your tribe outside, gazing off past the trail of smoke, alone together with their own thoughts. Tom suggested whittling.

"Whittling?"

"Yes, just take a little piece of wood and carve it. Sit on the porch. Whittle. If that's what you need is a reason to be out there. Or knit."

"Knitting was a disaster when I last tried it, and it's bad enough having to use a sharp knife for cooking."

He was teasing her, of course, but no one wanted her to quit more than him. It was hard for him to be around it. In the hospital, he's surrounded by smokers.

She stubs out the cigarette and sits a moment longer before going back in. Maybe Doris has it right about selling the house, maybe the key to quitting—for Linda anyway—is to not have a porch.

LUCKILY, SHE HAPPENS to glance out the window and see Emily coming up the walk with Ryan before they can ring the doorbell. Despite the time of day Tom is upstairs, still sleeping. Linda opens the door, startling them.

"Good evening. And to what do I owe this visit?"

Ryan stands in front of his mother, but he's suddenly shy. She's used to this.

"Gimme five."

Slowly a purple mitten rises up and slaps Linda's hand. She is rewarded with a small smile.

"Oh. Bert!" Emily makes a swipe for the cat but he slips through her hands and disappears around the side of the house.

"Don't worry about it. Can't help those who won't help themselves."

"I haven't seen you around for a few days," says Emily.

"No, I was in the city. Here, come on in. Is it okay if I put the TV on for Ryan?"

They settle themselves into the living room and Linda busies herself finding the kids' channel. Emily sits down but fidgets with her hands, finally coming out and asking if Linda will babysit. "I really hate to ask. I tried the sitter from before, but she hasn't returned my call and it's tomorrow morning...."

She doesn't need to check her schedule. It's been cleared for Tom.

"He's so comfortable with you, Linda, it might not even be a full day...."

She'll say yes, she'll ease Emily into the idea of Tom. She doesn't need to hear the whole story yet.

"I'd love to."

"Oh God. Thank you, Linda."

"But there's something I should tell you. My son. He's the reason I was in the city over the past few days."

"I hope he's okay."

"Oh yes, he gets ill sometimes." She can't bring herself to say it. Martin may as well be sitting in the room, a finger to his lips, *shhh.* "Anyway, he's staying with me for a bit, just resting up."

"He's here? I'm sorry, I hope we didn't wake him."

"No, love. Don't worry about that."

Emily looks like she wants to ask more, but Ryan pipes up.

"Mummy, I need to go potty."

"Oops, can we use your bathroom?"

"Go ahead, you know where it is."

Linda listens to their muffled chatter and wonders if she should just leave the story at that. She can go over to their house to mind Ryan. Tom sleeps most of the morning right now, so he might not even be around.

"Sorry, Linda, he was a bit late telling me. We have to get some new pants and then we'd better head into town. We have the dentist in an hour."

"It's fine. I'll look forward to spending time with you tomorrow, Ryan. Maybe you can help me bake some cookies."

"Oh." Emily turns back. "I was going to ask you...." She glances at Ryan and seems to consider something. "Were there ever any... break-ins at our place?"

"No. I mean, I don't think so."

Emily blinks at her, biting her lip.

"Mummy, my bum's cold."

"Never mind. I'll talk to you tomorrow. It can wait."

LINDA DECIDES IT'S best to do the cookies at her house. First off, she couldn't find Emily's baking powder and then it was the oven. Surely it is simple enough, it's just that she's used to turning a knob, not all these buttons. The display flashed 375 degrees, then made a series of alarming beeps before going blank again. The house would probably be on fire by the time Emily got home. So, the production was moved down the hill, and the dog decided he'd come along too.

It's hard to remember how old Tom was when she first attempted this kind of activity with him, but after five minutes with Ryan she's certain he was older than three. In the end, Ryan stays in the kitchen with her while she finishes the dough. He's assigned the task of washing the dishes. Glancing at his progress, she decides she can just wash them again once he's done. It looks as if the counter and floor will be clean though.

"You can turn off the water, sweetie." Linda points at the faucet with her spatula and Ryan turns it on full blast before working out that it's the other direction. But there's still a hissing sound. She stares at the water for a moment then realizes it's coming from upstairs. It's followed by a deeper groan, both mournful and threatening.

"Shoot. Hoover? Hoover."

Linda stomps upstairs—spatula still in hand—and finds Tom's door open. The cat is at the foot of the bed, his tail fat, eyes angry pools of black. Beneath him, Hoover is sniffing, close enough to get his nose bloodied.

The room is dim, Tom just starting to stir from sleep.

"What the?"

"It's Hoover, the neighbour's dog."

He sits up and the movement spooks Bert into leaping from the bed. The dog follows in clumsy pursuit.

"Blasted cat. Can you get him outside? I've got to keep an eye on Ryan…."

The house fills with noise, Ryan giggling and dripping sudsy water across the living room carpet. Tom overtakes Linda on the stairs. He plucks the cat from the top of the television and wrestles him to the front door. There's a scuffle as Tom attempts to lower Bert to the ground outside the door—the cat clearly wants to stay in higher places—and he tries to climb his shirt. Tom wins the battle and closes the door before the dog can wedge his way out too. When he turns around, Linda can see twin red marks down his neck.

"Looks like he got you."

He bends to touch the dog. "What's his name?"

"Hoover. And right here"—she taps Ryan's head—"this is Ryan."

"Hey, buddy." Tom only glances at Ryan. He's picking up the dog's ears, admiring the length and weight of them. "Quite a burden, these. Can he fly?" He directs the question at Ryan. "Can your dog fly?"

"No. He's a *basket* hound, he just poops a lot."

It's hard to know if it's what he says or the gravity with which the words are delivered that strikes Tom as hilarious, but his face folds up and he starts to laugh in a way Linda has not witnessed in years.

CHAPTER 6

By early afternoon, the orientation is complete and the trainees are sent home. Emily drops crumbs from her sandwich on her lap as she drives. She's tempted to spend an hour at a mall; she could browse or get her hair cut but either one means spending money, and what's the point of shopping without buying? Better to get home, tackle the laundry. Linda didn't sign up for babysitting while Emily pampered herself. How would it look—coming through the door with a new do, a cluster of those fancy paper bags they give you at clothing stores? Don't look a gift horse in the mouth.

The house is empty when she gets in. Hoover isn't in his usual position. They must be over at Linda's. It's the first time she's ever been entirely alone in the house. She calls out for them and listens, just in case. Maybe it's hide-and-seek? She's answered with giggle-free silence and then, just as she turns toward the front door, there's a thud.

She turns, suppressing a scream, but only catches the movement of a small feather clinging to the window. The bird is on the ground, wings outstretched, panting. She watches it, willing it to get up. It flutters onto its side and continues to lie there, its breaths slowing. She presses her forehead to the glass.

"Come on."

Holding her breath, she keeps her eyes trained on the tiny chest for movement, but she can tell that it's gone. It must have been flying full out, believing it was heading for wide open sky and not a wall of glass. She should go and pick it up before Ryan finds it, or Hoover.

"Damn windows."

She slips on boots and pushes the door open before she stops to think of how she'll pick it up. Back inside, she finds a small plastic bag. Then she steps outside and scans the ground. But it's gone. Her relief doesn't last long. Bert sits near his favoured spot at the cliff. The bird is between his paws; he narrows his eyes at her, ready to defend his catch. She can't tell if it's just the wind moving its wings.

"Fuck!" she shouts at the cat.

LINDA'S HOUSE SMELLS like cinnamon and hound when she lets herself in.

"Hello?" The sound of the TV comes from the living room.

Hoover woofs and rushes her ankles. He's made himself at home; lines of drool on the carpet lead from a larger puddle next to a bowl. Ryan is right behind him, his cheeks decorated with crumbs and he's followed by a floury Linda.

"Sheesh. You must be a quick study. It's not even two o'clock."

"They had a group of school kids arrive this afternoon, so she told us to head out early. Did you save Mummy a cookie?"

Ryan nods and skips off to the kitchen. A door closes upstairs and Emily turns to Linda.

"Oh, it's my son. I'll introduce you. He and Ryan were playing this morning—"

"Here, Mummy." He holds out a nibbled cookie.

Emily glances toward the stairs. "How's he doing?"

"Much better."

"I'm sorry, I forgot he'd be here."

"No, love." She reaches down and strokes Ryan's hair. "It's no bother. Really. We were over at your house most of the time, anyway. It's good for him, he likes kids, and he's been rolling around on the floor with Hoover."

"That's great. But I still owe you."

"Don't think anything of it."

Ryan disappears just when she's about to tug him out the door. So she picks up Hoover's bowl and heads to the kitchen sink to wash it out. From behind her, she hears Linda.

"Emily's here, I want to introduce you."

She turns, curious to see him. He's younger than she thought, healthier too. Didn't she say he was ill? He steps close and takes her damp hand, though she hadn't offered it.

"Tom," he says, searching her face. "You have a charming son."

His hair is wet from the shower; she can smell his shampoo, peaches.

"Oh, thanks. Sorry." She glances at her hand in his. "I was just rinsing out the bowl."

He has Linda's grey eyes. She pulls her hand back but he doesn't take the hint, she can feel the blood rush to her face.

"You remind me of someone," he says. "Is your hair permed?"

Christ, when was the last time Daniel made any kind of comment about her hair, beyond complaining about it being stuck to things?

"Unfortunately, no." Emily laughs. There's a slight smile on his face. "Um," she continues, "au naturel, or as I call it *ugh naturel*." He laughs and she manages to remove her hand from his.

"Tom surfs," Linda says. "Emily takes Ryan to watch them sometimes."

"Are you one of those guys out there in the winter?"

"No. Late spring, maybe. I don't have the gear for the winter."

"Looks like fun."

"The surf shop gives lessons...."

"Right. One day. Me and your mum. Hey, Linda?"

Hoover lets out a bark at the front door that startles them all into laughter.

"He probably needs to go out," says Emily. "We should be going. Nice to meet you. And Linda, thanks again."

Ryan doesn't have a coat. He and Linda must have skipped between the houses while the sun was strong at midday. Ryan hops the whole way, with an excess of fuel in the system.

"Did you have fun?" she says, pushing open the front door.

"Yup. Cookies."

"Did you like Tom?" She's lining up their shoes and Ryan is draped over her back hugging her. Kids love it when adults get down to their level.

"Rocket Man."

She goes still.

"Rocket Man?"

"Yup. Three, one, two."

She straightens and turns to him. "Is *Tom* Rocket Man?"

"Yup."

"*He* came here and gave you the candy?"

"Lollipop." He smiles, unaware of the electricity coming from her.

"Okay. Okay."

"Read me a book?"

She stares past him. The cat is just outside the living room window, a flurry of downy feathers surrounding him like a halo.

⁓

Tom sits across from her as she tries to stifle a cough. She probably inhaled too much flour today.

"Sounds worse."

"Don't worry," she croaks.

At least when you live alone, you don't have to talk to people when you can't breathe. She needs him out of the house so he can stop looking at her like that. It's plain to see he's about to start up. If only it was garbage day or they had some snow to be shovelled.

"Find Bert?"

"Huh?" He makes her work for it.

"Outside." She points toward the front door. "The cat."

He lets out a long breath. It doesn't seem like he'll budge, but he finally stands up, plunking a box of tissues next to her before leaving the room.

Did it go well? Emily had looked startled at first, but then she seemed to relax. Not that it should make a difference. It's just that it would be easier, and easier is underrated.

It's true, that expression about the cat who swallowed the canary. Bert is smug. She fixes on that, instead of murkier thoughts of Tom. It wouldn't be right to shriek curses at the cat in front of Ryan. So she turns her back on him.

Ryan returns to his neglected toys. Each one gets a countdown and a very wet-sounding *blast-off*, over and over. Each launch is louder than the one before.

It feels like something is lodged in her throat.

The kitchen sink is piled with dishes. She has to remove them all to get at the plug. This morning's porridge has cemented to the pot. With a dirty knife, she scrapes and chips at it. *I'll wait and talk to her after Dan gets home.*

The running water muffles Ryan's voice. She stares at her fingers in a cloud of bubbles, thinking of Tom's grip on her wet hand.

Something makes her look up. It's him, jacket gaping, hair still wet. He walks up her front path then veers across the front lawn. He pauses at the side of the house. She watches his mouth make the shape of the cat's name.

He doesn't seem to be aware she is watching. He smiles and bends at the waist. Bert appears at his feet and rubs his leg in that way people think of as affection. Ownership is what it is. They leave their scent on you; their subtle stink. He stoops and picks him up, plucking a feather from his fur and holding it up for the wind to carry away. That's when he notices her and waves. Her hands stay put in the sink but she dips her head in acknowledgement and pulls her mouth into a brief smile.

It's late and Linda is lost in thought, snugged deep into her smoking jacket on the porch. She doesn't see Emily approaching, so the voice in the dark startles her.

"Lord have mercy. What are you doing up?"

"Sorry. Thought I'd catch you on your own. Where's Tom?"

"Inside. What's up?" She stands and waves for Emily to follow her inside.

"If you don't mind, can we stay out here?" Emily's tone is wrong, business-friendly.

"Take a seat."

"Thank you so much for babysitting...."

"Never mind that." Nothing worse than delaying it.

"Okay. Um. I didn't get a chance to tell you about this. I thought maybe someone broke in. But, I think that Tom came into our house the other day. I was in the shower. Someone gave Ryan a lollipop—"

"You were in the shower?" She remembers Tom pacing the living room.

"He was gone before I got out...."

"When, exactly?"

"Um. Thursday."

The curtains were closed.

"Linda. Would he do that?"

Emily twists in her seat, staring, but Linda can't seem to pull her gaze away from her own knees. This is not the way she wanted this to happen. She'd hoped they'd get to know him a little first and see him as a person—a kind and funny and creative human being—before the label was slapped on. She hears herself tell the story of his diagnosis. Her voice sounds weak.

"Tom sometimes carries candy," she finishes. "Other patients smoke, he has a sucker."

They sit listening to the distant thrum of the ocean.

"Why didn't he at least say something?"

"He doesn't always recall afterwards." Would it have helped if he'd told her?

She offers reassurances. Says he's harmless, that he loves kids and animals. Not that it made a difference with the others. It wears her out. Emily leaves, apologizing...for something.

⁓

"It was him?" Daniel shakes his head at her as if he hopes she's joking. "Why are you so calm about this?"

Not calm, numb. He'd been on his way upstairs, heading for bed, when she came in from Linda's. She debated telling him at all, but he'd read her face.

"You need to meet him, Daniel."

"Fuck." He runs his hand through his hair. "You remember that story—we watched it on the news. That guy who was found *not criminally responsible* for stabbing his mother to death."

It takes her breath away. She had put that one out of her mind. They stare at each other.

"She says he's never been violent…."

"But you just can't know." He must realize his voice is too loud. He glances towards Ryan's room. "I'm sorry." He pulls her into a hug. "I want to go over there and talk to them."

She pulls away, frowning. "I don't think you should."

"Why not?"

"It's late for one thing. Let's just leave it—for now."

He drops his arms to his sides. She can see his mind racing; his eyes won't stay still. He raises a finger and points upwards.

"It's him you need to worry about."

"You think I don't know that?"

"I get it. Your own history and…but you're a mother."

He grew up in a family where things went as planned. Nobody close to him has died yet. He has an unshakeable sense of right and wrong. It's one of the things that first drew her to him, his certainty.

"Maybe…you should keep a distance."

Something tells her he was planning to say something else.

"I don't know if I can do that."

"What else has she held back?"

"Think about it, if it was Ryan. Would it be the first thing you'd tell your neighbours?"

He stares past her.

"Yes, I think it would."

EMILY WAKES TO crying. The heaviness of her body, as she swings her feet to the floor, tells her she's only just fallen asleep. Daniel groans from his side of the bed while she feels her way to Ryan's room, minus her glasses.

"Mummy." His cheeks are wet and his skin is hot.

She wipes away the tears with her hands and climbs in beside him to stroke his hair. A bad dream or the first sign of illness? He reaches his hand into her hair and winds a curl around his fingers. He did this as a baby when he was feeding, his eyes wide and searching. They gaze at each other. Emily hums "Row, Row, Row Your Boat." Each blink gets heavier until his fingers fall from her hair. She lies there watching his face. At these moments, the love for him spreads through her like a heat, blotting out the tantrums, the screams, the *I-do-its* of the waking hours.

It's hard to imagine him independent; driving a car, getting a job and a mortgage. What must it be like for Linda, facing a lifetime of caring for her son, not knowing if he is safe from his own mind?

It was her mother who found her. Emily had pulled every bottle of pills from the bathroom cabinet and swallowed them. It would not have killed her, the doctor said, but left her damaged. He didn't say how, only that she was lucky. *Lucky.* It rang in her head afterwards. They'd pumped the pills out of her and kept her in the hospital. She slept and slept, dreading the waking world.

Her doctor encouraged her to write it down. It would help her sort things out. She had a journal with a lock on it that she tucked under her mattress. It was hard to close, the pages got fatter with ink and tears. She scribbled in it every day for months, a groove worn into her finger from the pen. Then she came home one day to find it splayed on the kitchen counter. No one else was home. The open page contained one angry scrawl that tore through the paper in spots: *Why wasn't it mum who died?*

Her mother had arrived home a little while later. She came and sat at the end of the bed, fiddling with the folds of the blankets before returning the diary to Emily's bedside table. The lock was no longer usable.

"He said he found it when he was looking for a dictionary in here. He just wanted to make sure you weren't getting into any kind of trouble."

Emily had stared straight ahead, refusing to look at her face, but she caught a glimpse of the puffiness around her mother's eyes when she left the room. The diary stayed there for a week before she stuffed it into her backpack. She went to the harbour and threw it in, where it floated for several minutes. A hopeful gull landed nearby and pecked at it until it sank.

Ryan's breathing is louder than usual. He must be getting a cold. She pulls herself from his side and tiptoes from the room. Too awake to go back to bed, she heads downstairs to add a log to the fire. Hoover's tail thumps the floor even when the rest of his body appears to be in a dead sleep. She puts a hand on his chest and feels the slow *thrump thrump* of his heart.

She never apologized to her mother. Why should she? They were her private thoughts. Richard's house became a fortress with the medication, matches, and alcohol locked away. Trust was gone, on both sides.

The waking world was empty. In dreams, she could visit Da. She'd be in his study, watching him at his typewriter or down at the dock, oiling the wood in the cockpit. One night she woke to the pressure of him sitting on the bed, the way he did when she was small and he'd tell her stories. Before her eyes opened, she saw him, that way he used to look at her. No one else looked at her that way. His face was losing solidity, his features smearing at the edges as he reached out for her hand. Was it real, that touch on her wrist?

She closes the stove's door and watches the flames engulf the wood through the small window. Outside, a crescent moon is a smudge in the sky. The backyard is still against the movement of the water below. A cloud moves in and dulls the moonlight. She narrows her eyes at the horizon. It could be a sailboat. It's too far away. Still, she whispers, "Night, Da." The cloud drifts off and the boat's mast winks as it moves into the horizon, that subtle line beyond where the eye can see.

⌐

Linda's face turns up to the moon but she sees Tom, riding on Martin's shoulders. On the cushion beside her is the snapshot, taken by a stranger showing off his instant camera. The three of them are smiling, Tom ducks his head to place his cheek next to his father's. You can see their resemblance, the cheekbones and the sharp line of the jaw. It's fading into yellow tones now. One day it will probably disappear completely, but in her mind the image plays forward. Without the photo, the day might not have stuck in her mind like this.

Tom laughed, still perched on Martin's shoulders, he waved the little flag at the clowns tossing candy to the parade crowd. She stood back from them, the Polaroid held between her finger and thumb. The image was just materializing. Tom's head turned to the right as he watched the Shriners in their child-sized cars. Martin focused on something to the left. She might not have noticed except for his stillness. The smile dropped from his face and he seemed to shudder. He muttered a few words to Tom and placed him on the ground. At first Linda was too busy calming her son to notice as Martin slipped through the crowd. She straightened and located him, leaning on a wall. His face was ashen. Her only thought was to get to him and find out if he was sick. He fumbled for the cigarettes in his shirt pocket. She took Tom's hand and tried to follow. But Martin caught her eye. Just a subtle shake of his head, *stay away.*

Back in the car, she asked him about it but he said it was nothing, he thought he'd seen someone.

"Who?"

"Someone from a long time ago." And then, with his face turned away, he muttered, "Dad." He wouldn't look at her. Was he embarrassed, seeing ghosts in broad daylight?

A sharp pain brings her back to the present. The cigarette in her hand has singed the skin. She butts it out and lights another. It's worse when she can't sleep, as if her hands go about the business of lighting each one without her permission.

The Polaroid isn't the last one of them together as a family, but it is the last of the ones where Martin is holding his son. It sat on the mantle in a frame alongside their wedding photo and the ever-growing collection of Tom's class photos smiling in front of woodland fakery.

The following year Tom started school and Linda had her cleaning business. Martin withdrew bit by bit. He took jobs that had him travelling to work sites further away. He came home late, after they were in bed, and worked most weekends. When he was home he was in his chair, behind a newspaper, or in the basement with the television blaring the news. His hobby was collecting beer bottles, lining the basement room with them, after he emptied out the contents of course. A lot of men did that, Doris said. But this wasn't the same man she'd married.

People didn't talk about things like they do now. Just once, she suggested he bring it up to his doctor and he'd raised his eyebrows at her. It was before the business with Tom.

"You think I need a shrink?"

"I didn't say that."

"Then say what you mean."

"I did. I said you should talk to someone."

"Yeah, I know. A shrink. I'm not crazy, Linda. I'm fine."

He left the room. She should have tried again.

He only needed time. Maybe when Tom was grown up and out on his own, maybe in his retirement, when life stopped being so hectic: the things we tell ourselves to get through it all. Time, as it turned out, hadn't solved anything.

⌒

Normally, Emily would not have coffee late in the day, but it's her first shift this evening and she hasn't shaken the drowsiness from the previous nights. Three in the morning every time. Too late to take a sleeping pill, too early to get up. It's a sharp sound that wakes her, setting her heart off. No one else hears it. Last night she tried a glass of milk with a shot of Baileys.

"Hold onto my hand," she cautions Ryan as he jumps down from the car.

Inside, the lineup loops around the rope divider, snaking its way to the door. Taking up their spot at the end, she smiles at him. He gapes at a child in a nearby booth, slurping a drink with a small hill of whipped cream overflowing the sides.

"That," he says.

"I know."

Scanning the room, she sees her neighbour. Jim feeds his hot coffee into a cardboard sleeve. He's dressed for the early spring weather in heavy coveralls. *He must know about Tom.* He catches sight of them and waves. Smiling, she turns to the menu and makes a show of choosing what she'd like. But he comes over and pats the top of Ryan's head.

"How's Cap'n Ryan?"

"Mummy's getting me coffee!"

"Hot chocolate," she says. "You off to the boat?" There's a whiff of it coming from him. She'd know the smell anywhere.

"Just coming back. The wife's sending me out for groceries this afternoon. Saw Linda out with your young man last week."

"Yes, she babysat while I doing my training for the library."

"Oh, you're starting there, are ya? Good for you."

"Thanks. Yeah, Linda was very helpful."

It's not like she's been avoiding her, but the dog hasn't been for a walk in a week.

"I imagine she told you about it then. Linda?" Jim says. She nods and he pats her shoulder. "Sorry not to have brought it up. Seemed like a dark turn in conversation, especially around a little one. We were wondering how much those realtors pass on."

He turns his attention to the lid of his cup, trying to work the small tab open without spilling it.

"I'm sorry. The realtors?" Emily tilts her head. "Would they even know?"

"Oh, I think that when there has been a...." He stops himself, looking down at Ryan. "...when someone passes away on a property, they're supposed to disclose that. I suppose it's a tricky one since it was really the beach."

She's lost for words but starts to put it together.

"I was the one who found him, you know. Out walking my dog." He tries a sip of his drink and burns his lips.

"No, I didn't know. That must have been a shock," she offers, hoping he'll keep going.

"Yup. Thought maybe it was a drunk, until I got close." He brings his hand to the top of his head and grimaces. "I didn't even know him until they came and turned him over. Anyway, probably best not to talk about it here." Another glance downwards.

Emily decides there is no way around it.

"Um. I'm sorry, Jim. Are we talking about *Linda's* husband?"

His face falls.

"Oh, I'm sorry. Yes, Martin."

"You found Martin dead?" She doesn't edit her words. Ryan equates death with a battery that needs to be changed in a toy. Jim nods, the confusion clear on his face.

"I thought we were talking about...something else. Um. I did know that Martin died a few years ago, but she never told me how." She drops her voice to a whisper. "What happened?"

"Found him on the beach, he'd hit his head."

Another wave goes over her.

"You mean right behind our place?"

"Yes."

Her belly stirs like she's arced too high on a swing. A woman clears her throat behind them. The line has moved ahead. Emily steps aside, ushering Ryan over to a table with Jim following. She sinks into the plastic chair.

"I'm sorry. I thought she would have told you."

"She just said she was a widow." You don't ask people to tell you how it happened.

Ryan hangs from the back of her chair, making it swivel from one side to the other, oblivious to the air being sucked out of the coffee shop.

Jim sits opposite her, resting his elbows on the table.

"I feel like a right numbskull."

"I'm sure she was waiting for the right moment."

"True." He doesn't look convinced. "It's a striking house anyway. Great view and all that. Your husband sails you said, hey?"

She blinks hard at the shift. "Sure. We both do."

"Well, the whole lot of you are welcome to come out with me. And I could use a hand getting a few things done before May. You let him know. Nothing better than messing about in boats." He offers her a smile.

"Yes, thanks, Jim."

"Anyways, you come down to the house any time you need to talk, we'll put the kettle on."

"I'll do that. Thanks."

He stands to leave and she watches him walk past the window to his little truck. Ryan peers around her arm, his mouth wetting the sleeve of her coat.

"Coffee, Mummy?"

"Right. Let's get back in line."

She lets him take her hand and tug her sideways. Her mind seems to have shifted into a very low gear, assembling a puzzle without all the pieces.

CHAPTER 7

It takes so long for the door to open that Linda almost leaves. It could wait a little longer. Emily swings the door open, still in her bathrobe, but insists on inviting her in.

"There's still some coffee…."

The table is littered with crumbs and Emily has a kitchen cloth crumpled in her right hand. Linda heads into the living room and gets a hug from Ryan. Jam paints her sweater when she pulls away.

"Thanks for bringing it over." Emily puts the sugar bowl and a spoon out on the counter.

"It's probably just junk mail but I thought I'd let you figure that out for yourselves. How's the new job?"

"Good. I guess I haven't seen you since…." She's fidgety.

"You've been busy."

Emily tallies up her chores while she ferries dishes from the table to the kitchen sink.

After a slurp, Linda says, "I should've told you about Martin." Emily looks startled. "Jim was by with the dog yesterday. He felt bad he let it slip."

"Oh well. I can understand it would be hard to talk about...."

"I should have thought ahead to you hearing it from other people."

Hoover ploughs into Linda's shins in search of his greeting. She pats his head, distractedly.

"I guess I just assumed it was...natural causes."

"Yes," she says to Hoover's upturned face. "I prefer it that way, that assumption."

"Hang on, I'll set Ryan up with his crayons." She jogs up the stairs and reappears with a box marked *Crafts*. Ryan climbs onto a chair and dumps every crayon out on the table alongside the crumbs. Linda resists the urge to take charge of the kitchen cloth.

Emily settles onto a soft chair, tucking one leg beneath her.

"Don't feel like you have to tell me everything."

"I meant to thank you for being understanding about Tom. Not everybody would have let that slide." Jim's wife had called the police on him when she spotted him wandering through their yard, naked.

Emily nods and peers into her cup. "How is he?"

"Good. Back in his routine. For now."

"You must worry."

"It never stops, dear. You'll see."

"Martin dying must have been really hard on him."

"He handled it pretty well, considering.... It'll be three years this June." She stands and goes to the window with her coffee. "Before Tom was born, there was a little switchback, just there. He stopped climbing it years ago. But he'd still come up and watch the water. The police came to the door early in the morning. I remember thinking they had the wrong person, I figured he was still in bed. Sometimes he'd sleep in the spare room.... My knees went to jelly, like all my bones were gone. The officer had to catch me." She lets out a raspy laugh. "I just remembered that. I wonder how often that happens to them."

"Quite a bit, I imagine."

"Yeah. At first they wondered if he'd...meant to do it, but they had the experts in and...." She can't say it out loud for some reason. They'd said the fall wasn't enough to kill him. "His fingernails were dirty. So, they figured he'd climbed down."

"But it was an accident?"

"Right here, that's where it hit him." Linda shows her the spot on her own head. "They matched the rock with one from up top. It must have come loose just at that moment." It had her thinking about timing for months. She'd just sit there and think about that fraction of a second in which everything can change.

Emily lets out a long breath behind her. "I'm so sorry."

Turning from the window, Linda drains the last of her cup and goes back to sit down. "At least it was quick, I guess." They listen to Ryan singing to himself and then Linda continues. "About a year after, I was listening to the radio. They had a documentary about a girl whose mother went missing. They never found her. And I thought to myself how much harder that would be. Martin had over fifty years and he died painlessly, they think. I'm just grateful we could bury him."

It's not like she just sat still for that year though. That would have been a luxury. There was Tom to think about. And Doris kept yanking her out of the house, signing her up to help at the community centre or dragging her to card games. She did those things in a sort of automatic way. But her mind was caught in a loop—holding private conversations with Martin, dissecting that endless fall of the rock, until she found something for which to be grateful.

"You said something the other day. That Tom hears his voice?"

Linda shakes her head. "He didn't know how to talk to Tom when he was alive…."

Ryan appears at Emily's side. "Look, Mummy."

"Ah." She takes the piece of paper from him. "I like the colours. Is it water?"

"Mm hm. The sea."

"And here?"

"Sad man."

"Who is he?"

Ryan points out the window, his face serious.

"Out there, the sad man."

Linda can't help herself, she looks outside.

"That's his cat." He sounds proud of the orange smear.

"He has a cat?"

"Bert."

Linda puts her cup down on the coffee table with a clack.

"Ryan, were you listening to us?" Emily says gently.

He pulls his lips into his mouth and his eyebrows lower in concentration.

"Is this Tom?" asks Emily.

"No, Tom is the Rocket Man." He sounds exasperated.

"Oh. Good job, sweetie. Maybe you can go draw me a big sunshine, can you do that?"

He leaves her holding the paper and skips back to the table. Linda tries to suppress a cough.

"He still has quite a cast of imaginary friends, Linda. And Bert is here every day."

What was she thinking, talking about these things in front of him?

"I'm sorry." Linda stands and heads for the door.

Emily follows her. "I'll get you some water...."

"No, we'll talk later. Kids absorb these things." A rattle has started in her chest. She manages to croak out that she needs groceries and escapes through the front door.

EVERY SPRING IT'S hard to believe that winter is really over. Linda won't stow the shovel away until July. She's standing in her front yard enjoying the sight of tulips popping up from the soil when she hears the car. It's Bradley's blue Neon with Tom in the passenger's seat. He climbs out and goes to the rear of the car to pull out a duffle bag. Bradley rolls down his window.

"Sorry, Mum. I rushed him—told him he could have a ride if he left right away."

"Everything's okay?"

"Oh yeah. Says he wants to surf." Bradley makes it clear that he thinks surfing at this time of year is ill-advised.

Tom comes to stand beside her. "The news mentioned good conditions so I called Greg, he said to get out here."

Bradley winds up his window. "Sorry, gotta go." They wave him off.

Tom has had a haircut. She reaches up to his cheek. "You just shave?"

"Am I still bleeding?"

"Just a little spot." She points to her own chin.

"Should have left it. I need all the insulation I can get."

"Greg's picking you up?"

"Not until later. I said I'd call when I got here."

"How long has it been since you saw him?" They'd met at the play-ground when they were four.

"Three months? But we haven't surfed for years."

Greg's house was always packed with kids. Each of his four siblings dragged home friends after school. The first time Tom went there he reported back, wide-eyed, that one of the shelves in their fridge was "just milk." It was his second home for years, until the phone call came from Greg's mother. Tom scared the younger kids, talking to someone they couldn't see.

So Greg came by their house, when he could. It wasn't the same though. More and more, it was Tom climbing the hill home alone from the bus. Later there was Seth, but Martin put a stop to that, certain that Seth was trouble. Tom spent hours sketching in his room and less time in his wetsuit. At first, that part was a relief. She could never fully relax until she knew he was back on land.

"You ran it by Dr. Miller?"

"Yeah. I guess one of his kids is getting into it. It's not as dangerous as he thought, as long as I have a buddy."

"Greg has the checklist?"

"Doesn't need it, he's known me long enough." He puts his arm around her shoulders and gives her a light squeeze. "What about you? It feels like you haven't eaten a bite since I last saw you."

"Go on with you. I eat just fine."

"Well, come on. We better get in before a gust of wind comes along and blows you away."

⌣

Parking the car, Emily's happy to see the surfers out in the distance. Astride their boards, they're waiting for the next set of waves. The wind has a hint of warmth and she's hoping to spend the morning on the beach. Ryan runs ahead, wearing his backpack, arms held out from his sides.

"Fast airplane pffftttt…."

She follows with the dog leash in one hand. The bag over her shoulder contains a book and some snacks. Hoover vacuums things up at the side of the path—crab shells, old French fries, trash—the habit for which he was named. "Drop it," she mutters, tugging him along, wishing she'd left him home.

Anchoring a blanket with some stones, she sets up camp amongst the sand and the dried seaweed. She is trying to untangle the kite for Ryan when a surfer approaches.

"Emily?"

She puts her hand up to block the sun and make out the face. His hands are still dripping

"Hey. You're surfing?"

"Yeah. Well, you might call it that. I'm a little rusty." He turns and points to the water. "My buddy Greg, there he is, just getting up, he lent me the suit."

She's glad to have the task of working out the knots. It's hard to look right at him, her face might show everything.

"Hey, Hoov." Tom crouches down and lets the dog lick at the salty water on his hands.

Ryan taps on Tom's knee. "Look at my kite. It's an airplane."

"Yes, if I can ever get it untangled..." she says, yanking at a loop.

"May I?" Tom holds out his hands. "Good excuse to sit out this next set."

She watches the boarders behind him. One of them stands up briefly, then gets knocked sideways.

"It must be freezing."

Tom is in a full suit. Just his face is visible and his cheeks look raw. He pauses and glances at the water.

"The first wave is intense. It flows right through the suit and chills you to the bone. You have to get comfortable with it before you can start." He has almost got the main knot out. Ryan fingers the edge of the fabric, impatient to get it in the air. "But we have one secret weapon." He looks up. "If you, ah, urinate in the suit, it warms you up."

"No!" She laughs, thankful he didn't clue Ryan in, who has only just mastered the potty.

"You get so cold you don't care."

He hands the kite to Ryan.

"Can you say thanks?"

"Thanks." He leaps up, holding the kite above his head.

"In that case, do you want some tea?" She reaches for the Thermos.

"Maybe just a sip."

She pours it into the lid and he takes it, nodding his thanks, briefly meeting her eyes.

"Ryan, don't go too far! Oh, I should help him."

They watch him turn and run back, tripping over stones as he comes.

"I doubt he cares about really flying it," Tom says.

"True, he's totally wrapped up in his imagination. Doesn't know what's real half the time…." Christ almighty, she goes quiet.

"It's okay. It's easier when people just acknowledge it." He tips up the mug, draining it. "Actually, I came over here to say sorry. Mum told me that I was up at your place."

"You don't remember?"

"You ever have a dream that you've had a conversation with someone or you were sure you did something?"

"Mm hm."

"It's kind of like that. But for me, it's the flip side of it. There might be bits of it that come back, but they don't fit. I mean, Ryan looked familiar when I saw him over at our house, but I figured maybe I'd seen him out playing or something…." He squints at her. "Anyway, I'm sorry. It's not like I'd do that when I'm…*normal*." He enunciates the word.

"It's okay." Even though he's opened the door, she's not sure if she should walk through it. "Is it always like that?"

"No, sometimes I remember everything. Hard to know which one's worse."

Ryan abandons his kite near the water's edge, distracted by the sight of a partially built sandcastle. Emily heads over and retrieves it before the wind can carry it off, leaving him to demolish the castle with his hands.

"Not even five minutes. I don't know why I bother with toys." She gives a small laugh and settles down on a clean patch of blanket behind Hoover. Someone shouts Tom's name. "That your friend?"

He stands and raises a hand. "Gotta get back." He waves at Ryan. "Thanks for the tea."

"Nice talking to you."

He turns, picks up his board, and wades back out towards the knot of surfers in the distance.

Ryan ceases his running and comes to stand next to Emily, watching Tom get swallowed up in the waves.

SHE'S BRUSHING HER teeth when Daniel appears behind her.

"Hey," she mumbles around the brush. "Thought you were asleep."

"Just dozing. I went in the spare room in case you came in late."

"Ryan good?"

They have a lot of conversations this way, toothpaste escaping down their chins. Emily has often wondered if this is what kills the sex life in couples, sharing a bathroom.

"Yeah, he was good. My parents are back tomorrow. They invited us over for Saturday. Some of their friends will be there too. Lobster chowder. I know Ryan would love to see them. I told them you were probably working."

Turning off her toothbrush, she speaks to his reflection.

"Staying the night?"

"Yeah, I might want to have a drink."

"Okay." She turns the brush back on but he stays put. She turns it back off. "Something else?"

"Yeah, next week they want me in Calgary. The guy that replaced me there? He just found out he's stage three, cancer."

She spits into the sink and rinses before replying.

"George? God, he's only...."

"Our age."

Neither of them speaks for a moment.

"They want you there for how long?"

"A week, this time around."

"And again?"

"*To be determined* is how they put it in the email."

"I'll have to find someone for Ryan...."

"You could quit."

She doesn't reply. Instead, she pulls down her pyjama pants and takes a pee.

"Em, you could ask me to leave." He shakes his head.

"Sorry. I'm used to being around a small person."

He retreats to the bedroom.

Christ, he said it like it was such a great prize, quitting her job. She spends a few extra minutes in the mirror with a set of tweezers, tugging at sturdy hairs that don't belong. He's on his back looking at the ceiling when she gets in bed.

"I'm not sure I want to quit."

"It would be so much easier."

"Sure, for you."

"And for you."

"I'm just settling in there. If I quit now, they won't hire me again. When Ryan heads off to school in a couple of years I'll be looking. There's a better chance of getting on full-time if I stay."

"That's two years away."

"I like the people. They're grown-ups. Not one of them has peed on me."

"Give it time," he says.

"Let me think about it."

"Fair enough, but I could be in Calgary every second week."

"Maybe I can switch some shifts. Linda might be able to help out." She sees him tense.

"What? It's mostly evenings. It would just be getting him into bed. You're back every weekend, right?"

"I don't know yet." She waits for him to say it, that Linda comes with a big string attached. "Maybe my parents could come and stay?"

"Right, maybe."

"It might be too much for Linda. Especially here in this house," Daniel says.

"She's never said anything about that...."

"My mother could come out."

"Mm." Emily imagines her mother-in-law shadowing her around the house. Maggie holding her tongue, like when she'd come to the rescue when Ryan was an infant. And then Maggie's calls to Daniel at the office: they shouldn't be offering him a soother, they should be getting him out for more fresh air, and so on. "I'll figure something out." She pulls out the novel she's been reading, then closes it. "You leave next week?"

Daniel's face is buried in a pillow, she can barely make out his response. "Tuesday."

"I guess I'll have to drive you to the airport. Your parents will have taken their car back by then."

He sounds drowsy when he turns to her. "I think it's in the afternoon."

"Okay." She opens the book again and reads the page several times before giving up.

⌒

"You coming?"

Linda stalls out with the shopping cart, squinting at the fluorescent lights. Why do they always flicker?

"Coming," she says, rounding the aisle into housewares. She glimpses her reflection in a full-length mirror; this light makes her skin an awful colour.

"What is it you're after?" she asks.

"A lamp. My bedside one conked out."

"Well, there's one in the attic. Save you the money."

He checks the price tag on one. "Really? What one is that?"

"One we had in the den for ages. It's just plain."

"Hm." He puts down the lamp. "Anything else up there?"

God knows he doesn't exactly have a disposable income. She hates to see him buy even more stuff when the house is overflowing with things. One day it will all be his anyway.

"Dad's clothes, fishing gear, your old toy box...."

"We still have that?"

"Just the good stuff. Things you couldn't dismantle." He'd loved to take things apart as a kid to see how they worked.

"Mind if I have a look?"

"Help yourself. There might be a space heater that would be good for the apartment too."

"Cool. Want to get out of here? Swing by Tim's?"

In response, she lets go of the empty cart. It's refreshing to walk outside at this time of year, without the need to brace for the chill. No more scraping the windshield and stepping through snowbanks to get in the car. Dandelions are popping up alongside the road.

"You mind driving me back to the city later?" he says.

"No, I take it you want to check out the attic today then?"

"If it's all right. Kind of a pain going without the lamp. I read at night and I keep falling asleep with the overhead light on. Feels too much like the hospital."

She glances at him. "I don't mind."

"What were you thinking to do with my old toys?"

"I hadn't thought," she lies. The toy box had been saved for her grandchildren.

"Maybe the little guy would like them."

"Ryan?"

"As long as they don't mind."

"Worth a try. Maybe don't take the whole lot over."

"Mm. You talk to them much?"

"Well, whenever I see them out." She tells herself it's just that Emily is working at night.

"I apologized to her," he says.

"For…that day?"

"She seemed okay."

It's not fair, this illness. People don't feel the need to apologize for heart disease or a broken leg.

They pull up to the speaker in the drive-thru. "One large double double and a large tea."

"And a box of donuts," he says, poking at her collarbone. "Put some weight on you."

The day starts out too bright, painful to the eyes. Emily spent half the night awake again. It's like a hangover without all the fun. She drives Daniel to the airport in the late afternoon.

In the back seat Ryan sings Elton John. "Daddy is travelling tonight on a plane." Daniel watches the scenery whip past his window, saying nothing. It's her fault, she'd been humming the song. She always did that when they flew somewhere. Daniel gave up asking her to stop. It was one of her tics. She had a tune for every situation. She even irritated herself at times but it was the way her brain worked, tuned in to the same troublesome radio station for years.

Ryan belts out the chorus while she watches him in the rear-view mirror. "Oh I miss Daddy, ooh I miss him so much."

He seems pleased with himself. They'll make a killer karaoke team one day. She joins in. "Oh it looks like Daddy…."

Daniel gives them a slow clap at the end of their performance.

"All right, bud." Dan opens the back door and leans in. "Give Dad a big hug." After a minute, Emily has to get out of the car and peel Ryan's hands from Daniel. Somehow he had the idea that he was getting on the plane too.

"Call in sick if it gets too much," he says into her ear before heading for the revolving door with his suitcase.

The last ten minutes of the drive home are in thick fog. Emily creeps along the yellow line, hoping the driver behind her will be as cautious.

When she pulls into the driveway, it's unnaturally dark. Only a quarter to five on a spring night, but it could just as easily be after sunset. The mist clings to her thin shirt as she stands beside the car, trying to shake off the tension. She marvels at how fog steals your vision while enhancing sound. Memories of sailing come back—sounding the air horn every minute to make their presence known, squinting into the grey, hoping they'd have time to react if something appeared just in front of the bow.

Below, the surf is louder than usual. Waves thrash at the beach, as if they too are blinded by the fog. A gull swoops past, screeching as it nears her. It makes her drop her keys. "Pull yourself together," she mutters as she stoops to retrieve them.

She's unbuckling Ryan from his car seat, smiling into his eyes, when he says, cautiously, "Hello." She nuzzles his nose, thinking he's playing a game. "Hello," she repeats in the same tone. But he points to the windshield. She follows his gaze and catches a dark shape in the fog. But just as her eyes begin to focus, it's gone. They both stare.

"Did you see…someone, Ryan?" She keeps her eyes trained on the spot.

"Mm hm, a face."

She straightens up and peers around the side of the door, calls out: "Hello? Jim?" Maybe he is out walking his dog. Nothing, just the gulls and the waves and the fog. "Tom?" No answer. "Hm, I don't know, buddy." She listens for a moment longer. "Okay, bath time. Let's get in the house."

Hoover's deep, doleful howl comes from within the house. It comforts her as she unlocks the door and he bursts into his greeting. Kicking off her shoes, she heads straight for the bathroom.

"You sure it was a person?" she says over her shoulder. He wrestles with his shoes, with Hoover sniffing the cuffs of his pants, tail wagging.

"I think the sad man."

Emily has her arm under the tap, trying to gauge the temperature. *What did he say?* He is behind her when she straightens. One shoe is still on. She turns and looks at his serious expression.

"What's that?"

"Sadman."

"Salmon?" If only.

"He has a little bottle and he watches the sea." He's enjoying his own reflection in a little mirror she hung at his height. She leaves him to it and goes into the kitchen to pour a glass of wine.

When she returns to shut off the water, Ryan has begun to sing again; it's uncanny how children repeat things after hearing it only once. "Your eyes have eyes, but you see more than I...." The lyrics are wrong and he is off key. But he's happy.

She leans over to the far edge of the bathtub to gather a few toys for him and catches sight of herself in the water. It's a harsh angle, seeing her face from below, but she has noticed the new line between her brows lately. It's an expression of constant worry. She's trying to pull the skin taut with two fingers when she sees it. The face is beside her, so close, almost cheek to cheek. Ryan is right, a sad man. The face shatters when she drops Ryan's plastic boat in the water. She scrambles to get her balance, emitting a horrible scream as she lands on her son.

Thankfully, he's not hurt, but they're both rattled, for different reasons. She gets him in the tub and goes back to the kitchen for her wine.

"Mummy's juice," says Ryan, making his blue boat sink by flooding it with a scoop of water.

"Yup, Mum's juice. Not for kids."

"Not for kids." He shakes his head.

"You okay now?"

"Mm hm."

"Tell me, do you like your sad man?" She's trying to work out how to ask him if he's scared.

"He is not mine."

"Does he know your other friends?"

"Too old." Judging by his focus on anchoring the boat to his toe, he's moved on.

"I'll be back in a minute, okay?"

In the living room, she can hear his splashes well enough, so she dials Lola at work.

"Hey you. Daniel heading my way?"

"He's in the air right now."

"And you're calling to tell me to keep an eye on him?" says Lola.

"I am calling to ask you if you believe in ghosts."

"Ah. Yes."

"Just like that?"

"Mm hm. Why not? There are spectrums of light we can't see, sounds we can't hear—"

"I was hoping you'd say no."

"Because?"

"Do not tell Daniel this, should he pop in for a visit." Highly unlikely, as Daniel does not enjoy Lola's sense of humour. "But I think I just saw Ryan's imaginary friend."

"Cool."

"No, chilling." She fills her in on Ryan's description.

"Okay. Water is not a reliable mirror, Em. You literally live in the fog. You are tired. You need sleep."

They talk until Ryan's tub water is too cool. After he's tucked in bed she has a second glass of wine, as prescribed by Lola, and invites Hoover to share the bed with her.

CHAPTER 8

In the morning, the bedroom is filled with pale yellow light. The fog must have moved off. It seems absurd in the day. She decides that a spring cleaning might help clear her mind: put away the bulging winter coats and stash the snow shovels. She finds a hammer and nail to hang her Valentine's gift from Daniel. It's been migrating around horizontal surfaces in the kitchen and living room since the day it was unwrapped. She puts it next to the back door and stands back to admire her handiwork.

"How's it look?" she asks Ryan.

"Is it for emergency?"

"Hm?" She looks at his serious face, then back at the box on the wall. He's right, it looks a like one of those cases that house a fire extinguisher. He's always asking about them when they're in public buildings.

"No, it's a decoration. From Daddy. Remember?" She pulls it back off the wall and checks the nail. They haven't displayed much of their artwork. None of the walls seem to fit the frames they have.

"What's decoration?"

"Just a thing to look at." He considers this, his bottom lip protruding.

The doorbell makes her jump. It's not often that it rings, unless Ryan is playing with it. If given the chance, he'll spend an hour pressing the button and giggling. He beats her to the front door, going into a semi-controlled sock slide once he hits the tiles.

She cracks the door open, and it's Tom with a lump beneath his shirt.

"Is this okay? Mum was supposed to come up too…." He cocks his thumb towards Linda's place.

"Blast-off!" Ryan says.

"Sure." She opens the door wide enough for him to step in.

"Brought an old t-o-y for him. That okay?"

"Sure." What else is there to say? Ryan prods at his shirt and Tom lets him pull it up.

"I used to have one of those," she says, careful not to look at his flat stomach but at the little plastic record player. He places it on the floor and reaches into the back pocket of his pants for the miniature records. Ryan grabs the arm of the player and moves it back and forth, making machine sounds.

"It plays music." Tom puts one of the discs on the peg and winds it up. "Here, push this over and that turns it on, see?"

"What do you think, Ryan?" He doesn't seem to hear her. His ear is to the side of it. "Ryan, what do you say?"

"Thanks." He doesn't look up.

"I'll get out of your hair. See you, bud."

"No." Ryan scrambles to his feet and muckles onto a knee. "Blast-off?"

"Ryan, he has to go…."

It's embarrassing how quickly he can switch on the tears. She doesn't encourage the behaviour, but he seems to know when he can push it. Tom shrugs at her, looking for silent permission. "Totally up to you."

She nods.

"Three, two…." Just like that, the sniffling stops and a smile appears. Daniel dubbed it *crane rain*, the old movie trick for creating heavy downpours.

It doesn't seem right to continue standing there with her hand on the doorknob, so she shuts it. He won't stay long.

"You said Linda was coming up?" She hopes she's being subtle.

"She said she was but when I got down from the attic she was flat out in the armchair."

"Sleeping?"

He nods and lifts Ryan high above his head. Every time he does it, she has to look away. Something about that expanse of skin, the line of his hipbone—God, when did she become such a prude?

"I'm kind of worried about her. She seems to get worn out a lot faster now." He plops Ryan down. "Getting kind of tired myself, bud."

"Ryan, that's the last one, all right?" This time the bottom lip comes out and he hangs onto Tom's hand, tugging him toward the back of the house.

"Show you."

"Show me?"

He tows Tom toward the newly hung artwork.

"Oh. This is nice." He gazes into the frame. "Great shot."

"That's my dead Poppa," Ryan says proudly. Over lunch, he asked her why Poppa Charlie never visited, and she had to remind him that his grandpa was dead.

"My dad," Emily says.

Tom straightens up. "I'm sorry."

"I was ten."

"Has my name." Ryan crawls for Hoover's bed. The dog has yet to wake up and notice his visitor.

"His name was Ryan too?"

"No, Ryan's middle name is Charlie."

"This his boat?"

"Yeah. *Knotty Girl.*"

He scans the names on the chart. "You grew up here?"

"The South Shore."

"Huh, I thought you were from away."

"No, we were gone for about ten years."

"You miss it?" He straightens up and stretches.

"Most of our friends are out there…."

"No, sorry, I meant the boat." He's close enough that she can make out the scent of coffee clinging to his clothes. She edges back a step.

"Oh. Yes, we sailed a lot…me and Da."

"You still do?"

"Not since we've been back. I'm hoping we'll get out this summer." It's the way he doesn't break eye contact. It's as if she's pinned in place. "Jim invited us."

"Jim, right." He looks over at Ryan. "You've got it figured out already. Just push that button over. Yup." The music box plays "London Bridge is Falling Down." "I should get back."

"Thanks for the toy."

"If it's okay, I have more."

"Yes…of course. Thanks."

This time he doesn't say goodbye to Ryan. Emily closes the door quietly behind him so as not to draw attention to his departure. She watches him from the kitchen. He's in no hurry, poking at stones on the road with the toe of his shoe.

⌒⌐

Surely there's a fabric store closer to home, Linda thinks. It's just habit to go to the places she knows in the city, take familiar roads. Yesterday, she was wiping down the windowsill in the kitchen and the curtain kept getting in the way. It's as if it had not recovered from being pulled closed by Tom that day. When she tried to tug it back, the fabric ripped in her hand. How many years did it hang there, bleached by the sun and steamed by the kettle? It's time for a change anyway. She pulled down the floral valance and the decaying curtains. Maybe a roman shade. A sewing project is just the thing right now. If all goes well, all the windows could get a makeover.

She could take the New Bridge across the harbour—it's faster in the morning traffic—but she likes the old one. Even though the bridges have names, people continue to call them the Old and the New. Even Tom—born after the opening of both the Macdonald and the MacKay—refers to them that way.

At the toll booth, she comes to a complete stop to put in the change. Martin would barely slow down, his hand flicking out the window with the flash of a coin, then accelerating away. She was certain they'd collide with the traffic arm before it could fully rise out of their way, but it was all timed just so. It seemed like a bit of sport for him.

The cars in front of her slow as she reaches the middle of the bridge, and she's able to steal a glance at the water. It must be a drop of a hundred feet at this section. In both directions, she can spot sailboats—early season sailors taking advantage of a steady breeze. It must be nippy out there. The bridge lurches and sways at this halting pace. It's not that noticeable when the car is zipping along. Martin used to laugh at her gripping the door handle. *It has to do that, Lin, or it would snap. It's a suspension bridge.* Sometimes it doesn't make a lick of difference if you know a thing is supposed to move when the gut decides otherwise. Her lungs seem to stiffen too. *Slow breaths. Slow.* A crossing that should take a couple of minutes stretches into what seems like an hour. The radio keeps her company: tornadoes in the States, a suicide bomb in Chechnya, a sound bite of President Bush talking about Iraq…. She flips to a music station. Tom calls it classic rock. Classic. *What does that make me?* It's the Eagles; she can sing along and it's miles better than the news.

Tom will come with her on the return trip. The attic has become a project for him, and he's eager to get back to it. After fixing up the old lamp, he decided there were other things that could be improved with a bit of paint. He asked about updating some side tables and selling them. It seemed like a good idea. It would make the house less crowded and give him a little cash. So, the basement wafts fumes whenever he's around. It's a good thing it's warm enough to prop open the windows.

The toy box is thinning out too. The last time he went up with something for Ryan, she went with him. He took her elbow and tugged her along—thinking he was helping, no doubt. She was breathless on arrival and it made things awkward, being unable to speak to anyone for the first ten minutes. Emily kept glancing her way as if she wanted to say something. In contrast, Tom was on his back with the dog licking his face and Ryan bouncing up and down on his shins. It was impossible to speak to one another anyway above the din of laughter. God knows what Daniel thinks of this invasion of Fisher-Price on their home. Martin used to insist on toys being kept in Tom's room. The living room was strictly for the adults. That is clearly not the case at the McNallys'. The house is being slowly transformed into a playroom: the walls full of tiny handprints, the floors an obstacle course of coloured plastic, and clumps of dog hair scuttling out of the way whenever a door or window opens.

At long last, she is off the bridge and creeping up the hill on North Street. This route feels like her old city. The road off the Old Bridge is the same width, whereas the New Bridge feeds into multiple lanes of traffic, looping near the container pier with its leviathan cranes tending to the freighters. Things are a more human scale here. It's the city of her childhood. Every year, her family would drive in from the Valley to do a bit of shopping before Christmas. If they were lucky, they'd get to see a movie. Mum would put her hair in curlers the night before and take special care to braid Linda's. Some years they'd come in during the late summer, buy school clothes at Simpsons and have lunch at the Chickenburger on the way out of town. It still has the stone buildings and winding streets, but now there's more glass and steel. Something Martin welcomed with a wry smile: *they still need carpenters.*

A red light allows her to glance at her watch. Perfect, the store will be opening when she arrives. Touch wood, they won't have renovated and she'll find all she needs in a few minutes. They'll be home well before lunch.

Emily picks Daniel up from the airport and drops him and Ryan before leaving for her evening shift.

"Tired?" he asks as she heads back out the door.

"Little bit." ·

"Come here." He pulls her into a proper hug. "I haven't seen you for a week."

"I'm going to be late," she says, cheek squashed to his chest.

"Off you go then." He releases her. "See you at…?"

"Nine thirty."

But it's past ten when she gets in and he has fallen asleep with her bedside table light on. He's showered and put on his lucky underwear, purchased for him as a joke on their wedding anniversary. Nevertheless, they usually worked. Not this time.

In the morning, Daniel suggests an early lunch at Salty's Café. As they drive past Linda's, Tom comes out of the shed. Daniel pulls over and rolls down the window.

"Hey, Tom," she shouts, leaning over Daniel. "I have someone here you should meet."

He puts down his surfboard before sauntering over. Daniel thrusts his hand out the window.

"Tom, good to meet you."

Tom takes his hand and nods. "Daniel—" but he is drowned out by Ryan trying to be noticed in the back seat.

Leaning in the window, Tom laughs at Ryan like they're old friends. No facial twitches or awkward movements. It should set Daniel at ease.

"Okay, buddy. That's enough," says Daniel, catching Ryan's eye in the rear-view mirror. They drive away and she gets lost in thought, watching the scenery outside her window.

No one says anything until they reach the café. Ryan stops and plays on an old dory outside, left there for just that purpose. Daniel doesn't wait for them. He disappears inside, and by the time they join him, food has been delivered to their table.

Daniel cuts Ryan's fish. With a bit of luck, he'll eat more food than what ends up on the floor. Emily crunches her way through a salad, envying the fries on Ryan's plate.

"After this," Daniel says to Ryan, "we'll swing by the boat. Mummy can drop me off and you can head to the playground."

"Drop you?"

"I told you I'm helping Jim. He wants to launch it next week."

"Hm. I must have been out of earshot."

"Nope, I was right next to you."

"Mother brain."

She pops a fork full of salad in her mouth. The waitress appears instantly.

"How are the first bites?"

Emily bobs her head up and down and smiles around her lettuce.

"Good, let me know if I can get you anything else, love." She speeds away to the kitchen.

Emily catches Ryan's glass just as it's about to go over the edge of the table and pulls it to where he can't hit it with his elbow. "Three more bites." She leans over and looks him in the eye. "Then more chocolate milk."

"You still liking the library?" Daniel asks, grasping his lobster roll in both hands.

"It's okay."

Over the years they've been together, she must have had a dozen jobs. She envies people who know what they want to do. Whenever they're out socializing, she cringes when someone turns to her with the inevitable *and what do you do?* It makes her feel like a kid at the adults' table.

"Maybe once Ryan is in school, you can take some courses," he offers between bites.

"Yeah, maybe." She doesn't want to have this conversation. Right now, it's enough to keep the three of them fed, clothed, and moderately clean. Then she remembers something. "Tom is thinking of taking a darkroom course in the city…at the art school, I think."

Daniel puts down his sandwich. He picks up Ryan's fork and pops another bite of fish in before he can grab another fry.

"You want to take darkroom photography." Not a question, but a flat statement.

They lock eyes and Emily continues to chew. She knows exactly what he is poking at. It wasn't really her fault that she didn't finish the program. She'd discovered that her talent for doodling wasn't enough to make it as a graphic designer.

"I said Tom is taking it."

It was Daniel who looked up the cost of the computer and software she'd need. It's not like she went out and bought it. By then she was pregnant and the prospect of finishing the program was not as tempting.

"Or did you want to talk about how thoughtful it is of him to drop off the toys?"

Emily stares. "He's our neighbour, he's trying to help out."

"No, she's our neighbour." He picks up a napkin and wipes his mouth.

"What?"

Daniel's eyes flit to Ryan then back to her. "Nothing."

⌒

"You're still at that?"

Tom's face appears in the pool of light from Linda's sewing machine. "One more seam."

She'd been at it all day. Well that's not quite true. After lunch, she'd had a little lie-down and when she opened her eyes it was time to get back in the kitchen and pop the shepherd's pie in the oven.

"Want me to flip on the light?"

"Sure. The sun must have set."

"Yeah. Days are getting longer though."

She squints up at the clock on the wall. "Does that say nine?"

He pinches the edge of the fabric between his fingers. "Mm hm. This'll look nice." His words have to compete with the rumble of the machine.

"There," she says snipping the threads. "Now I just have to figure out how to hang it."

"I'm heading out."

"You are?"

"Greg. We're going to shoot some pool." He goes to the cupboard and pulls out a glass. "I'm keeping an eye out for his car." He pulls a bottle from the window sill and pops the cap. She watches him put the pill on his tongue and swallow it. Then he comes close and opens his mouth at her. It seems to have gone down his throat.

"Where?"

"Crazy Eight's."

"Never heard of it."

He shakes his head, smiling. "You're out of the loop, Mum." Lights trail across his face and they both turn to the window. "Must be him. I have my key."

She listens to the car door closing and the engine fading away, while she lays out the roman shade on the dining room table. She tests the strings that raise and lower it, still not confident that it will work according to the pattern's directions, but it does.

God knows if it helps, the charade of him with the medication. If he decides not to take it, he hides it, using some magic trick. Even the medical staff can't detect it. The patients must share their methods with each other when they're in treatment. Tests are their fallback, while she has to rely on instinct and the hope that he doesn't want to deceive her, at least not while he is *himself.*

She stands and goes to the open window. This project has kept her inside, slouching over a table for a couple of days. That's all right in the winter, but she can smell the soil now. Tomorrow, she'll get outside. First light, while she has a bit of energy. It might be too late to do anything in the garden but appreciate last year's plantings. Still, she could divide up one of the hostas for Emily. That barren front yard of hers would be much improved with some greenery. Or maybe she'll wait and ask her. It might be too many hand-me-downs all at once.

After this house was built, it took years to get things to grow properly. She was unprepared for that struggle after growing up in a place with such fertile soil. As a child, she helped plant seeds, water, and harvest everything, then stood alongside her mother in the fall, canning things for winter. In their fifth year, things finally took root. The shrubs and trees had grown high enough to provide a windbreak for the tender shoots. Her garden became a burst of colour, buzzing with fat bumblebees.

What she really wanted in those years was a brother or a sister for Tom. At first, Martin said that the budget was too tight. She started a business. Then it was that they'd need a larger house. She found a second-hand bunk bed. Then Martin was too tired.

One night he was home early enough to lie in bed with her. She came out of the bathroom holding the box, placed it on his belly and smiled.

"What's this?"

"I know you don't want to try right now," she said, perching beside him, "so, I got you these."

"Linda. If I wanted condoms I'd have got them myself. I can't stand these things, you can't feel. I been up on a damn roof swinging a hammer all day cause they're trying to save money on this project...."

Her mother's advice came right after the ceremony, clasping Linda's white-gloved hands in her own. "Just remember, sometimes the better comes after the worse." Her eyes shone as she stood back, appraising her daughter. What had she missed with her own parents?

Yes, the house up the hill needs something to soften its hard edges. Maybe Tom will lend her a hand with digging up the hosta. That, along with some bleeding hearts. Maybe something simple for Ryan too, marigolds to keep the cat out of the garden. Nothing grows if you don't get around to planting. She sighs and closes the window.

Emily wakes to muffled cursing. It's Daniel bumping into a wall, try-ing to come in without switching on lights. She must have dozed off. A fuzzy blanket is thrown over her on the couch.

"What time is it?" she asks, watching him collapse into the chair opposite her.

"Must be about midnight." His words are slurred. "You've been having a wild evening, I see." He indicates the book on her chest with his chin and punctuates his words with a stifled belch. "Sorry. How was your night?"

"Took a while to get him to fall asleep." Rolling on her side she sees his jeans are smudged with paint, his sweater sleeves are rolled up, and there's something else. "Were you smoking?"

"One." He holds up a crooked index finger. "Resisted for the first two beers, then I gave in. Jim's a social smoker, didn't want to do it alone."

They both used to enjoy having a cigarette with a beer. That was back when you could still smoke indoors at pubs.

"Mm." She yawns, pulling herself into a sitting position. "Get much done?"

"Oh yeah. Kept calling me a pencil-pusher if he thought I wasn't moving fast enough." He stretches his arms up and talks through a yawn. "He thought we were made of money, buying this place. Didn't believe me when I told him how much." He laughs. "We got a deal, I think. Good timing, right before the winter."

Emily stands up and heads into the kitchen with an empty glass.

"Then we headed back here and he invited me in for a drink. Been there since supper. God, I can't drink like I used to."

"Right," she says, smirking as she tosses Ryan's toys into the box in the corner. Out west he used to joke that his inability to hold his liquor was why he'd left the Maritimes—an embarrassment to his people.

"His wife, Meg, no Martha, yeah, she was asking about Tom. Said to be careful about him." He leans his head back on the chair and addresses the ceiling. "She saw him in the middle of one his episodes once, ranting, talking to ghosts."

Emily picks up her novel and dog-ears the page she was reading. "Linda told me. She said people find it pretty unsettling, but he's more at risk of hurting himself."

He doesn't say anything. She starts to wonder if he's fallen asleep until he says, "I'm just worried. You've never seen him like that. I'm not sure you could handle it."

She bristles. Handle it? She stares hard at him. The skin on his neck is dotted with pimples. His last shave must have been a bad one and now he's let the stubble grow in for a day or two.

"Actually, I've read quite a bit about it." That was one of the nice things about her job, she could read on her breaks. He raises an eyebrow at her, his chin just low enough on his chest that there's a roll of flesh beneath it. "You met him for thirty seconds."

"All I'm saying is that you should be careful."

He gets up and comes toward her, but the smell of stale smoke, industrial paint, and the sourness of beer make her turn her head away. It doesn't seem to register with him as he folds her into a hug, nuzzling her hair.

"He's not your responsibility, Em." Will he ever stop thinking of her as broken? A hiccup erupts from him. "C'mon, let's go to bed."

She pulls back and returns to the task of tidying the room. "I'll be up in a bit."

"All right." A minute later, the bed creaks under his weight. There's the sound of him punching his pillow into the right shape. Clearly, he hasn't bothered to brush his teeth. She stokes the fire and settles back on the couch, tucking the blanket over her.

IN THE MORNING, Daniel answers the phone downstairs and she strains to hear his side of the conversation. Then there are his footsteps on the stairs; his voice gets louder.

"Yup, she's still in bed...no, it's fine. I'm sure she wants to get up... here she is." Appearing, he mouths *your mother.* He looks irritated.

"Morning, Mum."

"I woke you."

"No, it's okay."

"You're not sick, are you?" *Jesus.* Emily glances at the clock. It's just past nine, not noon.

"I just had a hard time getting to sleep. When did you get back?"

"Thursday night. I thought we'd take a drive your way." We. "Come and see my grandson."

"Today?"

"If you're not working?"

"No, that's tomorrow. Okay, yeah."

She tiptoes to the top of the stairs. Ryan is at the table, munching cereal, one hand driving a small truck around the bowl. Daniel tends to the coffee pot.

Returning to the bedroom, she stands in front of the closet, frowning. When she finally crawled into bed last night, Daniel woke. Maybe he thought she was trying to rouse him. He threw a sweaty arm over her and started playing with her breast, his mouth near her ear, that sour breath again. She tried turning away but that didn't work, she had to tell him to leave off. And he had, without a word of argument. But it was the abruptness of it, the way he flipped his back to her.

She stiffens at the sound of footsteps behind her, saying nothing, and concentrates on her search for slimming clothes until she feels a tug on the back of her shirt. When she looks around, it's Ryan, wide-eyed. His cheeks are smeared with breakfast.

"Mummy?"

She deflates, sinking to her knees, and pulls him into an embrace, closing her eyes. He pulls away. "Can we take my kite to beach?"

"I don't know, your grandma is coming. You remember Gramma Mary?"

He shakes his head, unimpressed.

"Does she like kites?"

DANIEL WAITS IN the kitchen, fully dressed.

"I'm heading into the office. Catch up on a few things."

It's Sunday, he hadn't mentioned this before.

"Mum and Richard should be here in a couple of hours."

"You want me to stay." It would be a lead weight on an already heavy afternoon.

"No, go. It's fine," she says.

Ryan stands between them, his head moving like he is watching a slow tennis match. He hugs his kite, hoping the conversation will turn back to more important matters.

Minutes later Daniel is out the door, without a peck on the cheek. Even Ryan is shorted on the goodbye. Emily tidies the house and puts toys away while Ryan pulls different ones out behind her. It is futile.

When she was a kid, Da often read several books at a time, as if he needed one for each chair, another in bed, several on his desk. Rooms were littered with mugs of half-finished drinks. One of her weekly chores was to seek out his cups and put them in the dishwasher. The wood stove went all winter; a galaxy of ash hung in sunbeams. Thinking about this, she stops cleaning. They can see the house as it is.

Too soon, she hears a car door slam and glimpses them climbing out, gaping up at the house. It must not have been as windy in the city; her mother is in a bright sweater and white capris, ironed, of course.

"Ryan, they're here." She tries to sound enthusiastic. A three-year-old can really set the mood. "Let's go say hello."

At this, Hoover's head pops up, he looks around blearily, then stumbles out of bed, beating her to the door, which opens suddenly. Richard steps in, without knocking. Hoover stops dead and lets out a howl. Emily enjoys the alarm on Richard's face. His distaste for animals is clear in the way he avoids touching them.

Her mother appears behind him and smiles. "Ryan, dear, you're so big. I haven't seen you since you were…." She rattles on while removing her shoes. She tries to coax him closer for a hug, but he has one arm wrapped around Emily's leg, peering at the two strangers.

"Hello, young man," Richard says, as fond of children as he is of pets. "Emily." He leans in, giving her a kiss on each cheek. "Nice spot you have here."

"Oh, it's gorgeous," Mary chimes in, giving her a light hug, abandoning her efforts with her grandson. Pulling back, she searches the room behind Emily. "Where's Daniel?"

"He had to go to the office. There's a big meeting this week." She listens to herself, impressed at how convincing she sounds.

They tour the house, Ryan trailing behind them with his kite in hand. Richard eyes the toy-strewn floor of Ryan's room and the sticky walls of the hallway. His hands stay in his pockets.

Afterward, she stands at the counter filling the kettle. Richard is on the deck watching the sea—more likely, calculating the property value—and Ryan, defeated, plays with blocks.

"You seem a little tense."

Emily glances at her mother, surprised.

"I'm just tired." Her head pounds. "Listen, I didn't make lunch and I've not had much time for groceries. How about we head down to the beach, see if the café is open? Ryan wants to fly his kite."

"Okay," Mary says without enthusiasm.

"We'll have to take your car. I'll get Ryan's car seat."

THE WIND HITS them as soon as they open their doors. Emily is used to it, wearing layers, lashing her hair under a hat to keep it out of her face. Her mother has her arms wrapped tightly around her body.

"Will you be okay?" Emily asks.

"I think I have another sweater in the trunk." Mary smiles. "You go on ahead."

Ryan jumps up and down.

"Come on, Mummy!"

He grabs her hand, trying to tug her onward. They're not the only ones, another family is further down the beach. She breathes in through her nose and turns her face to the sun. There's a flat rock where she likes to sit not far from the stairs. Ryan runs along with his kite. She trimmed the string to just two feet and he's delighted, holding it slightly above his head. Mary wobbles toward her, wearing a blanket.

"This will do," she says, pulling the blanket tighter. The wind rakes her hair away from her forehead, Emily can make out the grey roots. "It always takes me a week or two to acclimatize when we get home."

"Where's Richard?"

"Oh, he stayed in the car. Wanted to make a call. He said the wind would be too loud."

Emily plays with the sand with one shoe, unearthing small shells and cigarette butts. After a long silence her mother says, "Happy to be home?"

"Yeah, it's great. Days like today make it even better."

"The house is nice. When you said you were moving back, you talked about getting something...small."

"It was sitting empty for a while so we got a deal. Maybe the commute to the city put people off." She doesn't mention Linda's husband. "It's more house than I wanted. Daniel loved it right away, of course."

"Yes, I can imagine he would. Is he enjoying—oh." Her eyes lock onto something. "Who is that man with Ryan?"

Someone squats down with Ryan but he's turned away. Then he's lifting him up high, the laughter carries on the wind. Her shoulders drop.

"It's okay." She waves and Tom starts towards them, beckoning for Ryan to follow.

As she makes the introductions, she watches her mother straighten her back and drop the blanket from her shoulders. "Tom, nice to meet you."

He smiles briefly before being impacted in the legs by Ryan. "Again!"

"Okay, little man, just hang on a sec." He offers a hand to Mary then turns his gaze on Emily.

"You going out?" she says, looking at his lack of wetsuit.

"Nah, just came down to pick up a friend. She said she'd go with me to pick out a new board."

"Oh, great."

He scoops up Ryan and whirls him around, moving closer to the water.

"Seems nice," Mary says, then taps Emily's arm and stage whispers, "Paul Newman eyes."

"Really? I hadn't noticed."

"You're quiet today."

"Just a bad night." That much is true. "We should get to the café. You look cold."

"I'm okay."

She puts her hand up to wave to Ryan and sees a female surfer wading out of the water, heading for Tom. She's willowy with a wide smile, framed by short-cropped hair. Tom allows her to hug him, laughing as his shirt gets soaked.

"Let's go, Ryan. Grandma's cold."

WHEN THEY GET home, she unloads the car seat, unhooking the various clips and belts. She thumps the back door shut and is surprised to find that Richard is still buckled into the driver's seat. He waves at her and backs out. She looks to her mother.

"Oh, he's keen on buying something nearby. He has a collection of antique model cars, I think that's what the call was about."

Emily can imagine the glass case of untouchable things. What doesn't fit is her mother's tone of voice.

"You don't like model cars?"

"Oh no, I don't mind them. But he's always heading off on these drives. Half the time he comes home empty-handed."

Emily says nothing, distracted with herding Ryan into the house.

"Glass of wine?" she says, dropping a sand-coated purse on the floor at the front door.

"Not for me, dear. Just a glass of water, but I can get it."

Emily shoos Ryan into the washroom to peel off his mustard-coated shirt. It's draining having a meal out without Daniel there as an extra set of eyes and hands. When she emerges, her mother is looking at the shadow box with the shackle inside.

"You still have it," Mary says quietly.

"Yeah." Emily watches her mother's face. She remembers closing her fingers around the brass, her mother's tears dripping onto her knuckles. "I still have it."

"You made a frame for it."

"Daniel did."

Mary doesn't seem to hear. "It's good that you kept it." Emily goes still. "I was your age when he died." She smoothes her hair. "I still had a lot to learn." Giving Emily a sad smile, she heads into the washroom, closing the door gently behind her.

CHAPTER 9

Linda is up at five, unable to sleep despite being tired. She sits on the porch under a blanket, taking small breaths of the cool air while the sun climbs the sky. Sometimes it's frightening, being alone.

After a while, she rises. Some light gardening might take her mind off it—pull some weeds and fluff the dirt. Now, the sun bathes her in heat. She kneels by the front flowerbed, a few unearthed dandelions wilt beside her.

"You're productive this morning," Emily says, appearing by her side holding Ryan's hand.

Linda puts down her hand rake and looks at Ryan with his hair covering one eye. "Just counting the ladybugs. See any, Ryan?"

He gets down on his knees and peers into the garden.

"You okay?" Emily says, kneeling beside her.

"Oh, it's…the sun's making my head worse. Help me up?"

Emily takes both of her hands, bracing her to stand.

"Thanks, love." Linda hunches into her cough. Her eyes water with the effort. In her pocket, she finds a tissue and spits into it.

"Linda, I think we need to get you inside." Emily puts an arm around her shoulders, steadying her steps. She can't argue, there's a whistle in her breath. When she gets to the porch she sits, gratefully, in the shade.

"I'm going to get you some water." Emily reappears moments later, glass in hand, and watches Linda sipping. "When was your last doctor's appointment?"

"I don't go in for a cold. Waste of their time." It's exhausting, just getting those words past her throat. Martin always complained he'd pick up more germs sitting in their waiting rooms.

"I don't think you have a cold," Emily says, gently.

Linda looks past her at Ryan inspecting the palm of his hand.

"Maybe not." She closes her eyes, leans her head back on the chair.

It can't be real, but there he is next to her, smoking one of his cigarettes. His eyes squint at the sky. He was always looking skyward, Martin. The smoke makes her chest tighten even more, but she manages to speak anyway.

"What do you see up there?"

He turns to her.

"Everything and nothing." She enjoys the lines around his eyes as he gives her his best Mona Lisa. "Bright blue right now. It'll give way to deep blue then darken all the way to black. It's changing from moment to moment. We're on a planet spinning at a thousand miles an hour, but we can't feel it. Sometimes I just sit here and try."

His words get quieter until he fades out like someone has fiddled with the volume knob, and then it's Emily crouching in front of her.

"Linda?"

⁓

"Your fingers are blue. You're sweating but your hands are freezing." Emily waits. "Linda?"

Her eyes pop open.

"Better, thanks."

Emily chews her lip. She goes into the kitchen, toting the water glass with her. There are several notes tacked to the fridge. Finally, she finds the number.

She tries Tom first but gets his voicemail so she leaves him a brief message. Then she piggybacks Ryan up to the house to pack a few things in a bag. He's buckled into his seat when she pulls over to Linda's driveway.

When she reaches Linda, she seems to have nodded off again. Emily hesitates, wondering if an ambulance might be wiser. Her eyes flutter open and she bends to cough into the crumpled tissue.

"Linda, I think you need to see a doctor. Your breathing, it's…."

"Just need rest," she manages between coughs.

"Come on, my car's waiting." Emily is impressed at how calm she sounds. She gets her left arm under Linda and heaves her up. "Not taking no for an answer."

THEY DON'T MESS around in Emerg when someone can't breathe. Emily is at the vending machine when she recognizes Tom's voice at the admitting desk.

"Tom." He turns, looking relieved. "They took her in about an hour ago, they didn't give me much information but they got her on oxygen right away."

"Tom Tom Tom." Ryan hugs his knees. Emily hands Ryan the full bag of chips, something she'd normally avoid.

"I was at work."

"Of course. Has she ever been like that before?"

"I don't know. She never says."

"They said she's going to be okay." He chews at a nail, his eyes scanning the room. "Come on. We're sitting just over there."

They sit side by side and stare at the TV screen. Ryan pretends his lap is the harbour, using chip crumbs as boats.

"I don't usually do this," Tom says, his eyes on the screen. "Watch TV."

Emily glances at him.

"Yeah. Bad habit. Sit across from me instead."

"Nah. There's a TV on that wall too."

A woman in scrubs appears in front of the screen looking down at a clipboard. "Thomas Morris?"

They find Linda behind a curtain, breathing into an oxygen mask. Her skin looks a better colour. She holds her hand out to Tom and he takes it, bending to kiss her forehead. Her eyes go to Emily.

"We'll just say a quick hello, they don't want a bunch of people in here."

Linda nods and holds her gaze, she wants Emily to come closer. She puts her ear next to Linda's mouth and listens to her words through the hiss of air. "Watch Tom, please."

Emily leans into her ear. "You got it." She straightens up, then thinks to lift Ryan up on her hip. He's been oddly silent, awed by the sight of flashing lights and beds on wheels. She hoists him into view and explains about the oxygen. "We'll leave the two of you alone." She puts Ryan down. "They said you're here overnight. Tom, I can give you a drive later."

He mumbles about taking a cab.

"No, I'll be back. We just need to run home for the dog." She'll have to call in sick to work with Daniel away. "You need anything from home?" Linda points at a square of paper on the table next to her. Emily smiles, she's already thought to write it down. If she's still organized, things can't be too bad.

"We'll be back before supper. Tom, can you call us and let us know where they take her?" He nods. He's stopped chewing his nails. Both hands are stowed in his pockets.

"Here." She holds out her phone to him. "The number is programmed in under *home*. Okay?"

⌒

Ryan hums along to the radio on the drive home. Her body aches from holding herself straight and forcing a mask of calm. At every red light, she'd glanced over at Linda slumped in the passenger seat, remembering the crack of the sails, fighting to keep them filled with wind until she got Da to the mouth of their inlet.

Hoover is wide awake when they get home. He pushes out the door and relieves himself without bothering to lift a leg. The house is as they left it, toys scattered, dishes in the sink. With Daniel away, they are at ease.

She goes straight to the phone and calls the library. While she waits for her boss to come on the line, she looks out the living room windows. There's a new oily smudge there, high up.

Her supervisor's voice is flat when she offers her sympathy. Before she hangs up, she reminds Emily of the weekend shift, Saturday at nine. Twice she says it, as if Emily is forgetful rather than unable to work.

There's a crow on the branch of a tree nearby. Closer to the window, she sees the other on the ground. It's larger than usual with shaggy throat feathers.

"What's that, Mum?"

"It must have hit the window."

"Is she okay?" All birds are female in Ryan's world.

"I don't know." She wants to do something. Mothers should know what to do. The bird's eye blinks and its beak moves slightly. The mate lands nearby and hops around, croaking. It must be a raven.

"Can we make her fly?"

He's at the back door trying to unlock it.

"Wait, sweetie."

Bert is out there, approaching with his ears lowered. He doesn't look as the other one takes flight. The injured bird moves its head, trying to look around. Emily joins Ryan at the door, ready to rush out. The other raven dips to the ground for a beat then flies directly over the cat and drops something. It bounces off Bert's back and rolls toward the house. The stone isn't big enough to injure the cat, but he's startled and disappears in a flat out run. Emily whoops, she can't help it; she'd spotted Bert's full dish of food in Linda's kitchen this morning.

Ryan stays at the window and watches. He reports it all to Emily as she makes up Hoover's food and does dishes. "She's patting her with his beak...now she's up...hopping...flying."

Just before leaving for the hospital, she goes into the backyard. Turning in a circle, she scans the treetops inland for any sign of them, but there's nothing. The only sign of life is the orange cat, back in his customary spot.

⌒

Tom bites his nails, sitting in the chair opposite Linda. The doctor just left, stressing that she should get some sleep. He'd spent some time with Linda, outlining her case and showing her how to breathe through her nose and then out through her lips, "like you are about to blow out the candles on your birthday cake. It gets rid of the trapped air in your lungs." He pronounced the *ed* in the word *trapped* as if it was its own syllable. It almost sounded like a good thing. "You must relax." The words were directed at her, but he was looking at Tom as he left the room.

"Do you have your meds with you?" Linda asks. It's nearly suppertime.

He shakes his head. "When was the last time you went to a doctor?" Tom's voice is low. He's turned away, looking out the window.

"A couple of years, I think." They'd asked her that before, and she couldn't work it out. Once, for certain, after Martin's death.

"You keep saying you're quitting."

The doctor was blunt. It's not like she didn't know the dangers. For some reason, when she thought of it at all, it was cancer, not emphysema. Still, it's a death sentence.

"I have been trying."

When he turns around, he reaches for the box of tissues and sits down again, blowing his nose. "Didn't it scare you?"

"I thought it was the flu." He holds her gaze. "I'll stop."

"If she hadn't come…."

"I'd have called someone." She's not sure. It was nice sitting there on the porch with Martin.

A nurse comes in, smiling. She inspects Linda's IV and jots something down on the chart. She's about Tom's age. Linda has never had the experience of him bringing home a serious girlfriend, only when he was much younger.

The nurse pauses at the end of the bed and introduces herself, says she'll be there all night, like she's a stand-up comic, and gives Tom a little wink. He watches her, now that she can't look back at him. The chair is at a diagonal to the bed, in a room of four. Other patients doze or watch their small televisions. The curtain doesn't provide a sound barrier. Earlier, Linda listened to a drama unfolding to her left. The woman next to her is silent now, but it had sounded as if she was listening to a marriage in its final throes.

Tom doesn't pursue his earlier line of questions, he sits in the almost pink chair holding his elbows in his palms like he's cold. As far as she knows, she and Bradley are his only visitors when he relapses. One day Brad will meet someone and not want to share an apartment with Tom. But she can't think that far. Every time she tries, it's like staring at a blank page. The future is a slippery thing.

Amidst the beeps and chatter of the hospital, Linda hears a familiar voice in the hallway. Emily appears in the door with Ryan. She can't help but notice how Tom's face rearranges. Letting go of his elbows, he leans forward and opens his arms to Ryan.

They're at the elevator watching the numbers light up. Ryan waits for the doors to open, having been promised that he can press the button for their floor.

"You want to eat here in the cafeteria before we head to your place?"

"Not here."

The metal doors slide open and Ryan tugs her forward, keen to get inside before anyone else can get near the panel of buttons.

"Right there, M, see it?" She guides his finger away from the bright red alarm button. "Okay then," she says to Tom, "pick something up on the way?"

"Sure."

"How is she, really?"

He runs a hand through his hair. "I don't think she realizes how close she cut it. You said her lips were blue." The elevator bounces and doors open to admit more people, and she has to pull Ryan back before he can charge out through the doors. "She's stubborn."

"She's used to being the caregiver. It's hard to switch roles."

They file out into the hallway and make their way to the main doors. Outside, a short distance from the entrance, a clump of people in hospital-issued gowns hang onto IV poles with one hand and cigarettes with the other. Tom says nothing but Emily catches his look, the set of his jaw.

They take their feast up to Tom's apartment and spread it out on the coffee table. Emily tries not to look around too much but she's curious. The TV is an older model, its plug dangles off the shelf. There's a short bookcase in the corner, containing one shelf of pharmaceutical reference books and two shelves of paperback novels. Emily chews her fries with her head held sideways, trying to make out some of the titles.

"Asimov?" she says looking at Tom.

"Yeah. Brad's." He pauses before taking a bite. "You like sci-fi?"

"I like the technology, like the replicator. Just speak out the name of the meal I want, and bam."

"Not a chef?"

"Nope."

Ryan chases some ketchup around his wrapper with his last fry and Emily catches it before the whole thing lands on the floor.

"Impressive," Tom says.

"Thank you."

He stands up and gathers their wrappers. "I'll get my things. You probably need to get him home to bed."

"Yeah." Emily herds Ryan down the hall towards the washroom. "You're going to fall asleep before we get home, right, bud?"

By the time she's finished cleaning up, Tom is back in the living room holding a small bag.

"Did you, remember the—?"

"Just took it."

She'd promised Linda.

"Try to watch him do it," Linda had said.

Linda hadn't had time to elaborate on how to do that, as he'd come back from the nurse's station just then. Linda squeezed her hand surprisingly hard before she left.

WHEN THEY ARRIVE at the house, Tom carries Ryan up to bed. Even the jubilant dog doesn't wake him.

"Tea?"

He nods and heads over to the bookshelves. She glances over her shoulder at him. He's looking at an old photo.

"What was it, your boat?"

"A wooden sloop, about nineteen feet. He'd single-hand it a lot, if I couldn't go out with him."

"What about your mum?"

Emily laughs. "God no. Sea sickness, or so she claimed."

The kettle clicks off and she heads into the kitchen. She comes back with a teapot and two mugs.

"Oh God. I forgot to call Daniel. I'm just going to try him."

She jogs up to the bedroom and finds the business card with the hotel number. He doesn't answer, he's probably at the office.

She leaves a message with the front desk and brings the handset down to the coffee table.

"In case he calls back."

"You guys talk every day?"

"Well, we try. I should have called him before." The raven drama had distracted her.

The fast food percolates in her gut. Her system has been fuelled on cleaner things of late, and it seems to be rebelling. Emily stands up and excuses herself. Naturally, the phone rings while she's on the toilet, but she makes out Tom's voice answering. When she gets back, he indicates the phone on the coffee table.

"I kept him on the line, just in case."

She picks up the receiver but there's no one there.

"Must have hung up."

Tom pulls his legs up on the couch, cradling the mug in his hands. He's poured hers too.

"He seemed a little confused, like he thought he'd dialled the wrong number."

"I'm going to call him from upstairs. Do you mind?" She walks over to the stereo and switches it on. The sound of the cello fills the room. "Change stations, if you like."

"No, this is good."

TOM APPEARS TO be asleep when she gets back. She's wondering if she should leave him or throw a blanket on him, when his eyes pop open. She laughs out loud, surprised.

"Just resting the eyes. I loved that last piece of music."

The hourly news is on, Emily turns down the volume.

"You're tired."

He swings his feet around and makes a show of looking more alert. "How's Daniel?"

"Busy. He's sorry to hear about your mum." That's not exactly right. There were a lot of long pauses on his end. If she'd been there she'd have read his face.

Tom nods. "I sat there this afternoon wondering what I'll do when she's gone." He stares into his cup.

She ought to sit with him, put her arm around him. Anyone else and she'd already be over there. "I think it scared her."

"Yeah." His eyes look glazed. He stands up and refills his mug from the teapot. She watches him settle back on the couch.

"A raven hit the window just there today." She points to the smudge.

"Did it fly away?"

"Yeah. Bert probably figured he'd hit the jackpot." She tells him about its mate dropping the stone. "You know, I saw footage of one stealing food from an eagle once? It had worked out that the eagle could only retaliate by letting go of its prey."

He smiles and gets a faraway look. "Dad used to feed the crows. It drove Mum nuts. Peanut shells all over the place and seagull shit." He smiles, studying his fingernails. "A few years before he died, one landed outside the window, a crow. It started pecking at the glass. It kept saying open it, open it, open it." He looks at her, maybe measuring her response. "I had to leave the room to get away from it."

"You didn't...open the window?"

He considers her question. "Those kinds of windows don't open."

"Oh." He was in the hospital.

"It's supposed to signal death, a wild bird flying into your house," Tom says.

"I've never heard that."

"It kept showing up." And then Martin died.

"Did you talk to it, tell it to go away?"

"Yes, it said it would stop when the window was open."

"Maybe it wanted you to come out?"

"Yes. Or to come in."

It's only a glimpse into his world. "Is it always like that?"

"Like the bird?" He squints up at the ceiling. "No. Sometimes, it's like rustling leaves. Like whispers. A bunch of them at first and then one takes over. It'll sound like someone I know, like they are right there." He holds his palm up to his ear. "What if someone walked in here right now—like Daniel—and told you I'm not here at all, that you'd been sitting here talking to a ghost? And what if you didn't know which one of them was real?"

She could tell him things of her own, but she shakes her head, *I don't know.* Since seeing the face in the water, she's avoided reflections at night. They sit in silence for what feels like a long time, listening to jazz and the soft yips of Hoover running in his dreamworld.

Emily manages a smile. "More tea?" She rubs at the goosebumps on her arms.

"Nah. I think I'm heading off to bed. They might discharge her in the morning, so I want to be there early."

"We can take you."

"No, I'll take Mum's car. It's okay, I do drive. Not much. But I'm fine."

"It's okay, I really don't mind." She'll have to beat him to the car in the morning, make an excuse about having to run some errand near the hospital. But there's no way he's driving on her watch.

⌣⟶

Doris arrives in the afternoon. She eases herself into the chair at the end of the bed and takes a minute to compose herself before launching in.

"You have to stop this habit of suffering in silence," she says, dabbing at the sweat forming on her brow with a limp tissue. "You should have told me. I could have diagnosed you myself. My mother-in-law had it. Will you have to keep the tank?"

She's referring to the oxygen tank. She interprets Linda's blink for a no and doesn't give her time to say anything more.

"Good thing. That would really keep you housebound. Once she had that, she hardly went anywhere but out to see the doc. What a life. She used to remind me of a goldfish in a bowl." Doris simulates the opening and closing of a fish's mouth. "Course she didn't give up the smokes till the bitter end." She takes a moment to look around the room. All of the beds are empty. Linda's neighbour has shuffled down to the lounge for a change of scenery. "What about Tom? You want me to look in on him?"

Linda shakes her head, no. Maybe a little too quickly. "Emily's next door."

"With the little boy?"

"Yes, they were in this morning. The nurses thought he was my grandson." And no one corrected them.

"Have you told her what he's like when he's psycho?"

"A psychosis—"

"You know what I mean. You told me yourself. He pretends very well—"

"He would never hurt them."

Doris presses her lips together.

"I didn't say that. But you don't know what he'll do, Linda. That time he just walked straight into the waves in January. Good thing someone saw him. And he nearly took the man down with him." She crosses herself, a grating habit of hers.

"He's all right. He's at work right now, and Brad's back from his trip tonight so he'll check in with me."

"Well, I'm here."

Daniel sits on the bed while Emily slathers moisturizer on her face.

"So how was he on the boat...really?" she says.

In front of Ryan, he'd boasted how good he was for his first time out. She had to work a shift at the library while they went out for their first sail.

"Into everything: ropes, wiring, winch handles, fenders...." He's tapping off each one on the fingers of his left hand.

"And Jim?"

"I don't think he has kids on board much anymore."

She climbs under the covers and props a pillow up behind her.

"How did it go when the boat started to heel?"

"Oh, he loved that. I had to grab onto his lifejacket because he wanted to hang over the low rail."

"Jesus."

"Yeah."

"But it didn't scare him?"

"Hell no. I made him go down below when I could see we were about to hit some wind. It was pretty gusty."

As a child, she'd loved it when the boat heeled; even better if water came over the rails. Up on the bow, she'd dangle a leg over each side and enjoy the spray. When she was a baby, Da rigged up a hammock while they were at anchor so she'd sway from the boom in her nest of blankets. *You'd fall straight to sleep.* Emily's mother wasn't as keen, especially when he'd talk of swinging the boom over the rail—his infant daughter suspended above the water in her nest—to give him some headroom in the cockpit. He said he trusted his knots.

Now she knows what her mother must have felt.

"Maybe he should be tethered when he's in the cockpit."

"Mm. I'm just glad he liked it."

Daniel's pale skin has a bit of colour, freckles show on his nose.

"And how did you do?"

"Jim does most of it. I'm used to newer boats. And of course, he's sailed here for years and I haven't been out in the harbour for…God, it must be almost twenty years."

Before Ryan, they'd split the cost of chartering a boat on the West Coast with Dan's brother. The boats were practically new and maintained meticulously. Most of them had the latest in navigation equipment too, unlike Jim's boat, which still had paper charts. Like a lot of wooden boat owners, he had a disdain for all things modern.

Daniel swings his feet up on the bed and lies back. It sends a puff of fur up around him. He turns his head to Emily, squinting.

"Has Hoover…?"

"He slept up here a couple of times."

Daniel fishes a piece of dog hair off his tongue with his finger.

"Why?" It was Daniel who had put a stop to Hoover sleeping with them.

"I was a little spooked." She tells him about the face reflected in the water.

He removes his glasses and rubs the bridge of his nose before responding. "I'm not sure what you want me to say, Em."

"You don't believe in it."

"I did as a kid. On Halloween. And at Christmas I believed in Santa." She examines her nails. "What you need is a good night's sleep." He stands and stretches. "Mum left a message saying they'd like to come out tomorrow. They haven't seen the house yet. Want me to invite them for supper?"

It's the last thing she wants to do: clean the house, cook…. His parents could have come many times since getting back from their trip, but they chose to wait until he was home. She debates saying this to him but decides against it.

"You barbecue and I'll do a salad."

⌒

When the doctor says her name, it sounds exotic. His eyes are fringed with dark lashes and he apologizes when he says that she must stop with the *cee-garettes*. The usual doctor, her GP, is a jogger and a vegetarian—she knows this because he tells her every time—and he's less tactful with his advice.

"*Leenda?* Your son can get you tomorrow?"

"Yes, thank you."

She watches him go, then turns her eyes to a water stain on the ceiling. She's had many hours to study it. It's like a map of Nova Scotia, with some of the more jagged edges of the coastline rubbed smooth.

As a child, Tom thought the province looked like a thin, cartoon whale with a lake for an eye. Cape Breton was its tail fin. Her childhood was spent in the Valley, head of the whale, and her adulthood in its belly. This was how she and Tom spoke of it. It was a wonderful way to look at the world. He always sought out faces in inanimate objects. Looking back, maybe that was a sign. Or maybe not.

Outside, the leaves on the trees flutter and the light playing across the stain could be ripples of water. He went through a whale stage. Kids do that with dinosaurs and fire trucks. He begged her to find a recording of whale sounds. It was an LP she had to order by mail. They sat in the living room listening; it was like a summer rainstorm, punctuated by guttural sounds. He was transfixed and claimed he understood. Every time she played it, he added to the story the whale told him. Should she have wondered then? No, it was a normal imagination at play. It's pointless to sift through the clues. None of them will change things now.

CHAPTER 10

L uckily, Daniel's father is a fellow wine enthusiast. Not only is he eager to accept a glass upon arrival but he brings along three new bottles: one from Napa and two from a vineyard in BC. Emily and Donald discuss the future of wineries in Canada, including the newer local ones in the Annapolis Valley, while Maggie gets the house tour from Daniel.

The fog rolled out mid-afternoon and they've left the door to the deck open to the breeze. Donald is content to stand out there with Emily, supervising the barbecue and watching the gulls.

She liked him the first time she met him. He's never in a rush to finish a sentence, and he has a permanent look of mischief. She often wonders if that alone contributes to his family's tendency to question his tales from the past, that ever-present smile in his eyes.

Maggie returns from her tour with Ryan on her hip. "Let me see that tummy. Let me see that...ugh. You're so skinny." She pokes at his belly button, eliciting giggles from her grandson.

"I thought you were talking to me," Emily says, hoping for a laugh. But Maggie doesn't take her eyes from Ryan.

"You have to eat all the food on your plate to grow big like Grandpa."

Donald is taller than both his sons. The family has a running banter about the height. Maggie says it's because they didn't heed her advice to eat all of their greens. Donald says it's nothing to do with the vegetables but everything to do with finding the boys sneaking cigarettes when they were adolescents. It came up at every holiday dinner and both boys would claim to remember a different version of events.

More likely, their height was tempered by Maggie's genes, she being a foot shorter than her husband and forever vowing to lose weight. Emily doesn't want to live in a world where her mother-in-law gets thin. At their house it's fresh-baked everything, homemade soups, real butter. In her day, people didn't ask if she *only* stayed home with her children.

"Does he drink his milk?"

Maggie looks at Daniel, but Emily answers. "He loves it, especially the brown kind." Maggie turns her head to Emily, a pinched look on her face. "Chocolate milk," Emily adds.

"I hope he doesn't *just* drink that." She looks at Ryan. "You have to drink the white milk. That's the good stuff for growing strong bones." Ryan sticks his tongue out, so Maggie appeals to Emily. "A dentist was on the radio the other day—so many toddlers are coming in with gum disease."

Donald lifts Emily's glass from her hand. "Now would you like to try that one from the vineyard in Osoyoos?"

"That would be great." She smiles, even though it would probably be better to have some food in her belly first. Relieving her of the glass, he gives his wife a wink and her face softens. After forty years, he still flirts.

"I got it as a special treat for today," Emily says to Maggie. "He promised he'd try a little bit of steak if he could have it with the chocolate milk."

JUST AS THEY'RE enjoying dessert she sees the raven. She's next to Ryan in the chair that faces the windows. Maggie is on about a little town they're considering, just north of the city of Nanaimo. The bird glides past, followed by the other. She puts her spoon down and heads for the windows, without excusing herself.

Daniel clears his throat. "What is it?"

"Ravens."

The pair sits on that same branch of the tree. She scans the back-yard and sees the cat walking the fenceline but on the outside edge; perhaps it's his way of sneaking up on the birds.

Ryan explains. "They hit Bert."

Emily watches, curious to see what they'll do.

"Hit who?" says Donald.

"Bert the cat." The rest of Ryan's story must consist of arm gestures accompanied by whooshing sound effects. Reluctantly, she turns her head and tells the story.

Daniel gets up to see for himself. "Where are they?"

She points to the tree, but they're gone.

"Huh, I don't see them," he says and heads back to the table. There's no sign of the birds or the cat.

Daniel tells them about Jim's boat. Tomorrow is to be their first time out, the whole famly. Emily's wine glass is full again. It's hard to work out how many it has been. Every time she takes a few sips, Donald tops her up. She touches the back of her hand to her cheek and feels the heat.

The McNallys never owned a boat, but they had a friend with a forty-foot ketch who took them out during the summer.

"We took turns in the galley," Donald tells Ryan. "Now, do you know what a galley is?" Ryan stares at his grandfather. "It's a kitchen on a boat."

"Galley," Ryan repeats.

"Anyway. I'm not the cook at home. But on a boat, everybody does their part and the captain said I had to cook a big fish that night." He holds up his arms to their full length. "It was huge, Ryan. I didn't know how I'd squash it into the oven. But worse than that was I'd no idea, none at all, about how to cook a fish. A little salt and pepper in the pan, that's all I'd ever done before this. And well, I'd said something about Gran's hair that morning and she said she'd not help me with the cooking."

Ryan seizes his moment and points at Emily's hair, which has reacted badly to the humidity today.

"Your mummy has beautiful curls, just like Gran." He gives Ryan a wink.

"Bee-yoo-ti-full."

"Right. And unless you know how to cook a fish the size of a dinosaur, you remember to tell her that."

Daniel lets out an exaggerated yawn.

"So, I looked at what we had and I saw salad dressing and a lot of rum." Maggie clears her throat. "Right. Anyway. You should have seen the beautiful job I did." Donald mimes the whole procedure. "Then I go to put it in the oven, and you know what? It won't fit. But it was my job, you see? So, I squashed the fish a wee bit. Like this." He takes his napkin and squashes it under his dessert bowl. "And I rammed it in the oven and shut the door before it could come back out. It was thirsty work, so I sat down and had a drink. Did I mention that we were still sailing? I could hear your dad up on deck working the winch to tack the main. That was his job. Anyway, in a boat, the oven is a little different than at home. It has to be able to move. It swings so that when the boat heels, the oven leans too. But when you're anchored, you can stop it from swinging around by putting across a little bolt. Well, I guess I'd been so busy with the problem of the big fish that I'd forgotten all about that. So, I'm looking out the porthole beside me and I see that we're starting to heel, just a nice gentle tilt. The water is getting closer to my window and that's when I think of it. But it's too late. Can you guess what happened?" Ryan's mouth gapes. "Well, the oven door let out a slow creak and...out came the fish. It shot across to the port side and straight into the open door of the head. That's the bathroom on a boat." Emily always covers her mouth with her hand at this part of the story. "You know what? I figure the fish was bound and determined to get back to the sea because it landed headfirst in the toilet. Probably trying to fit down the little hole back out to the ocean."

Ryan giggles. Did it swim back to the ocean through that little hole? What did they eat for supper?

Daniel clears the plates and Maggie rolls up her sleeves to get a start on the dishes. She shakes her head at Daniel as they head to the sink. "Ugh, your father and that story...."

"It was the best supper we had on the cruise." Another old refrain. "Straight to dessert for us, and the gulls got to have the fish."

Emily remains at the table, she doesn't share the McNally compulsion for leaping up to wash all of the dishes. Twirling the red liquid in her glass, she thinks how delicious it would be to go straight to bed, or to run the tub and just climb in herself, let the rest of them take care of things.

"Em? Em?"

"Hm?" How long has Daniel been talking to her?

"Where does this go?"

"Oh, top cupboard on the left." She ignores his look of annoyance. If he wants her to do dishes yet again, he can ask. Even her ears feel warm now, the flush has probably spread downwards from her neck too. It will be hard to read to Ryan at bedtime.

"Might as well finish this one off too," she hears Donald say, upending the bottle.

The knock on the door seems far away. Maggie answers, the dish-towel still in her hand. She must have spied Tom coming to the door from her spot at the kitchen sink. There's an exchange of names and fleeting smiles. Emily watches Maggie step back from Tom and send Donald a look.

What's that about?

Ryan leaps from his chair and barrels toward the door, ignoring Daniel's appeal to slow down. Tom scoops him up and plants a raspberry on his cheek. It's a good one, the sound cracks off the ceiling and walls. It's followed by a beat of silence that pulsates in her ears. Donald drapes an arm over his wife's shoulder and clears his throat.

Maybe we should have put on some dinner music.

"Bert was out back a few minutes ago," Daniel says, with his hand on the knob, opening the door a little wider.

"I'll come out with you." Emily stands and her chair scrapes against the floor. All heads turn and she feels her cheeks reach a new level of heat. "Let Hoover out for a pee." She concentrates on the dog. He's in his alert-sleeping pose, soggy lips draped over his paws. The excitement of having visitors has kept him awake for most of the day and now he's spent. "C'mon, Hoover." She puts a toe under his bum and gives him a little nudge.

Outside, Tom apologizes.

"Pffft." She waves at him.

He has a good look at her and a smile spreads across his face.

"What?" she says. It's the biggest smile she's ever seen on him.

"You're drunk."

"My father-in-law is a very tall man and he pours the wine according to his own—standards."

"Nice to see you so relaxed." It is nice.

There's a rap on the window. Ryan has been told to stay back. He squashes his face to the glass until Maggie peels him off.

"Christ. I still have to go back in there and bathe him." The wine seems to have taken full effect on standing.

They wander to the back of the house, Tom calling the cat. Hoover jogs ahead to the solitary tree in the side yard. He lifts his leg and Emily looks into the branches for signs of the ravens.

"You guys planning on leaving that tree up?"

"It's the only one we have. Why?" He shrugs looking up at it. A few branches have sprouted leaves, but most of it is barren.

"We'll burn that bridge when we come to it," she says.

The yard would have nothing without it, just a patch of grass reluctantly clinging to dry earth. On either side of the lawn the vegetation is scrubby, wispy native grasses and spiky things that cut bare legs. It's hard to say if the shrub near the tilting gate was planted there. Maybe it was one of the few green things allowed to stay when the lot was cleared for the house.

"He was right there a few minutes ago." She watches the wind push the gate against its restraint of twine.

"Jesus," Tom says, surveying the feathers on the ground. It seems that this is where Bert takes his prey.

"God knows how much happens when we're not around." She gestures vaguely behind her at the house. Today, it's like a massive mirror.

"Oh." He leans against the swaying fence, his eyes on the beach below.

"Get back," she says a little too sharply.

"I think I see him." He casts his eyes down at the rocks, inviting her to look.

"Down there?" It doesn't look like he landed on his feet. "Think he's okay?"

"I can't tell from here." He lifts a leg over the fence.

"No!" Is everything moving or is it the wine? She can't seem to modulate her volume. "I mean, it's all eroded…."

"I've done it before."

"What's going on?" Daniel's voice calls from the deck.

She doesn't want to lose sight of Tom.

"Emily?" Daniel must think she can't hear him. She turns and shouts, explaining about the cat. Tom has disappeared from view. He's already made it to the bottom. Leaning over, she spots him cradling the limp cat in his arms. He tilts his head up to her, frowning.

"Feel for a heartbeat."

He shakes his head, the small body clutched to his chest. She can't make out his words. Turning, he walks toward the water. On the deck they've made themselves comfortable, settling onto the patio chairs. Donald appears with another bottle.

Tom stops at the edge of the water, allowing the bigger waves to lick at the toes of his shoes. His mouth moves as if he's in deep conversation with someone beside him. Much further down the beach, there's a couple and a dog. They're too far for him to be talking to them. Is he talking to the cat? Something feels off. There's a prickle at the back of her neck.

Unwinding the twine from the gatepost, she scans the cliff and picks out the line he took. The wine softens her fear. No one protests as she finds her first foothold, but she doesn't look up to find out. It's okay when she is moving, though it crumbles under her fingertips. Only once does she dare to look below. It's best to focus on her holds, inching down until one foot finds the ground.

Tom is up to his knees in the water, still talking. The wind snatches away his words.

"Tom." He doesn't respond even though she's nearly shouting. She pulls off her shoes and rolls her pants up. The water is shocking against the heat of her skin, but she wades out through seaweed to stand beside him, still undetected. Putting a hand on his shoulder, she waits for him to acknowledge it. He's very still. When he does turn to her, his eyes are focused somewhere else.

"Come on," she says. There is a smear of blood on his arm; Bert's tongue hangs out, eyes open.

He looks down at the cat, and seems to remember that he is holding him. "He wants him," he says, tilting his chin at the waves.

Who is he?

Tom bends his knees and lowers Bert to the water.

"No! Tom, we can't do that. Here." She grabs for the cat, shivering at the lifeless sag of his body against her.

"Tom, we have to go. Come on." He hugs his elbows and watches the next wave coming for them. His height keeps the water just below his knees, but she can feel it inching up her thighs. Yet, she can't walk away from him. Can't leave him on his own. She repeats his name over the sound of the waves. She waits for him to turn, her bladder shrinking with the cold.

"Tom. We have to go."

She's trying to transfer the weight of the cat to one arm to reach out to him when he whirls around and splashes back to the sand. Her journey is less steady, with bare feet on the stones. Once there, she struggles to get her shoes on. His eyes look focused now and he waits while she hops on one leg to get a dripping, sand-covered foot lodged into her shoe.

They don't try to climb the cliff. They head toward the lane like it had been their plan all along. It will be a long walk up that hill. Her bladder feels bruised as she tries to walk without bouncing. The warm buzz of alcohol is now a budding headache, and the taste of grapes is acidic on her tongue. She wonders if it would be okay to squat in the long grass once they reach the lane.

"I'll call the vet when we get back."

"The vet?"

"You know, for burial...or cremation," she says.

Tom stops. They've reached the opening in the grass that leads to the lane. "Can't we...?"

Emily stares. "Bury him?"

"I guess."

Surely, he didn't mean cremation. She moves ahead of him to the path. Maybe she'll spot a place to pee in the grass, she's beyond caring about privacy, but there's a car there with its engine turned off. She wills it to drive away. But it's a familiar colour. Moving forward she makes out Daniel at the wheel. His face reveals nothing as she approaches. There's a mechanical pop and the trunk rises with a hiss. Bending at the waist, she nestles the sodden body amongst plastic beach toys and spare grocery bags before opening the car door for Tom.

They drive up the hill a little faster than usual. No chatting, no seat belts.

In the morning, there's a small grave in Linda's backyard. She stands at the window with her coffee. There were no tears for Bert, just a void. His bowl is still in the kitchen, half the food gone, a water bowl with a skim of dust, his scratch marks on the sofa punctuated by a few tufts of ginger fur. It will take time for her habits to go away: checking for him at bedtime, blocking doorways to hinder his escapes.

More unsettling than his departure is the location of his death and Tom's casual knowledge of how Bert fell. He told her all of it in a jumble, and it took her several minutes to realize that he hadn't actually *seen* it happen. He kept combing his fingers through his hair until it stood up in three ragged rows.

Quietly, she asked if he'd remembered his medication, trying for a casual tone. Yes, Emily had seen him. But that was days ago, and even while he said yes, his head moved faintly back and forth as if his body wanted her to know the truth. He retrieved the bottle of pills and showed her the contents, like she had been counting them, like she's one of those math whizzes who could tell at a glance, eighteen.

There's a snap out in the kitchen and she thinks it's the cat crunching his food. Only for a moment. Maybe it was an appliance cooling off. How many other house sounds did she attribute to Bert? It was like that with Martin too. One morning, three weeks after his death, she was coming downstairs, the staleness of sleep in her mouth, still half in a dream where he was still alive. She'd begun to live their marriage in reverse. That night she was back to their tenth anniversary.

She was almost down the stairs—her hand on the railing, luckily—when she registered the rythmic squeak. It was the La-Z-Boy in the corner, swivelled to face the wall, rocking slowly. Martin's thinking chair. That's what Tom called it as a small child. She stopped breathing on the inhale, her chest holding the air while her ears and eyes did their work. But it continued its slow sway, back and forth, a thin squeak with each gentle tip. No one in it, no one in the house, Tom was in the hospital. She was not dreaming, the varnished handrail solid in her hand, a crumb embedded in the carpet poking at the sole of one foot. Her mind empathizing with Tom? Or some other thing. She almost said his name, when the chair jolted forward, triggering a scream. Bert landed on the carpet, took a few steps, then sat with his tail curled tidily around his front paws; a furry fence between them. He regarded her with hooded eyes before picking up one paw and licking it, unmoved by her shriek.

He liked to clean himself at the foot of her bed in the middle of the night. The jiggling springs would force her eyes open to see him with one hind leg in the air like an antenna. "Arsehole," she'd mutter, her blood still speeding around her body.

She raises her mug to her lips. The grave is in a good spot to plant something. A fruit-bearing tree maybe. Something to nourish the feathered creatures he tormented in life while his food—with its essential fatty acids, vitamins, and minerals—sat untouched. Raising her mug to the window, she says, "To you, Bert, darncat. I'll miss you anyway."

Ryan wears swim goggles as he attempts to peel an orange. It's the closest he can get to matching Mum's sunglasses. She could do it for him, but this will keep him busy and there's a mop if Hoover's efforts below the table aren't sufficient. Behind the sunglasses, she can close her eyes without being asked if she is sleeping.

Last night, she'd come downstairs for a glass of water and saw Tom heading to the backyard with a shovel. It was almost two in the morning. She nearly picked up the phone to call Linda. But it could wait.

When she was seven the family dog had died. Da came home with the retriever in his arms, tears streaking his cheeks. He dug Sam's grave in the backyard and had a miniature wake for his best friend. She stood beside him with a glass of ginger ale. Sam used to let her dress him up in coats and hats for silly pictures, the perfect little brother. Da allowed her to hug him once more, stretching herself on the grass beside him, burying her nose in his matted fur before he'd gently tapped her on the back to say it was time.

Afterward, she stayed home from school for a few days. Her parents argued about it when they thought she was asleep. Mum thought the teachers wouldn't respect such an excuse. But Charlie said grief needed time, even for dogs, *especially for dogs*.

The spray of the orange brings her back to the table. She opens her eyes to a drop sliding down the lens of her sunglasses. Ryan has most of the peel off and is double-fisted, eating the orange like an apple, juice running down his arms.

"Good job. Tasty?" The orange bobs up and down in reply. "Good thing you have those goggles on."

She heads for the sink to deal with the sticky glasses. Daniel pops his head in the front door and calls out, "Ready? Jim said he'd meet us at the marina at ten."

"Just give us a few." When they'd said today, she hadn't imagined the hangover from Donald's wine and three hours of light sleep. Daniel seems vibrant today—louder, brighter, faster than usual.

"Okay," she says, smiling at her son's sticky orange face, "let's get you cleaned up."

⌒

Linda finishes up the dishes. Tom is usually up before noon, but even the smell of lunch didn't bring him downstairs. His muddy shoes are next to the back door. She's left them for now, he can clean up after himself.

Maybe he had trouble sleeping. His door isn't latched; it creaks open, revealing the empty bed. The sheets are rumpled but he's not known for making his bed. A pair of jeans are on the floor—underwear still inside, lovely. Her eyes stop at the desk where his wallet and keys sit. "Tom?" she calls out to the house. The effort makes her lungs tickle.

He's here somewhere. But she'd have seen him on the main floor. She checks every room anyway, finds herself looking under beds and in closets. In the basement, nothing. Outside in the shed. No. "Tom?" louder this time. The doctor's voice comes to her—*slow, even breaths, especially if you feel anxious.* She does this from her seat on the porch, allowing her eyes to continue the search.

⌒

The perk of all the business trips is that the office has given Daniel a few days off. He must have packed their lunch last night while she was reclining with a warm cloth on her forehead. The white wine is to blame. Red never does this. Only one of the bottles was white, but still, she knows it's the culprit.

Daniel glances over and begins to whistle a tune. A few more bends in the road and they'll be there. Every high note seems to intensify the brightness of the light seeping through her sunglasses.

"You take something?"

"A lot of ibuprofen. It'll pass."

Ryan is fiddling with an old cellphone, a gift from his grandfather. The battery was removed, but that doesn't dull the usefulness of something with so many buttons.

Daniel fills her in on the marine forecast. "It should die down mid-afternoon and give us a steady breeze."

Jim meets them at the car.

"Awfully sorry. The mother-in-law has a plumbing emergency. Duty calls." He holds out a small key to them and rest his elbows on Emily's window. "Still, you two could take her out or just sit in the cockpit and have a picnic. I hate to put a damper on things." His eyes drift to the back seat.

They debate it without getting out of the car, while Jim climbs into his truck and pulls away.

"The rest of the week is supposed to be rainy," Daniel says, drumming his fingers on the steering wheel. It's agreed, at the very least, they'll hang out and have a snack.

Climbing out, she's greeted by the music of a boatyard—wind thwacking metal clips against masts, creaking docks rising and falling with the waves. The bumps and squeaks and crying gulls.

Ryan skips ahead, his lifejacket strapped over shorts and a T-shirt. She and Daniel follow behind with a bag each.

"You brought some warmer layers?" She's done none of the preparation and suddenly remembers that time they went swimming and Daniel didn't bring towels.

"In the bag you're carrying."

The wood of the cockpit is a rich, reddish brown. It gleams in the sun. Emily pulls off her sandals and steps in with bare feet. Jim must have known they'd say yes; the hatch to the cabin has been left off. Down below, there's the glint of brass. She bends down and drops the duffle bag onto the quarter berth. It looks as if it sleeps about four, if a table is shifted out of the way and the people don't mind being cozy. In the cabin adults would need to move about in a stooped position, but it has a little stove for cooking and a head with sink and toilet.

"It's his baby," Daniel says, handing her a bag.

"Sure is." She lowers herself into the cabin and breathes it in. There's nothing like sleeping on a boat, the rocking, the slap of water just beyond your ear. She pulls things from the bag: her own lifejacket, a set of binoculars, a small camera.

Above deck they've opened a package of crackers. She joins them and attempts to sweep the errant crumbs into the water as they spill from Ryan's mouth. People bump coolers along the wooden slips and call hello. One passerby doesn't leave; he climbs into the cockpit and perches on the rail. "Bob's the name." He grins. "Mine's just down that way. The Boston whaler." He's known Jim for too many years to count. He's adamant that they take the boat out. "Too nice a day to be stuck here." He seems to be talking directly to Jim's boat. The conversation quickly evolves into Bob questioning Dan's virility.

"Jim had his little ones out every summer. Good for kids to be out on the water." He seems to size up Ryan with his pale hair and skin. "Here, I'll show you how to start the motor...."

Daniel humours him for too long. And that is how they find themselves chugging out into the harbour.

"Did we actually decide to come out?" Emily says.

"I'm not sure." They can still make out the figure of Bob on the wharf. "You know, that's not the first time I've met him. I kept waiting for him to remember me."

She picks up the binoculars and points them at the shore. Bob's waving at them, a bottle in one hand. It must have been stowed in his jacket the whole time.

"I don't think he's a details guy." She lifts a hand and waves back.

"I just wanted to get going before he taught Ryan any more words."

"Where are we heading?"

The water is deep blue, silky, flat.

"I don't know. Out in the harbour, maybe around the island?"

⌒

He isn't far off. God knows how long he's been there. The McNallys must have driven away this morning without glimpsing him in the long grass beside their house. *Small mercies.* The wind lifts the hem of her shirt, chilling her spine as she coaxes him to stand. It's not the first time he's found his way to the base of that tree.

He's nude and filthy with his legs crossed like a yogi. The scratches on his skin are already scabbed over. His hands clutch the grass so that his arms are held out from his sides like Jesus on the cross. Tears spring to her eyes. She can't help it. And the foul smell, what terror makes a person do that? He goes back to the house with her, even allowing her to get him in the shower and rinse off the worst of it. But he refuses to get dressed or even dry off. He bats away the bottle of pills, his eyes wide, like it's alive and venomous. It rolls behind the toilet, the pills rattling within like a maraca.

He paces the house, his skin a landscape of tiny bumps. He wants to leave. She stands with her back against the front door, afraid he'll push her out of the way or simply leave by a window or the back door, but some part of his mind keeps him from it. She listens in on half of a conversation, most of which he responds to with *no*. Sometimes it's low and pleading, sometimes a shout.

If she has to guess, it is the water that calls to him. Even inside the house his ear turns in that direction: the whisper of waves right through layers of drywall and wood.

There's no question of driving him there herself. They have to come here and sedate him first. It's agony to watch.

SHE IS PROPPED up in the waiting room, her inhaler held in her right hand in the absence of a cigarette. He insisted he hadn't skipped meds and there was no point in arguing it, these lapses can happen even when he follows the regime.

Two years into it Martin said the unthinkable. "We might have to let him go."

They'd been talking for an hour. It was past time for sleep. Tom was in the hospital. This time, he'd left in the early hours of morning without his wetsuit. It was early March. Another surfer spotted him. A stranger out to assess the waves before deciding his plans for the day.

Martin's words had come after a long silence, shattering her own thoughts. She'd stared at his mouth.

"What do you mean?"

"I mean, we can't save him from himself, Lin. We can't watch him every minute of every day."

It was the kind of thing she'd expect from someone else, an acquaintance or a politician. Someone looking at the numbers only.

"I know that. But what does *let him go* mean?"

As if Martin had been an easy man to live with for the past ten years, slipping past his family like a fish, always just out of reach.

"He's not the same person. It's taking him somewhere else. You heard the doctor. It's not something he'll recover from."

What she'd heard was that he might have a chance of leading a normal life with the right support.

"I read about this woman who was much worse than him, and she still finished university and became a professor. She does public speaking now."

But Martin was moving his head side to side. "We don't know when he'll do it again. Or something worse. What if one of his hallucinations is that we are the enemy?"

"That won't happen."

"He doesn't even believe that he's sick."

"That's not unusual. Once he's stabilized…."

"And when will that be?"

She rubbed her forehead. When she took her hands away, his face had changed, maybe realizing how harsh he'd sounded.

"I think we need to prepare ourselves. He might get worse. At best, he may spend a lot of his life in hospital."

"And at worst?" Her voice was shaking.

"You know the worst."

Martin's face was filled with lines. His hair had leached of colour in the past two years. Both of them had lost their appetites, and she could see the hollow below his cheekbones in the dimness of the living room.

"Let's go for a smoke. Look at the stars." They'd shuffled outside and sat in silence, Martin making smoke rings while Linda tried to imagine Tom married, coming home to visit with kids in tow. But it fizzled out like the rings of smoke.

⌣

"You sure he has one?" She's rifling through a shallow drawer down below.

Daniel's at the tiller. "Pretty sure."

Finally, she locates it under one of the berths. Jim had used the cushion to keep the charts flat. A familiar smell puffs out as she drops it back in place—what Da called the *yarr* smell. It makes her smile. She smoothes out the paper on the navigation table. Chances are, Jim hasn't had to check it in years, but she spots a few faded pencil marks where he must have taken a fix.

"Da never bothered with charts," she says, taking a seat in the cockpit.

Daniel says nothing, looking up at the mainsail.

"We going under the bridge?" she asks. Daniel is pointing them toward the Basin.

"No, I think I'll turn around in a minute."

Behind them the ferry chugs its way into the terminal, tourists pose for photos on the top deck with the city skyline. It's past rush hour on a weekday morning, but the harbour buzzes with life. Three lanes of traffic inch across the nearest bridge. What must it have been like before all of this was in place? She tries to picture it without two bridges and both ferries doing their work. If memory serves, it's a mile across at this narrow section. A crossing done by rowboat would have taken ages.

Ryan sits next to Daniel, his fingers working underneath one of the ropes wrapped around the mainsail's winch.

"Whoa! Ryan, don't play with that." The line is under a big load where they adjust the tension for the sail or *the gas pedal*, as she'd been taught. Her voice startles him and he jumps back, hitting his elbow. It's better than what would happen to the delicate bones of his fingers if he tried that while it was moving. He lets out a volley of high-pitched cries. Her fading headache returns.

"Almost ready? It'll be a jibe," Daniel says as if he's heard none of the exchange. The bridge supports loom ahead.

She shoos Ryan out of the way, toward the cabin door. A jibe can happen very suddenly with the boom swinging across the cockpit. As a girl, she confused the word with the jive. Da laughed and said that quick steps were needed for both.

"You got it?" he asks, leaning around her to see the bow. It's her job to handle the lines while he guides the boat around at just the right pace. "Coming about," he calls.

The sail goes from taut and wind-filled to a flapping chaos. She lets the port side go slack and scrambles to pull in the line on the starboard, bumping the handle of the tiller in the process.

"Watch out," Daniel shouts over the wind. She ducks just in time as the boom swings over, nearly connecting with her head.

Then they're sailing along in the opposite direction, heading for the mouth of the harbour. Ryan is sniffling. She scoots up next to him and pats his shoulder. It was a clumsy jibe.

"You came around too fast." She tosses the words over her shoulder.

"You're not used to this boat," he counters. He's no expert either; he's only been out with Jim a handful of times.

There's not a lot of manoeuvring room here, and Daniel has to sail close to the wind to avoid other vessels heading toward them. The boat starts to heel. Ryan wipes his nose and goes quiet. There's a smooth seat running from one side of the cockpit to the other. He straightens his legs under him so that he can slide toward the low side. She doesn't stop him right away. It's good to see him cheering up. Then a gust pushes them sideways and he slips too fast. His feet connect with the low side of the cockpit. His upper body pitches forward just as she catches the handle on his lifejacket and steadies him, glancing sideways at Daniel.

"Almost out of this bit," Daniel says, eyeing the water ahead.

But they tip another five degrees. She puts her left hand on Ryan's waist. He giggles and she braces her feet until she feels them straightening up again. She takes a deep breath and pushes it back out.

"You all right?"

"Think so." She swallows a lump in her throat. Not once was she seasick as a child. *Sailboats are supposed to heel.*

"Maybe it's because you were down below."

It was only while she was searching for the chart. "I'll be fine." There's a strange sensation in her arms, the slightest tremble, like when she's waited too long to eat lunch. "White wine."

"You and Dad polished off every bottle last night."

"Didn't you have some?"

"Half a glass. Mum didn't have any."

"I get the feeling she doesn't approve of me having any either."

"I don't think it was that." He gives her a look and leaves her to toss it around her in her head. *What, then?*

"Look, Ry." Daniel points ahead of them. There's a container ship making its way into the harbour, two tugboats nearby, fish swimming alongside the bulk of a whale. The shipping containers resemble Ryan's plastic blocks at home. "Cool, eh?" Emily steadies him as he stands on the seat to get a better view.

"You worried about him?" Daniel asks.

"No, I have him."

"Not *him*."

She turns and tries to read his face. Does he want to talk about this now? She shrugs.

"Linda's home. But he seemed…off."

Daniel is looking up at the mast. "Lost our wind."

Ahead of them the ship is growing larger.

Emily looks at the water in front of them. It's rippling.

"Here we go." It's like they're in a toy boat and an invisible hand puts the flat of its palm on the mast and shoves. But she's ready this time, gripping Ryan around the waist before he can skate sideways.

"Looks like it'll ease off in the lee of the island," Daniel calls, watching her face. She swallows hard. Her body is betraying her. *Deep breaths, look at the horizon.* They pop back up.

"You take the tiller? I'll start the motor before we get too close to that beast."

The tugs are close enough now that they can read some of the numbers on the sides. She arranges herself and Ryan on the seat at the stern while Dan hangs over the edge to swing the outboard down into the water.

"Jim hardly uses this when we're out."

"We didn't even have a motor on *Knotty Girl*. Da would sail right up to the mooring, or the dock when we'd sail to the pub."

"Course he did." At least that's what she thinks she hears, since his head is turned away.

"What's that?"

"Watch yourself, I have to give this a few good yanks."

There's not much room to get out of each other's way, with all three of them squashed in the stern. She leans as far away as she can with Ryan snugged between her knees.

Daniel pulls back the cord once, twice, three times. Nothing. He doesn't look at her. There is sweat forming at his hairline. Again. Five pulls. No life from the motor. He glances behind him at the ship. "Keep us pointed toward McNabs."

"I'm trying. But you were right about the wind." The telltales on the mainsail hang vertical. Without wind, they don't have much steerage. They seem to be drifting sideways like the container ship has its own field of gravity. "We have fuel?" she asks.

"Yes, we have fuel."

"Is it in the right position? The lever?" she asks, having never started an outboard. The charter boats out west had engines built in, and they worked with a twist of a key.

"Yes," he says, trying again. His lips pulled between his teeth. Nothing. He stops and squints up at the mast like he's willing the wind to come back.

"What did you do when you were becalmed on your dad's boat?"

"I think we had oars on-board...."

Daniel swivels around and pulls up one of the cockpit seats. When he straightens up he has a paddle in his hand.

"Better than nothing."

It doesn't look long enough, like it's meant for a dinghy. She keeps them pointed ahead while he splashes at the water. The ship lets out a deep, bone-rattling blast. Ryan responds by clinging to her and knocking her glasses askew. Her mouth has gone dry. The closer it gets, the more it looks like a tall building drifting through the water on its side. The deck is far above them, and above that still are the stacks of steel boxes.

"Dammit, Daniel, drop the paddle. We have to get the motor started."

⌣⌐

It takes fifteen minutes for Linda to walk to the closest convenience store from the hospital. It's not that far, but her pace isn't what it once was.

"Players? Pack of mints too." She counts out the bills.

She could have driven, but she'd told herself it was a walk. Lying to yourself is just another part of it. Now Martin, he didn't even pretend to want it: *quitting's for quitters*. At one point, he'd cut back, mostly because the price went up. It was just who he was. He decided he was a smoker like a minor character in a movie: the credits roll, *Smoker at Bar*.

Funny how we let things slide. If only life were like a movie, the solutions would have been tidy. In life, there are years of buildup, guilt over things said that can't be unsaid. And with Martin, there was the foggy expanse of his early life. He lost his mother when he was small.

He wasn't sure of the year, only that he was walking because he had one vivid memory of toddling toward her with his arms outstretched. Her gums showed when she smiled.

His father died a few years after. The obituary was brief, it's still tucked in an old Bible in the attic. A farming accident, kicked by a horse. It said Martin walked to the neighbour's house for help. But he was never able to access that memory. God knows she asked. Every time they were near a horse, she'd search his face. It always seemed odd, that he'd remember his mother but not his father who was in his life longer. It was as if it happened to someone else, he said. There was nothing but a blank from before, except for the glimmers he had of his mother. After, he was put into the system. No one wanted to adopt an older boy. *Put into the system*, it always made her think of a digestive tract: Martin, swallowed, travelling through twisting tubes until he was crapped out the other side.

She doesn't wander far from the store before lighting up. Things are changing in the world. She can see the looks smokers get now. It's not like when she started. It was almost glamorous then. After two drags, she crushes it under her heel and pulls the puffer from her pocket.

She'd met Martin while on her break at the diner. He was in his twenties. She was in her teens, having cigarettes on the sly, hoping Father wouldn't find out. She was leaning against the wall out back, still wearing her nametag, when he swaggered through, a pack rolled up in his sleeve. Even then, he had a little line on one side of his mouth when he asked if she had a light. Would they have met without that match? He made her laugh right from the outset. None of the boys had done that. With them, it was all pink, sweaty skin and nervous fumbling, while Martin knew things. He wasn't shy of silence either. It didn't put her off. *Still waters run deep*, her mother used to say.

Even though he was still an apprentice carpenter, he had plans to build his own house. It had to be near the water, not hemmed in by trees. Until then, she'd never thought of living anywhere but the Valley, where life went from growing season to growing season. Her parents watched the sky with caution, what it might or, just as bad, might not bring for them each year. But Martin looked up and talked of the future, of getting in his truck and driving as far south as he could. Why not?

You don't just fall in love with another person, you fall for the way they see you, the reflection. That's what he did, blowing his smoke rings and smiling; she liked who she was in his eyes. It felt as if she'd been holding her breath all her life and he taught her how to let it out.

An ambulance screeches past and turns into the hospital ahead. Christ, still five more blocks to go.

⌒

Another blast from the ship jolts them. It seems to go on for several minutes, though it's only seconds. Ryan slithers up and buries his wet face in her hair. Is it meant for them?

"We know," Daniel yells at the ship.

"The fuel tank, check it again." Emily is focused on the outboard, running her hand over it in hopes of seeing something obvious. A large red button reading *on* would be perfect.

Daniel's mouth hangs open.

"Yes. The lid." He's down on his knees unscrewing the black cap on the tank. "It needs to vent."

He tries it again. It takes a few pulls but the motor sputters to life this time. They start to inch away from the ship. Emily points them towards the island, taking deep breaths. The smell of fuel fills the cockpit and her stomach clenches.

Daniel collapses on the seat. "Totally forgot I'd closed that. Remember, Bob was on about how Jim hates to have the smell of gas in here?" She nods. He had a lot of advice. "It's him that opens and closes it usually. Stupid." He's muttering to himself. The ship is now at their stern, but it casts a shadow across them.

"I COULD GET the foresail set up while the wind is quiet," he says.

"How far do you want to go?" They still haven't agreed on their course.

"Out beyond the island? We'll have the wind behind us on the way back." That point of sail makes for less heeling.

It would be nice to be home right now with a warm mug in her hand, but she doesn't say it. This was what she'd pined for all winter. The stomach will settle if she keeps her eyes on the horizon. Ryan edges in a little tighter under her chin.

"You okay, Ryan?" Every hair on his arm is standing up. "Cold? Dan, can you get him a jacket or something?" He's still in clothes meant for on shore. Kids don't seem to register these simple needs. Instead, they twine themselves around something warm and whine. Daniel is in the cabin wrestling a sail bag out through a hatch. He grabs their duffle bag and tosses it to her.

"Okay, Ryan. Let's find you something warm." Unzipping the bag, she moves around the contents with one hand.

"Where are we going?" Daniel shouts at her from the bow. He's clipping the foresail to the front stay so he can raise it.

"Sorry." She must have wrenched the tiller over and has them pirouetting. Inside, she finds two large adult sweaters and an extra T-shirt for Ryan. *Fuck.* "Grab the blue one, Ryan, we'll just snuggle you in that one."

With one hand, she helps him don the sweater over his lifejacket. It hangs over him like a tent. There's no point in trying to get the sleeves on his arms. He stands unsteadily in the cockpit, gazing at his toes, just peeking out the bottom until he discovers that he can flap the loose sleeves like wings.

"Okay," Daniel says, stepping down from the deck, "I'm going to raise the sail. Is that my sweater?" She doesn't need to answer. He grabs the bag at his feet and dumps everything out, but doesn't find anything more. "Looks better on you, bud," he says. She keeps her eyes on the boat approaching on their starboard side. The people aboard raise their hands and she returns their greeting.

"Okay, raising. Watch out, Ryan." Daniel puts his back into it, grunting and pulling a face, but something is wrong. Pausing, he squints at it then glances at her.

"You hanked it on upside down." She means it to sound light, but she has to raise her voice above the motor.

"*You* want to go up on deck?"

"No, I'm fine." Normally she would, but the body can't be trusted just now. Sitting still and keeping her eyes on the horizon is better for the innards.

Ryan inches over to the companionway and Emily tells him it's okay to go below.

Above, the telltales are starting to lift in the wind. They're nearing the tip of the island. Daniel stands, having redone the clips.

"Just in time," she says. He gives her a look like he's determined to take everything she says the wrong way.

"Point us into the wind when we're round the tip of the island…." As if he needs to tell her what to do so they can raise the sails.

"What did you say earlier about your mum not being upset about me drinking?"

"You didn't notice?"

"Notice what?"

"Tom. He was practically standing on her toes."

"No. So what?"

"So, it rattled her. Him getting so close. And then you stagger off with him and disappear over the edge…."

"I wasn't staggering."

"You weren't yourself either. Looks like we're clear of the shoal. Point us into the wind."

When the sail is up, she kills the engine and finds a good point of sail. Daniel adjusts the lines.

"Might as well head out a little further before we turn around?" He waves towards open water. Maybe he's trying to soften things, give her a chance to enjoy it out of the harbour with the noise of the engine gone. He leans down and screws the cap tight on the gas tank. They fly along, tilting their faces up to the light. She can feel the keel digging into the water below as the wind sucks them forward. Daniel shouts and points at the shining head of a seal alongside them. She smiles, wishing Ryan was looking, but he's still below, rolling around on the V-berth. Dogs of the sea. No wonder people dream of mermaids. She used to wish she could leap overboard and follow the seals into the depths.

Daniel has retrieved the chart from below. "Duncan's Cove. Why don't we head that way? Then we'll point toward the Passage and head back home. Drake's Gut." He's talking to himself now. "That looks wider…."

She's found a good position now, leaning on her right elbow, able to see ahead and glance up at the sails from time to time. The water breaks into a curve of bubbles by the hull. The bow rises and falls on the waves. Gulls fly overhead. The wooden boat is doing its work, lines groaning with the strain. She could close her eyes and be a girl again.

Next year, Duck. We'll head south. Don't think I won't make you do your school work though. Da winked at her and took a swig from his mug. He never mentioned her mother when he told her of his plan to pull her out of school. She was always afraid to ask and break the spell.

"You have a choice between PB&J or ham and cheese." Daniel's voice brings her back.

"Either one."

"Chips." Ryan stands on the top step of the companionway. "Chips?"

"Sorry, buddy. Just a sandwich each."

Dan casts a look her way. Jim must have set a snack precedent.

They eat without talking. She nibbles on hers, still not sure how her stomach will receive it. Daniel gathers crumbs and throws them overboard for the fish.

"What's that?" Ryan smudges the protective case with a peanut butter–coated finger.

"That," says Daniel, rubbing it clean with his sleeve, "tells us how far the bottom is from the boat. Did you know that this harbour is one of the deepest in the world?"

Ryan shakes his head, unimpressed, reaching out to touch the button on the depth meter.

The horizon has a muddy look. She's been watching a ship approaching, but it seems to have had a shroud pulled around it.

"Did they mention fog?" she says to Daniel between bites.

"Later in the day." He follows her gaze. "It might not come in. Sometimes it just hugs that part of the coast."

⌒

When Linda gets back to the hospital, they say he's not ready to see her yet.

"There's a good place to eat just that way."

Linda glances at her watch.

"Thanks. I'll come back in an hour." Better to get away from the plastic chairs and the wall of well-meaning pamphlets.

This time, she takes the car. It's only a couple sets of lights before she sees a little strip mall. There's a Lebanese takeout at the end and a hair salon with its sign illuminated: *Walk-ins welcome.* These blips with Tom tend to kill the appetite, and spicy food doesn't appeal just now.

It's been months since her last haircut. The brittle ends have split and multiplied into a halo of frizz.

The salon appears to be empty, but the clang of the bell alerts someone in the back. She pokes her head out. "Be right with you." Her hair is a lively shade of red, and there's a fork in her hand.

Linda takes a seat and eyes the torn magazines. Clients must pull out the pages that interest them and leave the coffee-stained remains for others, the high-fashion stuff that no one would get away with around here. She's reaching for one when the woman reappears. A girl, really, now that she's closer.

"Sorry 'bout that." She chews a wad of gum. "What can I do for you?"

"Do you have time for a cut?"

A book is consulted on the counter and she glances up. "Wash and cut? Sure."

She herds Linda to the furthest of three chairs. "What are we thinking?" she says, tilting her head in the mirror.

"Oh, just a tidy up."

She lifts sections of hair, examining the ends, her mouth working away at the gum. "Take off about this much?" Linda nods. "You ever colour it?"

"Oh, years ago."

She snaps open a large black cape and drapes it around her. "Even a few lowlights might be a nice change."

"No thanks. Just a cut for today."

Leading her to the sink, the girl says, "I did some on my grandmother and she looks awesome." Water running next to her ears muffles the rest of it. *Does she think I'm old enough to be her grandmother?* Closing her eyes, she hopes she'll get the message. It's right up there with the dentist posing questions as soon as he gets his fingers in her mouth.

The water is a tad hot, but she's not going to mention it. Better to just let it work into the scalp and enjoy the sensation. Floating in warm water, arms outstretched. Martin taught her to do that on their honeymoon. They drove down to Florida in his truck and found a place with a pool in the courtyard. At night, the motel staff switched off all the outside lights and padlocked the gate shut. But the chain-link fence was low enough that they could hop over. People didn't have security cameras all over the place then. They slipped into the water just after midnight. It was still as warm as a summer day at home. There was no moon. All night they'd been nursing a bottle of bourbon, and he'd been teaching her more things about her body, bending into the pleasure of it. She pushed off from the wall and went into a lazy backstroke toward the shallow end. He caught up with her under the water, surfacing beside her face, smiling. With the flat of his palm he pushed up lightly on her back. "Stop kicking." They had to keep their voices at a whisper. "Just float." It took effort to relax at first. Her ears were under the water, listening to the distorted sounds of her own heart. Her hair was long then and floated around as if it had come to life. The pressure of his hand moved away from the small of her back while she stayed weightless and safe. Then his fingers, lightly—so as not to disturb her balance—crept inside the elastic of her swimsuit. She wasn't shy with him anymore, she looked at his face surrounded by the night sky. They couldn't speak if they wanted to. It was just the swirl of water, his warm fingers probing so gently. She let her legs move apart in the water and watched his eyes. It didn't take long. Something about the subtle movements made it more intense than the softness of the motel bed. The warmth and the cool ripples, his eyes wandering her face, memorizing it.

"Okay, let's get you into the chair."

Her eyes snap open to the white lights. The instant the tap is shut off her head seems to cool off. A towel is wrapped around her and the girl puts a hand on her back to lift her up.

"Man, you were somewhere else. Nothing like a head massage, eh?"

⁓

Emily can feel it on her skin before she looks. An icy touch, even while the sun is still shining. Wisps of fog are racing ahead of the bank as though eager to be aboard the boat with them. The sails are still up, but they've made little progress since they turned for home. At a speed of two knots, they're probably travelling sideways more than forward.

She wraps her arms tighter around Ryan. The wind ruffles his hair and tickles at her cheeks. Daniel has the helm. He points out some cormorants on a bell buoy ahead.

"They're drying their wings." They've always made her think of men in black overcoats.

"Why?" says Ryan, a popular word.

"They dive for fish. Look, over there," Daniel says. "Did you see?"

Ryan follows his father's finger, squinting hard at the bubbles in the water.

"They have a special kind of feather that makes it easier for them to dive."

"Why?"

It's best not to reply to every why, it only invites more. Instead, Daniel points out Devil's Island. It's just coming into view.

"What's a devil?"

"Well. A devil is—well, a bad guy. Emily, I'm going to start the motor. We should drop the sails."

She nods and whispers in Ryan's ear for him to go below. This time the outboard roars to life without any difficulty. Daniel hands off the tiller and hops up on the foredeck to gather in the jib. By the time it's stowed in the sail bag, the fog has wrapped around them like a cold curtain. Dammit, they should have taken a fix. Now they're blind.

"Shoot. Dan, grab the chart for me before you drop the main." She'll have to dead reckon as best she can. Devil's Island to starboard, but what was to port? The compass will have to do.

"It might not stick around." He doesn't sound sure.

At least there were no boats around them when last she looked.

"Did you say Drake's Gut?" Her finger finds the gap on the chart between the two islands closest to the mainland.

"Mm hm."

"Which way does Jim go?"

"Not sure." He gives the sail a yank and it clatters down to the boom. "We didn't come out this way."

"Well, I'm not sure where we are." She won't say it but she'd give her teeth for a GPS right now.

"I'll get the air horn." Daniel puts the last of the sail ties on. He's done a sloppy job, but they might need to raise it again later.

It's a busy harbour and they are a small vessel. Although Jim's radar reflector would show them as a tiny dot on the screens of the larger ships, smaller boats aren't equipped with such things and the ships wouldn't take this route anyway. And smaller boats are just as problematic when you bump into them in the fog. Plenty of fishing boats come this way.

He's coming up the ladder with the air horn when the motor sputters. They lock eyes and share a silent curse. Daniel scrambles to his knees and reports that the fuel tank is now empty.

"It's okay, there's a spare below the seat. Ryan, stay there." He need not have said it, Ryan is huddled in the cabin. The oversized sweater was too limiting and he's back to his T-shirt. The temperature must have dropped ten degrees.

She continues to study the chart as Daniel works. Drake's Gut is wider, but the other route looks deeper. It was the ebb tide when they left. It's hard to say if it was going in or out. These are the things she'd expected Jim to know. What were they thinking, coming out in unfamiliar waters in someone else's boat?

The outboard coughs on the first pull. On the second it gives a sound they'd later describe as a gasp. On the third, nothing.

"No!" Daniel says, slapping the side of it. "No."

⌒⌐

The stylist whips off the cape and cool air rushes into what was a humid cocoon. Levering herself out of the chair is like getting out of bed after a long sleep. The chair is encircled by a hedge of hair clippings. Her head feels lighter. The girl uses a straightener and it looks unusually glossy, like the cashier's at the grocery store. The hairspray she refuses, her lungs still thick from the efforts of the day.

Without the scarf of hair, her neck is exposed when she steps outside. It's a summer night but she can feel needles of moisture in the air. Fog?

Tom notices right away. His expression is flat. It's hard to know if he likes the change, and she doesn't fish for a compliment. Usually, she'd have stayed with him. Does he resent that she didn't?

"I'll go to your place and get you some things."

His voice is hoarse. "My other jeans."

"Sure."

"And the rest is at home. The book I'm reading too."

"What was it this time?"

"The crow. It's all quiet now though." He taps a finger to his head, his eyes look heavy.

THE ROADS ARE quiet. Pulling up to a stoplight, she glimpses a large TV in a window displaying the evening news. She runs a hand over her hair. That salon shampoo, she doesn't smell like herself. *What is my smell?* It's not like people can really know their own scent, be able to describe it. Lately, she's noticed a new odour on her skin, or maybe it's her hair. It's not unpleasant but not quite right either. Can other people detect it? Or is it her sense of smell that is changing? Isn't it a sign of a seizure when you smell burnt toast, or is that a brain tumour...?

Already, she's reached his apartment. It can't be a good thing that she has no memory of making all the turns to get here. The apartment has a scent that's easily identified, garbage that should have been taken out a day or two before. Trying not to breathe through her nose, she ties up the bag and plops it in the hallway to take to the dumpster on her way out. Afterwards, she looks around for a scrap of paper so she can keep Brad in the loop. There's a pad near the phone. An old message is scribbled on top for Tom. Brad is in the habit of recording the date and time for his work—and it mentions a name she hasn't heard in years, *Seth*. She taps the pen on the counter.

Martin was sure it was the marijuana that started it. He needed something to blame. And though he'd stopped short of starting a fight with Seth's father, Tom was forbidden to spend time with him afterwards. But he's an adult now. She'd hardly thought of him in years, but from the sound of this note they haven't been out of touch at all.

⌒

They sit a moment in disbelief before remembering the horn. Daniel lets out a blast, without warning anyone. In the vacuum of quiet that follows there comes the sound of whimpering. Ryan appears at the top of the ladder wide-eyed and trembling.

"It's okay, bud, I have to use the horn because of the fog."

"Why?"

No one answers.

"The radio," she murmurs, looking at Daniel. "We'll need the name of the vessel and the position...." It's been a while since she's had to use a VHF.

"Mummy, I'm cold."

"Yes, yes. I'm coming."

Daniel says nothing, just moves to take the tiller from her.

The wet air intensifies the smell in the cabin. What was a whiff from under a cushion now overwhelms her nose: petrifying wood, mould spores, and the chemicals meant to preserve it all. She can taste it.

The radio is a newer model, there's a red button labelled *distress*. Thank God. It will automatically relay their position to the coastguard. But the *on* button does nothing.

"Is the battery on down here?" She cranes out of the opening and gulps fresh air.

"Um, no. There's a switch just there...."

She ducks her head and tries the switch. Shallow breaths as the boat sways. Nothing. She tries another switch. Nothing. It's dim down here, it takes her a moment to see it. The wires on the wall are pulled free and tangled around something—a small plastic man.

"Ryan! Did you do this?" She rounds on him.

He is still sniffling from the horn blast, shivering, peanut butter smeared on one cheek. The sight of him makes her sag. It's their fault, oblivious up in the cockpit with a small child loose down here.

Still, they're dead in the water, in the fog.

She swallows hard and stoops close to Ryan's face. His eyes are still big.

"I want home," he says.

Me too. The poor dog is probably desperate to go out by now.

"I need to figure things out. Can you sit right there?" Powering off everything, she runs her fingers along the wires. Maybe it's a matter of stuffing them back in the opening.

Another blast of the horn. She staggers against the nav table and waits for the sound to end. Ryan leaps to his feet and wraps his arms around her legs.

"A little warning on the next one?" she yells up at Daniel.

The radio's face remains blank. She fiddles with the angle and tries a few more times.

"Okay, let's get a sweater on you." She reaches into the duffle bag and feels the shape of a cellphone. It's just the old one Ryan was playing with earlier. As she pulls the sweater over his head, she calls behind her.

"You don't have your cell on you by chance?" Hers had a dead battery this morning and she can picture it on the kitchen counter next to the empty wine bottles. In reply, he holds up an index finger, deep in concentration.

"Shhh."

She climbs into the cockpit. There's something. A rumble. Then it's gone. She's hoping not to hear breaking surf or the hum of a fast approaching engine. Her limbs feel weak after the few minutes in the cabin. The waves roll them side to side.

"Cellphone?"

He pats his pockets and almost smiles when he retrieves it. "No hope for the radio then?"

"You're welcome to try." She doesn't mean to sound angry. It's all the movement. Oh to be warm and dry and stationary.

He flips the phone open. "Not much of a signal."

He dials Jim and puts the glow of the phone to his cheek. Daylight is weakening. Three rings, four, five. He leaves a message, apologetic and anxious, and snaps the phone closed. He calls out a warning to Ryan before blasting the horn.

What on earth can Jim do anyway? Call the coastguard and give them a vague idea of his boat's position?

The nausea rises. This time she can't force it back down. She hangs over the edge just in time. Even so, plenty of it gets on the boat and her hair drags through it. Hunks of bread and ham drift astern, her head swims.

"Sorry," she mutters before another hot wave of it comes up. She hoists herself higher, letting the side of the boat dig into her ribs. With one hand, she attempts to keep her hair out of the way. There's a rumbling drawing closer. The horn blasts. Voices are muffled behind her. Is it Daniel shouting? Right now she is only capable of expelling. Useless. Weak.

A voice seems nearer, a high whisper—*Mummy*—and she turns her head enough to see Ryan through strands of wet hair. He's crawled up on the seat beside her. Things go into slow motion in the dim light. He's on his knees but he's trying to stand and the dangling sleeve of the sweater gets in his way. The boat twitches to port and he lurches forward, his arms trapped. Releasing her grip on the boat she reaches for him but only catches a sleeve as he tumbles. Her fingers clamp onto what she has of him but he's falling. Her effort only pulls his head close to the boat as he goes and the crack of his skull on the side slices right through her. She doesn't hear the splash as he hits the water over her own roar. She bawls his name with her throat still crowded with acidic lumps. The sweater rips free. The water is just there, just beyond her fingertips. The lifejacket keeps him afloat but his face is hidden by the sweater. She keeps her eyes trained on him, he's being swallowed by fog. Her body acts on its own, moving to jump in, but Daniel clamps onto her arm. "Wait." He pulls the life ring and tosses it, uselessly, toward Ryan. Splash, it's a body's length away.

There are other voices. Time rushes ahead. Ryan is smaller, darker, noiseless. Her arm is still held by Daniel as she leans toward the water. The shape of a hull materializes right next to him. She blinks. Daniel is shouting out the alarm. She catches a hint of yellow in motion.

"Boat hook, to port, port, yes, got him—we got him…." Watery sounds, bumping. A dripping figure is fished from the water with a pole. She's on her knees, straining to see the silhouettes in the murk.

CHAPTER 11

The hallway is dim but the hospital staff have assured them that visiting hours don't apply to parents. It's better if they're here when he wakes, so that he's not alone in this alien environment. Daniel rests his elbows on the covers and watches Ryan's face. They haven't spoken since the doctor left. She'd started several times but bitten back the words.

"One of us needs to go home," she says, "for the dog." He blinks at her and she watches the words sink in. So, he'd forgotten. "Can *you* go?"

He doesn't move to stand.

She should want to scrub the stink from her and change. In the bathroom she'd done her best, pulled the dried bits of vomit from her hair and tied it back. She washed her face with the liquid soap they use here, but the bitter smell lingers.

"I can't leave him," she says. It's as if a physical tether has formed between them. If she were to stand up and move away, he'd be dragged in her wake. *So lucky*, they said. Without the other boat, what? She'd have jumped in. And then what? Better to have drowned with him.

"Maybe Linda…" he starts, but she shakes her head.

"I tried, twice already."

He shuts his eyes and digs his fingers into his hair. The ventilator measures the time while she waits: whoosh, thump, thump. Whoosh, thump, thump.

"I'll do it. Then I'll come back."

"Maybe you should sleep. Come back in the morning?" He looks at her like she's slapped him. "Daniel, there's nothing you can do. As long as one of us is here…."

"I'm coming back."

Whoosh, thump, thump. Whoosh, thump, thump.

It wasn't like *she'd* put them up to it. *Standard procedure*, they said. Any time a child is injured, the parents have to be questioned. It was, oddly enough, the fresh bruise on his elbow that made them dig a little deeper. When asked, Emily confirmed that Ryan had done it himself. She sees him again, jumping back from her warning about the winch and wishes she hadn't been so stern. They seemed satisfied after that.

It's the first time she's seen Dan cry like that. He was okay all the way to the hospital, leaning into Ryan's ear in the back of the ambulance with calming words, sure that he could hear him. It was when the staff blocked him, when Ryan was wheeled beyond them, beyond doors and curtains, that's what did it. He turned from the room of faces and hugged himself, as if he could keep it in like that, lash everything down. She touched his shoulder but he didn't turn into her arms. It was just as well.

Maybe he can feel it from her, waves of it reaching him. Why was he not watching? How could he not have seen? Why did *he* not move to dive in? But he'd give it right back to her; if *she'd* been watching, if *she* hadn't had so much to drink again…. So they avoid looking at each other.

He stands up and pats his pockets, finding the jangle of keys. Reaching down, he brushes a lock of hair back from Ryan's ear and whispers something. Then he turns and leaves, rubber soles squeaking against the tiles, speed-walking the corridor. He doesn't say goodbye or ask her if she needs anything.

Standing up, she stretches her back. There's an extra pillow on the chair that Daniel has vacated. She sinks into it, it's still warm from his body. She hugs the cushion to her.

"You should shut your eyes." It's a different nurse from before. She glances at Emily, busy with checking the numbers. "The monitors will tell us if there's any change."

"Thanks."

Shifting her hips in the chair, she finds a comfortable way to lean her head and watch his face. Do his cheeks look a little pinker?

The fisherman that pulled him from the water might be just as restless tonight. If only she'd said something kind to him. Did Daniel? It's a blur. The man was enormous, clad in yellow gear, streaked with black and red. He stammered that it was the first time he'd given CPR. Then EMTs swooped in, speaking code to one another, shiny instruments, a wool blanket thrown over Ryan like a dark wing. And then they were speeding through the streets, weaving their way through the city to the hospital for children with that siren wailing above them.

Her eyes must close for longer than a blink. She opens them to a flurry of people in scrubs entering the room.

"If you can just move aside…" said in that overly calm tone.

Alarms.

"What is it? What's wrong? Is he…."

His face is a deep red now, she can hear him wheezing, see blue around his mouth. She is backed out the door. A woman in a white lab coat comes down the corridor toward her, not quite running. The CT scan on his head had been clear. What was it they'd said? All it took was a tablespoon of liquid in the lungs.

She fixes her hand to the doorframe. *No further than this.*

"His PO$_2$ has dropped."

Helpless.

"Temperature is up two degrees."

Someone has her by the shoulders—brown eyes over a paper mask fix on hers, making sure she is hearing—"…he's in good hands."

She nods. He's awake now, his head jerking away from the tube held by the nurse. In between coughs, she hears him trying to say Mum. It's killing her, not going to him. In her pocket, she clutches an invisible brass shackle.

SLOWLY, RYAN SWIMS back up to the world. Every time he wakes, he looks at the IV on his arm with panic. The staff have taped it on firmly. Whenever they have to change it, a new sticker is applied like a badge. Superman, Spiderman, Ninja Turtles.

"I won't do it again," he whispers, his eyes pleading. "I won't moan-yah."

"It's pneu-mon-ia." She says it slowly for him. "Here." She touches his chest. "Where you breathe. Not your fault, it was an accident."

"I promise," he says. "Can't we go home?" He misses the dog, he misses his blocks, he wants his own room.

"Sadman is alone." He squeezes her fingers.

"No, he isn't. He's right there. See?"

She points and he obliges, attempting to sit up for a better view.

"No, Mummy." He sinks down, disappointed. "Will Tom come?"

"Maybe."

"Daddy said Tom's mad."

"Oh, no." Did he overhear something between Daniel and Maggie? "Tom isn't mad at you."

Maggie is there every day, always toting a new trinket from the gift shop for her grandson.

The room isn't meant for that many people, so Emily finds an excuse to leave, walking the halls or sitting in a corner of the cafeteria. They brighten up the building as much as they can with primary colours, but it's hard to see gaunt children, and parents trying to hold themselves together.

On the fourth morning, Daniel arrives, his hair damp from the shower, and finds her stashing toys in plastic bags.

"They're moving him?"

"Yes." She watches his shoulders drop.

"That's great news, Ryan." He goes to the bed and ruffles his hair.

"Maybe now Tom can come?"

Daniel behaves as if he hasn't heard, stooping down to scoop up a stuffed animal. "I wonder if we can go for a little walk this afternoon," he says, overly cheerful. He has the twitch he gets when something irks him.

"They did say he could go to the lounge, maybe play with some other kids."

"You heading out?" He looks at her coat, but she's only put it on to avoid carrying it.

"In a bit. I wanted to ask you about your trip."

"No, they get it. I can probably phone in." He'd said it could lead to the expansion of the firm, not just nationally but throughout North America.

"Well, they said he might be good to come home in a few more days," she says.

"I'll talk to his doctor later." His cheek pulses. She goes back to pulling things from the drawer.

"Fine. I just wanted you to know, we'd be okay if you have to go."

He doesn't reply and when she looks up, he's not even in the room.

∿

It's a hot, wet summer day. The rain is welcome after two dry weeks, plants were beginning to crisp in gardens. Linda tries running the defogger, but they end up driving with the windows down. The hum of the city, the smell of wet pavement rush into the car with them.

"Are you babysitting tonight?" Tom asks.

"No, Emily quit the library. I didn't tell you?"

"No." She knows she didn't tell him. It might have led to talk of Ryan's accident.

The rain challenges the wipers, and she's focused on the car in front of her with its brake lights on. Out of the corner of her eye she catches him chewing his nails. He's brimming with energy, she can feel it like static before a lightning strike. After this, she'll drop him at his group session. Maybe it will settle him, sharing things out loud that he can't, or won't, tell her.

He goes into the apartment while she waits in the car.

She switches off the engine and watches the window for any sign of him. The rain has stopped and steam rises from the pavement. She pulls out her inhaler and gives it a shake. Everyone else is in short sleeves, but she's just fine in a light cotton sweater. The heat barely touches her, but she can feel the stickiness in the air clogging up the pathways within. Tilting her chin, she pushes all the air out of her lungs before pressing down on the canister.

Tom appears at the passenger door just as she's finishing. His mouth twitches.

"What?" she says.

"Nothing." He looks out his window then back at her. "It just made me imagine you sitting here taking a hit off your bong."

"Bong?"

"Never mind."

Clearly, he doesn't think she's heard of such a thing. As if it was invented for his generation. "Speaking of that, you see much of Seth these days?" She catches the faintest flinch from him.

"Sometimes, yeah."

"How is he?" She tries for a softer tone. It wasn't she who disliked him so much.

"Up and down. He's working right now. Seems happy enough."

She starts the engine and backs out. "Well, he ought to come by the house some time." It had been a mistake cutting him off. Some things take stronger root when you try to bury them.

"Yeah, maybe." He shrugs.

Better the devil you know.

⌣

Ryan's first day home from the hospital feels too quiet. They haven't been together in the house for over a week. Emily gathers an armful of blankets and helps Ryan build a fort on the deck with lawn chairs. It allows him to be outside without really leaving the house. He's itching to get back to the beach with summer in full swing, but he's still weak.

In the evening, Daniel finds her at the kitchen sink, scraping something blackened and stubborn on a pan. He picks up the towel to dry.

"So it's down to our firm and one other in the design competition."

"That's promising." But he doesn't sound happy about it.

"They'd like me there, to walk the client through it."

"I already said we'd be okay if you need to go—"

"I mean, I can do it remotely, but they think it might hurt our chance."

"Go." It's the answer he wanted, wasn't it? But there's a long silence after.

He is on a flight the next day.

Without her job, the days stretch into one another. It should feel good. But she misses it. The only scheduled thing is the phone call from Daniel. She listens to Ryan's half, waiting her turn. She has to remind him to keep it close to his mouth and not play with the buttons.

"Bye, Daddy." Ryan shoves the phone at her and she catches it just as his fingers let go.

"I think he's back to his old energy level…. You still there? Daniel?" She waits in case it's a hiccup in technology. "Ryan, did you press any buttons?"

He doesn't hear her. Hoover is licking his face. She pushes redial.

"No, it wasn't him. I hung up," Daniel says.

"Oh."

She twists a finger into her hair while looking at Da's shackle, trapped in its glass box.

"Never mind. I just thought I'd make sure."

"Gotta go. Love ya."

Love ya, he says that to his brother.

"Okay, Ryan, let's get you into pyjamas before Linda comes over."

Lola had suggested it. "Drinking alone is a slippery slope." Emily is quite happy to drink alone, less judgement.

Linda said she'd come up and read Ryan a story before bed. *That's one less thing.*

Tonight, with any luck, she won't wake up and tiptoe to his room to listen to him breathe. Her dreams are flooded with sea water. Ryan is just out of reach. Every time, she wakes to a sound. *Did he cough?* Lying there, she wonders if her heart is audible to the outside world. It might not be for the right reasons, but she misses Daniel, the house feels wrong at night. Ryan's imaginary friends don't set her much at ease either, his talk of the sad man and his cat, pointing out the window, inviting her to see.

"Okay, Ryan, time to brush the teeth."

⁓

Outside Emily's front door is a row of blue bags. They clink as Linda brushes past.

"Hello," she calls out. Emily said to just come in as they might not hear her in the bathroom.

"Upstairs."

She puts a bottle on the counter but notes that Emily already has one on the go.

"Come on up, he's all set for you."

"Is there a bottle drive on?" The Scouts often leave a flyer around this time of year, they get money back for them.

"Huh? Oh no, just cleaning up the kitchen."

"Winnie!" says Ryan, holding up a book for her.

"Winnie the Pooh, good choice."

Later, when Linda comes out of his bedroom, Emily is in the living room with a glass in each hand. She glances behind her at the dimmed room. It doesn't feel complete. With Tom, she used to pull the door shut and tiptoe away. Here, there's just a bend in the wall, like with public washrooms. It makes sense, avoiding the transfer of germs from thousands of hands overlapping on the same damp handle. But here?

"Is he asleep?" Emily asks once Linda reaches the last step.

"No, close though." She takes the proffered glass.

"Thanks, Linda, it's a treat for him. And me."

Emily's glass is half full, a smudge from her lips on the edge

"Ugh, no need to thank me." She settles onto the couch. "Seems like he's doing all right, since?"

"So far, so good. Did he show you the scar?"

It was easy to spot. They'd shaved away some of his pale hair to clean the wound.

"Yes, I told him he looks like a pirate."

"Mm. He'll like that."

She scans for a place to put her glass down but both tables are crowded: fingerpaints, storybooks, toys, and flyers.

Emily follows her gaze. "Sorry." She plucks an empty tissue box from the coffee table and drops it on the floor. "There you go."

"So, no other problems?"

"I had him in yesterday. At least they're not worried about his head. All the tests were clean." She squeezes her eyes shut. "If you'd heard it, the sound of him hitting the side of the boat." She shudders. "They said it might have been good that he was knocked out. At least he didn't panic and pull in more water. But every time he coughs I freeze." She takes a gulp of wine.

"Does he know how to swim?"

"Not really, I've been meaning to sign him up." She puts a fingernail in her mouth and works at the edge. "How's Tom?"

"Fixing things. My coffee maker was fine until he decided it should be taken apart to clean." It's not the kind of thing she can discourage. He's trying to be useful. "Time I had a new one, I suppose. I'm heading over to the hardware store tomorrow." The old one is Harvest Gold. It matched the stove, and the fridge, until it died last year. "Maybe Ryan could come along?"

Emily nods as if her mind is elsewhere. She's flushed.

"Kids like hardware stores," Linda adds, hoping to pull her back from wherever she is. "Machines and gadgets."

"Right, sure, as long as you don't mind. Refill?" She reaches for Linda's glass on the coffee table but finds it's still full.

"I'm a sipper." She shrugs.

"Where's Tom tonight?" The sound of liquid glugging from a bottle comes from the kitchen.

"Out with his friend Greg."

"Someone you don't like?"

"Hm? No, I like him well enough." It's only that it might not *just* be Greg. If it's Seth, why not tell her?

"I thought he might have been working."

"No, they took him off the schedule." They had to while he was in the hospital. "They're overstaffed with students for the summer."

They switch to talk of landscaping and after half an hour, she thinks she has Emily convinced that it's possible to grow things here. "I'll go to the garden centre with you." Still, there's something simmering. There are gaps of silence. "Will you take him out in the boat again?" Might as well prod a little bit.

"Hm? Oh yes, we'll get him out again." Emily's eyes shine. "Did I ever tell you my father's nickname for me?" Linda shakes her head. "Duck. Because I was always jumping in. Whenever he'd drop the anchor I'd swim laps around the boat. He'd play 'Ride of the Valkyries.' Do you know it?" She hums a bit. "I'd swim and swim until it ended. My record was twelve laps."

"You loved the water."

"I wanted to be in it all the time. You know how it is. I had no fear." Emily swirls her wine. "That last time, it was a scorcher. We were out most of that day. On the way back, Da told me to take the tiller. I was tired but it was a reward, giving me the helm. He'd do that sometimes. He was often…sleepy when we were out. I could always tell, he'd start to sound more Irish." She smiles. "First, he said it was something he ate, then he said it was the flu. I was used to steering, but with his help. It was hard to handle all the lines. And when it was time to tack and he didn't help—he couldn't—I should've called a Mayday right then. Just let the sails go. But he said to get us home, that I could do it." She stares into her glass.

"But you got him back?"

"I got us to the mouth of our river. Then the wind went out of the sails. I could see the roof of our house. He wasn't talking anymore. I just started yelling for help. His skin was a terrible colour."

Yes, that colour is hard to forget.

"Two boats came out for us and towed us in. I could hear the sirens coming forever, echoing across the water." The light from the kitchen casts shadows below her eyes. "I was too late."

"You were just a child."

"Yes. But he never let me think that." Emily straightens her back and lets out a long breath. "It was a heart attack. Same as his dad. I never met him." She looks around the room, pulls herself out of it.

"You're still talking to Daniel every day? On the phone?"

"Mm." She lifts a shoulder.

You'd think they'd be overjoyed—a healthy boy with a future ahead of him, sleeping in the room upstairs.

"Hang in there, love." Linda claims her glass from the table and has another sip. Wine is hard on her throat, drying it out more than wetting it. If only she could spout some wisdom like her own mother, something comforting, a proverb. They settle for silence and the sound of the dog snoring in the corner. She nurses the glass of wine until it is almost empty, but she is outpaced by Emily. At nine, she leaves, yawning.

Outside, she stops to look at the tree in the side yard. Tom must have been a little older than Ryan when this mark was made on its trunk. Martin balanced Tom on his lap, coaching him to steer the car down their driveway and along the road. They were the last house on the hill then, years before this house was built. Good thing too; Tom steered right at the tree. Martin spilled out of the car, laughing as Linda pulled Tom back to the house. Bumpers on cars were tougher back then.

LINDA PICKS UP Ryan after breakfast for their hardware store outing, offering to keep him until the afternoon. No sooner does she drive away than Tom is on Emily's front step in a wetsuit, the top of it worn open around his hips. It's impossible not to notice the contours of his muscles. Emily crouches down and strokes Hoover's ears while Tom makes the case for her trial surf lesson. She wants to say no—every fibre of her screams for a nap. She says as much.

"Okay, but I'll ask you every day until you cave. And it's warm out there today."

"Just this once," she says, holding up her hands in surrender. An hour in the water and back home to bed.

The rental shop looks her up and down and produces a wetsuit, still damp from its last use. She goes behind a curtain and tries to shimmy into it. Surely, they've given her the wrong size. But once it clears the top of her thighs it seems like it might make it. When she bends to gather up her things, a ring of sand lies at her feet. Tom zips her up.

"Cool, you got it on the right way." He sounds approving. Thankfully, she is observant enough to notice the zipper goes in the back. The thought of having to do that twice…ugh.

"I'm not sure how I'll get it back off." In the mirror, she does a half turn and is pleased to see that it's smoothed things out, even if it makes it hard to bend knees and elbows.

"Don't worry, the water eases things up. No good having it too loose."

Off they go, with boards propped out the back window of her car. It is only one bend in the road to the spot Tom has in mind.

They practise on the sand before going in the water. "Too far back and it'll flip up on you, too far forward and you're arse over teakettle."

It feels good in the water, on her belly, paddling the board out to where the waves gather. But she can't feel when to go, the way the water drops under her.

"That's your moment. Grab it on either side and pop up to your feet. One motion."

She gets to her knees and stays for a count of two seconds then scrapes herself along the rocks, emerging with hair across her face and snot flying. His praise is lavish.

After a half-hour she needs to sit. From the beach, she watches him. He's on his feet, hands out to the side, balancing. It looks comfortable, soft. The crest of the wave brings him closer with the ease of an escalator.

She tucks her knees up to her chest and examines the top of her feet. Both of them have taken a battering. Bruises are already visible. Her skin has that waterlogged look, paler than when it's dry. He's right though, tonight she'll sleep.

"Hey." A shadow blocks her sunlight. She looks up to see a guy with a piece of seagrass between his teeth. "You out with Tom?"

"Um, yes."

"He's a friend." He doesn't wait for an invitation, just lowers himself to the sand beside her. "I'm Seth." He offers her a hand.

"Emily."

"He been out long?"

"Maybe an hour." She glances at her wrist, remembering all over again that everything is locked in the glove compartment, the keys stashed in her sandal. "I'm not sure."

"I told him I'd come out later. See if he wanted to…do something."

"Ah." Don't judge, she tells herself. He's too thin, chicken legs inside sagging jeans that seem to be trying to escape his hips, a long-sleeved T-shirt featuring bones and blood on a hot afternoon. And all of it a faded black.

"You known him long? Tom?" he says.

"His mother lives next door. A few months, I guess."

"So you know about him then?"

She nods. Why is he smiling like that?

Seth produces a cigarette from behind one ear. He lights it and crumples the grass in his other hand.

"You surf?" she asks, even though he doesn't look the type.

"Not when it's just ankle busters," he scoffs, jutting his chin at the water. "Want one?" He holds out the cigarette from his mouth, squinting, remembering his manners.

"No. Thanks."

"Greg out here too?" He scans the beach.

"I don't think so."

"He's got to have someone out here with him, you know. Just in case it starts to *come alive* for him." He mimes it for her, jazz hands, the cigarette hanging limp from one corner of his mouth.

Tom has paddled out further. He sits on the board, watching behind him for a good set to arrive.

"I guess that's me today," she says.

"Tell you the truth, sometimes I kinda envy the guy." He waits for her to ask, and when she doesn't he goes on. "It's like he's *trippin'* all the time. I have to smoke some good shit to get that way." He laughs, pulling the air back in his throat like a donkey. "No offense."

"None taken," she says with her eyes trained on Tom, willing him to notice that his friend has joined them.

"The stuff about his dad though, that would freak me right out."

She glances at him. He's propped up with one hand so he's angled towards her, making himself right at home.

"He ever tell you that shit?"

She shakes her head.

"Talks to him. He sees him, with his head, you know—like after the fall?" He grimaces, a Boy Scout telling a ghost story.

"Seth," Tom calls, putting the board down on the sand.

"Tom boy." Already, the sound of his voice grates. He gets to his feet, brushing sand from his jeans.

"I'm going to give this another shot." She pushes herself up, stiff from sitting too long.

"You'll be all right?" Tom asks as she stoops to put the strap back on her ankle. Without this tether, the board would have been sucked out to sea by now.

"Sure." She has no intention of attempting to stand this time, she only wants to get away. "The toughest part is getting back in."

If she ever does this again, she'll wear something on her feet, those booties some of the surfers have. Working her way in, bracing the board to her hip, she wobbles on the stones. Tom must have tough feet. Each wave pushes and tugs, but she's determined not to fall in front of Seth.

As soon as the water is around her chest, she pulls herself up to lie on her belly and paddles out. She switches to a sitting position, proud that she doesn't fall off. This part is comfortable enough, a leg slung over either side. She settles in, pretending to watch for the right moment to join a wave.

Seth is on his feet. He talks with his hands, while Tom stands a few inches from him. He must be dripping on his friend's toes at that distance. He runs a hand through his wet hair and turns his face her way, then he gives a quick nod and waves, indicating what, she's not sure. Reaching into her sandal, he pulls out the keys and the two of them turn for the car. *What the hell?* But his board is still on the sand.

The water is flat, she glances behind her and sees a swell. Why not? Dropping to her front, she propels herself forward. One motion, onto her feet for the first time. God, if only someone was looking. Her elation evaporates as the front of the board hits a rock, larger than the others, and she's dumped sideways. Seawater floods her nose as she puts a hand out to stop the board from whacking her head. She's just straightening up, pushing the hair from her eyes, when she sees him coming back, alone.

"You didn't see," she shouts at him, smiling.

"You got up?"

"Briefly."

As soon as she's out of the reach of the waves, she plunks down the board and pulls the Velcro apart at her ankle. *Quit while you're ahead.*

"Your friend coming back?"

"No, he's gone." He drops the keys back in her sandal and holds out a banana for her. Just went to retrieve a snack for them, did he?

"Ah, thank you. Sweet with salty."

"Sorry about that," he says.

"Old friend?"

"Known him since I was five. Even then he didn't make a great first impression."

She doesn't respond. Daniel has one of those in his life.

"He gets nervous around women. His mother—she took off on them when we were kids. He's had a rough go."

"Mm." She's bitten off too much banana. It saves her from commenting. They chew in silence, watching others try their luck on the larger waves off to the right.

"You're a strong swimmer."

"Thanks." Does Linda share their conversations?

"I know a good lake. It's about twenty minutes from here. It's shallow, warm, and there's a gradual sandy beach for getting in. Might be a good place to get him back in the water."

It's the second time he's brought it up today, the need to *get Ryan back in.*

"Good idea. This is probably not a great spot to teach him." There are kids further along the beach but they're building sandcastles, far from the lapping of the waves. Here, the water seems hungry, it roars with the sound of a million stones clattering against one another as the ocean drags them away.

"I could come along. Two sets of eyes?"

Daniel will be back in a couple of days, just as soon as they make the announcement on which firm gets the project.

"Yeah," she says, stifling a yawn. "Maybe." It's time to get back to the rental shop and use the last of her energy to peel off the suit.

"Think you'll try this again?"

There's a pair of women walking past them, each carrying a board with ease. One glances her way and nods, mistaking her for one of them. They're light on their feet, supple, unafraid of falling.

"Never say never."

⟞

Hardware stores were Martin's domain. He had to go there for supplies several times a week. They knew him by his first name. The owner had been at his funeral, offered to help out if she needed anything. After that, she was loyal to this store, coming here for anything she needed, even when it was a better price somewhere else.

"Linda." Well, speak of the devil. "How are things?"

"Good, good." She searches her memory for his name.

"Well then, who is this?"

"Oh." Ryan has the steering wheel of a ride-on lawnmower wrenched to one side. "I hope this is okay?"

"We don't mind, as long as they have an adult with them."

"Ryan lives next door."

"Pleased to meet you. I'm Harley." He proffers a large hand.

"I thought I'd bring him along, give his mum a break."

"Well, we can always use a hand around here." He winks. "I'll show you what kids like. You want to follow me?"

Ryan climbs down and they trail behind him to the back where a tent is set up. They've created an indoor campsite with a barbecue, lawn chairs, and sleeping bags. "Go on in, test it out."

"You have grandkids?" She can't remember the age of his children.

"No." He laughs. "They're still *finding themselves*. Paul's travelling for a year and Susie is working in the city, thinking about going out west."

"You'll be lonely."

"Yeah. Well, they grow up, get their own lives." He shrugs. "Part of the deal."

"Your wife…?"

"Five years ago now. Sat me down and said she was done."

Jesus, Joseph, and Mary. So matter-of-fact.

"I'm sorry."

"Better to know, I guess. She could have stayed and pretended."

"Still."

"I was always busy. The store, the kids…."

They watch Ryan working the button on a lantern in the tent, chattering away to himself.

"I know what you mean."

An employee wheels past them, the cart piled high with flats of bottles. Harley nods toward it.

"We're stocking water. See if we can put together a kit for storm supplies." He shrugs. "Hard to compete with big box places."

"Good idea."

"Can I help you find something?" He straightens.

"My coffee maker bit the dust."

He smiles and tugs at his belt. "Doc has me down to the three cups a day. Used to always have a mug on the go." He uses a clipboard to point. "Down aisle seven."

"Thanks."

"Must get into the back," he says, checking his watch.

She settles into a folding lawn chair and accepts tin mugs of imaginary drinks from Ryan.

"This one for Tom." Ryan balances a second cup on the empty chair.

"Oh, he'll like that."

"Is he here?" Ryan squints hard at the empty chair.

"No, no, Tom's not here, love." He was just coming downstairs when she left the house.

"He could be. He's got secret powers," he whispers.

"Does he?"

Ryan gazes at her seriously, waiting for her to agree or maybe fill him in.

"He told me. But it's secret." He places a finger to his lips.

"Okay. We ought to go soon. I have to find a few things here in the store."

"Five more."

"Five more minutes? Okay."

Inland, the sun feels stronger. Emily rummages in the cooler for some snacks, keeping an eye on Ryan. Tom sits alongside him in the lake, showing him how to put on a diving mask. The idea is to get him comfortable putting his face in the water. Hoover is tied in the shade of a tree, barking at ants.

"Good job! Now blow out, like this. Make some bubbles." Tom dips his head to show him.

She's about to call out for them to join her but decides not to interrupt. They stand and move out a little further.

"Now, it's treasure time." Tom throws some coins in the water and leans over to pick one up, putting his head just under.

"Is it real?"

"Yes, it's real. That's a loonie."

"Can I keep it?"

"Only if you find it."

"Coo-wool." That's all it takes. Ryan forgets to freak out about his head going under. They do this until all of the change is picked up.

"Okay, come on. I've got watermelon."

While Ryan is occupied with eating, she rubs him down with more sunscreen. Without his shirt, he looks ghostly white.

"You going to come in with us?" Tom says, taking the tube of sunscreen and rubbing it on his shoulders.

"Of course, I just wanted to make sure Hoover settled." He's rolled onto his side, an ear covering his eye. The watermelon is perfect, but it drips all over her legs. Tom plops down beside her on the blanket. "I'll pay you back for the coins."

"No, you won't." He turns, smiling. "You're looking a little toasty on your back, you want me to?"

Her fingers are covered in juice. "Um, sure."

His hands are chilled from being in the lake. It sends a shiver up her spine.

"Sorry."

"No, it's good."

"You have a strand of hair here." He blows on the nape of her neck to clear it away. That against the heat of the day and the sweetness in her mouth sends a tingle through her. His fingers work around her neck and down her spine.

"Thanks." She can't look at him until they are in the cool of the lake, both of them focused on Ryan.

DANIEL'S PLANE LANDS just after ten in the morning. He tells them they can just pull up and he'll be waiting outside. Ryan skips the hello.

"I dive now, Dad!"

"You do?"

Emily watches the parking attendant in the rear-view mirror. They don't take well to people spending too long in the loading zone.

"I didn't get a chance to tell you," she says, pulling out. They'd missed their call yesterday, with him catching his plane last night.

"I'm a good swimmer now!"

Daniel swivels in his seat to give an awkward high-five. "Wow, Ryan."

"We were at the lake yesterday—" she starts.

"Tom put my head under the water!"

Daniel's head snaps in her direction. She keeps her eyes on the road ahead; cars are merging from the left.

"He had you look under with the mask," she corrects, catching Ryan's eye in the mirror. "He was *really* good with him."

"That's great, buddy." It's quite a trick, Daniel makes it sound enthusiastic for Ryan while conveying the opposite to her with his posture.

"It's not far from us and there's a little beach for him to play. We could go."

"Wow. Swimming *and* surfing lessons." Ryan doesn't pick up on sarcasm yet. Daniel leans against his door to look at her.

"You miss us?" Her sunburn suddenly feels unbearable against the fabric of her shirt.

"Did you miss me?"

"Of course. We missed Daddy, right?" But she's on her own, Ryan has discovered a snorkel in the back seat. Tom's. He'd shown him how to put it on. "You were the one who was too busy to talk."

"I would've talked," he says. "You seemed uninterested."

"When?" She risks a longer look at him. They're on the divided highway now.

"Wednesday." He's going to make her work for it.

"About the competition?"

"My job, us...."

So that's it. She'd switched the subject when he wasn't finished telling her about how they'd like him go to the West Coast office—when and if they open it. But if she hadn't at least mentioned the surfing, he'd have accused her of hiding it.

"You seriously want us to think about moving? There's still a couple of boxes that aren't unpacked...."

"Pretty soon my parents will be out there. Dave's already there." His brother has been out there for years.

"This is home." She holds out a hand to the windshield, as if she could cradle the heavy grey sky.

"Really? Your mother, when she's not down south? Richard? Or the house?" At least he doesn't bring up the neighbours.

Then he turns on the radio at just the right volume to make conversation impossible and lets his head rest on the seat. Ryan hums along to the song, his mouth inside the snorkel, playing it like a kazoo.

The drive home is a pot coming to a slow boil.

⌒

There's a blinking light on the answering machine when Linda gets in from groceries. And it's not Doris, or anything to do with medical reports, or prescriptions, or appointments. It's Harley.

The coffee machine she'd purchased is going on sale next week. He'll be happy to honour the new price for her if she comes back in. Then there's a bit of throat clearing before he musters the right words. Maybe she'll consider having one with him—a coffee. She wouldn't have to make it for him, they'd go out. Someplace nice. Maybe eat something.

She played the message three times, reaching a full smile by the third one. What a luxury to have the time to absorb it, in all its fumbling charm, and form a reply. It's been a very long time since a man has asked her out. So long, in fact, that they were boys, not men.

Physically, he couldn't be less like Martin. No hard edges. And he has kind eyes. He doesn't overdo it on the cologne, and there is no excess jewellery. God knows he's handy. Maybe she'll regret it. But she'll say yes, to both his offers.

Right on schedule, there's a bang on the door and Doris lets herself in. Just coming by for a tea before she goes to a thing in the city. She'd called yesterday, accusing Linda of being a shut-in, waving off her health problems like they were a convenient excuse to avoid socializing.

"I'll just run to your loo."

When Doris hasn't returned by the time the tea is steaming in two mugs, Linda goes looking for her. She finds her in the basement, arms crossed, staring at the dryer. It's still in bits. Tools are scattered around it, as if Tom will be back any minute.

"I know what your boy needs." She still talks of him as if he's a teenager. "I'm going to make a call."

She marches up the stairs, not bothering to ask to use the phone. It's a brief conversation, she bends the person on the other end to her will. She should have gone into politics or something that used her skills. Doris was the one to buy the cigarettes when they were girls. She's always carried herself like that. When it suited her, she could hold a silence too, unflinching until the other blinked.

"Property maintenance. He'll need a few weeks of training." She scrawls the name and address on a notepad. "It's good pay for...." For what? Never mind. She straightens up and glances around the kitchen. "New machine?" The coffee pot is un-boxed but there is still a Styrofoam disk nestled between the carafe and the machine. "Stainless steel. Look at you."

Linda shrugs and decides against sharing the news of her potential date. It's hard to know if Doris will be in the *it's about time* camp or the scandalized *at your age* one. Either way, she'd be firm about it, and it's more fun to enjoy it for now.

Doris bustles off shortly after, apologizing for not staying long enough to see Tom and share the news. Good thing too. Those two are like oil and water.

⁓

After the talk with Daniel, Emily drives away with no planned destination. A rare luxury seized in spite. He implied that she wasn't concerned about Ryan's safety when it was the other way around; teaching him to swim could only help. Clearly, it was about Tom, but he wouldn't say it, the twitch in his cheek told her that. She drives toward the city, toying with sitting at a pub for an hour, but decides on the liquor store instead. She browses the various countries, reads some labels rather than seizing the largest one on special. In the car, she realizes it will require a corkscrew and a glass and she is not ready to go home. What the hell, she does know someone downtown.

It's fun, just to see the look on her mother's face. Even though she's had time to compose herself between buzzing Emily in and awaiting her arrival on the top floor, it's clear that she's taken aback. She's in her nightgown and a cardigan, but still wearing full makeup. An unannounced visit from Emily is unprecedented. And there is the matter of the time of night, when she'd normally be home with Ryan. The bottle-shaped brown bag makes it three things that she has never done before.

"What a lovely surprise." Mary says, showing some teeth.

"Thought I deserved to get out of the house. Come and see you." Emily leans in for a light hug, thudding the bottle against her mother's back.

"Sorry, I forgot I was holding that."

Mary straightens and looks at the bag. "Would you like to stay the night?"

"Let's see how many glasses I have first." She elbows her mother, who doesn't laugh. Has she ever seen her look relaxed?

"Where's Daniel?"

"At home. With Ryan, before you ask."

She can sense her mother's hesitation but she carries on, pulling off her shoes at the door, heading for the living room and its panoramic view of the harbour.

"You still enjoying this?" she says, waving at the window.

"Oh yes, every morning we have our coffee and watch the boat traffic."

They stand side by side, the lights of the city reflecting in the water. The ferry is halfway across.

"Where is he?"

Mary gives her a look, she doesn't need to say it—*you mean your stepfather?*

"A golf trip."

"I thought he hated golf."

Richard had attended many business golf tournaments before retirement, always claiming that it wasn't his idea of a good time, just for work.

"Well, *hate* is a strong word." It's a refrain of her mother's. "But you're right, I didn't think he liked it much either." There's an edge to her voice as she holds her hand out for the bottle. "Shall I pour?"

"Please." Emily watches her dig through a drawer and come out with a wing corkscrew. "Want me to do that?"

"No," Mary says, threading it in. Her arms quiver with the effort of pulling it free. It's hard to sit there and do nothing. Finally, there's a satisfying pop.

"It's a good one," Mary says, holding the bottle as far from her as her arm will allow.

"Yup." Normally she keeps it under fifteen dollars. Lately, though, the bank account seems to be holding steady.

Mary gets out a glass and pours.

"You're having one too," Emily says, coming forward to claim it.

She glances at the clock and sighs. "I don't like to after supper but…."

"So, tell me what's going on with you," Emily says, sinking into the armchair.

"Not much really. I've been doing some shopping for Christmas."

For decades, she's prided herself on getting her list crossed off well before the start of the school year. She was usually down south before the holidays, so she would deliver all the gifts in October.

"There's a place just off Spring Garden with a sale on clothes, they're closing next week. You should come with me in the morning."

Emily brushes a clump of fur off the knee of her stretchy pants and watches it flutter to the white rug. "New clothes are not really a priority right now. I'm just home with Ryan."

She can see her mother deciding not to say something. If she was still a teenager it would have been something along the lines of *you could be so much prettier with well-fitting clothes.*

"I'd like to get you something for Christmas though, and this would help take the guesswork out of it."

She listens to her mother recount the deals she's scouted, wondering why she didn't just head to the pub where she could have really opened up to the bartender.

"Emily?"

"Mm?"

"You're somewhere else." She gives a pause, an opportunity to fill in the gap. "I asked what Daniel would like."

A wife who is content to just wave politely at the neighbours?

"Maybe a Tilley hat?" Mary offers, watching her face. "Does he have one?"

"No. No, he doesn't." She has no idea what that is, but he hates wearing hats. It's perfect.

"I'm going to have a look at the spare room, make sure the bed's made," says Mary.

Should she call him or let him worry? It might be the first time she's been away from Ryan overnight. But he'd go to find her at dawn, she usually woke up with him trying to stretch his arms around her back for a hug. *Let's keep sleeping,* she'd whisper, but it never worked.

Ryan was up in this condo once, when he was a toddler. Richard kept blocking him from the breakables like a goalie. They hadn't bothered to put things away, figuring they could *just watch him.* All four adults were quickly worn out, and they took him off to a nearby playground after a lengthy twenty minutes. That might have been the last time she was here. Yes, it was.

She tips her glass up and heads to the kitchen for a refill. Reaching into her purse, she finds her cell doesn't have any messages. A stalemate. This was their pattern before, when Emily could retreat to Lola's place.

"It's all made up for you when you're ready."

She reappears and catches Emily topping up her glass. "How's my grandson?" Maybe it seems like safe territory.

"Feisty, of late." Emily points to the bruise on her shin. "Rocks at the playground." He'd whipped a handful at her.

"Oh yes, you were like that at his age too. Your dad had a term for it. What was it? Oh, you were *up to ninety.* That was it."

She feels the ache that comes when her mother doles out a memory. She shakes her head. "What was that?"

"You were ready to explode, I think. He was good with you when you were like that. Not me." An unusual confession for her. "He'd just look amused. He said he could tell you'd be independent."

Is that a compliment?

"I'm finding this year harder. I thought it was supposed to be the terrible twos...."

Mary shakes her head. "I cried a lot when you were three."

"You did? I don't remember that."

"Well, you were too young. And not in front of you. I'd go in the bathroom."

She does remember closed doors, wanting them to open, wanting to be held.

"Why?"

"It's hard to remember all the reasons now. I was young, remember? Now most people wait. I went straight from my parents' home to being a parent myself. Charlie grew up in a place where the kids ran as a pack, the big ones caring for the little a lot of the time. He took to it easily. Just carried on doing things, like you'd always been there. Showed you off all over the place."

She listens, afraid to break the spell.

Mary rubs at her eyes delicately, careful not to smudge her mascara. "I never told you any of this?"

Emily shakes her head.

"I wanted to come and help with Ryan when he was born." She had offered but Emily had put her off, saying Dan's parents would be staying indefinitely. It was true, but they both knew the real reason. Or reasons. "I was so tired after your birth." She knows the story: two days of labour. "I didn't hold you right away—to feed you." She glances over. "They make sure to do that these days, right? Charlie was right there. So, I just let him do it." She lets out a breath. "After that, it was like you'd imprinted on him. He was the one who could make you stop crying. He was the one to see your first smile. You lived for him." She turns and smiles sadly. The makeup has dried out around her mouth, making the lines in her skin appear deeper. Her lower eyelids droop slightly, like Hoover's. Why has she always worked so hard to keep this from people, the cracks?

"How did you meet him? You said you were still living at home."

"Oh, yes. I'd finished school and was taking a secretarial course, but I was still underage for drinking. Anyway, I went to a dance with a couple of girls from school. The young men were so...inhibited. All of them, except your dad. He came straight over, started telling us all a story. We didn't understand half of what he said, his accent was stronger then. God, he was funny, you'll remember. He could tell a story like no one else. After that, we danced until they turned the lights on."

She had heard the story, but it was from Da's point of view. In his version, Mary had forced him to dance with her, even though he was all left feet. He said she was a *tapestry of bruises* the next day.

"Oh, that was all a joke, he wasn't half bad on his feet."

Their courtship had been short. Mary discovered she was pregnant in their fourth month of dating. She never talked about that part. Emily had been sworn to secrecy by her father, who'd let it slip one day when they were out sailing. He'd been planning to return to Ireland after two years in Canada, but her birth changed that. She often wonders what it would have been like, if he'd brought the whole family back to Dublin, lived next door to her uncle Seamus. Instead, he'd found more work here and stayed on.

"More wine?" Mary has managed to finish an entire glass.

"Oh, why not?"

She ought to pour the rest into her mother's glass; it seems to be having a good effect on her.

"That young man we met, your neighbour. Do you see much of him?"

"Tom?"

"I'm terrible with names, the surfer."

"Yeah, Tom. Sure, I see him." Emily puts the glass in front of her.

"Is Daniel okay with that?"

"Not really."

She looks startled, perhaps expecting to work a little harder to get at the truth.

"Is that why you're here?"

That's when it occurs to her, she hasn't even filled her in on Ryan's accident. While Maggie and Donald were notified the next day, she'd put off calling her mother. It was hard enough to put on a brave face for Ryan. Clearly, this isn't lost on Mary as she listens, one hand milking the hem of her sweater.

It's always been this way with her mum. It's the wine that has made Mary bold enough to talk this much. Maybe that's what drew her to Charlie in the beginning, his apparent ease with people. And later she'd latched onto Richard. Both older men, both stable, in their own way.

"I'm sure Maggie was a huge help to you," Mary says.

If it's meant as a dig, Emily can't tell from her tone of voice. "She was there every day. Anyway, I guess you could say the argument was a bit to do with Tom, but not really."

Mary stares into her glass.

"Is Richard all right with *you* having male friends?"

It's the first time she's seen her mother laugh in surprise, an open-mouthed, heaving-forward, all-out guffaw. She nearly spills red wine on the pristine couch.

"He gets annoyed if I talk to a waiter for too long. Not that it's an issue, at my age."

"You're not old. God." She tries to remember her mother's age. "Now Richard, he's old." They both laugh.

"This is kind of fun," Mary says, putting her glass on the table. "We should do this, you and me, every once in a while. If you don't mind."

"That would be nice," she says, even though she can't imagine them repeating this particular evening.

Mary stands. "I think I'll head off to bed. I need my beauty sleep." Emily yawns, and nods. "The phone's on the kitchen counter, if you want to call him. You two will get through this," she says, before closing her door.

He lets it go to voicemail. Maybe he really is asleep, but she imagines him looking at the call display next to the bed and rolling away from the phone. She stays a little longer in the living room with the lights out, watching the harbour, thinking of her parents whirling around a dance floor.

⌒

Harley suggested a place he had spotted near a large mall because he didn't know the city very well. "Plenty of parking," he'd assured her.

They hadn't called it a date. Linda planned to run her errands afterwards. Even so, she spent too long gazing in the mirror before leaving the house, trying on smiles, pulling the skin under her chin upwards.

They hold up the line, reading through the catalogue of tea and coffee. "Who puts ice in a coffee?" Harley seems genuinely mystified, gazing at the chalkboard behind the cashier. In the end, they both settle upon decaffeinated brewed coffee, once they realize it's an option.

The cleanest of the tables has a dusting of sugar, and Linda's chair has the partial remains of a cinnamon bun in the centre of the seat. Harley makes an extra trip for napkins and cleans it off before he allows her to sit. She smiles as he pulls out her chair, a paper napkin over one arm.

"Thank you."

In the corner, there's a girl with a sticker-plastered laptop, her hair an oily shade of black. She's plugged her computer into the wall and has her feet propped up on the chair opposite. Three silver hoops pierce her nose.

"Susie got a nose ring. Hers is just a little stud. Seems like a bad idea to me." He takes a sip, keeps his voice low. "I mean what do you do when you have a cold? And who hires someone with too many holes in their face?"

"Did you ask her that?"

"She told me that lots of people do it. Tattoos too. She called me old." He gives a little snort. "Used to be, sailors came back with piercings and ink. Now kids think they just need to apply the look and people will believe they're worldly."

"I guess I can put you down as not in favour?"

"Nah. It's fine. It's just too much like branding. Trying so hard to be different that they all end up looking the same."

She nods even though she's not given it any thought.

"What about Tom? He have any marks?"

"Oh no. He's never bothered."

"Probably has one where *you* can't see it."

"No, I would have seen it." Harley gives her a look, *how would you know?* "When he's...having an episode, he sometimes takes off his clothes."

She watches him struggle with the image, a limp smile on his face while he reaches for a napkin.

"How are things with him?" He doesn't look her in the eye.

It seems too weighty a topic for a coffee shop with the clamour of cups and the hiss of the espresso machine. "I don't want to burden you."

Only three days into his job training, Tom comes in the door, eats, and heads off to bed. It's either a good thing or a bad thing. For now, it's best to take his word for it; it's better than his last job.

"Well, it's okay if you don't want to...." Harley holds up a hand as if to block her words.

"Then again," she continues, "sometimes the rumours are worse."
He looks away. "You *have* heard rumours?"

He shrugs. "I try not to listen to that stuff."

"I see." What had she expected them to talk about, if not their lives?

"At the store, people talk. I mean it's not really about Tom but, you know, the other guy on the news." He can't say it. "Thought his mother was an alien or something."

The coffee is just halfway down her throat, but she manages to keep it from coming back up.

"That boy had violent tendencies. Tom's never shown any sign of that." She waits for him to look up. "How about I tell you about the worst time? Then, maybe you'll get it."

He tears the edges of a napkin so that it has a fringe all the way around. "Okay."

"After the funeral. Martin's. A couple of weeks, I guess. I could see it starting. He stopped washing. He might go down to the beach and wade into the water, but that was it. No baths, no showers, his hair got tangled and greasy. He lived with us then. With me, I mean. He became a vegetarian. One night he took all of the stuff from the freezer and burned it in the yard in some ceremony. My ground beef, my casseroles, the turkey I was keeping for Thanksgiving. Still in their dishes and plastic wrap too. What an awful mess. And the wasted food." She closes her eyes, seeing the heap of smoking glass and plastic in her yard. "I was still grieving for Martin, so I guess I didn't control myself well."

"Understandable," he says.

She shakes her head. "I treated him like he could control that stuff. I yelled at him. I said I'd have him locked up. Of course, he took off. In my car."

"Jesus."

"I was hysterical, I just stood at the end of the driveway yelling for him to come back like he could hear me." It was the first time she'd had to bear it entirely alone. Anger had been Martin's role, while she did things, kept life rolling along. "I called the police." She reaches in her pocket, pulls out her inhaler, and lays it on the table. "It turned out, he only drove it as far as the beach. He got out, left the keys in it, and disappeared."

"And you thought he...?"

"I imagined planning a second funeral." The statistics weren't in his favour. "Everyone was looking for him. I thought he might have gone to his friend Greg's place. I hoped. But no such luck. It was on the radio…."

"So where did he go?"

"Hitched a ride with a German couple on holiday. They took him way up the coast. I guess they spoke very little English, and they probably weren't listening to the local news. He camped with them a night. Said he slept out under the stars. Then in the morning he woke up and they were gone. He had nothing with him. No money, no water, no food, no shoes even. He got up and walked, followed a seagull to a rocky beach, then a cloud in the shape of a mountain. The sky was sending him messages. His knees and feet were a mess after."

"How did he keep going without water?"

"Puddles. Dew on leaves. When he's in that state he reverts, he behaves like the animals around him. I think that's what made him a vegetarian. He's always had a deep empathy for others. Anyway, the weather turned cold. There was a cottage out on its own. He found a way in, thought he'd just stay there for a bit, he said, then go when the sky cleared. But the people came back and they found this dirty guy sleeping on their couch."

"And they called the police?"

"Not at first. There was *an altercation*, as the police like to put it. The man wanted to be the hero. Tom ran and that's when they called the police. He spent another night outside before they found him. A farmer spotted him sleeping under a tree. Thank God. When they called me, they had him in an ambulance."

"It sounds exhausting."

She's talked too much and needs to breathe.

Harley looks thoughtful. "This might sound harsh, but can't you—I don't know the term—have him committed?"

Years ago, she would have been livid at the question. But she's since realized how little she knew of it, before Tom. It's better that he just says it. Most people probably just don't.

"If there was a place around here that could really help him. But no, he's better off this way. He's not dangerous, like that guy. And that boy, he was untreated, they didn't even know that he was ill until after…."

"Figures," Harley mutters. "Sorry, just seems kinda convenient, keeps him out of prison."

She decides to ignore this. She could point out that he is needlessly making a pile of clean napkins unusable.

"Anyway. He has more normal days than not." The napkin is no more. He gathers the pieces and balls them up in his hand. "I know how it sounds, but there's more to him. You should see him with the little boy from next door."

"The boy you brought by the store?"

"And Emily, his mother, she seems glad of the help." It seems like his eyes keep drifting to the table behind her, the chatter of young women discussing their previous night out.

"That's good. I take it she knows that he's...?"

"She does."

"It's a good thing, him having a girl."

"Oh. They're not—no, she's married. Her husband is just away a lot."

"Sorry, my mistake." Harley looks away.

She leans back and practises what the doctor had shown her. Whenever she's short of breath, he said to push everything out with all the bad air, slow things down.

"Everything all right?"

"Fine." She'll just have to speak softer.

He excuses himself and pulls out his cellphone to check his voice-mail. The coffee shop has emptied out, and she can make out the music. When did people start listening to crooners again?

"Is that Old Blue Eyes?" she says, tilting an ear toward the speaker. He snaps the phone shut, wedging it back into the pocket of his work shirt.

"Susie calls him Mr. Bubbles. But it's Boo-blay, I think." He's looking at her, waiting for her to set him straight.

"Huh, I could have sworn it was Sinatra. I wonder if I still have Martin's records downstairs."

"I was never a fan."

"No?"

"It was kind of our parents' music."

"True, I guess. Martin used to listen to him when we were first together."

"My wife too. Actually, that was one of the first signs. She bought a bunch of the old stuff on CD, said she wanted to listen to *her own music.*"

Linda leans her chin on her hand. "What did she listen to before that?"

"Nothing, I guess. It seemed like she just had the kids' favourite radio station on or the TV with the news. It's like she woke up one day and started resenting us, like we'd made her stop being herself. Or I did."

"That happens with parenthood. We lose ourselves."

Harley seems to be considering her, looking at her hair, her face, then he stands up with his fist full of napkin. "Be right back."

She watches him cross the room and put the paper in the garbage, not the recycling. She wants to go home and dig in the basement for Martin's records, remember the first year together, when they'd go for drives together, no destination in mind, it must have been on the eight-track.

"You want another coffee?" He's still standing, his body turned towards the door.

She glances at her watch, not really noting the time. "Thanks, but I should be going. I have a lot of things to get done."

They say goodbye at the door. He shakes her hand while looking at her mouth. She has to sit in her car a few minutes before trusting herself to drive. She's not used to the body language of regular people anymore. She's not sure if he'll call her again. Maybe that's okay. It's not just a partnership with her. She wraps her arms around herself, sitting at the wheel, looking across the parking lot at a young couple heading into the café. He opens the door for her without letting go of her hand and she tilts her chin up, laughing at something he says.

CHAPTER 12

I t's Daniel who opens the door.

"Morning, Linda."

"Oh, I'm sorry. The car's gone so I thought you must be at work."

"No, sorry to disappoint." He's still in pyjama bottoms and the sound of children singing on TV comes from behind him.

"Oh, go on with you. I just thought I'd bring these up for her. We were talking gardening the other day."

"Emily? Was talking about plants?"

"I'll just put them in the shade."

She can't get away from him fast enough. It's like his face is too heavy for the smile. None of her business.

Inside the house, it's blissfully cool. Tom has lugged home an old air-conditioning unit and rammed it in the living room window. A perk of his new job, getting the appliances that no longer match the building. It's not pretty, but it sucks the dampness from the air. Outside it's like breathing sludge.

She finds Tom hunched over the kitchen table with a bowl of cereal.

"Where were you?"

"Up the hill. Thought I'd take Emily a few plants."

He nods, his eyes scanning the paper from last week. "See this? That huge power outage last month." He uses his spoon to point at the story of how the major centres came to a standstill. "'Most widespread blackout in the history of electrical civilization,'" he reads. "So, is Emily out digging in the dirt?"

"Oh, she wasn't there. He was."

He stops chewing and squints. "What?"

"Daniel. I should have waited until later in the day. What are you up to?"

"I might get out on the water."

"With Greg?"

"Maybe." He drops his gaze to the cereal bowl. *Not Greg then.* "Oh, the hardware store called. I wrote it down." He indicates the small whiteboard on the fridge. There's a phone number and a price.

"Did they leave a name?"

"Handy's."

"No, I mean the caller. Was it a man or a woman?"

"Man."

"Was it the owner?"

"He just said he was calling about the coffee pot. Why?"

She turns to the kitchen sink and peels off her gardening gloves.

"Oh, just wondering."

"Next time I will be sure to ask for a full name." She can hear his smile without turning to look.

⌒

They're at the table when Emily gets in. Hoover, on alert for the drop of crumbs, gives her a proper greeting while Ryan, obediently, stays in his chair. Despite the food painted across his face, she goes straight to him for a hug. Daniel stays put, studying his hands.

"I was at my mother's."

"I know."

"She called?"

"You left your socks there."

"I'm going to have a shower. Change into clean clothes," she says, wiping away the splotch of raspberry yogurt on her sleeve with the kitchen cloth. "But, we should go for a walk on the beach." On the drive home she'd decided. There's no way she can wait until the evening, for Ryan to be asleep.

"Sure."

She closes the cupboard door on her way through the kitchen. "This is the one. It's always swinging open during the night." She makes certain it clicks and glances his way, but he's got his eyes fixed straight ahead.

THEY DRIVE TO a sandy beach, instead of the one nearer them. It's better for walking. Ryan holds the dog's leash with two hands and Hoover tugs him through the dunes, his nose glued to the sand.

"You can't just take off like that," Daniel says.

"I had my phone with me. And I *did* call."

"You could've left a message."

A young couple comes toward them holding hands, splashing bare feet through the water. They don't even seem to notice Emily and Daniel, but she waits for them to be out of earshot anyway.

"I'm tired, Daniel. Aren't you?" She stops to face him.

"Between this and work? Yes." Hoover and Ryan are coming out of the long grass. The dog is chewing on something—great. "I was talking to Dave last night." Daniel keeps in touch with his brother more than she does with Lola. "He reminded me that Mum and Dad went through a rough patch." Maybe she shouldn't resent him telling Dave, but she does. "Dad left for about a week. Stayed with our grandparents."

She tries to picture Maggie and Donald swearing at each other, hurling objects across the room.

"Why?"

He shrugs. "We were really little. It's weird. Dave remembers it better than me, even though he was younger."

"How is this helpful?"

"You've seen them. I mean, if it can happen to them...."

"Ryan, please don't throw seaweed at Hoover." She pulls a clump of it from the dog's head.

"Can I throw it at the water?"

"Sure." She grabs the leash just as Ryan dashes off, his arm whirling with a strand of kelp like a propeller.

"You're always picking at me," she says.

"I'm worried about you."

"I am taking care of myself—and him."

"You don't see it. I have nothing against a glass of wine here and there, but I just paid off our credit card—you're at the liquor store every week. And Ryan talks about Tom—he thinks he's telepathic. They talk about ghosts like they're family members."

"So? You make his toothbrush talk to him."

He drops his hands to his sides.

"And it's a glass of wine at the end of the day. It's not like I'm a—"

"Watch out, Mummy."

She sidesteps just in time for a web of seaweed to thwack Daniel in the knees. Ryan retreats, giggling. Daniel peels the sandy clump from his legs and, wearing a stiff smile, tosses it towards the water.

He sits with a sigh and strokes Hoover's back absentmindedly. "I'm just concerned about us." She lowers herself beside him, an arm's length away. Hoover switches sides, moving his damp body to lean against hers. Too many thoughts rush around her head. After a long silence he turns his head toward her. "I'm sorry."

He doesn't look away and she can feel herself welling up. It would be simpler if he didn't apologize. All of the words she'd rehearsed this morning seem to be fading. What was it she'd planned to say? It had made perfect sense. Reaching a hand over the dog, his fingers brush her cheek.

"Tonight, let's put him to bed early. I'll cook."

"Okay," she says, if only to keep from falling apart in front of Ryan.

⌒

Linda waits at the counter with the box in her arms. It might have been easier to return it while he was out back. But instinct made her ask them to page him.

"Linda," she hears him say, coming up behind her. "You didn't have to bring it back in to get the discount." His cheeks are full of colour, like he's been doing something strenuous behind the scenes.

He seems undecided about what to do with Beth, the cashier, watching them. He can't very well shake her hand with the box in her arms, and a kiss would be an outright scandal. He settles for patting her shoulder. Beth seems to get the message anyway and asks if he can cover for her while she runs to the washroom.

"Actually, I'm returning it. Tom fixed the old one after all."

"Did he?"

"This one's too pretty for my kitchen, and I needed to come in and pick up some other things anyway." *Not really.*

"Well, if you're sure." He moves behind the cash and takes the box from her. "Learning some new tricks on the job, is he?"

"Seems so. You spoke to him the other day. On the phone?"

"Oh, right. That was him, then."

"I don't have any other men living with me." She hopes to make him laugh.

"He's living with you now?" The question comes too quickly.

"Just staying with me for a while." Although, she can't see him leaving any time soon.

"Right." He turns his attention to the counting of cash.

She debates whether to refer to their date, invite a repeat. But they both let the moment pass and then Beth is back, straightening her nametag.

"Sorry, Linda. I have to get back there before they think I've abandoned them. Beth can help you find things, if you need help. Nice seeing you…." A business smile flashes across his face.

"You too."

In a daze, she purchases window cleaner and an overpriced package of paper towels before escaping to the muggy air outside. She's forced to put down the plastic bags and get her breath under control before continuing to her car. At her age, she should be able to read people, but it's all just as baffling as it was when she was a girl.

⌒

Daniel disappears for the rest of afternoon to gather ingredients while she tries to behave naturally for Ryan. He asks her why her face looks mad.

"Just tired."

"Sadman's tired too." He nods knowingly and turns his head toward the window. It sends a chill through her.

"Come here and give me a hug." That's all she wants to do, snuggle with him on the couch and smell his hair. He gives her the briefest embrace then goes back to lining up a series of small cars along the edge of the rug. There's a new leanness to him, his cheeks are losing their baby fat; it's easy to imagine the boy he'll soon be.

Daniel pushes through the front door with an armload. He has to make two trips from the car but insists on doing it himself. Oh Christ, he's purchased lobster.

"I know what you're thinking," he says, "but I got some tips at the store. It won't be like last time."

"Can I sit outside while you do it?"

"Of course." He tips the container up at her. "And see? Totally secure in there."

"You plan on showing him what's in there?" She casts her eyes toward Ryan's room.

He doesn't answer, just closes the door with one foot and lurches into the kitchen with his load.

IT'S ONE OF his better attempts. Every once in a while Dan believes himself a chef in the wrong career. Half the time his creations are delicious. At least he tries. Cooking is only a chore for her.

"So, buddy? You liked getting a chance to use tools at the table?"

Ryan blinks at his father, his face dripping with butter. "I feel sorry for him."

"The lobster?" She can't think of anything comforting to say that isn't a lie.

"But it was tasty?" Daniel asks.

"Yup."

He even does the dishes, then opens all the windows to air things out. It feels like a beach house with the salt air tunnelling through; sand still sticks to her feet from earlier, and the hint of seafood clings to her fingers.

When she comes out of Ryan's room later, Daniel has set them up on the deck, a throw blanket for each of them slung over the chairs and two steaming mugs of coffee.

"Nice," she says, taking a seat. The heat of the day is waning and the breeze brings goosebumps to her skin.

"I was just thinking that if we had glass panels on the railings, we'd be able to spend more time out here." He stands up and shows her the height he has in mind. "That would do it, wouldn't it?"

"Probably."

"I was at a restaurant last week and that's what they did on their deck. The waiter said they're out there almost all year."

"Not much space out here though, it might feel strange…."

"I'd extend the deck too, put a firepit out here, sunken in like at Dave's place, and then we could build in some storage underneath for the wood and the lawnmower."

"It would be nice," she says, as if he's talking about winning the lottery.

He sits back down. "I know you don't want to move again."

"We haven't given it a chance—"

"I agree." He lifts a shoulder. "I dropped in and saw Dad this afternoon. He…clarified a few things for me." Thank you, Donald. "We ought to give it another year here."

They finish the wine from supper and talk of changes, other ways to make the house more their own. Daniel's face has a telltale glow, though he's only had the same amount to drink as her.

"Let's go inside," she says, not meaning upstairs, but he tugs her hand and they climb to the bedroom, leaving the lights off.

"We need doors," she whispers as he tugs at her shorts. "He can come in any time."

"I know." He ducks his head and all words are lost. She clenches her jaw to keep from making a sound, but everything else seems to seize up too. He feels it. "What?" Looking up. "Do you hear something?"

"I just can't relax." The heat is rapidly evaporating from her skin. "Let's get under the covers, at least," she says.

He shoves the blanket down to the foot of the bed and pulls the sheet over them. "Tomorrow morning," he says, running the whiskers of his chin lightly over the skin at the crook of her neck, "I'm redesigning the house to have doors."

WHILE HE SLEEPS through the night beside her, snoring, she stares at the ceiling. Twice, she sneaks into Ryan's room to check on him. It's harder to hear him with Daniel next to her.

Maybe it's a cough or maybe a guttural sound leaking from deep in Daniel's throat. Either way, she can't settle without knowing for certain. Four hours is all she gets. That's even worse than her usual.

But Daniel feels none of that, whistling as he rinses out his cereal bowl in the sink.

"That looks like Richard's car," she hears him say. He's staring out the kitchen window.

"What?"

"Your mother's here. Was she planning to come by?"

"Not that I know of."

Daniel doesn't move for the door so she gets up and opens it, catching Mary mid-knock.

"I'm sorry." There's a small suitcase at heel, handle extended. "I didn't know where else to go." Her makeup is intact, but there's a pinched look about her and her eyes are pink.

"What's happened?" Emily says, reaching for the suitcase.

Manners first, she catches sight of Daniel in the kitchen and Ryan beyond. "I'm very sorry to barge in like this."

"Mum, stop it. Just come in, for God's sake."

She pulls her lips back into a smile and scuttles down the hallway into the bathroom, beckoning Emily to follow.

"I think Richard has someone else."

Years ago, Emily might have gloated, finally proven right.

"You *think* he might?"

"No." She stands a little taller. "I'm sure of it."

"Did you ask him?" Mary closes her eyes and takes a deep breath. "Don't you want his side?"

"He joined a gym last month. Last week he coloured his hair. Highlights and everything."

"Okay."

"And I found this in his pocket." She produces a tube of lipstick. Clearly, it's not a Mary shade.

"The bastard," Emily whispers, not knowing what else to say.

"Grandma, what are you doing in the toilet?"

"Oh, hello, Ryan."

"Just talking, sweetie. Do you need to come in?"

"Gotta poop."

Are all kids wired to interrupt at moments like this?

"I'm sorry, Mum. I'll just help him."

Mary pastes on a smile and backs out of the room.

"There's coffee," Emily calls.

⁓

Linda slips downstairs while Tom sleeps. One drag then she'll stamp it out, making sure it's extinguished before concealing it in the bin. How much damage can one drag do, really? It's progress. But Tom would be livid, and it would cost her too much air to explain it.

Steam rises as the sun warms the ground, softening everything. There's no wind. There's the distant sound of waves. It's not often that she can hear them with the buffer of scrubby trees that ring their property. Martin insisted they leave them, even though they would have had the coveted ocean view with them gone. But in the storms, they were better sheltered.

She grinds the cigarette out with her heel and bends to pick it up. It makes her dizzy. It's getting worse. The doctor said she'd soon need a machine to take away the CO_2 in her lungs while she sleeps. Then it will be oxygen. Down the line, a lung transplant. But not yet.

She takes it slow through the front yard. Around back she finds the spot where she'd left the plants, empty. Odd. Maybe Emily picked them up. She catches a movement in Tom's window, the curtains sway. His ride will be here soon.

Inside, there's the hiss of the shower from upstairs. She puts the old coffee pot through its paces and feeds two pieces of bread into the toaster, confident that he'll be down and fully dressed by the time it pops. Oh, to be young and limber.

Sure enough, he's there just as the bread leaps up. He pours them both a coffee and sits down.

"Those plants out back—" she starts.

"Already did it."

"Did what?"

"Put them in," he says. She fixes him with a stare. "At Emily's, I thought I'd surprise her."

"When?"

"Night before last."

"At night?" How deeply she's been sleeping with the air conditioner in the house.

"New moon planting. I was up anyway." He butters his toast, not looking at her. Is he pulling her leg? All her life she's been growing things and not once has she gone out in the dark to put something in the soil.

"But how did you know where she wanted it?"

"She'll like it there." He smiles, crumbs dotting his front teeth. "There was an overgrown bed, I just dug things up. Same side of the house they were on here."

"And she's not noticed?"

"Don't know. I didn't go up yesterday." As if he goes up daily.

"Had you talked about it?"

"No, I thought *you* talked to her."

She sighs. "Just Daniel."

His eyes are clear. He's clean, good appetite, no tremors. "I don't think you should be up there…without asking."

"We're friends."

"He's home now, Tom."

Popping the last bite of toast in his mouth, he nods. "I'm just helping out."

The dishwasher door makes a grinding sound as he opens it to put in his plate. He pauses to peer at the hinge. God knows he'll have that in pieces soon.

"You supposed to babysit this week?" he asks, opening and closing the door.

"Not now that she's unemployed."

He leans his back against the counter and crosses his arms.

"She did all right on the surfboard, you know."

"So you've said."

"Oh, he's here. Gotta run." He grabs a paper bag from the fridge and heads for the door. "I'm going to shoot some pool after work so, no supper." He shuts the front door before she can ask anything else.

⌒

Emily and Daniel are still in bed.

"How long is she staying?" he whispers.

"I don't think she knows."

"And she said nothing to him?"

"I heard her leave a message for him last night." If nothing else, this house is great for eavesdropping. "Said she was staying here to help *me* out."

"So, she's lying to avoid confronting him about his lies?"

"I know. But she'll do it her own way."

"It might be a good thing, extra hands, with me heading out on Wednesday."

"Sure." Ryan hasn't exactly warmed up to her.

He swings his legs over the edge of the bed and stretches. "I have a guy coming over this afternoon. He'll give us an estimate for the deck. I figured I'd ask for a quote on the fence too."

"Can we afford that?"

"It should be okay. I checked the bank account yesterday." Her stomach gives a twist; spending chunks of money always does that. "My overtime hours are helping. And I'll start sketching out some interior changes myself," he says, winking.

Ryan didn't wake up the other night, but now there is her mother downstairs. It's not just the lack of doors. It's too much, this flood of affection. He keeps throwing his arm over her in his sleep, clamping her to the bed, weighting her spine. She lifts it off but it wanders back over, like it has a life of its own.

"You showering?" he says, pulling out his clothes for the day.

"You go first." It'll give her a few minutes to herself, as Ryan's usually in here by now.

She closes her eyes and lies on her back in the middle of the bed, listening to the sound of running water. It's not like Mary can't afford a hotel; she's here for a reason. Should she be prodding her to do the right thing—whatever that is? The older she gets the less black and white it all seems.

There's a bang, followed by the sound of shattering glass from downstairs, accompanied by a shriek. She leaps from the bed, her pulse racing. Hoover howls. From the top of the stairs she sees Mary in her nightgown, clutching her chest. The shards of glass extend nearly to her bare feet. The shadow box has fallen.

"My God. I wasn't even near it," Mary gasps.

"Don't move, the glass is everywhere." Emily points a finger at the dog. "Stay, Hoover!" He's on his bed, inches from the debris, standing up with his nose working hard at the air.

"I just came out of the bedroom and I thought I'd just look out at the water—"

"Just watch Hoover for me."

She scrambles under her bed for a pair of old sneakers.

"Mummy?" His bottom lip is trembling.

"You stay up here while I clean up. Daniel," she calls into the bathroom, "that was my Valentine's gift falling from the wall."

"What?" He sounds bewildered, his hearing dulled with his head under the shower.

Halfway down the stairs Hoover forgets her command. It's his habit to get out of bed for a stretch and a roll on the rug. His paw finds a shard of glass and he lets out a yelp.

"Fuck," she spits out, unable to hold it back.

"Lie down," she barks. He doesn't hear her and begins to investigate the source of pain with his mouth. His tongue will be punctured next. She shoves him back onto his bed, holding him on his side with her knee. The glass glints from the centre of his right front paw. Quickly, she grasps it with her fingers and yanks it out. Blood drips to his bed and he tries to nip her. "No!"

"Oh dear," Mary says from behind her. She's swivelled around, standing on one leg trying to pick out a clear path of escape. "I think I'm okay. I'll just…." She makes a wobbly leap and lands free of the wreckage. "I'll get the broom?"

"Yes, Mum. And toss a roll of paper towel this way?"

By the time Daniel appears, Mary is doing a second pass with the vacuum.

"No one is to come down here without shoes on," Emily says, pointing at Ryan's bare feet.

The dog has been banished to the deck where he's working hard to free his paw of the wad of paper towel held there by duct tape.

"How did it—?"

"Mum said it just fell, all on its own." Her breath is stale from sleep and she needs water. The adrenalin is starting to wear off, and she feels like lying down.

"What a pity," Mary says. "That was a thoughtful gift, Daniel."

"Maybe it could be repaired," he says, helping Ryan push his feet into a pair of shoes.

Kneeling to lay the box on its back, she pretends not to hear. It's not hard to rip the loop of rope free of the nautical chart. She inspects it for glass in a shaft of sunlight.

"I'm going to get dressed. Dan, can you call the vet? It looks pretty deep."

Back in the bedroom, she undoes the knot and pulls the shackle free. What if it had fallen in the night? She's holding it in her palm staring at it when Ryan sniffles from the doorway.

"He did it."

"Who did it?"

"Sadman."

"Oh no, it was just the drywall crumbling...."

If you'd used a screw instead of a nail, Daniel pointed out.

"He's not sorry."

"Come here." She opens her arms to him. "These things happen. It's nothing to do with you."

"Not me."

"Or your friend. Sometimes things just fall."

Afterwards, she dresses, choosing jeans for once, just so that she can tuck the shackle away in her pocket.

⁓

Linda's answering machine goes back to its usual job of collecting medical appointment confirmations, except that now half of them are for her. She goes into the kitchen. There's a mark on the floor, a circle where it's shinier than the rest, where Bert's dish used to sit.

What to do today? She could attempt another of Tom's vegetarian recipes. The last one wasn't as bad as the one before. He told her not to fuss, content to live on veggie burgers and pre-packaged bean soups. But there's a brick of tofu awaiting her in the fridge, and she's never been one to waste food.

The sound of a car makes her look out the window. Emily eases Hoover down from the back seat, wearing one of those lamp shades. One paw is encased in a bright pink bandage. The plastic cone gets caught when he dips his nose too low, and Emily has to free him so he can move forward.

Then she spots Jim, ambling past with his mutt. The dog stops to water the post of her newspaper holder. That explains the state of the grass just there. He spies her in the window and waves. Nothing for it, she goes to the door.

"Haven't seen you in a while." He squints.

"I've been keeping indoors with the heat." She claps a hand to her chest. His dog takes the opportunity to squat on her lawn.

"Wallace," he admonishes, as if his dog is trained to use a toilet in the house. He searches his pockets and comes up empty-handed. A charade, if she's ever seen one. Not once has she witnessed Jim pick up after the dog.

"Don't worry about it." It's the neighbourly thing to say, but he must make an awful mess of the beach on his walks.

"Tom home?"

"He's got a job with Shore Property Maintenance," she says.

Jim says he knows the owner's brother. But he's too quick with his enthusiasm, like Tom is a child in a man's job.

Jim's dog barks at Hoover. Emily turns and shades her eyes with her hand. Waving with the other, she starts down the hill toward them.

"They doing all right since the accident? Haven't seen Daniel around much," Jim says quietly, before Emily gets within earshot.

"They've got him working in their Calgary office."

"Ah," says Jim.

"What's happened?" Linda calls as Emily gets closer.

"Ugh. A gash on his paw this morning. Three hundred dollars at the vet and pills twice a day for a week."

Jim nods along. "Wallace met up with a porcupine a few years back. Cost us a fortune. But what can you do?" Hoover has hobbled down to meet Wallace, and they watch the dogs assess one another. "I'm out most days on the boat, if you'd like to join me. I promise not to abandon you this time." All talk leads to boats.

Emily smiles briefly. "You didn't abandon us Jim. It's just that my mother is staying with us right now. Oh," she says, turning to Linda, "thanks for the plants. Daniel just pointed them out."

"I'd meant to ask you first, but I got my wires crossed with Tom. I hope that's all right?"

"Of course. It's just that we might be ripping up the deck, but I'm sure we can shift them."

"Well," Jim says, "time to see about mowing the lawn."

They watch him go.

"Tom surfing today?"

"No, working."

"Ryan's been asking for him. Daniel's a little…." She looks at the house.

"No need to explain, love."

She lets out a long breath, shaking her head. "He's on a plane tomorrow. You should come over for supper. Just some 'izza' from down the road."

"It's the kids, you know. Always stealing the P." She can just see someone like Seth with a bedroom full of small plastic Ps.

"I figured they just couldn't be bothered to replace it."

"Oh no, it's been a target for years. They have a Wanted poster up in the store, near the cash."

"I like living in a place where that counts as crime. Anyway, tomorrow? Tom too. You can meet my mother."

"Your stepfather must be away?" It's the most tactful way she can think to ask.

"No." Emily glances back at the house. "They're taking some time apart." She widens her eyes at Linda. "Ugh, hang on." Hoover's cone is hung up on Linda's front step. "I have to get him up to the house. He shouldn't be walking around too much."

"Need a hand?"

"No, he'll make it." She tugs at his coller. "Around six tomorrow?"

~⁓

Emily is sopping up spilled tea on the coffee table. "God, it's like I can't see straight these days."

"It's all right, dear," Mary says. "You didn't get me."

She straightens up and brushes her hair from her face. "Yesterday, I went through a red light, right after I dropped Daniel off at the airport." She's surprised to hear herself confess to her mother. "It was weird. I stopped and then—I guess I'm getting used to four-ways around here—I just put my foot on the gas and went."

"Was there anyone else around?"

"There was a car right behind me. It blared its horn, but I was already halfway through the intersection." She shrugs. "I guess I was on autopilot."

"Was he with you?" She tilts her head towards Ryan's bedroom.

"He was. Don't tell Daniel."

"Why don't you sleep in tomorrow? I'll get up with him."

"He'll come looking for me...."

"I'm up early. I could take them both for a walk."

"That would be great." If it happens.

"Do you have trouble falling asleep?"

"It's not that so much as I don't *stay* asleep. It's the ghost, I guess." She smiles to make light of it. But her mother looks thoughtful.

"After your dad died, I didn't sleep for a month. I thought I was going crazy. I kept seeing him, hearing him, smelling him."

"You never told me that."

"No. They prescribed pills but I think I was worried I'd be unconscious if you needed me. Without sleep, everything is off. Everything."

"I wish I'd known."

"Why?"

"Because you were so...it would have helped me to understand. How long did we stay in the house before we moved to the city?"

"Oh, a few months. Remember you started the school year there, then you did the second half in Halifax?"

"Right. We weren't in that apartment long though."

"No, just over a year."

"That long?" In her memory, they'd been there a matter of weeks before moving into Richard's house. "But you and Richard were together before then."

Mary looks hard at her. "Together? I met him at the funeral, of all places."

"Da's?"

She nods. "He came with a friend of mine. She moved away years ago. Anyway, he was very kind. He'd lost his sister weeks before, so he was still grieving too. He gave me his business card, said to call him if I needed to talk. So that's what I did, often very late at night."

"Why did I not know that?"

"I thought you did. But you were grieving. It was even harder on you—the way it happened. You needed to be angry at someone alive. That's what the doctor told me."

"God."

For once, Mary's hands are still, her fingers wrapped around her empty mug of tea. They've said more to each other in the past week than in the last twenty years.

"I tried to keep things light between us. Sometimes that worked. I'd get you out shopping. Richard thought long drives were the answer."

"I hated those."

"I told him as much." She shrugs. "The man loves cars the way Charlie loved boats. Men."

There's a faint knock on the front door and then it opens, making both of them jump. Tom steps in and smiles at their surprised faces.

"Jesus, Tom."

"Sorry, ladies."

"No, I suppose you *did* knock."

"Oh, where I grew up we were in and out of each other's houses all the time," says Mary, smoothing things over, even if she doesn't seem entirely relaxed. "Different times."

"Is he asleep?" He pulls his shoulders up to his ears like a shield, as if the upper floor might come crashing down on him with the waking of a child.

"A rare nap," she says. "What do you have there? Tom's been digging up his old toys for Ryan," she says to Mary.

"Think he'll like this?"

"A View-Master. God yes, maybe he'll leave the binoculars alone."

"Hoo-hoo-Hoover," Tom says, leaning over to rub the dog's belly. He likes to get him howling whenever he can. Hoover seems defeated by the cone on his head, sleeping even more than usual. "It's only got one card. I'll see if I can find any more in the basement."

"One's plenty. Your mum on her way up?" she asks, putting the toy up against her glasses. "Hey, it's the Roadrunner." She looks up to locate Tom but he's not in the room. Mary indicates the kitchen, where he's filling a glass with water. "I would have gotten that for you."

"No worries," he says. "Mum's right behind me. The phone rang just as we were leaving and she shooed me out." He raises his eyebrows.

"I'll just freshen up before the pizza man gets here," says Mary, rising from her chair. Tom smiles as if she's made a joke, but she's quite serious.

He settles himself on the couch next to Emily, his legs splayed out so that his knee brushes hers. She waits a beat, not to be too obvious, then stands up.

"I'm just going to grab my wallet."

"You need any cash?"

"No, thanks."

⌒⌒

Just when she'd decided it was done, Harley calls with another invitation. No time to brood about it, she moves about the house sealing up windows and doors. The air conditioner is set to its coldest; all the numbers have worn off and someone has placed a tiny penguin sticker on the maximum setting. The house should be good and chilly when they get back.

She knocks on the door twice before Emily appears.

"Sorry, Linda, I figured you'd let yourself in." She gives a curious smile and heads back over to the kitchen where a wine bottle has an opener jammed halfway into a cork. The doors to the deck are wide open, moving the thick air. It feels like a greenhouse minus the plants.

In the living room, Tom squints at the windows. "Do you know if they had that one replaced?" he says, glancing at her.

"Why should I know?" Clearly, she's walked in on some maintenance discussion. So now he's the authority on these things after a few weeks on the job.

"There's some condensation between the panes. Do any of them leak, Em?"

"Not that I've noticed."

"The common room in one of the apartment buildings has a wall of windows like this. They replaced a bunch of them last year."

Emily places the open bottle on the kitchen island and comes over to gape at where he's pointing.

"I'm surprised Daniel hasn't noticed that."

"Oh, I'm sure he has," Mary says. "He's probably got a plan." Then she turns and puts out a hand. "You must be Linda."

"Oh, sorry," Emily says, "I totally forgot."

"Never you mind. It's good to meet you, Mary."

They're saved from small talk by the simultaneous arrival of the pizza and Ryan waking to discover Tom in the house.

Two pizza boxes dominate the dining room table. "Sit wherever you like," says Emily, grabbing a roll of paper towel from the kitchen.

"You're in Daddy's chair," Ryan says to Tom.

"Uh oh. Am I sitting on him?"

"No! It's his *chair*, silly!"

"Anyone else for a knife and fork?" calls Mary from the kitchen.

Everyone has a slice in hand already.

"Daddy doesn't do the rocket right," Ryan tells Tom. He's eating his pizza crust-first, the toppings sliding onto his placemat. Emily watches but doesn't move to stop it.

"He doesn't?" Tom lets his mouth hang open which causes Ryan to mimic him. It's a display of half-chewed crust and tomato sauce.

No one gets a word in amid the chewing and the banter between Ryan and Tom, all of it set to the squeak and clatter of Mary's utensils. Emily's eyes look glassy as she lifts her wine to her lips.

Meanwhile, there's the puzzle of Harley. He's proposed bowling. She should have asked if it's just the two of them. But all she could think of was Tom's eighth birthday party. Half his class had piled into two cars and gone to the alley in the city. He had so many friends then.

Silence. Everyone is looking at her.

"What's that?"

"I was telling Ryan that his mum is a natural on a surfboard."

"Oh yes, that's what I've been told." She gives her biggest smile to Ryan.

"Pfft," Emily says, even though it's clear that she's pleased her son finds this piece of news fascinating. "I almost stood up at one point, but you didn't see it because you went off with your buddy."

"Greg?" Linda offers.

"No, whatsisname…." Emily snaps her fingers.

"Well," says Mary, "I don't think I could do it. But you were always happiest in the water."

Tom nabs a lump of cheese from Ryan's plate and pops it in his mouth, causing the boy to retaliate by reaching for Tom's gnawed crust. Mary's utensils go quiet as she watches mid-chew.

Emily clears her throat. "I'm sorry to say that the new plants might have to relocate. I had an email from Daniel saying that they can start work on the deck next week."

What a relief to know that ramshackle fence will be gone.

"I'll move them," Tom says. "I'll get some help from the little man." There's a distant ringing. "That your cell?" he says, looking at Emily.

"No, it's mine. I'll leave it," Mary says, laying her knife and fork parallel on her plate, not meeting her daughter's stare. "Nice of you to do that, Tom."

"It's nothing."

"Will you put me to bed tonight?" Ryan turns sideways to face Tom. "I can—"

"Will you tell me that story again about the talking sea?"

Instead of answering, Tom looks at Emily and gets a little nod.

"It looks like you need a bath first," he says, taking a swipe at Ryan's tomato-sauce beard with his napkin.

"I'll do that part." Mary stands with her empty plate. "I'm all done. You can sit and enjoy your wine," she says to Emily, who looks startled.

"Okay. Just open the cupboard for him, he's allowed three toys. Oh! Make sure he pees before he goes in."

Mary nods, herding him away, careful not to let his hands touch her shirt.

Linda waits until the bathroom door clicks shut. "Nice having her here?"

"Yes," she says, but there's a telltale twitch. "It's good to have someone here at night."

Tom wanders into the living room.

"She thinks he's having an affair," Emily says in a low voice, just for Linda.

Right, the stepfather. A lot of things went unsaid with Martin, but she'd have spotted that on him like a stain.

"Good that she has you."

Emily shrugs, looking toward the bathroom. The tap has turned off now, so they might be overheard.

"Yes, I suppose so."

⌒

Hoover interrupts a good sleep, nudging her with a damp nose to be let out. Christ, if only she could sleep through one night.

"Go pee," Emily mutters opening the back door, trying to hang onto a thread from her dream. Maybe she can slip back under the sheets and just pick up where she left off. He's only inches out the door when his tail flicks and a rumble starts in his throat. She catches a whiff of something as she moves to grab his collar.

"It's just me," says a voice from the side of the house.

"Jesus, Tom, you scared me."

"Sorry, couldn't sleep." He crosses the lawn, picking his way around the edge of the newly framed deck. Something is pinched between his fingers, the source of the smell. He holds it towards her as he draws close.

"Oh, why not? I need something to help cram my heart back in my chest."

She inhales a small amount at first. It's been years since she's had a joint. It'll probably knock her flat.

"Let me guess," she says with the smoke escaping her lips, "Seth?"

He smiles, not answering. She takes a longer pull before handing it back to him.

"How's Ryan?"

"Funny you should ask." She leans back against the house. "I discovered his secret treasure today. This morning, I got a nasty letter about our taxes. Good thing I caught him shoving it behind the bottom drawer of his dresser. Half our mail, invoices, bills...." She'd like to kick herself for not investigating why the drawer hadn't been shutting properly for months.

"How did he get his hands on all that?"

"My fault." Thanks to the joint, she's able to smile. "I showed him how to get it from the box."

He holds out the roach to her and she takes it. Her body feels lighter already.

"Dan's been getting extra pay, so I lost track." She puts it to her lips, careful not to burn them.

"But, you'll be okay."

"Yeah, except for all this." She sweeps her arm at the piles of new lumber, the line of the fence forming along the edge, the sheets of glass for the new wind-sheltered deck. Too bad they'd signed off on this before discovering Ryan's stash. Damn lucky the power hadn't been cut off. Suddenly it seems funny. Ryan, the tiny accountant in his room. He was distraught when she dug it all out. The drawer also contained Daniel's missing prescription clip-on sunglasses and several of her unused (thank God) tampons along with the original tax bill. Her shoulders start to shake. Tom plucks the joint from between her fingers before she drops it.

"And you?" She wipes tears from her eyes. "What are you doing out here?"

The way he's moving, it's like he doesn't have bones.

"I just come to be near the water."

"I thought you weren't supposed to do this."

"I don't…much." She tries to give him a serious look, but the corners of her mouth float up. He continues, "I'll just get a little buzz and save the rest for later. But, no. Not recommended."

"You gotta live though." Is she starting to sound stoned? "I'm always wound up tight."

"Not me, the meds flatten everything."

She pictures him like a lump of pie dough being rolled out on Linda's floury kitchen counter.

"Jesus. Have you looked at the stars?" It's like deep space is suddenly visible. The oily blackness makes the starlight that much brighter, and that wisp that might be cloud is the Milky Way. "Am I high?" she says, not daring to look away from the spectacle. It feels nearer than usual.

"I'd say so." She can hear his smile.

"Man, I feel good." All the weight of it gone—the awkward intimacies of marriage, her mother's fragility, the responsibility of her words around Ryan. It's just the two of them.

He sinks to the ground and leans against the wall. She follows suit and reaches out for his hand, threading her fingers into his, rubbing them together. He allows it, staying silent. The skin of their hands is so different. His fingers are long and straight with calluses on the pads, and there's a tiny scar running along his wrist.

"After my dad died, I tried to kill myself," she says, unashamed with him. "Even after Ryan was born I wasn't sure I could handle things." His fingers tighten around hers. "These thoughts…like I didn't belong." She looks to the Milky Way again. It's comforting, this feeling of smallness. "But we're just bits of dust. Aren't we?"

"We are. Just pieces." His voice is soft. He presses her hand to the ground between them. Their fingers move together, sifting fragments of soil, rolling small stones between their palms. "Just listen," he says. And she does. There's the wind and the waves and a faint thumping. Her hand moves to his chest feeling for his heartbeat. It's fast. Is that what she heard? Or was it her own? Hoover appears. He shoves his nose into their laps, licking and rooting for a treat. The giggles leak out of her.

Then another voice is there.

"What *are* you doing over there?" Her mother at the back door in her ankle-length nightgown, a sleeping mask around her throat like a bulky necklace. Now the laughter is boiling up. Tom lets go of her hand and the air is cool when he stands up. Mary shoos Hoover away from them. Tom says he's sorry. It's a streak of colour as she moves into the house. Apologies and goodnights and *quiet, you'll wake him, get ahold of yourself.*

Mary shuffles off to bed, and through the kitchen window Emily watches Tom ambling home. She's feverish. His touch brought her to the brink of understanding something. But what was it? She pulls a box of crackers from the cupboard, drinks apple juice right from the carton, the sweet and the salty and the crunch. On the couch, she lies down and contemplates the height of the ceiling, imagines herself floating into that night sky, touching points of light.

Ryan finds her there in the morning, on a pillow of crumbs.

⁓

Tom must have thought she wouldn't mind him taking the car. But it's a bit much. Twice in the past two weeks she's discovered an empty driveway and a hasty note where her keys should be. She's regretting saying yes to lending it to him for getting to the beach.

"Mind if I tag along?" Linda asks. Tom turns at the back door, a wetsuit flung over his shoulder. "I feel like I've been cooped up all summer."

"Okay. I might be out for a couple of hours."

September days are drier. It's a pleasant kind of heat during the day, and the nights are cooler. The sea is at its warmest of the season. Maybe she'll dip a toe in.

In the car, he twists to reverse out of the driveway. "You driving me to my meeting tomorrow night? If not, I can stay in the city after work, but I'll need a ride back."

"I'd planned on it. Thought I'd see a friend while I'm at it."

"Doris?"

"No."

"Handy?"

"Harley," she corrects.

She doesn't like his smirk. This is exactly why she's said nothing to him or anyone else. As far as she can tell, they're just friends, even though she did not make a good fourth on his bowling team. Bringing her vehicle would avoid Harley driving her home and the goodbye in the car, feeling like a clumsy teenager.

"What'll you do?"

"He suggested an early movie."

He sniffs. "You think all the new stuff is terrible."

"It's time I give Hollywood another chance."

"What one?"

"Some action thing with Arnold Whatshisname."

Tom doesn't need to say it, the latest Terminator won't change her opinion on wasting money at the theatre. But they can sit beside each other, in a dark, cool building. No more bowling.

"All right," he says, like he's giving her his reluctant approval.

"What about you? Any girls in your life?"

"Emily." He keeps his face straight, but he's always had Martin's dry wit.

"What about Greg's little sister?" Hadn't he mentioned her asking him out?

"I went and looked at boards with her a while ago," he says, raising his eyebrows at her. "That would be weird."

Because they've known each other since they were kids? Or because she knows about him? Or because of Greg? He doesn't say, putting the car in park and handing her the keys. Standing, he reaches behind and pulls up the zipper on his suit. He puts his sunglasses in the cup holder. "Just keeping it simple, Mum." It's the advice his doctor likes to spoon out at the end of a session.

Another surfer wanders past and stops to talk. She can't make out the words.

"Someone you know?" she calls out.

"No, he was just wondering if we'll get some swells from that hurricane. Isabel?"

The thought of people out there on the edge of a storm. She barely hears the rest of what he says, his words drowned out as he feeds the board out of the back seat. "Too far south...."

She takes her time climbing the stairs. He's already wading out. It never ceases to amaze her how the dunes can muffle the full roar. On this side, it's like hearing the very earth breathe, one gasping intake of air, like it has the same shoddy lungs as her.

To the left of the stairs, she takes shelter from the breeze. It's too close to a garbage bin, but there's nothing for it if she doesn't want sand in her eyes. The smell is mostly carried off except when it whirls around and delivers a whopping stench of ripe dog poop her way.

She easily picks him out from the others. His hair has gotten long since that cut back in the spring, wavy strands hang over his eyes. When he started this as a kid, she drove him down on the weekends, as long as she wasn't working. Otherwise, he'd catch a ride with a friend. Martin came along a couple of times. But he had the sport pegged as a *bunch of hippies* right from the get-go. He preferred his fishing. In his line of work, he didn't need to seek out extra physical activity; on his feet all the time, outdoors and hefting tools around kept him in shape. Tom responded by calling him a redneck, something Martin pretended not to find insulting.

She undoes her sandals. Might as well be able to say she's touched the water this year. She wanders down to the edge and roots her feet in the sand. Wriggling her toes in, she enjoys the sensation of water sucking the ground out from under her, until it feels like she's standing on two small islands. Nearby, a crab scuttles beneath a strand of seaweed. To think, most of the earth is covered with water, a whole other alien world. Martin used to tell bedtime stories of lost cities under the sea. But that was when Tom was small. Little did he know, the spell he'd woven on his son.

"Look at you."

Somehow he's snuck up on her.

"You weren't out long."

"Too crowded today. I'm thinking of heading out, unless you want to stay?"

"No, I've done my bit for another year or two."

He offers a soggy hand and they head for the car.

⌒

"One built a house of sticks." Emily is squashed into the armchair with Ryan, a book open between them. She glimpses Mary heading into the spare room with the phone in her hand. Who is she calling? Such secrecy.

She's developed a knack for reading aloud while letting her mind drift.

"Mummy, it's *pig*, not pink."

"Sorry. Little pig, little pig, let me come in...." They plough through the rest of the book, and then he grows restless and wanders off to pull more toys from the box in the corner. She doesn't get up, enjoying a moment free of requests. When Daniel gets home today, she'll have to tell him about the taxes. Maybe they can pay with credit and delay things for another month.

"I think I might need to do some laundry, dear." Mary's voice startles her.

"Okay. I just need to get a load out of the dryer." She uses the arms of the chair to boost herself up.

They leave Ryan in the living room, jamming plastic discs on and off the peg of the toy record player.

"Was that Richard?"

"Yes."

"You two still haven't talked about it."

"He knows." Her lips clamp shut. Up until now she hasn't pushed, knowing that her mother will take it as her being unwelcome here. But it's been weeks.

"Have you actually said the words?" She yanks open the dryer and pulls out the tangle of sheets.

"I shouldn't need to. It's up to him, if you ask me."

"So, what do you say to him? On the phone?" The lint trap is thick with fluff from more than one load.

"I tell him about things around here." As if he's interested in that. "And before you criticize me for keeping things bottled up, let's not forget that you asked me not to mention your visitor the other night."

There it is.

"I'd tell him if he wouldn't jump to conclusions, but you know Daniel."

"Still." Christ, the whole room is covered in a layer of dust. She swipes a hand across the top of the dryer then balls it up between her palms.

"Mum, you know he'd think there was something else going on."

"I've seen the way he looks at you."

"Tom?"

"You haven't?"

It was clear enough that her mother didn't approve of him putting Ryan to bed after their pizza night.

"It's not like that at all." She pulls the detergent from the high shelf. It's sticky with drips and nearly empty. "He's a friend. We shared a joint." It was a good decision, not telling her about his illness or about the first time he'd been here.

"I thought things were…better with Daniel."

He thinks so too. "It's fine." On the phone he'd suggested they try for a second child. "What are you scared of, Mum? You have us."

Mary starts adding her whites to the machine, placing each item apart from the other rather than ramming it all in, and choosing the cold setting.

"I'm just trying to prepare myself for what he'll say. You're young, you don't know what it feels like to face this kind of thing at…this stage of life."

Emily begins to pull apart the lump of sheets. It's still damp in the centre.

"Is Richard the love of your life?"

"No."

They both pause at how quickly the answer arrives.

"I'm a grown woman," says Emily. "What's to stop you from living life for yourself now? Take courses. Travel. Join a club. Or just hang out with us."

"You've never liked him." Mary pauses and shoots a weak smile over her shoulder. "It's okay to say it."

Emily shrugs. "He's an asshole."

"It's all a front. He's insecure."

Emily rubs her neck and looks at the ceiling. "That's no excuse for some of the things he said to me over the years."

"Think about it." Mary glances toward the living room, but Ryan is chattering away to himself. "His first time being a parent was to an adolescent girl who wanted her real father to come back to life."

"Okay, it might have been hard."

"He never had a chance with you, darling." Mary places a hand on her shoulder and Emily stops sorting and stares at a pair of tiny socks with boats on them.

"All that aside, he cheated on you. Don't let him get away with that." Mary takes her hand away to close the lid to the washer.

"Maybe he never had a chance with me either."

EMILY IS TOE to toe on the couch with Mary, watching the late news, a blanket thrown over the two of them.

"Sure you don't want a glass?" says Emily. Her mother refused to join her, saying it gets her up in the night.

"No, dear. I'm off to bed in a minute." She stretches her arms above her head and yawns. "You usually read at night, don't you?"

"Mm. I can't concentrate lately." They've been sitting in front of the TV, but she's absorbed none of it. It's all speculation about the approaching storm. She's been hashing over things from years ago, wondering about Richard, replaying their arguments. *Don't go thinking your dad was a saint, missy.*

Mary stands and tucks the blanket back over Emily's legs. "Well, don't stay up too much—" She goes still, her eyes fixed on something.

"What is it?"

"Something outside."

"Probably Tom."

"No, not Tom." She goes to the window. "Oh, it was probably my own reflection." She gives an embarrassed laugh.

Emily sighs. "That's the thing about these windows. You can't see out when we have the lights on at night. It freaks me out sometimes." She leans over and switches off the lamp on the side table. "There. Anything?"

"No. I'm just tired."

Emily leaves the light off and stretches out on the couch. On the screen, a kayaker leans on a paddle; there's a closeup of a filthy beer bottle. The background looks familiar, maybe it's nearby. She turns up the volume but they flash to the next thing before she can catch it.

"Night, dear."

"Night, Mum." There's the click of her door.

Of course her dad wasn't a saint. No one is. But what had Richard been getting at? She tries to imagine what he took on with her and her mother back then. A bachelor in his forties, used to doing things his own way. She'd resented him for loving her mother. Hated him. She's on her back facing the windows, her eyes out of focus, seeing his house for the first time, smelling it. It had been cleaned, it wafted of bleach and fake pine. That's how it started off, her impression of him linked to that sterile environment. Her mother tried to quiet her when she muttered something about embalming fluid. It must have felt like a slap from the girl he was taking in.

There is a movement near the window. She's on her feet without thinking about it, going straight for that spot with her heart racing. If Tom wants to smoke a joint with her, he can tell her, not stare through the window. Or Jim or whoever. Hoover is with her, stumbling to his feet, his nose twitching. She cracks open the back door and has a good look. "Tom? Are you out there?" Hoover nudges the door open and trots to the back fence, his nose to the ground. He lets out a woof and wags at her. There's something glinting on the ground.

"What is it?"

She goes out, barefoot, hoping it's not another dead bird. But it's Da's shackle, nestled in the grass instead of in the jewellery box where she left it this morning.

CHAPTER 13

L inda discovers the box on Sunday morning. It's sitting on the porch. A sticker on the side reads *Handy's Hardware*. She can't lift it, she'll have to ask Tom for help to take it inside. There's a crate of water, candles, two small propane tanks and a burner to fit on top, several cans of food, a first aid kit, a small radio, and an enormous bag of chips. Underneath it all is a six-pack of beer with a yellow sticky note, no words, just a smiley face.

"What a romantic."

It was on the news yesterday, another storm. Her basement still has a stockpile from last season. Oh well. She can run the box back to the store during the week. If there's a power outage—more than likely—she'll be needing more ice for the cooler.

"What's that?" Tom says from the doorway, his voice hoarse from just waking up.

"Hurricane kit."

"You ordered a kit?"

"No. Harley must have dropped it off." Tom scratches his head and walks into the kitchen. "I don't think we really need it." She straightens up and goes to stand in the kitchen door. "I'll send it back."

He fills the kettle and turns to her with a lopsided smile. "Methinks she dost protest too much." Tom was forced to memorize Shakespeare in high school, and Linda was the one who tested him on it.

"Well, it's a waste."

"*They* might need it," he says, meaning Emily. "Everything's closed today."

"Right, it's Sunday. Have you heard an update?"

"Nope." Tom's avoidance of the TV often keeps him in a bubble. "But I had a message from Greg."

"What message?"

"I think it was, *it's got a name now, let's get down there.*"

"And that makes sense to you because…?"

"They only name them if they're hurricanes. He's hoping we'll get some double overhead." She continues to stare. "Big waves, Mum." He's scooping loose tea into a strainer, but he catches her look. "Don't worry. My board's not up for that kind of punishment. Where's the honey?"

"Promise me you won't."

"Found it." He pulls his lips under his teeth as he strains to get it open. "Who puts these lids on?" He's smiling but she won't be distracted.

"Tom."

"What?"

"Promise me you won't go out there in the storm."

"Don't worry. The waves are good ahead of it, not during."

She watches his back. His shoulders are relaxed, he's stirring honey into his mug. She starts to say something then stops herself. "Are you done there? A woman needs her coffee."

⌣⟶

Emily stands behind her mother, trying not to look as she punches her code into the machine. "You're absolutely sure you want to do this?"

"It's my money too," Mary says, pulling an envelope from the slot on the wall.

"I doubt you can withdraw that much."

"Then I'll get what I can today and we'll see about more next week. I want to help."

It should ease the knot in her gut. Mary suggested they have a little dinner party out on the deck, as soon as the renovation is done. Ryan's fourth birthday is fast approaching. But all of it meant one thing to Emily, spending money. Her mother pressed her, wondering why she'd resist a simple dinner. She ended up confessing about the unpaid bills. After adjusting their account balance for the payments, they'd be short for their mortgage this month.

"Well, that's something anyway." Mary stuffs the cash in the envelope and hands it over. "Now would you mind running us home before going to the airport?"

She swaps spots with her mother and enters her code.

"You're okay to keep Ryan with you?"

"As long as that's okay?" Mary says.

Ryan claimed it was the Sadman that took the shackle, not him. With forced calm, she told him he'd never get in trouble for telling her the truth. Still, he shook his head, bottom lip stuck out.

"I don't mind bringing him with me," Emily says. But a glance at her mother's face makes it clear that she sees this as some kind of test. "That would be great though."

The machine pulls in the fat envelope and spits out her card.

"You two might want some time alone, anyway," says Mary.

SHE'S LATE TO pick up Daniel. He's standing by the curb with his suitcase, checking his watch.

"Want me to drive?" he says, throwing his case into the back seat.

"No, it's okay, you've had a long day already."

"It was lucky I got through. The boards are filling up with cancellations."

"Why's that?"

He turns in his seat to look at her. "The big storm?"

"Oh right, is it supposed to hit here?"

"Oh, they have no idea." He sighs. "That one last week was supposed to be a one-hundred-year storm and tear right through the Carolinas. The media was all excited. Then pffft. Anyway. How's the work looking?"

"The fence is done. The deck's pretty close, they just have to get the firepit in."

"Does it look all right?"

"Yeah."

"But?"

Now is as good a time as any to tell him about the bills, so she spits it out.

"I wish you'd said something to me before taking their money."

"*Her* money."

"I'm surprised at you." He shakes his head. She'd always turned them down, not wanting to be in Richard's debt.

"We'll pay it back," she says, glancing at him. Money can't buy happiness, but it seems quite capable of killing it.

⌒

Linda stands in front of the TV, her hand covering her mouth. The news anchor leans on a glossy desk. "It appears to be a modern-day message in a bottle. Peter?"

"At first the man who found it thought it might be much older, because the bottle is that of a local brewing company that hasn't made this particular ale in over fifty years."

It was the mention of the bottle's brand that made her stop her search for batteries. An image of the handwritten note comes on screen. Then the camera turns to a man leaning on a paddle.

"I'm hoping to get it back to the person. I don't have much to go on. The museum said it's only a few years old. Maybe someone will know the handwriting."

Back to the reporter's stoic gaze. "The note is very personal in nature, so we are not releasing many details." Again, they show it. She gropes her way to the couch and plops down. "…contact the station…."

She can't jot down the information. She'll have to look it up in the phone book later. Instead, she recovers sufficiently to wobble down to the basement, hanging tight to the rail. A wide shelf runs the perimeter of the house on this side. It holds Martin's bottle collection. It is a fixture, part of the foundation. He'd always kept a bottle from each of his favourite breweries and rounded it out with the occasional yard sale treasure.

"Constantly changing some little thing on the label," he'd say. "They'll be collector's items one day. You'll see, we'll retire on my bottle collection. Go somewhere we don't have to shovel snow."

It was a long-running joke, Martin's only investment. She circles the basement until she sees the gap. One missing. Maybe it fell below into the pile of bags filled with old clothing. But there's no sign of it.

The back door creaks and slams. "You in here, Mum?"

"Downstairs." Her voice is not loud enough to be heard over the TV. She should locate her inhaler. She hears his footsteps head for the kitchen, calling for her. "Down here." Her voice is a croak.

"You okay?" His tone rises in pitch.

"I need my puffer."

"Where?"

"Kitchen table."

"You should lie down," he says, watching her.

"Help me up to the living room."

Once installed on the couch she asks for the phone book.

"What's happened?"

"Did you take, or move any"—she's forced to breathe in between the words—"beer bottles?"

"Dad's?"

She nods.

"No, why?"

"I think…maybe…he sent a message."

⌁

Splashing greets them when they get in.

"What happened?" Emily says, seeking out her mother in the bathroom.

"Nothing," Mary answers, her eyebrows up.

"Daddy here?" Ryan says from underneath a beard of soap bubbles.

"I just thought he'd like a bath," says Mary.

Daniel peers around the edge of the door. "Hey, buddy, I'll help you dry off when you get out okay? I just want to see our new deck."

Emily trails behind him as he runs his hand along the new railing.

"Not bad," he says over his shoulder.

"You're happy?"

"I think it's great."

The workers left the spare bits of lumber in a neat stack. The patio furniture is still down on the grass, along with the barbecue.

"The wind might get strong enough to throw this stuff around," she says.

He shrugs. "I'll haul the wood under the deck."

"We ought to bring the table and chairs inside."

"What is it?" he says, looking at her expression.

"Earwigs."

The sight of her shuddering seems to ease a bit of the tension. They're both remembering the night she found an earwig under her pillow and screamed loud enough to start the dog howling.

Inside, a cellphone is vibrating on the kitchen counter. She grabs it before it plunges over the edge.

"Mum." She jogs to the bathroom to hand it off before the caller can hang up. "For you."

⁓

Linda pulls into a parking lot next to a white van with the news anchor's smiling face on the side: grey suit, polkadot tie, with Peggys Cove lighthouse over his right shoulder.

Inside, the receptionist has a phone to her ear. She smiles and points to a seat. Oversized pictures of familiar TV faces beam down. She turns her attention to her cuticles and begins work on a jagged one.

"Sorry about that, can I help you?"

"I'm Linda Morris, I called."

"Oh, right." Her heels click down a short hallway. Moments later she returns with him in tow. He's much smaller than she expected, his face more angular than on television.

"Mrs. Morris?"

"Linda." There's an extra blink from him when she says it.

He invites her into a room down the short hallway.

"I understand that you believe your husband wrote the letter?" he says, once they're seated at a table.

"I do." From her purse, she pulls a birthday card he'd given her years ago and places it on the table. "My late husband's name was Martin." She can see his mind working, looking at her like she's a story.

"Anyway, if this is a note left by him it might...help."

He nods. "This isn't the original. We used a copy for the story so that we could black out some of the words."

"Right."

"I'll be right back." He pauses in the doorway. "I don't suppose you'd be willing to go on air? It would be closure for the story, the note finding its proper owner."

"I'm not really comfortable—"

"It would just be the four of us, with my cameraman. Very low-key."

"I'm sorry, I couldn't."

"Right. That's quite all right. I'm sure we'll have our hands full with the storm," he says with a weak smile. He's gone for a matter of seconds, returning with a yellow envelope.

She pulls the paper out enough to see the top: *the doctor told me to write it down.* What doctor?

"He names you in it, and he mentions your son."

She looks up from the page, trying to refocus her eyes.

"I'll put you in touch with Terry—the man who found the bottle. Just leave your contact info at the desk."

She nods mutely and leaves the station with the envelope hugged to her.

⸺

Emily pushes around the contents of the freezer and yanks out a large lasagna. She hesitates before reaching in for a pizza.

"Hungry?" Dan says over her shoulder.

"I was just thinking that if the power does go out, these won't cook as well on a barbecue."

"Sure." Daniel has had nothing but restaurant food for three weeks with no need to plan ahead. It's one of her favourite things about travelling, getting out of bed and heading down to a buffet, just walking away from dirty dishes.

Afterwards, she turns to the living room and considers the windows. Is there anything to be done with them?

Daniel finds her dragging the lawn chairs inside.

"You planning on putting that food in the oven?" He indicates the frozen meals thawing on the counter.

"Oh yeah, I guess I got distracted."

"You don't have to do this. We can leave them outside, I can tie it all down."

"I'd just feel better—"

"Fine." He holds up his hands as if he's surrendering.

"What?"

"You remember the one in '96?"

"No."

"Exactly. A lot of wind and rain. It'll probably weaken before it gets to us." He sniffs and goes toward the oven. "What temperature for these things?"

"I don't know, try four hundred. I'll check in a few minutes." Like he can't read the carton himself.

It's not the best place to find privacy. Regulars like to hold court over entire sections of the coffee shop with their canes and walkers parked between tables. But it was on her way back from the city, and the last thing she wanted to do was rush home without time to absorb it. Linda scans the words for a third time. Martin had been seeing a therapist. How did she not know that? How did he pay for it?

At a nearby table, a man slurps a bowl of soup. Behind her, people compare stories about hurricanes. It's close to supper and her tea has gone cold. Leaving her sweater draped over her chair, she goes up to the counter and orders a bowl of soup. Tom can help himself to leftovers in the fridge.

She dreads bringing it all up again, not knowing how he'll take it. He'd wanted to come with her, but she asked him to tuck things away in the yard while she was gone. Nothing out there was much worth saving, he'd pointed out, threadbare from years of weathering. But it would make a hell of a mess if it hit the house, she'd argued, slipping on shoes.

Settling back at the table with her tray, she catches sight of someone familiar holding the door open for people. "Welcome," he mutters. Yes, it's Seth. That drooping posture he's had since he was a scrawny kid. If he looks her way, she'll wave, but he tips his ballcap to hide his eyes. He orders a black coffee and leaves without looking around. Oh well.

The folded note sits next to her. He was planning to tell her everything. It's as if he's occupying the extra chair at the table, watching her scoop split pea soup into her mouth. Did he think she'd reject him, blame him? It stings. Of all people, he should have known her better.

"Mind if I sit here?" A woman stands before her with a hand on the back of the chair. Linda looks around and realizes the tables have filled up.

"No, please. I should be going anyway."

"But you're not finished," the woman says, indicating the bowl.

"Oh, I never finish anything these days," Linda says. A full stomach presses on the lungs and makes breathing that much harder.

Outside, there is still no hint of the storm to come. Maybe they'll be spared this time around.

⁓

Daniel descends the stairs from Ryan's bedroom holding his glasses.

"Little...guy broke them." Clearly he'd have chosen a different word if his son was asleep.

"Oh. That's the yell I heard."

She lifts the last lawn chair to the top of the stack. Everything is crammed in here now. The patio table is on its side with Ryan's boxes of toys held between its outstretched legs.

"I was just leaning in to kiss his cheek goodnight and he flung out his arm. They've snapped right here." He holds them close to his eyes in the light of the lamp.

"Don't you have a backup pair?"

He looks up, unable to focus on her face just a few feet away. "We donated a bunch of stuff before the move, remember? The old prescription was a lot weaker anyway. I'll have to take them in."

"So, a wad of tape in the meantime?"

"Looks that way. I don't get it. He was hot and cold. It's like he doesn't want me to touch him."

"He's three. It's not you, it's him."

Something catches his attention out the window and he holds his glasses up to his eyes. "What's he doing out there?"

She follows his gaze and sees Tom leaning against the old tree.

"Probably just watching the water."

"Is he smoking?" He doesn't give her time to answer. "I found a couple of butts, like hand-rolled ones."

"He's not bothering us." The power of suggestion.

"Can't he do it over there?"

"Him and Linda in that little house all the time? I think they're still getting used to someone living here." She keeps her voice casual even though she'd like to put the question to Tom herself.

"Anyway, the butts were right *here*, by the house," he says.

A polite cough stops him.

"Oh. Hey, Mum. We thought you'd gone off to bed."

"I'm heading there now. I just wanted to talk to you both first."

Now that Daniel is home she seems to feel the need to dial up the formality. Working her way between the furniture, she takes a seat on the edge of a chair. Emily perches on the arm of the couch while Daniel continues standing where he can keep an eye on Tom.

"First of all, the money. I don't want to be paid back." She holds up a hand as Emily opens her mouth. "I won't hear any more of it. It's a gift. You've never let me help before, and I consider it my right."

"But Richard. ..." Emily says.

"He knows and he agrees." She gives a little nod, her mouth in a hard line. "Second. We've talked about it now. He's come clean, as you put it, Emily."

"Have you decided anything?"

Her fingers are laced tightly in her lap. "Not yet. Right now, it's enough to have it all out."

"You were on the phone all that time?"

Mary lifts a shoulder.

"Well, I guess that's good then, Mary. And we're grateful...for the lend. The gift."

Christ, Daniel sounds stiffer than her mother.

Two knocks on the front door and then the sound of the weather stripping sliding across the wood floor.

"Hello?" Daniel looks alarmed.

"Tom?" Emily stands.

"I was just thinking about the windows." He walks into the living room, his feet bare; grass is stuck between the toes of his left foot. "You should tape them up."

"What?" Emily's smile is tight.

"Painter's tape in an X." He draws the shape in the air for her with an extra line intersecting the other two. "It should give them a little support."

"It's getting kind of late—" Daniel starts.

"There's a ladder in the shed to get up to the top ones." He doesn't even glance at Daniel; his eyes are trained on the windows.

"Thanks for thinking of it, Tom," Mary says, looking at Emily.

He turns his head her way, his eyes bright, then he scans the room, taking them all in. "Where's Ryan?"

"In bed," Emily says. It feels like there's not enough air in the house.

A groan comes from Hoover's bed. He rolls from his side to his back, showing off his belly to Tom.

"Hey, Hoovey." She can smell him as he moves past her to greet the dog. Daniel's mouth is twitching as if there are too many words in there to be held in much longer.

"The ladder?" she says. "I'll come with you and get it…if you don't mind."

⌒⌐

It's getting dim outside when she gets in. Not a light is on inside the house. She pads across the living room carpet and scans the backyard. No sign of him. He still hasn't put things away, but the shed door flaps open. In her gut it's part relief, part worry, a familiar sensation.

The air conditioner has been given a break while she was out, so she dials it to high. Leaving the lights off, she climbs the stairs to find any open windows. That's when she hears their voices.

Emily and Tom are shadows, moving toward the side of the house. He's talking too fast about suction and forces. Nearing the window, she catches sight of him and everything inside her sinks. No shoes. One hand is jammed in the pocket of his jeans and his elbow has a tremor. She watches them pull the ladder from the shed. It's awkward but Emily grabs the middle and insists on carrying it alone. What on earth are they up to?

"I've got it. You stay here."

"You'll need—"

"No thanks. Really." Her voice shakes either from the effort of lifting or holding something back. She's about to call out, but it seems like Emily has won, staggering away in a pair of flip-flops.

He's coming through the front door when she gets back downstairs. "What are you up to?"

"They need to strengthen the glass. I can feel it changing."

"Tom, can you close things up out there? Put away the chairs and things?"

She makes her voice almost too quiet to be heard; he has to turn her way and listen. He tilts his head slightly, like a bird. She repeats herself. "Remember?" she prompts.

He blinks a few times and nods.

While he's outside she searches for his pills in the usual spots. It's all right, maybe he's stashed them in a drawer or something. If he's out though, or if he's disposed of them, she can guess what's rattled him. Now is not the time to run into the city. If they can just make it through tonight, they'll get to the drop-in clinic in the morning.

⌒

The first pane is done thoroughly with interlocking Xs of bright green painter's tape. Bracing the ladder from below, Daniel gives multiple explanations of the utter futility of this exercise. He stops short of using words like *crazy* or *insane,* but it's clear what he wants to say. Then he tells her it will be hell to clean off the residue later. When she asks him for a better plan, he offers up the idea of bracing the whole wall with large beams of wood, bolted to the floor. She doesn't need to point out that they don't have those supplies on hand. Each piece of glass gets a little less tape until they run out at the midpoint.

"Oh well." She frowns and drops the empty cardboard ring to the floor.

"I'm off to bed." He yawns.

"Let the dog out first?" she says, smoothing a loose end of tape. Her arms and back ache from arching and stretching.

It's eleven when they find themselves side by side in bed. Daniel's breathing changes almost the moment the light goes out. Turning her head to the window, she watches the blur of distant trees jiggle and sway and wonders if she'll be able to sleep.

Her mother looked flattened by the day. They'd met in the kitchen, Mary with a glass of water and a small blue pill in the palm of her hand. "I don't often, but the mind is busy tonight. Want one?"

She should have said yes.

"He's suspicious about the smoking," Mary whispered, her eyes glancing upstairs where they can make out the sound of Daniel brushing his teeth. "He wanted to know if Tom's *okay now*."

"What'd you say?"

"Just that I've only met him a few times, and that he's good to Ryan." Her eyebrows are arched, seeking more.

"He is okay. Well, maybe a little off, but Linda's there with him."

"What do you mean, off?"

"He has an illness."

"A mental illness?" The words are enunciated like a school teacher's.

"It's okay, Mum. He's okay."

Her eyebrows remain up. She shouldn't have said *okay* twice. Who is she trying to reassure?

"I wish you'd told me that before."

"It's not like our family is all that *normal*," she says, wishing she'd just gone upstairs and left the subject for another day. But her mother surprised her.

"I suppose that's true. No saint, your dad."

"Da?" She'd meant everyone in the family but him.

Mary popped the pill in her mouth and took a sip of water. "Anyway, we'll talk in the morning."

Lying in bed, she's thirsty—too much caffeine and almost no water. Closing her eyes, she sees Da in the cockpit. His knee braces the tiller and in his hand is not a book but a bottle. There's a slack smile on his face and his eyes water slightly. He's pale but for the spider legs of pink at the surface on his cheeks and nose, where he always had a rosy hue. The wind stirs up his aftershave, along with his odour, that sweetness sat too long in the sun.

He's packed the picnic for the sail, or so he said. She searches the bag again then looks up.

"Da?"

"Mm, Duck?" He's not taking his eyes from the horizon.

"I can't find anything in here."

"Look harder, surely there's something."

She plops the bag at his feet, zipper gaping open.

"Sure, an empty Thermos and that sandwich from last week." Mould has done rather well in the interim, making it look as if the bread has been packed in with cotton balls.

"Oh," he says, barely registering concern.

"So, there's nothing for *me* to drink," she adds. "Not even water." Her tongue feels thick in her mouth. That smell from the cabin seeps into her. "What am I supposed to drink?"

Her voice rises to a roar, hurting her ears. Her head aches from hours of bright sun, light bouncing up from the water. Charlie moves things around in the bag with one hand, coming up with nothing. Then he eyes the bottle in his other hand and presents it to her, one side of his mouth curling up. It's getting harder to focus on his face; the light is blinding. He says something but she can't make it out above the noise. It's not coming from her, it's above and all around, the sails creaking and slapping, the whole boat quivers. Inside her belly, there comes a sense of dread, the body readying itself for something, like the hours before birthing. So thirsty, and the maddening sound of water everywhere but in her mouth.

Her eyes flutter open. Hoover is at the bedside wagging, squeaking, then panting. She rolls toward him. His tail is wet.

⁓

Linda kneels by the tub. With these winds, the power will go out. She can't hear if Tom has come back in with the white noise of the running water filling the room. It's slow progress, getting back up, with her feet numb. The air has thickened since she left the coffee shop. Resting her hands on the sink, she does a slow jig until the pins and needles go away. Stagnant—a word from her crossword the other day—no movement or flow. It's just the word for her life. It's the message Doris has been shouting for years, *move.*

Would he have told her? Maybe she was there as he wrote it. She only wishes she could have told him that it was not his fault.

She turns off the water.

"Tom?" she calls from the top of the stairs. Rain drums the roof. The house is in darkness except for the light over the stairs. The motion of the trees has changed, the house has begun its inhale and exhale, the blind slaps the sill in the kitchen. One window left to seal. It's begun to rain.

The lights are out at Emily's. Too late to call and ask if he's there. If he's out there, she hopes the rain will soon chase him in.

Slap, slap, slap goes his tail. Little sprays of water hitting the bedclothes.

"How're you wet?" she mumbles, trying to focus.

The wind has gained force. The sounds from her dream are in here, raindrops gunning the glass at the back of the house. There's cracking and slapping and the wind whistles through the window nearest her, despite being closed. And water, like the tap is on in the bathroom. She turns to the clock but the face is blank. Daniel is on his back, his lower jaw hangs open, lazily exhaling every few seconds. Perching her glasses on her nose, she makes her way out of the room with Hoover pressed to her shin.

Surveying the living room below, she tries to make sense of what she sees. The floor is shining, a few of Ryan's blocks floating slowly toward the front of the house. Water runs down the inside wall of windows, so much like those Zen water features she's seen in public buildings.

"What the fuck?" It should wake up the others, but her words don't compete with the thrumming of the roof. Mary is downstairs, likely wearing her sleeping mask and earplugs.

Her stomach heaves, like she's still on-board with Da, the cabin rocking. Maybe this is part of the dream.

Daniel doesn't wake easily—she has to put both hands on his chest and shout his name. When his eyes finally settle on her, she says, "We're flooding."

He tries to close his eyes again. "We're on a hill," he mumbles.

"It's coming through the back windows."

Hoover boosts his wet paws onto the pillow and slurps Daniel's cheek. It does the trick.

They stand at the top railing like it's the bridge of a ship. "Not much we can do except mop it up right now." It's odd, having to raise their voices to speak to each other in the middle of the night inside their own house.

"Mum's sleeping down there."

"She can come up."

"What? In bed with us?"

"Or she can probably stay there. The water's not going to float her away."

"Fuck." Emily's looking at the sponge that is Hoover's bed, the new-ish rug.

"The windows haven't leaked before this?"

"Not that I know of."

"Is someone out there?" Daniel says, squinting at the windows.

They don't have time to react, but Emily catches sight of a dark shape in that fraction of a second before it hits the topmost window. It's the second pane she'd taped. One moment it is a delicate branch from a living tree, useful for so many things—tiny bird feet perching for a rest between flights—and the next it's the spear that makes the first cut. The glass breaks neatly along the taped lines into six triangles that cascade to the living room floor, shattering as they connect with the patio table and chairs.

The wind is several octaves higher through this new opening. She doesn't scream, just pulls in a lungful of air and holds it there. The scream is from the bedroom behind her.

"Mummy's here," she says into Ryan's ear. He looks at her wide-eyed.

"Woof."

"What?" She needs to think. Get all of them into the master bedroom.

"Big bad wolf." He cringes and ducks his head. She lets him slide away. He gets on his knees and crawls under his bed.

"It's just wind, Ryan. The storm."

Maybe it's better that he's under there. The dog is trying to squeeze under too.

A new smell is in the room. Shit. Hoover has taken a squat in the corner. She stands above it wondering what to do, dizzy.

"Oh dear." Mary totters into the room, the bottom of her cotton nightgown damp and clinging to her legs. Her sleeping mask pushes her hair up into a mushroom shape, like a mad scientist's.

"Don't step over here."

"Oh dear," Mary says again, the back of her hand going to her nose.

"Grandma, the wolf is here." Ryan's voice is shrill.

"Where's Dan?" Emily asks, still guarding the corner, like the most important thing is that no one soils their feet.

"Outside, I think."

"Can you stay up here?"

Mary nods, both hands pressed to her collarbone as if she has to restrain her heart.

At the railing, Emily pauses, Daniel passes by the back windows. *What the hell is he doing?*

She splashes through her living room, thinking of the sinking *Titanic*; the ship groaning, water rising around Kate Winslet's thin dress. In the laundry room, she rams her wet feet into rubber boots.

She keeps a hand on the house as she makes her way to the backyard. Daniel is under the deck, rooting through a pile of tools.

"What are you looking for?" she yells. It's darker under here, and he holds his broken glasses on with one hand.

"An axe or a saw or something."

"Dan, you can't do any of that now. It's too late."

"Did you look at that tree? It's already broken one window."

"So, you're going to chop down a tree in a hurricane?"

"Just the branches."

Clearly, he's not fully awake. Yes, he can split a log for the fire better than she can, but she's never seen him attempt anything more with an axe. His strength is in hiring the right workers for the job.

"Just come inside."

He pauses his search. "Just let me see if I can find what I'm looking for."

"Fine. But I'm going back in."

THE THREE OF THEM gather in the master bedroom. Despite disposing of the dog's mess, the stench lingers. Emily and Mary sit on top of the queen-size bed while Ryan and the dog shelter underneath. The only consolation for Ryan is the use of a flashlight, usually tucked away on a high shelf.

"I keep telling him it's the wind," Emily says. "But he thinks it's the big bad wolf."

"You loved that one when you were small," says Mary. She sits at the foot of the bed, as if she is there to read a bedtime story.

"At least we're not in a boat."

"And your insurance will cover things," Mary says.

Insurance. Did she even read the policy details? They'd chosen the cheapest one, signed their names. Done.

"Is it getting stronger?" Emily says.

Mary doesn't hear her, so she asks again. Her mother only nods and looks up at the ceiling.

"I'm going back out."

Partway down the stairs, she sees a second figure outside.

She ducks at the sound of a crash, another piece of glass shatters on hardwood below.

⌒

Linda's power clicked off a while ago. She didn't go to bed. There's no point in trying to sleep. It's better to be downstairs, further from the roof. But it's also the best place to watch for him at both doors. She's turned sideways on the couch. Legs curled under a throw blanket. There is a candle next to her and a pack of matches when she tires of the darkness.

She hears glass breaking. The car window, maybe. She'd like to know what it is but she is rooted here, unable to stand let alone walk the dozen or so steps it would take.

The air is heavy. Breathing is a conscious activity. She wants to find Tom, help calm him, pull him out of his spiral of thoughts, but she has to reach for the inhaler, deal first with the ability to remain awake and lucid.

"Don't panic." It's Martin beside her, even though she knows he's not. But she sees him over the edge of the inhaler. "That's right, relief is coming." He's covered in sand, the bottle lies across his lap, empty of its message. "Count to ten." He lifts a hand and raises a thumb, then index finger, then middle. There's burning at the back of her throat, her heart picks up momentum. He ticks off the fingers, he's onto the second hand now, six, seven….

The inhaler slips from her hand.

"Eight, nine…."

⌒

The front of the house is in the lee of the wind. It doesn't fully hit her until she corners the house, and that's when she sees him fully.

"Tom." Emily ducks under the lurching branches of the old tree. Her words are thrown back by the wind. He sits at the base of the tree, his clothes scattered on the ground around him, moving with each gust as if they have a life of their own. Mud smears his face and his hands press into the earth, grasping the roots. His lips move. "Tom." His eyes are shut. "You have to come inside. The storm is getting worse." At the word *storm*, his eyes snap open and lock onto her.

"I am talking to it. I have to calm it with my hands, but it wants two, yin and yang." He snatches her sleeve. "It's my fault, I have to fix it. We have to fix it."

"Storms are not your fault." She places her hand over his, hoping he'll loosen his grip. The chill of him spreads through her. "It's dangerous out here. Come with me."

He clutches her other arm and hauls her toward him. She's losing balance. He has the advantage, cross-legged on the ground, an anchor.

"I need you." As he pulls her nearer she sees that he's gone hard. She turns her head, trying not to look.

"Please, let me go, Tom."

An arm wraps around her waist and tugs. "Let go." It's Daniel, drenched and angry. His voice snaps Tom to full alertness. Shit. There's no time to plea for rationality with Daniel.

Tom pulls himself up, knocking Emily aside, lunging at Daniel, who is holding a saw. He grabs Daniel by the head and clamps one hand to his mouth. "Shut up shut up shut up." Daniel drops the saw and wheels his arms, trying to stay upright. "You're dead. Stay dead." It's not Daniel he sees. The two of them stumble together as she rights herself. Tom's voice roars: "I saw it hit you, but you never shut up. Now you talk to her too."

They hit the ground together. The impact hits another switch in Tom. Scrambling back under the tree, he crouches with his hands over his ears, cowering from whatever voice is yelling back at him.

She makes her way to her husband on hands and knees. "Daniel, are you okay?" Even in the dim light she can see his pallor. His glasses are gone. He nods, still on his back. She leans in close. "He's talking to his father, not you." The rain is heavier now. "We need to get Linda."

"I'll go down." He winces as he sits up, one arm protecting his ribs. "You go in and make sure they're okay."

"I might be able to get him inside."

"No. Just look at him. And the fucking tree is going to go." It's rocking. "We have to get away."

All the more reason for her to try one more time. She holds out a hand to Dan and hauls him up. He limps towards Linda's house, not looking back.

"Tom." She stays beyond his arm's reach. "Come in the house."

His eyes are open but he doesn't see. He pleads, "Just stop, stop, stop." In his terror, he's defecated. Recoiling, she watches his scattered movements.

"I'll be back," she tells him, even though she's not sure.

IN THE HOUSE, she climbs the stairs, soaked through and trembling. Ryan is still under the bed, Mary reaching with a hand, trying to pat his head like a dog. The house groans, as if trying to hold itself together. The floorboards hum with stress—it travels through her bones, into her chest.

Going back to the railing she squints out, trying to locate Tom. The tree leans drunkenly away from the house then snaps forward, hardwood turned to rubber. Finally it breaks free, tumbling in slow motion, the top bounces at the edge of the roof. She holds her breath, watching for Tom. It rests there, maybe it won't break through. Is that him, moving toward the back fence? There's a growl as the mass of roots pulls free of the earth. Emily has time to retreat to the bedroom before the wall of glass shatters.

Now, it's like a hive filled with fury. Every nail, screw, and beam squeaks with strain.

"Mummy!" Ryan screeches.

It's like something grabs the corner of the ceiling and gives a violent yank. The pressure changes in her ears. She shouldn't look up, she should be protecting her head, but she has to see. The ceiling fragments, a cloud of powder obscures her vision, and there's a pop followed by an awful ripping. Some things fall, others are lifted and whisked off. The roof peels away, entire sections taking flight, leaving ragged bits over their heads. The wind gnaws at that too. The nightmare sky is above, drywall and debris whirl around them, biting at her skin as they rake past. Rain licks at everything while more of the roof is sucked away.

Mary drops to the floor and Emily follows. They huddle at the base of the bed, rain whipping their backs. Hard things clunk about the room. Mary clutches at her, Ryan wails into his teddy bear.

It's Hoover that makes the first move. Squirming past the knot of bodies, he scrambles through the mess that was a bedroom, gets to the doorway, and disappears. She wrenches Ryan from under the bed, ignoring his howls.

"Follow me," she yells at her mother.

It's hard to find a stable place for each step through the wreckage. A silver picture frame just misses her cheek. She doesn't have time to see the photograph, but it's the one with Daniel's arms draped around her shoulders, both of them facing the camera, her hands showcasing the sonogram of Ryan, still floating in her womb, the size of a plum.

Ryan has to be carried—wriggling wildly—glass is everywhere. Hoover must have made it down the stairs, he adds his baying to the sounds. It's all one discordant shriek.

At the front door, the ceiling is still intact. She thinks to grab her purse, hung for once on a hook. As she opens the door, a slosh of water carries one of Ryan's tiny plastic boats ahead of them.

Outside, the rain is pure salt. Emily strains to see through wet glasses in the dark. Things are not where they should be: a section of the brand-new fence lies across the hood of their car; insulation, roof beams, and tiles litter the front lawn and driveway. All of it is shoved along by the wind toward the squat trees across the lane. She's too stunned to keep an eye on the dog, only catches sight of him skidding past a branch as it whirls near his rear end, tail tucked between his legs. He doesn't hear her yell. The front of the house blocks the full force of the wind. As soon as they leave its patch of shelter, she has to lean sideways into it. Ryan locks his arms around her neck, pressing into her windpipe while air rushes up her nostrils, smothering her.

Her legs are heavy. It's like that dream where she runs like mad but can't move an inch.

"Go on, Duck." The words are spoken so clearly that she snaps her head around, but there's no one there.

Daniel holds open the door at Linda's.

"Thank God," she says to him. It's blackness within. Salt runs down her cheeks as she eases Ryan to his feet.

"Linda?"

"She just fell down. I was trying to help her with her inhaler."

She gropes around in her pocket for the little flashlight. Ryan clings to her knees. "It's okay now, Ryan." It's not okay. Linda is on the floor, her mouth gaping.

Mary bends to Ryan's height and opens her arms.

～

"That's better isn't it?"

Martin reaches into his shirt pocket and pulls out a package, the lighter version of what he used to smoke. He pops one into the corner of his mouth and shrugs a shoulder.

"Got tired of the reds." He tilts the package towards her, and she finds she's able to reach out and take one.

"S'okay, Lin. We won't light up in the house. I know that drove you nuts. Just hold it." Martin nods, his eyes smiling.

She blinks a little too long, and when she opens her eyes again the room is sideways. Faces clamour around her, saying her name.

The light has changed on Martin's face.

"I found the travel brochure in your bedside table," Linda says. "It's been my bookmark for years. I always wanted to ask you about it."

"Just like our honeymoon," he says. "Come with me?" A little wink with his left eye.

"I couldn't leave him."

"No, you wouldn't."

～

With Da, Emily couldn't help. No training in first aid, and her arms weren't strong enough to pump his chest with the ferocity required to snap his heart back into its rhythm.

It's thanks to Ryan that she drops beside Linda, pulls her onto her back, and checks her mouth for an obstruction. She went to a first aid class when he was still in her belly, listened with horror at how little time she'd have to bring her infant back if something stopped him from breathing.

"How long has she been like this?"

"I don't know." Daniel is beside her, holding the flashlight.

A strangled hiss comes from Linda. It's been a few years, and Emily's training was not for an adult; she pinches her fingers over the nose and puffs a breath into her mouth. It's like a balloon, fresh out of the package, the resistance of air within. Placing her hands on Linda's chest, she tries to find the apex of her ribs, hopes she's remembering it correctly, hopes that adults are not like a different species for CPR. She pushes sharply down. The instructor said to sing the song from *Saturday Night Fever* to get the right rhythm. But how many times? How hard?

She tries not to sing it but it helps. "Ah ah ah ah, stayin' alive, stayin' alive."

Ryan crouches beside her. "Wake up, Lin—"

"No dear," interrupts Mary gently, "let your mum help."

Emily keeps her eyes on Linda's, pumping through four rounds of the chorus. The flashlight directed at her own knees, casting long shadows across Linda's face. *How many times?* She takes a rest, hangs over Linda's face.

"Come on, Linda, breathe."

Mary finds candles and lights them. Shadows swim around the room.

Daniel has a phone to his ear, relaying information as she strains to hear a breath. It's a small consolation while they wait for an ambulance.

"You told them about her inhaler?"

Daniel nods, he'd found it with his heel.

"How long?" she asks, glancing at his face, trying to tell if he's listening to her or the 911 person.

"They're coming but roads are blocked all over the place.."

She glances over her shoulder. Mary has wrapped a throw blanket around herself and Ryan. Her mother's blonde hair is red on one side. "Mum, are you okay? Your head."

She touches fingers to the spot and winces. "I'm sure it's fine."

"Look outside for Tom," Emily says to Daniel, feeling like she's piloting an erratic vehicle. Her thoughts are a whirl, cycling through the ruin of the night.

"Breathe, Linda. Come on." Pump pump pump pump, *stayin' alive, stayin' alive.* Trying to count the compressions. Time speeds up, slows down.

"Tom needs you," she tries. Is that a flutter of eyelids? "Linda?"

The room fills with flashing lights, they've turned off their sirens. Daniel opens the front door and they come in. She backs away and watches as tubes are uncoiled. They talk to each other in numbers and jargon, asking about her medical history. It takes too little time for Emily to tell them what she knows. She needs Tom.

"I have to get him."

"No," says Dan. "Don't."

"She'll want me to go after him. I'll see if he's near the house."

"You stay, I'll go."

She shakes her head. "You'll set him off. Just give me a few minutes."

THE FIGHT HAS gone out of the wind. It's now possible to take a regular breath. She moves past parts of her roof, skirts large tufts of insulation like cotton candy. Over there, the bulk of her barbecue, minus its tank. *Don't think of that now.*

"Tom?"

The flashlight only shows her a tight circle of light. Flicking it off she tucks it in her pocket, puts her hands to the sides of her mouth, and hollers his name.

Her house is like a Hollywood set with only the front wall intact.

It's only a thing, says Da's mild voice in her head. So clear.

There's Tom, sitting on the edge where the fence was a few hours ago. She crouches to move closer but avoids touching him. His skin is streaked brown. Cuts on his shoulders bleed freely.

"They're taking your mother to the hospital." The soil has crumbled here where the fence has been dragged down the slope.

He shakes his head, *no.*

"Tom, please come with me."

He turns his upper body, pulling one foot up as though to stand, and reaches for her. She flinches, tucking her hands behind her.

"No, Tom. We have to go." She tries to use a calming tone, backing away. "What are you doing?"

"Just let it all go," he says.

"*We* have to go. The ambulance is here for your mum."

"He won't stop talking, Emily."

She nods. *What are the right words?*

"He says there is no end." He gets to his hands and knees. "You can hear it."

"I can't hear it." Just the booming of the sea.

He kneels in front of her. "There's a voice in it. Listen."

Does he think they are the same?

"Come on." Both hands are held out for her, filthy.

She takes another step back.

"Where?" What is this place he has in his head?

In answer, he stands up and turns to the sea, sheets of white foam are carried on the air.

"You'll drown."

He shakes his head. "It's just a deeper part of this world. Things most people don't see."

"No, you'll die, Tom. Don't." She backs away, afraid he'll grab for her. A streak of lightning ignites the sky green.

"I have to. It's the only way he'll stop."

Her glasses are smeared with salt water.

She yells his name, uselessly, as he steps into emptiness. Underneath, the ground quivers with thunder.

She crawls to the edge, still yelling for him.

He's swallowed into churning water; a glimpse of an arm, the back of his head, a sliver of skin. Then the sea inhales, sucking in every loose thing.

She squints. Another jagged line of light flits across the sky. Her stomach lurches. How can this be the same place as yesterday?

A movement catches her eye, a seagull's pale feathers, diving into an air current, wings holding still, tilting its body to catch an updraft. Just beyond, another gull rides the storm. For what reason—desperation, survival, joy?

⌒

Above Linda, an IV bag swings from a hook on the ceiling. A man sits beside her, talking into something, her name, age, medical history. She's lying down but moving, the sound of her own breath a mechanical whoosh in and out. They keep stopping and starting.

"My son?" she says inside the hiss of the mask, but the man is not looking at her, he's peering up front, grumbling about fallen trees. "My son."

Martin looks down on her, his eyes dark pools.

"I knew what you did to him," she says.

He continues to look at her, saying nothing.

The first break happened when Tom was fifteen. She'd been in the hall talking to his doctor. He'd just told her the diagnosis. Tom was still unconscious. She found Martin sitting, watching his son as he slept, looking hard at him. Tom's face was swollen on the right side. Martin leaned on his elbows, one hand cradling the knuckles of the other. Tom stirred, his eyes opened and saw his father. Something passed between them, before Tom turned his head away. Martin looked up, jammed his hands in his pockets, and left the room.

"I should have made you talk," she says.

But she just sat in the still-warm chair beside the bed and watched Tom breathing. Sometimes, moments pass and you just leave them there in the murky wake.

CHAPTER 14

J im wakes them up, thumping on the front door, yelling, "Linda!"
Emily coaxes one eye open. On the opposite end of the couch
is Dan, an afghan thrown over his upper body. Mary reclines in
the La-Z-Boy with Ryan across her lap. "I'll go," she croaks at
Daniel. Sun streams through the windows. Her clothes are still damp,
she realizes, leaving the warmth of the sofa.

"Oh good, you're here," Jim says when she opens the door. At his
feet is Hoover, sagging more than usual, a plastic bag taped to his front
paw, the same one as before.

Emily shuts the door behind her and crouches down to hug her dog.
Hoover presses his nose into her armpit and groans.

"We cleaned it up and that bandage is fresh. Found him hiding
under my old dinghy in the backyard. Poor fella."

She should have thought to ask for Jim's help during the night.

"An ambulance came for Linda last night," she says. Jim turns to look at Emily's house, roofless and surrounded by debris. "No, she was here at home, she couldn't breathe." Emily taps her throat and recounts how they found her. "I'm going to call the hospital in a minute."

"I thought I'd come help." He gestures behind him where he's left a chainsaw and gas can. "I don't know how I missed the ambulance. I, we, were in the basement. I had no idea it was so—"

"Also." She just needs to get it out. "Tom...he went into the water. I couldn't stop him."

Jim stares, his face slack.

"He was in a state."

"You called the police?"

She nods. They said a search crew would be out, but these were *exceptional circumstances*. "I don't think he could have survived it, Jim. I've never seen it like that." She runs her hands down Hoover's ears, glad of his quiet company, his reassuring old-sock odour.

"It's not the first time, Emily." Jim's tone is soft.

"I know. I know." So achingly tired. She'd stayed there, watching the crashing waves until first light when Daniel came and took her by the hand.

"She'll be okay," he says, as if he can know. "And Tom, well...." He turns and looks up the hill. "Do you want me to check out the house?"

"No, it's okay. We'll get to it. Thanks for bringing him home."

"Just glad he didn't stray too far."

He doesn't offer to walk along the shore, see if he can find what she couldn't in the gloom, and she won't ask him. She can't.

DANIEL POURS HER a cold coffee from Linda's carafe. She must have brewed it last night, knowing what to expect. If she was here, she'd probably have warmed it on her barbecue. But Daniel doesn't bother. There is cream in the rapidly warming fridge and sugar to counter the staleness. Emily takes a sip before picking up the phone. It takes a few tries to find the right hospital, then the right department, and she's not a family member so they can only say so much. She gets enough though. Linda was admitted. She's stable. They offer to connect her to the phone in her room, but Emily declines. Not until she knows, for sure, about Tom.

Mary stays back with Ryan, scraping together a breakfast for him from Linda's cupboards. The sky is clear, the air filled with salt and soil. Shredded leaves coat Linda's car like green confetti. On the breeze is the sound of chainsaws. It's not just Jim, distant neighbours hack through the wreckage of their yards. They sit in Linda's car and listen to the news before starting it up. Many streets are impassable with fallen trees. Power is out everywhere and likely to stay that way. Emily drives them down to the lane. In the trunk, they have a pair of binoculars and an old wool blanket. They don't speak, only the necessary words to carry on with this day.

The beach has claimed the lane as its own. Boulders and sand and heaps of seaweed occupy the spot where they used to park the car. Emily stops on the road and climbs out. Daniel pops the trunk and lags behind her as she wobbles over the shifting rocks. *What will we find?* Within the hour, more will arrive to take up the search. Daniel catches up, offers her the blanket.

"It's not for me," she says.

"I know." But he drapes it over her shoulders, and that's when she realizes she's shivering.

The shoreline is full of chasms, sand lugged to new places, fresh islands of stones. Only the sky has returned to its usual self.

"I don't think we can go much further," she says, eyeing the size of the waves.

"No." Daniel's words are laboured. His ribs are broken and breathing hurts.

He offers her the binoculars. Without his glasses, all things visual are assigned to her. She scans slowly, starting from the left, and stops at a lump along the sand. It might be. But it's someone's lost float from a dock. "You haven't said I told you so," she says without looking at him.

"I know."

She lowers the binoculars. "Thank you."

His eyes are wet but he doesn't look away.

"Tom never did anything like that before."

Daniel nods.

⌐⌐

Linda knows where she is before opening her eyes: the smell, the sounds, the stiffness of the sheets, the crackle of the pillow beneath her head.

"Welcome back," a woman says, touching a tube in her arm. A young face, hair in tiny braids decorated with beads, her scrubs feature pumpkins riding bicycles. "You missed the big storm. The city is a mess today. I walked here. Good thing."

"My son," Linda wheezes.

"Oh, honey, I'm sure he'll get here when he can. Just rest." The nurse pats her arm and stands up. "Back in a bit."

There's nothing to do but stare at the ceiling and mine her memories.

⌒⌒

What if he is still alive and suffering? Her head aches from trying to sort out the glistening shapes through the binoculars. For some reason, she just feels it. He's gone. He wanted to go. And how could he *not* have drowned in that chaos? But maybe he was swept around to the next bay, hung onto something floating. He's a surfer and the body has its own will to survive.

The thump of a door pulls her out of her thoughts. A white truck is there, an emblem on the side. A man and a woman climb out, both wearing dark uniforms and reflective vests. They talk to Daniel first, resting on a chunk of driftwood nearer the car. Then they march straight to her, with somber faces.

It's the woman who speaks. They must have worked this out in the truck. She touches Emily's shoulder as she says the words, confirming what her gut has been telling her.

"Spotted by someone just down near the inn." She points. "They're taking his body in. They'll need to speak to his family."

The picture of police showing up at Linda's hospital bed is too much. She finds herself bent forward with a horrible sound emitting from her. Too much to hold in. She's still in pyjamas and rubber boots. The woman drops to her knees on the sand beside her and allows Emily's tears and snot to smear the shoulder of her uniform. Apologies spill from her lips. Through her tears, Daniel weaves toward her. The world is wavy. It's one thing to feel that he's dead and another to know it. Daniel stops short at the other one, the man. Words are exchanged and a business card is passed over.

After a while it's Daniel beside her, murmuring. They stay there for what seems like days, the chill of wet sand soaking through their bones.

MARY TAKES ONE look at her and knows. She opens her arms and Emily walks into them. "Ryan's sleeping in Linda's room," she whispers, patting Emily's back. Daniel goes to the kitchen and finds a bottle of water for himself and Emily.

"Come, sit down, dear." She guides Emily to the La-Z-Boy and opens the bottle for her.

"How's your head, Mary?" Daniel asks, easing himself onto the sofa.

"It'll be fine. I've patched it up with things from the medicine cabinet."

"What's this?" Emily picks up a folded piece of paper on the side table.

"Ryan found it between the cushions on the couch."

It's a photocopy of a handwritten letter. She scans it, then looks up. "Jesus. It's from Martin."

"Oh dear, we shouldn't. It was meant for her," Mary says, brushing Hoover's hair from the armrest of the sofa.

"No, you're right. I'll take it to her." Emily leans forward, pressing cool fingers around the swollen lids of her eyes. "But Tom...." He'd said something last night.

"There's nothing you could have said to stop him," says Daniel. "Nothing you could have done."

"Someone might have been able to get through to him." Others had saved him before. "I should go see her."

"You can't go right now," says Daniel. "You're still shaking."

"Suicide is such a waste of a life," says Mary, settling in the rocking chair.

"Mum. Don't say stuff like that. First of all, that's not what he thought he was doing. Second, you don't know." It's a return to the old Emily.

"Em, she didn't mean it as a criticism."

"Still, you won't say that to Linda. What will she have without him? He was such a good person. I know you couldn't see past it all, Dan. Mum, you'd just met him. But he had this gentleness. Ryan will be...." She can't finish, her throat gets too hot.

"Dear, you should go upstairs and lie down with Ryan. Get warm, shut your eyes."

As much as she feels she should go straight to Linda, Emily takes her mother's advice. Climbing the few stairs makes her legs burn with fatigue. She stops at Tom's door, his unmade bed, a pair of jeans crumpled on the floor.

Ryan is on his back, mouth open, arms flung overhead. His biggest loss, until now, was the kite whose string snapped and flew off to sea. Even that she spun into a tale of his toy untethered and forever touring the earth.

⟋

The same nurse shakes her awake. Pumpkins. Her chipper tone is replaced with something serious, careful.

"Ma'am, there's an officer here to see you."

"My son?"

The nurse averts her eyes, backs away from the bed so that the officer can step in, hat in hand. This is never good. It's a female officer. At the end of the bed is a doctor and a second nurse. They are not looking at her but watching her vitals on the machines behind her, watching as her breath shortens and her heart cracks open.

⟋

"Mummy, where are we?"

His words are insistent, like he's been asking for a while.

"Linda's house." The square of light through the window is dimmer than a moment ago. It feels as if she just lay down and blinked. How long has she slept?

"When can we go home?"

It all comes rushing back.

"Did Grandma show you what happened in the storm?"

"Yes, but Daddy can fix it."

Has Mary told him this? "It will be a while."

"What about my blue boat?" Better his toys than asking about Tom.

They discuss the possibility of removing things from the house until his stomach interrupts.

"Did I just hear a lion roaring?" says Emily. He smiles and pulls her hand to his belly. They lie there waiting for the next growl. She marvels at how things can feel normal for a few seconds.

Emily swings her legs out from under the covers. Sitting up makes her head throb. Ryan shows no sign of fatigue, running ahead of her down the stairs. She hears Mary greeting him and hangs back. Staring at her legs, still in the pajama pants. She can't go the hospital like this.

In the kitchen, Ryan watches his grandmother make a peanut butter and jam cracker.

"Want one?" Mary says, looking up.

"No thanks, I'm a little queasy."

"It'll pass. You're running on three hours of sleep."

Emily opens a bottle of water and sinks into a kitchen chair. "You're dressed," she says, noting her mother's skirt and T-shirt.

"Daniel has been over to the house with some neighbours from across the hill. They're out there now." She glances at the window. "Sorting through things. I think the blue bag by the door is from your closet." Outside are several vehicles. Some people are taking pictures.

"Oh, good."

"Someone from the news was here earlier. I put them off. Dan's not looking so good." Mary puts the plate on the table and helps Ryan onto a chair. "I told him he ought to lie down when you get up, but he says he wants to see Linda with you." Emily takes a long breath. "But, I bumped into Jim's wife a few minutes ago, and she said she could watch Ryan for a few hours."

"Okay?" Emily's groggy mind is not following.

"So, I'll go with you to the city and Dan can get some rest."

"But when did you sleep?"

"I rarely get more than a few hours at night. The gift of menopause."

"Gift?" says Ryan, licking peanut butter from a thumb.

"Just a joke, buddy. Grammy is being funny." She turns to her mother. "You're sure you want to?"

"I don't have to come right in with you." She sweeps Ryan's crumbs into her hand and deposits them on the floor for Hoover, something she wouldn't have done a few weeks ago. Someone has dug up his "cone of shame" from the house and it's strapped around his neck once again, preventing him from yanking the bandage from his foot. He resembles a canister vacuum more than ever.

"Thanks, Mum, I'd appreciate that."

MARY CLIMBS INTO the driver's seat. Her hood is dented, while Emily and Daniel's car is still underneath a section of fence.

"First sign of an open coffee shop and we're stopping," says Emily.

"I'm sure the hospital has something." Mary takes it slow on the road out of the community; they stop a few times to gawk at the damage. It's odd to see boats flung far from the water. Several trees are horizontal, tangles of roots and soil dominating front yards. The "izza" place no longer has a sign. People are tacking up plywood in the front window.

"Nice to see so many people out helping," says Mary.

But Emily sits in silence, thinking of her house, currently filled with neighbours she's never met.

"What will you say to her?" says Mary. "Of Tom?"

"I don't know. Everything, I guess. Or maybe I'll just sit with her. I don't know." The phrase *don't kill the messenger* keeps running through her mind. She fingers the folded piece of paper in her lap.

Mary glances her way. "You think you know someone when you first get married. You think it'll just grow from that. Deepen. But it's so much more...complicated." She must have started to read the letter too.

Emily studies her mother's profile as she drives. No makeup and her hair pinned back. There's something else...her clothes aren't ironed, that's it. Without her eyebrows pencilled in, her face seems more open. Excepting the rare glimpses of Mary on her way to the washroom in the morning, Emily can't recall seeing her this way.

"Just before everything started last night, I had the dream."

"In the boat?" Mary says, stealing a look at her.

"Mm. But it was vivid. More like I could...taste it. Da was at the tiller."

"You used to wake up screaming."

"I remember."

"You only wanted him."

"I know." It's blurred purples and reds, her mother leaning over her pillow, backlit by the light from the hallway, shushing her. "In this dream, I was mad. He'd said something about the boat, but I can't remember what it was." Mary checks the rear-view mirror and stays silent. "Was that just in my dream or was there something about *Knotty Girl?*"

"He'd lost it."

"Lost the boat?"

"In a bet."

"But he didn't gamble." Mary says nothing but they seem to be speeding up. "Watch it, Mum, another tree is down ahead." She slows and they swerve around a small pine, thrown onto the double yellow line.

"You were too young to know about all that." All *that?* "To you, he was always funny and ready for adventure."

"I thought you sold it right after."

Mary shakes her head, *no.* "Good thing I filled up the tank before," she says, pointing to the queue at the gas station. It snakes out onto the road and continues around a bend. Some people are on foot with red plastic cans resting at their feet. "No, he'd signed it over to someone the week before. I had to find out from the lawyer."

"I thought it was going to be mine when I grew up." What had he said to her?

"That's what he used to tell you."

Emily waits for more but Mary doesn't go on. They pull over to let an ambulance pass. Then there's a line of army trucks chugging along ahead, just part of the crew called in to help.

"Seventy thousand," says Mary as they pull in behind the trucks. "That's what they said on the news. Seventy thousand trees."

"And Tom."

LINDA'S BED IS in the upright position and a tray of food sits untouched on the table beside her. She doesn't notice Emily in the doorway, her focus is on something outside the window. *I could just leave and she wouldn't know I was here.* There's a twist in her stomach, an urge to run.

"Linda?"

Her head turns and the corners of her mouth lift slightly. It's not a smile. How could it be? Somehow, she's still Linda. Emily doesn't know what she was expecting. A mess; she was imagining blubbering incoherence, anger and howling.

"I'm so sorry." Emily moves in to hug her then realizes there are tubes, so she reaches for her hand and squeezes. Her hand is cold, a tissue wadded in her palm.

"He promised me he wouldn't go out in it."

"In the storm?"

"I knew it would take him one day. The water. I always knew." Her voice is flat, her eyes dry.

"I'm so sorry." Is there anything else to say? Then she remembers the letter from Martin. "I brought this."

"Did you read it?" She lets go of Emily's hand to take it, unfolding the paper.

"I started to but I stopped." She pulls a chair closer to the bed and sits.

"Is everyone all right at your house?"

Emily shakes her head and gives the briefest possible description. It seems trivial compared to Linda's loss. "We won't know until they have the insurance company assess it. I hope it's okay that we're at your place. We'll go and stay with Dan's parents. It was just the panic of it all."

"I like that you're there." She looks down at the note. "I wish he could have talked to me. He meant to."

"Martin?"

"Just read it." Linda holds it out to her.

Emily reads it twice, afraid to look up until she knows what to say. But Linda beats her to it.

"There was a family history, so he blamed himself. I was planning to tell Tom, to show it to him, but not right away."

"But he knew about this?"

Linda nods.

Something he'd said in the storm when he lunged at Daniel. *I saw it hit you.*

"What did the police tell you?" asks Emily.

"That they found him this morning, near the inn. You reported him missing. He was…."

"I was with him before. He was by the tree." Linda must see what Tom would have been like, something changes in her expression. "And the wind was just wild. It was going to come down any minute." Emily stops, her throat feels like it's closing.

"It's okay, it's okay."

"I couldn't get through to him." She leaves Daniel out of it, Martin too, and skips to the water, his idea about going somewhere deeper.

"Was he angry with me?" Linda's voice is a whisper.

"No, Linda. He was just, lost."

Emily bows her head and watches tears hit her knees. When she looks up, Linda is staring up at the ceiling dry-eyed.

"I have to write his obituary."

"Not right now."

"Will you help me?"

Emily jots things down as Linda remembers them. Memories bubble up and Linda has to tell her about the time Tom fell off his bike or how he once wanted to be a bug farmer and so on. She forgets to use past tense—*Tom is*—then corrects herself. She tells her about photo albums they need to dig up for the service.

"Thank you," Linda says, watching Emily tuck the obituary into her purse. "Doris will make the phone calls."

"I'll type it up."

They sit holding hands for a few minutes, something they've never done before.

IT LOOKS AS if her mother is dozing behind the wheel when Emily opens the passenger door, but her eyes snap open at the sound. It's been nearly two hours.

"That bad?" Mary says, passing her a box of tissues.

"She's in shock, I guess. I did all the crying for the two of us."

"I got you a coffee."

Emily picks it up and works the lid open. "It's still warm. Thanks."

"Straight home?"

"You're sure you don't want to go to your place?" It would be quieter there, and she has her things.

"Not yet. Tomorrow."

"As straight as possible then." The city was filled with detours on the way in, not to mention the people driving at snail speed, snapping photos and video of the damage.

"How long will she be in?"

"Not sure. A day or two." Emily rolls down her window and inhales. She finally identifies the smell outside, tree sap. "She's planning a funeral from her hospital bed."

"Oh dear."

"She has a friend who is doing a lot of it." Doris had arrived as she was leaving. The first thing she did was inspect the food tray and march back out the door with it. "I didn't tell her everything about last night." She'd related it all to her mother, Daniel had filled in the gaps.

"No?"

"I'm not sure if it was the right thing to do."

"For now, it is." She reaches a hand across and pats Emily's hand.

AFTER EVERYTHING SALVAGEABLE has been removed from the house, they move in with Maggie and Don. Emily and Dan share what was his room, still decorated from his university days. Ryan sleeps in Uncle Dave's old room. It's his first time in a twin bed. Emily lines the floor with pillows in case he rolls out during the night.

Daniel waits until after the funeral to bring it up.

"You probably don't want to stay with Mum and Dad too much longer."

"Well, they're selling the place so, no, it's not the best solution." As much as she enjoys the extra help with Ryan, she misses their privacy, and Hoover has begun to dig holes in their backyard.

"We got the project."

"On the Island?"

"Yup." He smiles. Good news for a change. "And since we're now homeless, they've sweetened the deal, offering us a rental place for six months." He sees the look on her face. "Fully furnished."

"So we can just...go."

He nods, watching her shoulders drop.

MARY INSISTS ON helping them get ready for the trip. Daniel takes Ryan out to play in the yard while they pack the final suitcase.

"He's good for you, you know? Daniel. You balance each other out."

"Yeah, well, like you said, it's complicated," Emily says, watching Mary roll up Ryan's pants and tuck them into a neat row.

"It doesn't get any easier, dear. No relationship does." If that's a jab at her, she deserves it.

"I was so hateful to you after he died."

Mary looks up, surprised. "You were in a lot of pain."

"Still, I wish I'd been kinder." All those wasted years. Something has been bugging her. "Why was it that we moved to the city, after?"

"We couldn't keep the house, we were bankrupt."

"Right." Mary had sold most of their furniture, packed the remaining boxes, and drove the moving van herself. "But you let me think it was all you. You could have told me that he drank it all away."

She pauses and considers before answering. "It would have taken him away from you all over again. And you were too young to understand."

"But, later?"

"When you were a teenager? You were...troubled. I guess I was afraid you'd follow his example or think I was lying. It just didn't feel right." For years she'd thought of her mother as weak, self-centred.

"He let me believe those things of you." She was thinking out loud, all Charlie's little jokes, eroding her mother in her eyes.

Mary watches her. "It's only useful to look behind if it helps guide us forward, dear. Otherwise you're just blinding yourself." She turns away to zip up the suitcase. "Something I read the other day." She clears a space and sits on the bed. "Did you tell Linda?"

Emily takes a seat beside her.

"No. And I don't think I will."

⌒

On Christmas Eve, there is a knock on the door. Linda looks at the clock. If it's Harley, he's early. She hasn't even changed yet. He said six. But it's not him.

"Merry Christmas." He holds out a gift.

"Seth?" No ball cap, his head freshly shorn. Thin as ever in his baggy pants. "Well, thank you," she says, taking the gift from him. It feels like a box of chocolates. Last time she saw him was at the funeral.

"Just something small."

"Well, it's nice of you. You want to come in?"

"No, I should probably go—"

"Coffee? Tea?"

She steps back, opening the door a little wider. Stale smoke wafts from him. It's been weeks since her last one.

"Coffee, if you're having some." He ambles into the kitchen, pulls out a chair, then stands there as if he's not sure.

"Go on, have a seat." She pulls two mugs from the cupboard. "Thanks for speaking for Tom at the funeral," she says, scooping coffee into the filter. At the service he was one of the few who got up to talk, if you could call it that. He put his elbows on the podium and sniffled into the microphone. The only words anyone made out was that Tom was "a good shit." Her own voice had been too weak to deliver a speech. In the end, she'd written a few things down for Doris to say.

"Things have been hard since," says Seth, looking at his socks.

Linda turns to him. "I'm sorry."

"He was solid, Tom. I mean, he had his shit going on, but he knew the right stuff to say."

She nods. "He was a good listener."

"Yeah, but he helped people out, you know? Not just me."

"I didn't."

"Little stuff. Helped me with doing up a job application. Course I went and got fired." One knee starts to jump up and down. "Got me out of more than one fight too."

"I'm glad to know it." She turns back to the counter to hide her face. Of course, he had a whole other life in the city.

"It's got me thinking a lot since he...since he's gone."

Linda busies herself with wiping the counter, unwilling to sit across the table from him just yet.

"I been going to meetings. Trying to get, you know, on track."

"That's great."

"I feel like he's helping me in some weird way." He drops his head and rubs at his eyes. "I guess I wondered." He looks up at her. "I wondered if maybe you felt that too."

"Like he's...?"

"With you or something?"

"Oh, Seth. It's like that with people that go and we're left here. Yes, sometimes I feel him." No need to tell him that she carries on full conversations with him. That she can hear him in his room sometimes. "Sugar?" He blinks at her. "Cream?"

"Oh, no, just black, thanks."

"Let's go in the other room." She leads him into the living room where she's strung some Christmas lights on a plant.

"I won't stay long. I said I'd visit Dad."

"He still in the same house?"

"No, he rents a room from my aunt. Seems okay." Seth takes Martin's La-Z-Boy, spilling coffee on himself when it rocks forward. "Sorry."

"Don't be. It's all going soon. Going to downsize myself."

"You are? Where are you going?" This news seems to bother him more than she would have guessed.

"Oh, I don't know just yet, but it's time."

"You're getting better then?" He glances at the oxygen tank in the corner.

You don't get better from this, but she can't tell him that, with that look on his face. "I'm feeling better all the time. Considering."

"Yeah." He nods. "You making a turkey tomorrow?"

"No, not for just me. A friend is having me over. Midnight mass and lunch tomorrow." Between Harley and Doris, she's out most days. Doris polices the place for any sign of smoking. Harley takes her out for food.

"That's good." He reaches for his pocket and starts to pull out his cigarettes. She can see his thought process, his eyes drifting to the oxygen tank. He picks up his mug instead and gulps down the rest of his coffee. Jittery. "I should let you get back to things."

She follows him to the door, where he stoops to jam his feet into scuffed sneakers.

"I appreciate you coming by," she says when he stands. He's so thin.

"Thanks for coffee."

"Keep in touch, will you?" She holds her arms out and he steps into an awkward hug. "I mean it."

She watches him light up in the car before driving away, feeling something spark in her.

CHAPTER 15

Emily sits at the edge of the water. Sometimes, when the ferry is out, a little family of otters plays near the shore. They're not here today, so she amuses herself by counting the starfish, their shimmering purple. Clouds skim along the reflective surface, gentle waves making them sway together, carried along by tides and currents.

She glances at her watch then back out at the horizon. Here it comes, the ferry moving along where there was nothing a minute ago. It's time to drive the car over to the pickup area.

Lola wheels a bag behind her, hair a foot longer than the last time she saw her. A puffy winter coat in the crook of her arm. She spots Emily before she's even off the ramp, does a little jog to get there quicker, everything bouncing and swaying.

"Look at you," she says, dropping everything and pulling her into a hug. Emily's throat tightens and her eyes are wet when Lola finally releases her.

"I've missed you too," Lola says, not waiting for words to be possible.

They drive with the windows open, Lola gulping the air. In Nanaimo, they stop at a grocery store to stock up on candy for the kids' Easter egg hunt.

"Jesus, you must be happy," says Lola. "It's still winter everywhere but here."

"That part's great." Emily adjusts her sunglasses.

"You guys always talked about moving here." Lola leans forward, looking up at the massive cedars. "But?" she says, eyeing Emily.

"We don't know yet."

They drive west across the Island and then turn north for Tofino. Daniel and Ryan went ahead with his brother and their family. They'd already spent a night in the cabin there. Three hours gives Emily and Lola time to catch up.

"I recorded some of the news coverage," Lola says. "It looked like a pretty cool house."

"When it was in one piece, it was. Did you see that thing about the photo?"

"The picture frame in the shrub? Yeah. That was freaky."

"Not a scratch on it." It was upright in the scrubby bushes beside the house, Charlie's smiling face looking up. "Daniel wasn't so lucky, he had to wear an old pair of my glasses for a week." This makes Lola tilt her head up and laugh. "Nothing was open." It feels good, finding some humour in things. Until now, it felt wrong to smile.

"How's Hoover?"

"Oh, he's okay. Pretty timid whenever there's a storm now, and he walks with a limp."

"And Ryan?"

"I don't know, he's just swept up in the present, whatever is in front of him. Now he's all about Uncle Dave."

"Oh, Dan's sexy little brother?"

"Dan's married younger brother who now has a baby."

"Mm." Lola says it like they're discussing dessert. "I'm just messing with you, Em. You know that."

"*I* know that."

LATE ON SUNDAY she gets away to the beach with just Ryan. She flips off her shoes and watches him dig around in the sand. She's brought a book with her, in case he settles enough to let her read. It was Dave's idea for the family to gather here for Easter, thinking they could start a new family tradition. They went whale watching and spent a lot of time drinking tea and watching Ryan try to talk to his baby cousin.

"Tom!" Ryan's sprinting down the beach after a guy with a surfboard. He moves like him, his hair is even the right colour. Ryan reaches out and touches the back edge of the board. The man turns, surprised at the tug. He smiles down at Ryan. She stops short, the wind makes her eyes water. She hears him say "little man." Then he scans the beach and sees her standing there. He gives Ryan a little salute and walks into the water.

"That's not Tom." She crouches next to him.

"No," he says. His eyes are serious. "Tom's out there." He points. They watch until the surfer catches his first wave, wobbles, and is dumped into the water. No matter how many times she corrects him, he continues to believe that Tom is in the sea.

"Come on, sweetie." She takes his hand and they walk back down the beach.

WHEN EVERYONE ELSE has gone to bed, she takes out the postcard from Linda. On the front, a resort town in Mexico, on the back, her neat printing.

> *Place on the front's not where we're staying. Ours an hour by car, a bargain. Realtors been showing the house. Dread packing. Next year coming back here on my own if house sells, then maybe to see you. Turns out that Doris can speak Spanish, or thinks she can. Suits me fine. I just sit and watch the clouds while she talks to the locals. Keeps telling me to smile, says I scare people off. Not her, me (snort). Keep dreaming of them both, it's like they're with me. Hoping you feel better now. Thank you for trying. Squeeze that little boy. It all goes too fast.*

Turning it over she stares at the blue of that ocean, then tucks it into the novel she's been reading.

"You're still up." Daniel yawns. She pats the cushion next to her. "Reading?"

"I was." She pulls out the postcard and shows him.

"Ah"

"Have you read it?"

He nods. "Sounds like she's doing all right."

"I think she's still in shock. Nothing's holding her anymore."

"Yeah."

He takes the book from her lap and reaches for her hand. They sit side by side, like they're on a first date in another era, then she lets her head fall to his shoulder.

"Mum sent me an email. She's booked her flights."

"She's coming?"

"For a whole month."

"Happy?"

"I was getting used to her. And I like this revised version of him."

"He's not coming, is he?"

"No. It's part of their new deal, she gets to do trips on her own. Said she wants to do this every year."

"God, then they'll all be here."

"And they'll be so disappointed when we leave again," whispers Emily. There's still a spot for Dan in the Halifax office, if they decide to go back.

"I started sketching out something. This one has doors and I'm looking into some glass that has a pattern built in."

"For the birds?"

"Mm hm. But we still get the view of the water."

"Nice."

"Time for bed," he says, patting her leg.

"I'll be right behind you." With nine people in the house, it's hard to find a few minutes alone.

"Remember, the small people get up early."

She watches him go before pulling the shackle from her pocket. It was almost chucked out while tossing the ruined items from the house. She turns the small bolt at the end, opening it up then closing it. It resembles a horseshoe when it's open. *It's only a thing.* Da's words again. That's what he'd said of their sailboat after dangling it before her, talking of the big trip they'd do together when she was old enough, then saying it was gone. Just like that. Someone else owned it. *It's only a thing.*

She puts the shackle on the coffee table and it's still there the next morning. Ryan snatches it, a magpie drawn to a shiny thing.

"Ryan, that's Mum's. Give it here," says Daniel, holding out a hand.

"You know what, Dan? It's okay. Let him play with it."

"Sure?"

"Mm hm." She smiles at Ryan, "I'll show you how it works later."

⌒

The doctor told me to write it down. That's the first step. If I can't say it out loud, just put it on paper and tear it up or burn it, but he said it will do me good to let it out.

I guess it was all buried pretty deep, until Tom. The mind does that with some things, protecting itself. So, until it happened to him—the ghosts showing up—I didn't remember. It was just my mother, from the early years, and the way she said my name, Martenn. I knew she was good, that she loved me. We lived in the country, grew our own food. It was pretty isolated, so when she died it was just me and Dad. Until then, she must have kept him away when he wasn't himself.

He told me the baby killed her. It scared me, that something could grow inside your stomach and then kill you. I was too young to know about any of that. I hadn't even started school.

Anyway, without my mother he had me do more chores. I remember he had me watch him kill the chickens and the pigs, saying I'd be doing it one day. He was always talking, like there were other people following him around. Then, sometimes he wouldn't know me, he'd look at me like I was a monster. But the worst thing was at night when he wanted to cuddle. Maybe he thought I was my mother. So, whenever it was warm enough, I'd bed down in the barn, hiding behind the bales of straw.

It was me that borrowed the neighbour's horse that day. He didn't do well with people and I liked going next door. It always smelled of fresh bread and it was a good, long walk. I was holding the mare's bridle while my father hooked up the plough. But there was something off with him and animals sense these things. She wouldn't stay still, eyeing him behind her. Her hoof caught him in the side of the head and he went down, limp. I don't know how long I stood there, terrified he'd get back up and belt me for doing a bad job. But he never did.

After, my grandparents said they were too old to raise a child, so I went into a bunch of different homes. I learned how to take care of myself and not to say too much.

Tom was still a little kid when I started seeing my dad's face. It was just this feeling of shame that I couldn't place, and I couldn't talk to her about it. I drank to make him go away. Then later, when I saw it in Tom, I just wanted him to be quiet. I couldn't protect myself when I was little. So I hit him, more than once, my own son. It scared me.

Linda needed a partner, not another patient. And she was good at it, being calm with him. So I stayed away. I thought it was the best thing for all of us.

A while ago, the police pulled me over on the way back from the Legion. I was lucky, I knew one of them and they let me go with a warning. But the deal was that I'd talk to someone. And I keep my word.

I see it now. By keeping it bottled up, I've passed on Dad's abuse. It's eating away at my own marriage, and that isn't right. We started out well enough, me and Linda. It's time to level with her. In time, maybe she'll forgive me for these years. Maybe one day she'll let me take her on that trip we talked about.

⌣⌐

"That was for you," Doris says, lowering herself into the lawn chair by the pool as if she's reached the end of a race.

"What was?" Linda's back is to the motel, sitting on the edge with her feet in the water.

"Phone. Harley calling from the house to say things are okay."

That was the deal, he'd call from her place whenever he checked on it, that way she'd pay the long distance. The man had a thing about giving phone companies his money. At least she's found out one of his quirks early on.

"Anything else?"

"He said the machines finished off the neighbour's house."

So Emily's house is no more. Better that than the pile of rubble, an awful reminder. Most of their stuff is in a storage place just outside the city now, furniture that wasn't soaked or smashed. Emily had offered to let her keep a few boxes there too, if the house sold quickly.

"Oh and Seth is working out, whatever that means. I tried to get more out of him, but you know what he's like."

"That's good."

"Who's Seth?"

"You met him at the service, one of Tom's friends. He got up and spoke?"

"The homeless guy?"

"He's not homeless." Although, at least one of Tom's friends was. "Just a little ragged. Harley gave him a job."

"He's all right," Doris says, meaning Harley.

Pushing herself off with her hands, Linda drops into the pool.

"What are you doing?" Doris says, her voice an octave higher than usual.

"Just going for a float. Why?"

"It's the first time you've gone past your ankles, that's why."

She follows the slope of the pool until the cool of it reaches her ribs.

"You got a letter from Emily the other day too, right?"

"Mm hmm." Must she know everyone's business?

"Well?"

"They'll be back in August for a week. They'll stay with me, if I still have the house." It was unlikely they'd all squeeze in the condo with Mary.

It feels so good now that she's in.

"Will they move back?" Doris's words are clear enough, but her ears are just going in the water. It's easy enough to pretend she's not heard her, a skill she's learned, sharing a suite for a few weeks.

Slowly she lifts her feet, her arms stretch out to the sides, and she relaxes on her back. Gazing up at a cloudless sky, floating and weightless as a child, she closes her eyes and allows herself to drift.

ACKNOWLEDGEMENTS

I could not have done this without a lot of good people. An ocean of gratitude to:

The wonderful community that is the Writers' Federation of Nova Scotia (WFNS) for accepting me to the Alistair MacLeod Mentorship Program and pairing me with the warm and gifted Carol Bruneau. The team at Nimbus/Vagrant (especially Whitney Moran), who foster the writers of Atlantic Canada. My talented editor, Kate Kennedy, for pinpointing the foggy parts of the manuscript.

The illustrious Donna Morrissey, whose workshops fired up my brain and gave me the confidence to start a novel. A big, mushy hug to my fellow writers and first readers, Rick Alexander and Theresa Babb, who provided feedback on the first drafts and said I should finish it. My writing group, who always have great questions to stir the imagination. Cathy Spence, a lifelong friend who knows what happens behind the scenes at hospitals.

My dad, Frank Eppell, for proofreading all those essays. My mum, Jen Eppell, for getting me my first library card. My sister, Sue George, for that bottle of wine that got me pondering what I had not yet done in life. Family, friends, and blog followers, for reading my words through the years and encouraging me to write.

My husband, Chris, who purchased my membership to the WFNS for my birthday (it was just the right nudge), then gave me the gift of time to write.

My son, Dylan, who never says no to one of my stories.

NOTE FROM THE
AUTHOR

Much of the insight into Tom's character, and the effect schizophrenia has on loved ones, was drawn from *Henry's Demons: A Father and Son's Journey Out of Madness* by Patrick and Henry Cockburn, published by Simon & Schuster. The documentary *Living with Schizophrenia: A Call for Hope and Recovery* by Janssen, Division of Ortho-McNeil-Janssen Pharmaceuticals Inc., provided first-hand accounts of people living with schizophrenia. Other resources included The Schizophrenia Society of Nova Scotia and *Learning About Schizophrenia: Rays of Hope*, a reference manual for families and caregivers produced by the Schizophrenia Society of Canada.

Nicola Davison is a portrait photographer living in Dartmouth, Nova Scotia, with her family and neighborhood-famous basset hound. In 2013, she returned to Nova Scotia after living too far above sea level for thirteen years. She studied English at Dalhousie University and serves as a board member with the Writers' Federation of Nova Scotia. In 2016, she completed the Alistair Macleod Mentorship program (under the guidance of Carol Bruneau) through the WFNS. *In the Wake* is her first book.